VALKYRIE'S CALL

AN ASPECT SOCIETY NOVEL

MICHELLE MANUS

Valkyrie's Call Copyright © August 2021 by Michelle Manus
ebook ISBN: 978-1-954400-06-1
Paperback ISBN: 978-1-954400-23-8
Publisher: Seclusion Publishing
Cover Design: Indigo Chick Designs

This one's for you

The spiderweb splayed across the hedges a foot from Valkyrie Winters' face seemed like a too-apt depiction of her life. The web was a beautiful, intricate trap, and she was the squirming bug caught in the sticky threads. The spider, very like the monster that existed in her own life, was nowhere to be seen. But she was certain it lingered, just out of sight, waiting for the perfect moment to reveal itself.

She resisted the urge to tear the web down. The spider was simply existing as nature had designed it to. It wasn't the spider's fault that Valkyrie found a little too much to sympathize with where the trapped bug was concerned.

She drew her focus from the intricate silk threads, turning her gaze to the small house beyond the hedges. Property wards hummed an inch from her nose, announcing to anyone with power that this land belonged to someone with Aspect, and that someone did not desire company.

Property wards were a given for any home that belonged to a member of Aspect Society, so their presence, in and of itself, wasn't unusual. What *was* unusual was that these particular wards were only two—maybe three—hours old and the shattered remnants of a much weaker ward lay beneath them.

"We should call for backup," the woman crouched next to Valkyrie whispered. A couple inches shy of Valkyrie's own six feet, Meredith Townsend was pretty and slender, with long blonde hair that was currently hidden beneath a brown knit hat.

Valkyrie barely spared a glance at the woman who had once been her friend and was now simply a useful resource. Meredith *always* said they should call for backup. Every damn time.

She gave the reply that, by now, was as familiar as breathing. "I can't call for backup because this isn't a Council-sanctioned mission. Also, I don't *need* backup."

"That attitude's going to get you killed one day. And it could *be* a Council-sanctioned mission if you would just tell them where you're getting your information."

True enough, but Valkyrie had no interest in telling the Aspect Society Council anything. Not when two six-year-old girls waited in the house beyond the hedges, both of whom were the unwilling recipients of illegal Aspect experimentation, and both of whom stood to pay the price if the Council handled the situation badly.

Considering that the madman who had experimented on the girls was an Illusion Aspecter who had also impersonated one of the Council's employees for months without their knowledge, Valkyrie wasn't going to give them a shot at fucking this up. Not when they'd bungled their chance to bring him to justice so badly that, not only was he still on the loose, but they still didn't even know his real name. She was forced to refer to him as Danvers, the name of the Council employee whose identity he'd taken on.

After she'd liberated the girls, after they were in the custody of someone she trusted, then she would report this to the Council. Not before.

"If you don't want to be here," Valkyrie told Meredith, "go home." She had gotten what she needed out of Meredith for the night. Trackers weren't rare, but Trackers of Meredith's caliber were. There wasn't another person in the state who could have led Valkyrie to this house.

"You said if I helped you, you would let me explain. I have done nothing but help you for months," Meredith said.

"And you aren't finished helping yet." There were more houses like this one. Quiet, seemingly normal looking homes where the victims of Danvers' experiments were kept under constant watch. If it weren't for Lucille, the young Oracle who had been liberated from Danvers' clutches six months ago, those victims would have remained unknown.

They might have continued to remain unknown if not for the girl's grandfather, his years of Oracular experience able to pull sense from Lucille's ramblings and weave them into something Meredith could Track.

"We may *never* be finished," Meredith snapped. "Lucille hasn't stopped talking since she came home."

"Then you may never get the chance to explain." Which would suit Valkyrie just fine. Her brother, Jace, might be able to forgive what the woman had done to him, but Valkyrie had no interest in doing so. Jace was the forgiving sort and, being newly married, his head was fogged with marital bliss, besides.

Valkyrie *wasn't* the forgiving sort. And her head would never be fogged with marital bliss.

"Val—"

"I'm going in," Valkyrie said. Slightly reckless, but while she had no doubt that whoever had erected the new property ward was inside, waiting for her, she also hadn't seen any evidence that they would pose a true challenge. "Come with me or don't. I don't care."

She pulled two daggers, rose to her feet and drove the first dagger into the invisible wall of the property's wards. They shuddered as the runes in her blade, inscribed from the well of her own Battle Aspect, hammered her power at the wards like a battering ram. The wall trembled, the manifestation of her will and anger thundering through it. Cracks splintered its surface, stretched and grew.

The wards groaned. The last rune in the blade unleashed its Aspect and the wards shattered like untempered glass.

Valkyrie dove through the maelstrom of falling pieces. A ward shard struck her, opening a slice of skin along her cheek, and she accepted the small pain as a reminder that she was alive. Few other things made her feel so, anymore.

The power of her Aspect crackled along her body. It gave an edge to her strength and speed, a sharpness to her hearing and sight. The front door of the house opened and four people stepped out, three men and a woman. The woman and two of the men bore blades.

Their own Aspect danced down those sharp steel edges, and Valkyrie recognized theirs as kindred to hers. It was hardly a surprise—most Aspecters who went into the mercenary fields bore a Battle affinity.

Only the fourth man, standing out of the way by the door, his hands empty, remained an unknown to her. Until he actively called his Aspect, she wouldn't know what affinity he bore.

Valkyrie kept the potential of his threat in the back of her mind as she shifted the dagger to her left hand and pulled her short sword with her right. One of the men approached, his katana held in a low-level defensive posture.

He closed the distance between them and swung the katana in an upward strike. Valkyrie parried with her short sword, gauging his skill, his strength in terms of Aspect potential. She deflected a second strike, dampening the amount of strength her Aspect funneled into her when she discovered that his was less than she'd expected. With three others to fight, there was no sense in wasting power on what skill would do as well or better.

As she drove his blade up with her own she spun on a rush of Aspect-aided speed and slashed across the top of his thigh with her dagger. The blade sliced deep, which told her he either wasn't good enough to hold Aspect armor over his skin, or he'd been arrogant enough to think he wouldn't need it.

She knew it was the former when, rather than use Aspect like a butterfly bandage to hold the leg wound closed, he pulled recklessly on his reserves, channeling power into a flurry of attacks.

It was too little, too late. The fight had been over the moment her dagger tore through his leg. They both knew it. The others, waiting in a holding pattern around them, knew it. Valkyrie parried the man's increasingly frantic blows until her dagger slashed the underside of both wrists and his nerveless fingers dropped the katana.

Before his knees even hit the ground, the woman with the scimitars moved in, twin blades slashing for Valkyrie's exposed back. Valkyrie tucked her shoulder and rolled, a deft twist of her Aspect making what would have been a risky evasion carry her far enough away from pursuit to gain her feet and parry the barrage of attacks that followed.

The woman was good. Her Aspect was a thin, well-placed enhancement—it added a touch of strength and speed, but she relied more on her skill with her blades than on the power that ran in her veins.

Fighting her was a simple pleasure, one Valkyrie let herself revel in until the woman lost one blade, then the other. Valkyrie knocked her out with a right hook that needed no Aspect enhancement to do its job.

Dispatching the third swordsman took less effort than the second, but she had barely put him down when the ground lurched beneath her feet. A shaky tremor through the soles of her boots was the only warning sign she was given before the earth tore open. She dropped both blades and caught herself on the edge of the chasm that had seconds before been solid ground.

Goddess-damned Elementals. So *that's* what the fourth man was: Earth.

The ground beneath her fingers crumbled. She scrambled for

the earth behind it, only to have the new handhold dissolve into loose soil in her hands. She strove for solid purchase but it disappeared again and again, until her movements had far too much in common with swimming through quicksand.

But the Elemental was tiring. Each time she took hold of the edge, it was slower to crumble, until finally she caught firm ground that held. A twist of Aspect zinged through her, delivering a burst of speed, and she swung her leg up over the lip. She gained her feet, ran as the Elemental renewed his efforts and the ground once more dissolved. She sprinted ahead of its collapse, and when the cave-ins finally stopped, she knew the Elemental was spent.

She turned to face the fifteen foot wide chasm that now separated her from the house. She backed up several feet and took a running start. Her Aspect punched the ground when she pushed off the edge and carried her high into the air as she somersaulted across the gap.

The Elemental pulled a gun as she landed. She barely saw it, barely had time to snap a shield of Aspect around her before she heard the bark of the pistol and a bullet slammed into her shield. It was followed by another, and another, eight bullets firing in rapid succession until the gun clicked empty.

Most Aspecters did not traffic with guns. Battle Aspect, born for war in a time when guns were not even a glimmer of thought in man's mind, was entirely incompatible with them. They simply failed to fire in the hands of Battle users. Other branches of Aspect—such as Elemental—were more compatible, but Aspect always added a factor of volatility. Given that volatility, few Aspecters bothered with guns, unwilling to risk the possibility of one exploding when they pulled the trigger. Especially when an Aspect shield could stop a bullet as easily as it could stop a blade.

But every now and then you got an idiot like this one who was willing to risk it in the hopes the unexpectedness of the weapon would win the battle for them.

Valkyrie turned a glare on the man that could clear a room in under ten seconds, but it wasn't her look that had his already pale face blanching corpse white. No, that would be due to the Aspect that stretched from the other side of the chasm. From Meredith.

Her eyes were unfocused, her hands held loosely at her sides, palms upturned as ribbons of her Aspect wound around the Elemental. Those ribbons of power slithered and writhed, gripping him tighter and tighter.

Meredith might be a world-class Tracker, but that wasn't all she was, wasn't even the core of what she was. That core was lit up like a blaze in the dark of night, now, its truth shining out from her. Because her core *was* truth, and if most Truthfinders stuck to being human lie detectors, the darker side of their power was that they could wrap a person in the absolute veracity of their own darkest moments.

It was called a Truthfinder's Telling, and there were few people who failed to be affected by it, who had accepted the truth of what they were—of *who* they were—so completely that they didn't crumple into a ball at a Telling's touch.

The Elemental was not among the few. A scream tore from his throat. He dropped the gun and fell to his knees, clutching his head and sobbing.

Meredith wore a serene expression. She looked like a benevolent goddess dispensing mercy, not a woman who had a man screaming on his knees as if he'd just lost everything that had ever mattered to him.

And people said *Valkyrie* was scary. At least everything Valkyrie did to a person, she did without rooting around inside their mind.

The man's eyes rolled back into his head and he slumped into unconsciousness. Meredith's power spun back into her and she opened her eyes, catching Valkyrie's.

"You couldn't have done that a little earlier?" Valkyrie asked. "Say, before he tried to drop me into the ground?"

Meredith shrugged. "Didn't know he'd try. Besides, you get prickly when people interfere in your fights."

"Truthfinders," Valkyrie muttered.

"What's that?" Meredith called sunnily.

"Just get your ass over here."

While Meredith walked up the surprisingly intact driveway, Valkyrie tied up the three unconscious people and divested them of their remaining weapons. The only death had been the first man she'd fought. She hadn't enjoyed the killing, but she'd long ago ceased to be bothered by it.

Death was inevitable in her position contracting for the Council, a job she'd taken as soon as she'd passed her Academy finals, because that was what her father had expected of her. She had learned at a young age, and the hard way, that it was best to do what Elijah Winters expected.

"Basking in the afterglow of victory?" Meredith asked.

Valkyrie snapped out of thoughts of her father, ignoring the phantom ache his memory had brought to her wrists. The invisible chains of power that lurked there, just beneath her skin, had been dormant since her father's disappearance a year before— since he'd been captured by the same man who liked to experiment on the Aspect of young children.

If she had anything to say about it, those chains would *stay* dormant. So she needed to handle this situation—find Danvers so she could find Elijah, and fix two problems at the same time.

She picked up the female mercenary's scimitars and slapped the woman awake with the flat of one. The blades did not, to Valkyrie's mind, make up for the loss of her own short sword and dagger to the chasm's depths, but they would do, for now.

The woman's eyes flicked open.

"Do your thing, Mer." Valkyrie motioned Meredith forward. Meredith came, her Aspect sparking as she took the woman's hand.

The woman's eyes went wide as she understood what Meredith was. Then they hardened. "You may be able to tell if

I'm lying," she spat, "but you can't make me talk. I'm not going to tell you anything."

"*She* can't make you talk," Valkyrie agreed—although she wasn't entirely convinced that was the case. "But I can." She pressed the tip of one scimitar to the woman's stomach.

Meredith's lips tightened and she let go of the woman's hand, breaking the physical contact necessary for a Truthfinder to determine the veracity of a person's words. "I won't be a party to torture."

Valkyrie rolled her eyes. "Fine. Keep your moral high ground, Mer, and we won't know if what she starts spouting off is the truth, or if she's just yapping because her guts are spilling out on the ground."

"Do you even *have* a heart, Val?"

Yes, she thought, *and life would be a great deal easier if I didn't.* "Not that I'm aware of." She grinned.

Meredith cursed and took the woman's hand again. It was an old act between them, one started because it had worked so well the first time they'd actually had this argument.

"Would you prefer I start with your guts or your fingers?" Valkyrie asked. "On the one hand, having your guts spill out is terribly painful. On the other hand, modern medicine is probably better at putting your insides back in than they are at reattaching all of your fingers with the dexterity needed for you to hold a blade again."

The woman blanched. "What do you want to know?"

"What's your name?"

"Amy."

"Amy, do you know what's inside that house?"

"The job," she spat.

"And the job would be?"

"Keep anyone from getting to the kids."

"Hmm. But did you know those kids were taken from their parents shortly after they were born? Did you know someone tampered with their Aspect, which is a violation of Council law?"

"No."

Meredith *tsked*. "You didn't even try to mean that lie."

Valkyrie pressed the tip of the scimitar in, just enough to pierce the skin, until blood blossomed on the woman's white shirt.

"I didn't know the particulars," she said quickly. "Sal books the jobs."

"Sal?"

The woman nodded at the dead man.

"Ah. So you didn't know the particulars. But you knew something."

"Maybe I heard some rumors about Aspect experimentation. Didn't really believe them. After everything with the Savage woman came to light, everyone was seeing Aspect experimentation everywhere."

The "Savage" woman was Siren Savage, Valkyrie's new sister-in-law. Siren had been one of Danvers' first experiments in Aspect alteration. He had locked her Aspect inside her when she was only one day old. She hadn't even realized she *had* power until she was sixteen, hadn't known there were others like her until she'd stumbled into Seclusion—and Jace's arms—a year ago.

If the Council had just tried to help Siren, instead of treating her as if she were responsible for what had been done to her, they might have Danvers in custody right now. Instead, the Illusion Aspecter was free in the wind, and no one had a clue what his real face looked like.

Valkyrie wasn't having any luck finding Danvers—she'd beaten her head against that brick wall until her brains liquefied —but she *could* find the other victims of his experiments.

"Did you hear any other rumors about children like the ones inside?"

Amy shrugged. "Some. Nothing you'll find useful."

Valkyrie asked a dozen questions after that, but the woman was right about one thing: she didn't have any useful information. Just like all the others.

"Who is inside, other than the children?"

"The adoptive parents."

"Are they dangerous?"

Amy snorted. "The first has so little power he spent it in the first two minutes after we arrived. The other one's Broken." Broken was the word Aspect Society used for a person who had spent their Aspect down to the last spark inside them, spent it so entirely that it never regenerated again. After that they read, to all appearances, as a Null—someone born without Aspect.

Valkyrie narrowed her eyes. It was something about the way the woman said *Broken* and *adoptive* that bothered her. "Do the parents know anything about this?"

"No."

"Thank you," Valkyrie said, "for your honesty." Then she knocked her out again.

Inside the house, Valkyrie and Meredith found the parents and the two twin girls in the girls' bedroom.

One man held the two terrified children to his side and the other stepped in front of them protectively. "Don't hurt our daughters."

"I have no intention of hurting anyone," Valkyrie said. "My name is Valkyrie Winters. You know who I am?"

The man hesitated, then nodded. Most of the time, Valkyrie hated that her name was recognizable to pretty much anyone in the town of Seclusion, Arkansas. It was the peril of having a father on the Council who then mysteriously disappeared without a trace. But sometimes, like now, it had its benefits.

"Good. What's your name?"

"Shane Anders."

"All right, Shane. This is Meredith Townsend. She's a Truthfinder. It is in your best interests, at this moment, to submit to her for our line of questioning."

"Why? What is going on? Who were the people who attacked us?"

"Mercenaries. Here to ensure they," she pointed at the girls, "remain unknown to the Council."

Shane frowned. "Why would the Council care about our daughters?"

"Was your adoption of them typical?" Valkyrie asked, rather than answer.

"It was legal, if that's what you're asking," he said hotly.

"It's not."

Shane shared a glance with his husband, then turned back to Valkyrie. "We aren't saying anything until you tell us what's going on. We have rights. We want a lawyer."

"You will likely need one," she answered. "Those children were taken from their biological parents when they were six months old. You are familiar with my sister-in-law, Siren Savage's story?"

The two men nodded.

"Your girls were taken by the same man, their Aspects altered before he apparently adopted them out to you for safekeeping. No doubt he thought you were a good way station until he decided it was time to retrieve them."

Shane's face blanched of color, and he lowered his voice. "Can we talk about this away from Lacey and Taylor?"

Valkyrie's gaze swept the room. It had only the one exit and a lone window. The latter was small enough for the girls to get out but not the adults, and she'd hear the screen popping out if Lacey and Taylor tried. Not that they looked like they were going anywhere.

"We can move to the end of the hall," she conceded. "But the door stays open, the kids stay in sight." She nodded to Shane's husband. "He can stay with them or join the conversation."

The two shared a look and Shane's husband began telling the girls how they were going to play a game, or whatever bullshit it was good parents fed to their kids to make them unaware they were in a potentially traumatizing situation.

Valkyrie didn't get it. Her father would have given her a dagger and told her to guard the exits, and if she'd cried about it she'd have found herself running interval training every morning for the next month.

Bullshit firmly in place for the wellbeing of the children, Shane's husband joined them and they relocated to the end of the hall.

"I'm Derek," the other man said. "Are...are their parents alive?" he asked, barely a whisper.

"No."

He looked relieved first, then ashamed.

"You have two options," she told them. "One. You refuse to answer my questions and you all return with us to Council head-quarters. The girls will be placed in a temporary home until this mess is sorted out." The Council wouldn't be *happy* that Valkyrie had struck out on her own, but they were used to it by now. She'd call them and let them handle matters from here—*after* she'd gotten what she needed. After she'd learned if these men had any information that could lead her to Danvers and hope-fully, by extension, to her father.

"Option two?" Shane asked tersely.

"Option two is that you answer my questions, with Ms. Townsend to verify them. If I determine you had nothing to do with what happened to the girls, and no knowledge of it, I will guarantee you won't be separated from them while the Council reviews the situation." She could promise that much. "I cannot guarantee you anything about their longterm placement, as that isn't up to me."

Shane and Derek shared a look. It was Shane who held out his arm. "I'll do it."

Meredith rested her fingers atop his palm and the deep well of her Aspect spun out.

"How did you adopt the girls?" Valkyrie asked.

"We'd been trying to adopt for years. Somehow, despite five years of a solid marriage, both of us having stable, decent-paying jobs, home ownership, and regular volunteer work in the community, we were just never the right fit." He ran the hand unattached to Meredith over his short buzz cut. "We were approached by a private adoption agency. We were naturally suspicious. We researched the hell out of it. They are registered with the state. They are registered with the Council."

"Name of the agency?"

"New Beginnings."

Valkyrie frowned, but Meredith didn't halt Shane to indicate that he was lying. Very few parents in the Aspect community died without provisions for their children to be raised by a family member or a friend with Aspect. She only knew of one agency approved by the Council to handle Aspect adoptions, and it wasn't the one Shane had mentioned.

"They did all of the things they should," Shane continued. "Pre-placement interviews and home inspections. We had a lawyer look over the contract. The agency checked in after the adoption. Everything was above-board."

"Do you have the paperwork for the adoption here?"

"We have copies. The originals are in a safe deposit box."

"I would like the copies, and any other information you can remember on anyone you met from the agency." It wasn't likely to lead her directly to Danvers, but this was the first paper trail he'd left that she'd found. "Have the girls manifested?" Most Aspecters would have shown their talent by now, but there was the occasional late-bloomer who didn't show until eight or nine.

Shane nodded.

"Have you noticed anything unusual about their power?"

Both men shook their heads.

"They're Empaths," Derek said. "And though it doesn't matter to us, their Aspect isn't particularly strong. Certainly not unusual. Are you sure this isn't some kind of mistake? A mixup, or—"

"I'm sure."

He let out a slow breath. "So what happens now?"

"You pack. A security team will come to relocate you to a Council safehouse until a more permanent solution can be arranged. Do you have a pen and paper?"

Derek retrieved both and handed them to her. She wrote down two phone numbers and handed the paper back to him.

"What are these?"

"The first is the number for the best Aspect defense lawyer in the country. His name is Random Tremayne. You want the girls to stay with you? He is your best chance of ensuring that happens. Should you have difficulty covering the legal fees, the second number is for The Savage Foundation. My sister-in-law is extremely invested in helping others like her. Explain about the girls, and she will assist you in any way she can. I'll stay to ensure your safety until the Council's security team arrives."

"That's it?" Derek asked. Now that the shock of the situation was wearing off, anger was swiftly taking its place. "Just wait for a security team and hope our children aren't taken away from us? We were attacked. In our own home. Lacey and Taylor could have been killed and you want us to, what? Pack and make a couple phone calls?"

Valkyrie understood his anger, she really did. But she'd never done well at having anger directed *at* her. She gave him a hard look and he backed up a step. "I'm not good at the emotional support side of things, Mr. Anders. You want your fears assuaged and your emotions soothed, call Tremayne and Savage. That's what lawyers and philanthropists are for."

She walked away and dug her phone out as she stepped onto the Anders' front porch. Martin DuPont, the head of the Aspect Society Council, answered on the fourth ring.

"Can I assume I know why you're calling me at this unholy hour, Ms. Winters?"

"I found two more."

"I believe I was very clear the last time that you were to—"

"These have parents," she interrupted him. "Adoptive ones. Ms. Townsend confirmed they had no knowledge of what had been done to the children. You will not remove the children from their parents' care."

"You are in no position to be issuing orders."

"It's funny, DuPont, that every time you say that, nothing ever happens." It had taken her a long time to discern how a man who as bad at handling conflict as DuPont was had risen to become the head of the Council. Why her father, who believed no one could do anything better than him, had *let* DuPont become head of the Council. She hadn't liked the conclusion she'd come to. "Why is that, do you think?"

"I would tread the line you're walking very carefully."

"Will you send a security team to escort the children and their parents to a safehouse or not?"

"The team will be there within the hour. And Ms. Winters? I'd start looking for a new job. As of now, your clearance to contract for the Council has been revoked."

DuPont might not like direct conflict but he could, it seemed, be petty. She wondered if he knew the financial pressure the job loss would put on her, if he knew she had no access to her father's funds, or if he was simply striking at her with the only weapon he had. Either way, it gave her the opportunity to test a theory, since she no longer had a job to lose.

"My father will be disappointed to hear that."

DuPont inhaled sharply. "Elijah Winters is gone. He isn't coming back. No matter how many extensions you bargain for on his Council seat, that is never going to change." But his tone held an undercurrent of uncertainty, the wavering fear of a man who had just pissed in a wolf's den before it occurred to him that maybe the wolf wasn't gone, after all.

It told her everything she needed to know about him. "I'm sure you hope that's true. Goodnight, Martin."

Valkyrie hung up and let out a long breath. Losing contracting rights with the Council *did* hurt. Her father might be worth millions, but they were millions she couldn't touch. When he'd still been around, he had controlled everything. She'd worked for the Council since she was seventeen and every single dime she'd made had gone into a joint account with his name on it. He'd transferred out everything but a hundred dollars of every paycheck she made into his own accounts. If she tried to let the scraps he left her build up, he simply transferred them out, too. If she withdrew it in cash, he beat the shit out of her and didn't leave her anything for months.

It wasn't about the money, for him. It was about making certain she didn't have options. That *he* was the only thing she had to rely on. The first thing she'd done when he'd disappeared was open a new checking account and change her direct deposit information. She'd spent the next month in a cold sweat, jumping at every shadow, wondering what he would do when he came back, when he found out.

But he'd never come back. Not yet.

"You all right?" Meredith stepped onto the porch, looking concerned. It was irritating.

"Shouldn't you be mothering the children, or something?"

Meredith rolled her eyes. "You know, just because slinging swords around and gutting people isn't my thing doesn't mean I'm Suzy Homemaker. I'm not any better with children than you are."

"Everyone is better with children than me," Valkyrie answered.

The low rumble of a motorcycle split the night, the sleek black machine pulling up the drive and easing to a stop at the foot of the porch steps.

Damn it. She had hoped the security team would arrive before Random did, so she could leave before she had to see him. Unfortunately, now that she *had* seen him, she couldn't take her eyes off him.

He looked, as expected, perfect. Only Random Tremayne could arrive on a motorcycle and look like he'd just stepped out of a business meeting. His Aspect, which always ensured he looked just how he needed to, meant his suit was crisply pressed, his shoes spotless, and not a lock of dark black hair was out of place.

He had no right to look so goddess-damned *refreshed* at this time of night. His chocolate brown eyes were sharp and alert and his bronze skin practically glowed in the moonlight. He was sex personified, and no straight woman with a functioning libido had a chance in hell of not reacting to him.

He walked up the porch steps, his face all business, and passed her by without so much as flicking a glance in her direction.

"Are my clients inside?" he asked Meredith.

She nodded. He knocked on the door, waited until Shane opened it, and then disappeared inside. Meredith gave Valkyrie a what-the-hell look that Valkyrie ignored.

"What was that all about?" Meredith asked.

"What was *what* all about?"

"Uh, Random."

"He's here to be a lawyer. Did you miss the part where I gave Derek his number?"

"No. I also didn't miss the part where he acted as if you weren't in physical existence."

"Why should he?" Valkyrie tapped her fingers against her thigh. The sooner the damn security team got here, the better.

"The man's been pining over you for forever. He looks like a damn puppy dog every time he sees you. Hell, when he danced with you at Jace's wedding I thought he was one kneel shy of a proposal himself."

"Is this string of babbling nonsense going somewhere?"

"Yeah. What the hell did you do to make him act like *that*?"

"Nothing. Random and I are not involved, Meredith. We never have been, and we never will be." The roar of an arriving, armored SUV was music to Valkyrie's ears, and she set off down the steps to talk to the security team's leader. "Have a good night, Meredith. Or don't. I don't really give a damn."

"You know, one day you're going to wake up and realize it sucks not having any real friends. Trust me, I know. When that day comes, you know where to find me."

"If I'm your best option for a real friend," Valkyrie called back, "then you're more pathetic than I am."

"Oh, fuck you, Val."

"Right back at you, *Mer*." For good measure, she flipped her off.

Valkyrie had friends. She did. She had her brother, Jace. His wife, Siren. She couldn't possibly need more than two.

CHAPTER
TWO

Valkyrie's empty kitchen greeted her when she stumbled into it, peeling off clothes tacky with drying blood, leaving a trail from the door to the kitchen. The blood had ceased bothering her a long time ago, and it wasn't what bothered her now, wasn't the reason she just stopped in the middle of the kitchen in her underwear and stared at the stove.

The skillet sat atop it, spatula resting against its side, gathering dust. She might as well throw them in the trash. Random was never coming back to use them, and goddess knew *she* couldn't cook worth a damn.

Her chest constricted, a painful tightening that stole her breath. Here, alone, she could admit that the way Random had walked past her earlier without acknowledgment had hurt. Even if it was her fault. Because she'd lied to Meredith. She hadn't done *nothing* to make him treat her like that.

It had been two weeks. Two weeks since Jace's wedding, two weeks since she'd told Random—

She shook her head. There was no point in reliving it. She had carefully curated the words she'd spoken that day to achieve precisely this result: an empty kitchen. She pulled a Dos Equis from the fridge and pointedly ignored the stove. If she didn't look at it she could almost see him there, bronze skin and dark hair, those chocolate brown eyes with their perpetual undercurrent of laughter.

If she saw Random, she didn't have to think about the man she'd killed tonight. If she heard Random whistling, she didn't have to think about the fact that she wasn't any closer to finding Danvers *or* her father.

Now that Random was gone, now that he was never coming back, she could admit how much she'd liked having him here. She came home with the dawn most mornings, and in the safety of the garage she could smile at Random's motorcycle, lounging in the space next to hers as if it had every right to be there, despite the fact she'd never invited him and he didn't have a remote to her garage.

But then, Random didn't need anything as mundane as a remote. Unlike the power that ran in her veins and every other Aspecter's, Random's Aspect was just that: random. He was an anomaly, and no one really understood how his Aspect worked. When he'd been a child, his guardian had point-blank refused to allow anyone to, "Study him like some test subject." No one argued with the Queen of Death. No one called Random's great aunt that to her face, either. Not if they wanted to keep breathing.

If Random himself understood how his power worked, he'd never shared the secret. So it had been nice to find him here every morning and pretend it was because no ward or lock could ever keep him out of somewhere he wanted to be. Nice, to pretend he actually wanted to be here when she knew he'd shown up each morning out of a misplaced sense of guilt.

She'd let it go on for far too long, might have let it go on even longer if he hadn't pushed her at the wedding. Thank the goddess he'd pushed her. She'd snapped and pushed back and now he was gone. No more mornings making her breakfast, no more texts, no more contact.

He was gone, he was away from *her*, so he was safe.

She would need to find someone to scrub her records with the phone company, of course, erase any traceable evidence of his contact with her just in case all her plans went sideways. Just in case she failed.

And where the hell was she going to find the money to do that, now she didn't have a job? If the mortgage didn't pull directly out of her father's accounts, she'd be homeless by now.

She supposed she could always start pawning off the family antiques. Her father would beat her bloody for it, but what did it matter? A year out from under his control had given her perspective. It was time to plan. Her brother's decision to sell his place in Portland and stay in Seclusion permanently had cemented matters. If her father came back, he would use Jace against her. He'd done it once before, and she was never living like that again. She was going to solve the problem of Elijah Winters once and for all. She just had to find the damn man first.

But her father was proving to be just as elusive as the mysterious Danvers.

She pulled a frozen lasagna dinner from the freezer and popped it into the toaster oven, thinking longingly of one of Random's omelets. The man was an artist in the kitchen. She left the lasagna to heat, nursing the beer in the shower while she scrubbed blood off her skin. It swirled down the drain in mud-red eddies, but even once the water ran clear, she didn't think *she* would ever be clean.

If she'd believed in souls she would have said hers was stained with blood—her own, other peoples', other *things'*. In the end, she was as much a made creature as any Dark Aspect construct she'd ever hunted.

She drained the last of the beer and contemplated the empty bottle. Her father had never allowed her to drink, except at formal functions. Alcohol interfered with training. Alcohol made a person slow and lazy and weak.

He'd been gone for three months before she'd had the guts to break that rule. That first sip had set her entire body to trembling, her blood racing through her on a wave of fear-spiked adrenaline.

Twenty-nine years old and still doing what her father told her. Twenty-nine years old and still living in her father's house. She knew what everyone thought of her—that she'd never grown out of being Daddy's Little Girl. They liked to whisper it behind her back at Society functions—there goes poor, pathetic Valkyrie, no life of her own and trying so hard to please Elijah, thinking one day it might make up for the fact she isn't her father's biological daughter.

Her own brother thought it, though Jace likely left out *poor* and *pathetic* even in his internal thoughts. He didn't have a cruel bone in his body. So she had let him think it, because so long as he kept thinking it, he was safe.

She walked back into the kitchen just as the toaster oven dinged. She pulled the cardboard tray out to reveal the unappetizing lump of soggy noodles and tomato sauce passing itself off as food. She'd never minded the frozen dinners before. She'd never *noticed* them before.

Damn Random for getting her used to things she had known wouldn't last. She still wasn't sure why he'd tried so hard to convince her that he wanted something more than the one night they'd had together. Well, she did know the reason, and it was stupid. Which was why, when he'd shown up in her kitchen months ago and told her he was going to make her breakfast every day until she agreed to marry him, she'd known it was bullshit.

Random wasn't the marrying type. He wasn't even the dating type. He was the thanks-for-a-good-time type. Valkyrie had no interest in trying to make a person go against their nature, but when he'd kept showing up, morning after morning, a tiny, stupid part of her had liked it. Liked that for a few minutes she wasn't alone in this obscenely large house. Liked that it was *him* making her feel not alone.

She poked at her soggy lasagna. The overheated sauce hissed

as a trapped air bubble escaped, sending a splatter of red to land on a gold envelope lying on the kitchen island. A gold envelope that hadn't been there when she'd gone to shower.

She stiffened and dropped her fork, trading it for her dagger even though her instincts whispered that the kitchen, the house, was empty.

Instincts could lie as easily as people.

She swept the kitchen and the surrounding rooms, found them empty. Sweeping the entire house was pointless. It was enormous, and it would be all too easy for an intruder to slip through rooms one step ahead of her. The wards that were sunk into every inch of the house, into the grounds, whispered that everything was *fine, fine, fine.*

Everything was not fine. She took the envelope—she recognized it as one of the ones she'd sent the Gathering Ball invitations in months ago—and pulled out the very short note inside.

You want your father. I want something too. Meet me at Savado's at ten tonight. You'll recognize me.

Danvers, she thought. *It has to be Danvers.*

Her obsession with finding the Illusion Aspecter who liked to run human experiments had its roots sunk into so many portions of her life it bordered on the absurd. Danvers had altered her sister-in-law Siren's Aspect and nearly killed her, but long before that, his first experiment had been Valkyrie's mother, Evelyn. He had kidnapped Evelyn, tortured her, *broken* her, and when Elijah Winters had rescued her—the only good thing, in Valkyrie's opinion, that Elijah had ever done—she had been pregnant. With Valkyrie.

The dots connected all too easily, and Valkyrie did her best not to think about them. To make sure that when she thought the words, *my father,* she thought of Elijah. A missing father who, according to Siren, was in Danvers' captivity. She needed to track him down, deal with him before he found a way out of

Danvers' clutches and unleashed himself on the world, on *her*, again. She needed to take Danvers out at the same time.

Because the nightmare had to stop. She had to be able to make a decision without jumping at every shadow. She needed freedom. And the only way she was ever going to have it was if her fathers, biological *and* adoptive, were finally dead.

She stared at the letter, not quite daring to believe it was in her hands. She'd been hunting Danvers for *months*, and now he was hand-delivering messages to her kitchen and then slinking off without a trace?

Why not simply confront her here? Sure, she would be at an advantage in her home territory, with the property's wards to bolster her. Except this letter was proof that he could circumnavigate her wards, *without* her knowledge, and that—that didn't make any sense.

If Danvers really did have Elijah then maybe, *maybe*, Elijah had given him a way to slip through the wards. But Valkyrie doubted it. Elijah wasn't the type of man who broke. He was the type that did the breaking.

Which left only one person who could enter her home without her knowing about it. She couldn't imagine Random doing this, didn't know what the point would be. If he'd wanted to talk to her, he could have done that last night.

If this was some sort of emotional revenge, hitting her where he knew it would hurt, well, she couldn't see him doing *that* either. It was petty, and the Random she knew wasn't petty. But she had to be sure. Because the consequences of her being wrong were too monumental to leave the matter to chance.

RANDOM LOOSENED HIS TIE. His Aspect snugged it back up. He loosened it again and dared his power to do something about it. Some days, he wished he had some banal branch of Aspect like a water or wind affinity, some placid little power that would answer his call when he bid it to and shut the hell up when he didn't.

Instead, he got a jack-of-all-trades Aspect that did what it wanted eight times out of ten, and apparently wanted him to look presentable even when he didn't give a damn. He'd been awake since one-thirty in the morning making sure two worried fathers and their terrified children weren't going to be separated from each other. If he wanted to loosen his damn tie, he would.

Coffee. Coffee would solve all of his problems. He stood, ignoring the little pings from his Aspect telling him to stay here, stay *right here*. He'd been letting his Aspect drag him this way and that for the last year and where had it gotten him?

Nowhere good, that was for sure.

In the reception area, he threw his assistant a dazzling smile. "Would you like a coffee?"

Mrs. Harringford, a trim brunette in her early fifties, merely raised her reusable travel mug and went back to clacking away at her computer. When she'd applied for the position, he hadn't hired her because her skill set, job history, and references were stellar, even though they were. He'd had a dozen applicants with perfect resumes. He'd hired her because she was completely, utterly immune to him.

He smiled, she frowned. He charmed, she grew bored. It was delightfully refreshing and he still hadn't tired of it. Even if she did seem to think he had an unhealthy relationship with espresso.

The small suite where Random kept his law office was situated on Seclusion's Main Street, six stores down from the local coffee shop, Rise and Grind. He quickened his pace as he walked to it, gritting his teeth against the annoying and increasingly insistent pings of his Aspect insisting he return to the office.

He didn't want to return to the office, he wanted to have coffee. Exquisitely made, delicious coffee. The second he stepped into the shop and the pretty brunette at the end of the line turned and zeroed in on him, he wished he'd listened to his damn Aspect.

He just hadn't thought it was actually trying to help him in a way he wanted. Typically, when his Aspect was as irritating as it was right now, it was because it was trying to drag him headfirst toward Valkyrie Winters. Since he'd recently sworn to have nothing more to do with the woman, he hadn't been inclined to listen. Apparently, his Aspect had actually been trying to keep him out of the path of Lauren Hale, and he now felt like he owed his power an apology.

Lauren turned a blinding smile on him. "Random."

He found a smile and managed a, "Lauren," in return.

Lauren was stunningly pretty, with big doe eyes that presented the false impression that she was sweet. She was a shark in a summer dress, a social climber who had nothing more to worry about than what to spend her mother's money on. She was the type of woman who went for unattainable men simply to prove that she could obtain them. The harder to catch, the more interesting. Random, never once having been in an actual relationship, was apparently the ultimate challenge.

He was under no illusion she had any real interest in *him*, specifically. It was simply that he had a playboy reputation, and she didn't like being left out of the loop. If she could make him date her for a couple weeks, even better.

More than once, he'd contemplated just sleeping with her and getting it out of the way, so she'd decide he was no longer interesting and move on. Unfortunately for him, despite the many rumors to the contrary, he was actually quite selective about the women he slept with. Admittedly, in his early years he might have been thoughtlessly hurtful out of sheer stupidity, but he liked to think he'd gotten a handle on his situation relatively soon.

The situation was this: he'd always been hopelessly in love with Valkyrie Winters, whom he could never have, and he had no interest in anything serious with anyone else. The solution was simple: have fun with women who also only wanted to have fun. He was the perfect rebound man and the lifestyle had always suited him just fine.

Until Valkyrie had made him think he *could* have her. Until he'd spent the last year chasing her only to have her shove him off a cliff at the end of the race.

"So what do you think?" Lauren asked him. She'd been talking, but his brain had been a million miles away.

"About what?"

She laughed, soft and delicate. "You haven't heard a word I've said, have you?" Her words were teasing, but irritation showed at the corners of her eyes. She was used to getting her way, to being pandered to, and she didn't like being ignored.

"Guilty," he answered. "Long night."

"I suppose you wouldn't be up for another one, then?"

Oh, for goddess sake. "Of being dragged out of bed at one in the morning to help clients who are afraid their children are going to be taken away from them through no fault of their own? I'd rather not, but if necessary, I will."

That shut her up for all of the time it took both of them to order, after which she chattered on brightly while he prayed for the barista to screw up her order so he could sneak out while she was yelling at the poor bastard. It didn't happen, and he received the message from his Aspect loud and clear: he'd ignored it earlier, and it wouldn't be helping him now.

He'd once tried to explain to his best friend, Jace, that living with his Aspect was like having a completely separate entity inside him, one whose feelings were easily hurt. Jace hadn't believed him, but the fact he now had to walk back to his office with Lauren keeping step beside him was living proof of his Aspect's vindictive nature.

He actually had to stop at the door to his office and face her to keep her from following him in. "Have a good day," he told her. *Somewhere else. Anywhere else.*

"Actually, I need some advice. Legal advice."

He muttered a litany of curses in his head in Spanish. Spanish was a great deal better for cursing than English, and though his mother had never been interested in teaching him the language, his Aunt Ella had made sure he'd understood that half of his heritage.

"I have a client now," he lied. "But my assistant can make you an appointment."

"Oh, well, it's very *personal*. Maybe we could discuss it over dinner, or—"

"Things don't get much more personal than lawyer-client confidentiality, Ms. Hale. If you change your mind, Mrs. Harringford can make you an appointment during my office hours."

He escaped into his office suite and closed the door behind him. Maybe he would take the rest of the day off. He didn't actually have a client and he'd kept his case load low of late, only taking the cases from people who really needed his help and sending the others to colleagues well able to handle them.

He'd been distracted the last few months. He'd been down the last few days. Lauren Hale was a brilliant reminder that all of that needed to change. It was only natural that he'd floundered a bit after deciding the last year of his life had been a complete and utter waste, but it was time to stop wallowing and set himself to rights.

A day away from work would be just the thing. He could socialize with friends, if he still had any left after all but ignoring them for a full year, possibly get roaring drunk, and definitely *not* think about the attractive, infuriating, six-foot distraction that was Valkyrie Winters.

He looked to Mrs. Harringford, intending to tell her to clear his schedule, only to find her face twisted into the expression that said she had bad news to deliver.

"There is a woman here to see you."

He looked at the empty waiting chairs.

"She's in your office. I attempted to stop her but I rather got the impression she would murder me. You pay me well, Mr. Tremayne, but not quite well enough to die."

A sinking feeling spread through his gut. "Thank you, Mrs. Harringford."

He opened the door to his office. Valkyrie Winters sat in his chair, her booted feet up on his desk, a scowl on her face as she tapped an envelope idly against her thigh.

Of course, of *course* when he'd decided to do everything possible to avoid her, the universe all but threw her in his lap.

"Where the hell have you been?" she snapped.

"I didn't realize where I have or haven't been was any of your concern."

So Random was right, and so Valkyrie had been rude. Rationally, she understood that. Irrationally, she'd had to watch through the one-way glass in Random's office while Lauren Hale flirted with him and it had pissed her off.

Surely Random wasn't dumb enough to go swimming in *those* shark infested waters. Yes, Lauren was all shapely legs and had a sundress collection that brought most men to salivating attention, but she was also a conniving bitch. For years, Lauren had been telling anyone in Seclusion who would listen that she was just the woman to make Random Tremayne finally settle down, if she ever decided to put her mind to it.

"Is there something I can help you with, Ms. Winters, or are you just here to sit in my chair and brood?" His voice, which usually flowed with warmth and laughter, was a bored, glacial monotone. Almost as if he were imitating, well, *her*.

And *Ms. Winters*? She'd known him since she was twelve and he was eight. Her fingers tightened on the envelope in her hand. She wasn't here to be irritated by Lauren flirting with him, or to worry about the coldness in his voice. She wasn't here to worry about *him*.

"I'm here about this." She tossed the enveloped onto the side of the desk where he stood.

Random glanced at it. She watched him for any flicker of recognition or surprise. All she got was that bored, empty exterior that was so unlike Random she felt like she'd slipped into a mirror-world where everything was upside down.

"I'm confused," he drawled. "Have you started a mail courier service, or do you just enjoy throwing things at me?"

"Tell me you had nothing to do with this."

"I have no idea what *this*" —he tapped his fingers to the envelope— "is."

"It's a letter—"

"You don't say?"

"—that was left in my home. In my kitchen. While I was in the shower."

The cold shell surrounding him broke and for a moment he was Random again, *her* Random, concern painting his features. It told her everything she'd already known in her heart. He hadn't had anything to do with this.

Had she really thought he might have, or had she just wanted to see him again?

He reached for the envelope, clearly intending to examine its contents. She pulled her feet down and lunged forward, snatching it away.

"Kyrie—"

She cut him off, because *Kyrie* was bad, bad news. Kyrie meant his helpful, protective side was kicking in, overshadowing the recent hurt she'd caused, and that hadn't been her intention in coming here. "Was it you, or not?" she demanded.

His mouth clicked shut, anger battling against concern. But the concern was still there, and if she was going to get rid of it, she would have to be harsher. She was so fucking tired of being harsh with him. Of delivering the words she knew would strike at his core, would *hurt*.

What did it say about her, that she always knew which ones to choose?

"Are you that fucking obsessed with me, Random? I told you I didn't want you, so you decided to start playing games?"

Brown wasn't a cold color, but his eyes did their best to make it one. He interlaced his fingers together and met her gaze head-on. He was gracing her with his court persona, that air of icy, official detachment that couldn't be riled, couldn't be ruffled, and never, ever lost.

"Someone came into your home without permission. Naturally, you thought of me. Let me clarify this for you, so you never again feel the need to rampage into my office to insult me.

"Recently, I expressed some affection for you. You responded with a very firm assertion that you would never return that interest and told me to—and I quote—'Stay the fuck out of my house, Random.' I have stayed the fuck out of your house. I have not been anywhere near it. I did not send you that" —he nodded at the envelope— "by any means.

"I don't stalk women, Valkyrie. You wanted me gone. I'm gone." He jerked his thumb toward the door. "I trust you can see yourself out."

She could. She *would*. Any moment now. She wouldn't keep staring at him, feeling like she was about to hyperventilate while he looked at her like she was nothing.

It didn't matter. Because she *was* nothing.

You're an arrow, Valkyrie. A blade. A weapon is nothing without a wielder.

She had been molded and forged by her wielder. She had been pushed to the limits of her abilities and she had come to understand that what her father had told her long ago was true. She *was* nothing without him. She was good for one thing and one thing only: destruction.

The man standing six feet away from her was proof enough of that. She stood, walked out, and didn't bother to shut the door behind her. The letter in her hands took on new meaning as she climbed into her Jeep and drove home. If Random hadn't left it then somehow, some way, Danvers had.

Whatever the reason, whatever his impetus to seek her out now, she didn't care. She only cared that she would finally, *finally*, be able to confront him. To find out where he held her father.

And once she did, she would take them *both* out, and set her world to rights.

Random considered the fact that he had last taken a vacation when his best friend, Jace, had needed help rescuing his now-wife, Siren, from her kidnappers. He then considered that he couldn't remember taking one before that, and so deduced that he only took vacations for terrible reasons.

Admittedly, his regular office hours were so irregular they drove Mrs. Harringford to the brink of insanity keeping track of them, so it wasn't as if he was a workaholic with no free time, but he didn't make time off official unless things had really gone to hell.

He'd just made it official. Mrs. Harringford had made a remark about him sending all of his business elsewhere anyway, so it wasn't as if she had a lot of rearranging to do, and would he be able to keep paying her salary if he continued to behave like a child skipping school?

Now that he was sitting on his back porch again, the vacation that had seemed so vital to getting him out of his stuffy office had morphed into the oppressive certainty that he had nothing at all to do. The entirety of his life for the last year had been focused on one Valkyrie Winters. Even when he'd *tried* to focus on other things she'd crept back in. His Aspect hadn't been above tugging him toward her every time she'd overextended herself and hadn't slept or eaten in two days.

It was why he'd started the stupid breakfast ritual. At least if he went to her house every morning and cooked for her his magic stopped waking him up at one in the morning to send him over there, where she was inevitably *training* while on the verge of passing out. She'd claimed she threw his food away, but he'd known otherwise when he'd finally started getting a good night's sleep again.

A flicker in his peripheral vision was his falcon, Nelsen, who dove to the porch and dropped a bleeding mouse at Random's feet.

"Thanks Nelsen, but I'm not hungry. You have it." Random's Aspect flared, twisting the words into something the falcon could understand. Nelsen retrieved the mouse and carried it off a ways before he ripped into it.

Random had found the bird when he was eight, right after his mother had died, a fallen nestling with a broken wing. Not even *his* Aspect could twist itself to the healing arts of Siren's Life Aspect, so he had sought out all information he could on caring for wounded birds. He'd needed the falcon to survive because his mother hadn't, and he'd wanted desperately for the bird to understand he was trying to help it.

That was only the second time in as many days that his Aspect had ever manifested. Eight years old was an abysmally late age for manifestation by the Society's standards. They had taken to calling him a dud by that point, even though all signs had indicated he'd *had* Aspect, it just didn't work.

Aspect fell into dozens of categories: Elemental, like Jace's affinity for water and lesser affinities for earth and air. Truthfinding or Tracking like Meredith's. Battle Aspect, like Valkyrie's, whose power poured itself into the strength of her body, the balance of her blade, the speed and certainty with which she moved. The common denominator being that each discipline was highly defined.

Random's Aspect didn't fit neatly into any mold—it just tried to make the things he wanted to happen, happen. Which was why his healthiest, most steadfast relationship was with a seventeen-year-old falcon. They were known to live around twenty years in captivity, and though Nelsen wasn't quite in captivity, the additional care the bird had received showed in his health.

Even so, Random knew it was only a matter of time before his oldest companion was gone. He had his best friend back, now that Jace had decided to return to Seclusion permanently at the behest of his lovely wife, and he had a handful of other friends. He wasn't alone—wouldn't *be* alone, when Nelsen died. But he'd hoped to have something more, something permanent, when the time came.

He still remembered every moment of the night he'd thought all his dreams about Valkyrie were coming true. He'd once buried those dreams at nineteen, when Jace's departure from town had meant Random hadn't had any reason to be around Valkyrie anymore. That was when the silly idea that she was somehow meant for him had been exposed for the schoolboy crush it was.

Fast-forward several years and her father had disappeared. A month after that disappearance, Random's Aspect had killed his motorcycle engine and left him stranded on the road for Valkyrie to find. She'd driven up, told him to get in her Jeep, and the world had just...stopped. He'd had to admit that it had never been just a schoolboy crush, and he hadn't buried anything at all.

When she'd driven him to his apartment and told him to take her inside, he'd barely gotten in the front door before her body had been perfectly, gloriously pressing against his. A part of him hadn't been able to believe it was actually happening.

So much so that he'd stupidly told her things he shouldn't have, and she'd shut down. He'd watched it happen. One moment she'd been with him and the next she had just been...gone. And no matter how hard he'd tried, he couldn't bring her back out.

In fact, it would be more accurate to say that the harder he'd tried, the more withdrawn she'd become. He'd been stupid enough to keep trying for the better part of a year, stupid enough to kiss her at Jace's wedding. For a moment, she had kissed him back, and he'd thought she felt *something* for him—but then she'd turned around and refused him so completely that the only logical response was to give up.

His phone buzzed and his friend Kagen's name flashed across the screen.

Hey, we're going to Finnigan's later, you in?

Random did not feel like going out. But sitting on his porch all day, alone, doing nothing, smelled strongly of a level of pathetic he had no desire to descend into. He had taken a vacation to *do* something, hadn't he? Frankly, it was a miracle his friends were still talking to him. He was typing in a rote acceptance when his Aspect flared, reminding him that Finnigan's was classy and respectable, and he wanted neither of those things.

Make it Savado's and I'll be there. Savado's was about as far from respectable as bars came.

Done. Ellipses appeared on the screen, before: *Carli's bringing a friend.*

Random groaned. Ever since Kagen had married Carli, the woman had become obsessed with the notion that Random would turn into a nice, reasonable human being if only he found his own marital bliss, and she had proceeded to parade a string of women in front of him, all presumably willing to take the job.

I'm not interested. He didn't get an answer to that, so he added, *Seriously. Carli brings a friend, she's Carli's problem.*

The last thing his evening needed was another bloody female. He should just stay home. Not risk it. But he had to get on with his life at some point.

Tonight was as good a night for it as any other.

CHAPTER

THREE

S avado's was a behemoth of an establishment situated in a converted warehouse. It sat off to the side of the highway, about a mile outside of town, and it attracted the sort of clientele who would frequent a bar that wasn't anywhere near another business. It was ten thousand square feet of undivided space, its only organization into sections provided by the intended use of a particular area.

To the right of the entrance sat a scattering of high tables and dart boards. The far wall opposite the entrance housed the establishment's first bar, the wide area in front of it marked out for dancing by the shift in flooring from tile to wood, the latter marking out a large, rectangular area in front. The second bar lounged in the corner left of the entrance and looked out on the sprawl of pool tables that claimed dominion over that side of the warehouse.

Valkyrie made her way to the first bar. She took the seat at the end, ordered a beer she didn't drink, and scanned the crowd. The place was a nightmare for keeping track of anyone. The sheer physical size alone made it almost impossible. It had a secondary entrance to the one Valkyrie had come through, and over half a dozen doors marked "exit only." On the one hand, all of those things were convenient if she needed to disappear. On the other hand, they were horridly inconvenient if she intended to gain the upper hand on Danvers.

The place was filling up, but it wasn't yet so packed that a methodical sweep of the establishment was impossible. Her aim in arriving an hour early had paid off—she hadn't recognized anyone yet, as Danvers had claimed she would, so she'd arrived first.

At least, she didn't recognize anyone until she swept the billiards area and her gaze snagged on a pool table. More specifically, on the figure bent lazily over it.

Random.

Her first thought was that he couldn't be here. Her second thought was that Danvers had used Illusion Aspect to wear Random's face for the evening, except Danvers wouldn't be hanging out with Kagen and Carli, and Danvers wouldn't have a brunette practically plastered against him.

Her third thought, if she could really be said to be thinking at all by that point, was that she wanted to go insert herself between him and the brunette.

Mine, her body, her Aspect, insisted. He was *hers*, and whoever the fuck that woman was she had no right to be so close to him, almost touching him, breathing the same air he did. Valkyrie's hand clenched around the pint of beer in front of her.

Random made his play, smoothly sinking the eight ball in the corner pocket. The brunette clapped, turned, and revealed the face of Lauren Hale.

Aspect coated Valkyrie's fist and the pint glass in her hand exploded. Shards of glass dug into her palm and drops of blood swirled to mix with the amber beer spreading across the bar. The barkeeper took a step toward her, towel in hand. Then he saw the look on her face and backpedaled so hard it would have been comical if Valkyrie hadn't been so angry.

She grabbed a nearby container of napkins and dumped it onto the mess. All that did was make it so that, instead of a spreading pool of beer, she had a mountain of beer-and-blood-soaked napkins. Wonderful.

What the hell was wrong with her? Random wasn't *hers*, wasn't even *close* to hers.

Liar, her body whispered. *He's yours, you* made *him yours.*

Despite her internal disagreement with herself, she wasn't so distracted that she didn't notice when someone moved into her personal space behind her.

"Need some help?"

"No," she replied without bothering to turn around.

"You sure?" The man stepped around to face her, a fresh napkin container in his hands. He looked to be in his early thirties, and she supposed he was good looking if you were into generic mundanity that looked pretty enough but had nothing unusual to recommend it.

"You can move along," she told him. "I'm not interested in company."

Typically, a well-placed glare was enough to drive most men from her. She'd long ago realized she exuded bitch to such a level that the average male never even bothered to approach her. The ones who did tended to either be very drunk or possessed of massive egos. Unfortunately, Savado's at night had plenty of men who were both.

"Oh, I think you are."

She looked him dead in the eye, prepared to tell him to fuck off in no uncertain terms, when his image flickered, revealing the face of the Council's former scribe, Gary Danvers, for all of half a second before reverting to the generically attractive façade.

Valkyrie's body came to full alertness. Her Aspect rolled to the tips of her fingers, eager for action. She hadn't honestly expected Danvers to come himself.

Her hands wanted to curl into fists. She pressed them flat to her thighs instead, and glass shards dug into her right palm. The pain was good. It kept her from doing anything stupid.

Like trying to kill him right there, right then, in front of the entirety of the bar's occupants.

∾

THE SOUND of shattering glass was the excuse Random needed to move left and regain a scant few inches of his personal space. He couldn't believe Kagen and Carli had brought fucking Lauren Hale with them.

He should have left as soon as he'd seen her, had been going to leave when Kagen had pulled him aside and sworn up and down that Lauren and Carli were BFFs now, or whatever, and Lauren's being here had nothing to do with Random. Then Kagen had asked him why he was "being this way" and he'd been convinced that maybe he was overreacting.

He hadn't been overreacting. All he'd wanted out of tonight was to get drunk and have a good time. Without a woman being involved. Instead, he had Lauren pressing herself to his side whenever the opportunity presented itself, and no one in their party seemed to have a problem with it except him.

The shattered glass that had bought him a moment's reprieve had come from the bar, where a woman with black hair and defined muscles, who could have been Valkyrie's double, sat at a barstool in front of a mess of broken beer glass. The bartender took a single step toward the woman before he froze at the glare on her face, and she dumped a container of napkins on the problem.

Not Valkyrie's double, then. Valkyrie. No one, *no one*, save Valkyrie made anyone backtrack as fast as the bartender just had. The only problem with this theory was that Valkyrie didn't go to bars. Valkyrie didn't do anything that remotely resembled fun, unless one considered galloping around on the seventeen-hand-tall monstrosities she called horses, but which were more like wingless dragons, fun. Random did not.

He briefly entertained the idea that she'd followed him here, but it was a ludicrous notion. She'd wanted *him* to leave *her* alone. She wouldn't waste her time trailing him.

A man stood behind her. He was good-looking, Random supposed, in that way someone could have features that were considered handsome in all the traditionally acceptable ways without actually being interesting. He said something and Kyrie turned.

Random leaned on his pool stick, prepared to enjoy the glorious show that would be Valkyrie telling the guy to fuck off. It would be nice to see her ire directed at someone other than him for a change. Maybe he could even commiserate with the poor bastard later, if only to feel like he had something in common with someone for the night.

Only she didn't tell the guy to fuck off. She smiled—*smiled* —and followed him to a table far enough away that Random could only barely make her out.

Random decided this couldn't be happening. There was no way, absolutely no physically possible way, that he was in the same bar with Valkyrie Winters and she was on a fucking date.

His Aspect surged and his pool stick broke in half.

THE SOUND of splintering wood snapped Valkyrie's gaze back across the room. She wished it hadn't. However Random's pool stick had severed, it had had the effect of molding Lauren against him. His back was turned to Valkyrie, and she watched as Lauren ran her hand over his shoulder. White-hot fury hazed Valkyrie's vision.

She took a deep breath and forced her gaze back to the man in front of her. She couldn't afford to be distracted right now, and Random—she clenched her fist beneath the table, digging the glass shards she still hadn't removed deeper into her palm— Random could let every woman on the planet touch him, if he was so inclined. Valkyrie herself had done everything she could to guarantee that someone else *would*.

As it had before, the pain from the glass in her palm helped, focused her attention where it should be. She doubted the face of the man before her was any more his true one than the one he'd briefly shown her a moment ago. No, his true face, she suspected, probably looked a great deal more like hers.

"Tell me," she said with false calm, "did you kill poor Danvers and impersonate him, or did you simply create a false persona to infiltrate the Council?"

"Neither. Danvers worked for me. When it was convenient, I took his place."

"Worked?"

The man shrugged, the casual, dismissive movement somehow familiar. "He was a loose end."

She supposed his movements *should* be familiar. She had sat in on plenty of Council meetings after Danvers' hiring, watching him scratching away as he recorded the meetings via the extremely antiquated system of ink and paper. She told herself that *that* was why his movements felt familiar. That it had nothing to do with the fact they might share DNA.

"Do you have a name of your own, then, or should I just call you Danvers?"

His mouth twisted into a grimace of distaste. "It is such a mundane name to live under. Names have power, you know. They convey a great many things to the people who bear them. Take yours, for instance. There is strength in the syllables. Do you really think you could have become what you are now if you'd been given a name like Daisy?"

The blow hit. But the fact he knew what her mother had *wanted* to name her didn't quite prove he did indeed have Elijah. She'd been operating under the assumption that he did, but she needed to know for certain.

"No answer?" he taunted.

The answer was *no*. No, because any man who could have

named her Daisy would not have had the desire and fortitude necessary to mold her into what Elijah Winters had made of her. A man who could name her Daisy might actually have treated her like a daughter.

"I didn't come here to discuss myself. Are you going to give me a name to call you or not?"

He shrugged. "You and your lot have been calling me Danvers for months. I imagine it will continue to do the job."

So much for hoping he'd give her a name that would tell her something—anything—about him. "Well then, Danvers, I can't decide if it speaks to your arrogance or your desperation that you came here yourself, after what Siren did to you."

If her words bothered him, he didn't show it. He relaxed, leaning back against his seat. "How *is* your new sister-in-law? I heard the wedding ceremony was touching."

"She's on honeymoon. How are your bones? I heard she broke half of them."

"Bones heal. A lesson you learned multiple times at fourteen, if I'm not mistaken."

Valkyrie's left hand twitched beneath the table. If she closed her eyes, she could still remember the feel of each finger on that hand snapping, one by one. She didn't close her eyes.

"So you *do* have my father, then." Elijah was the only one who could have told him that information. Not even Jace knew —Elijah had sent her away for the length of time it had taken the bones to heal, and she had been glad he had, glad she could protect her little brother from the truth.

She remained outwardly calm but the words, the knowledge, sent the first tinge of true discomfort through her. If her father had told this man about her hand—such a seemingly pointless piece of truth in the great sea of other truths—what else had Elijah told him? And why had Danvers wanted to know about her in the first place?

The man shrugged. "What is Elijah worth to you?"

Valkyrie schooled her voice into indifference. "We both know that isn't the real question. The real question is, what is he worth to you?"

He laughed, softly. "Oh, one might say his value to me is incalculable. I could hardly bear to part with him. Unless, of course, you brought me something of higher value."

"I'm listening."

"The Council's adnexus. I want it."

Valkyrie stiffened. "I don't know what you're—"

"There is *nothing*," he interrupted her, "Elijah Winters knows that I haven't pried out of him. So let's cut the bullshit. I want the adnexus, and I want you to get it for me."

Of all the directions she'd expected this evening to go, this one hadn't even been on the list. She could count on two fingers the number of people outside the councilors themselves who even knew the adnexus existed: one of those people was herself, and the other was Siren.

Now, she had to add Danvers to that list. If he managed to obtain the adnexus, he could destroy the Council. Something he'd already tried to do once.

He could also destroy *her*, which was a fact prior to this moment she'd have said only she, Siren, and Elijah knew. How much had Elijah told Danvers? More to the point, *why* had Elijah told him anything?

"And if I get the adnexus for you, you'll hand over my father?"

"Yes." He lied easily, smoothly.

"And if I don't believe you?"

"Then I'd say congratulations, you aren't an idiot. Unfortunately for you, neither am I."

The words were all the subtle warning it took for her Aspect to leap to readiness. She got halfway out of her seat before his own Aspect struck, reaching for a leash she had foolishly thought only Elijah could hold.

The cold chains around her wrists, links that had been inscribed there over countless hours, countless days, with power that had bit like acid into her skin, her muscles, her *soul*, awakened from the dormant state they'd slumbered in since Elijah's disappearance. Danvers caught the ends of those chains, wrapped them in a fist of power, and pulled.

Valkyrie froze. She didn't have any other choice

"As I said," Danvers said, leaning calmly back in his seat once more, "I know *everything* Elijah knows. Now sit."

She fought the command, fought as she hadn't fought since she was twelve, right after her mother had died, when Elijah Winters had first bound her in chains of Aspect and told her it was for her own good. She was too wild, he'd said, too prone to rages. She wasn't really his daughter. She was the daughter of someone terrible, someone capable of raping her mother, and evil like that ran through a bloodline.

He'd told her he wanted to love her. That he wanted to be proud of her, as if she *were* his own daughter. But if he was ever going to do either, he needed to control her. Until she could prove that she could be good.

She *had* raged, then. Against the chains that had bit beneath her flesh where no one would ever see the scars they left. She'd raged until the heat in her had burned out and she'd almost died. For weeks, months, after that she'd gone along quietly, until her strength had rebuilt enough to challenge those bonds again.

She had continued that way for years, trapped in an endless cycle of fighting a control she couldn't break. But her resistance had taken its toll on Elijah and she'd known that, given the time, she would wear him down enough to break his hold on her.

He'd known it too. So he'd found another lever to push. He had called her into his office one day and explained, in excruciating detail, how easily her brother could be killed. How easily it could be made to look like an accident. How irreversible death was.

It had worked as no threat to *her* ever could. Because her little brother, Jace, was *her* responsibility. One she treasured because he looked up to her, looked at her like she was strong and good and worth something. He was nothing like her, nothing like Elijah. He was everything like her mother had been. Smart, and kind, and sweet.

So she had stopped fighting. She had done everything she could to keep Jace safe. To keep him from ever knowing what a monster Elijah Winters truly was. She had succeeded, and she had been very, very careful to never care about anyone else enough that Elijah had more than one hold over her again.

Had succeeded with that, too, until Random came along. She'd managed to keep that desire hidden until Elijah had disappeared, and in the drunken euphoria his absence had produced, she'd been stupid enough to take what she wanted. The panic had set in later. The realization that she had no idea where her father was. That his disappearance could simply be a game. That in one selfish moment she could have already signed Random's death sentence.

She'd understood, then, what needed to be done. Freedom and safety, they came at a price, and that price was a death. But she couldn't kill a man she couldn't find.

And if she couldn't fight the chains that bound her yet again, she would simply become a different man's puppet.

Danvers snarled and pulled on her chains with a vicious twist of Aspect that slammed her back into her seat. The illusion that made up his appearance didn't show if the fight strained him, but she could smell the sweat he'd broken out in, knew she had cost him more than he would admit to. She was stronger—much stronger—than she'd been as a child, and even if this man knew enough about her to use Jace against her too, Jace was safely away on another continent right now.

There was nothing to keep her in check in this moment.

The hand that held her leash trembled.

"You always were a disappointment to Elijah, you know?" Danvers spat out. "Never quite everything he wanted, never quite good enough. A Valkyrie that never managed to take flight." He reached out, stroked the backs of his fingers across her cheek in a caricature of a loving gesture. His iron grip on her chains kept her from taking that hand off at the wrist. "Let's see if you can do better for me. Come."

He stood and held out his hand. She didn't take it willingly, didn't rise of her own accord. She made him work for every movement of her body, felt what it cost him to make her rise and walk with him out the door.

"TOUCH me again without my consent and you won't like the results." Random never should have had to say the words. He didn't touch a woman without her permission and he deserved the same respect.

He'd tried to see the evening out because he hadn't wanted to be rude, even if what was supposed to be a relaxing night for him to let off steam had turned into him clenching his teeth and trying to avoid all the casual touches he didn't want. But he had his limits, and Lauren had hit them when she had apparently decided he wasn't being *fun* enough and called him a tight-ass. He wouldn't have cared about the comment if she hadn't grabbed his ass to accentuate the point.

Now her big doe eyes were filling up with tears like he'd slapped her, and Kagen and Carli were staring at him like *he* was the one who'd done something wrong.

Carli gave Kagen a look that clearly said she expected him to deal with the situation.

"It was just a joke, man," Kagen said. "You're overreacting."

"Do you have any idea how often I hear that excuse in court?" Since he primarily represented victims of domestic abuse, sexual assault, and sexual harassment, it was practically a litany in his head at this point. *Your Honor, the defendant is clearly overreacting to the situation. If she didn't* want *my client's hand up her skirt, shouldn't she have made a bigger objection at the time?*

"I am not overreacting. I did not come here to get felt up, which I was quite clear about." He turned to Lauren. "And the next time you want to feel someone up, make damn sure the man you're putting your hands all over wants them there."

He left his pool stick against the side of the table and walked away to the sound of Carli's awkward laugh and her nervous, "Well, he's clearly in a mood. Maybe we should call it a night."

By all means, he thought as he headed for the bar, *call it a night.* Let *them* leave. Because he had come here with the intention of getting stupid drunk, and now that he was freed from obligations, he intended to do just that. He ordered a whiskey soda and was impatiently awaiting its arrival when he caught sight of Valkyrie.

He hadn't precisely forgotten that she was in the bar, it was more that avoiding Lauren had consumed all of his mental faculties, and he hadn't had time to think about Kyrie.

He couldn't *not* think about her now. Not when the man across from her leaned over and brushed his fingers along her cheek, then stood and held his hand out to her. Not when she rose and placed hers in his and let him lead her toward the door.

His Aspect leapt to wakefulness, pinging inside him with the instance that this wasn't right. Valkyrie didn't go to bars. She didn't date, and if she did, she wouldn't date a man like that. So plain and boring and *vanilla.*

Maybe Random was just jealous. Maybe he was so gone on her that he couldn't tell the ceiling from the floor. Maybe, no matter how badly she'd hurt him, he couldn't stand the thought of her with someone else.

But his instincts screamed that something was wrong. She had hesitated before she'd stood, and her stride now lacked its usual fluid grace.

He slid off the barstool and quietly followed after her. If he was wrong, if she *was* on a date, if she wanted to be leaving with whoever the hell this guy was, Random would respect that. She'd never even need to know he'd followed her. But like hell was he going to let the woman he loved walk out that door and into someone's vehicle if it wasn't what she wanted to be doing.

VALKYRIE USED the oldest trick she knew. Halfway across the parking lot, she quit fighting. The sudden release of tension caught Danvers by surprise, made him relax without meaning to. His hold on her lessened and she lunged at the opening, both mentally and physically.

She got a single physical blow in before his Aspect reached through the chains and crushed her like a full-body vise. She stood, frozen, while his fist slammed into her face. He released physical control of her as the blow landed and she went sprawling on the gravel lot.

"Kyrie!"

Random.

No. What the hell was he doing out here?

Fear hit her, then, as it hadn't when she had been the only one in danger. She opened her mouth to scream at him to leave, but her body wasn't under her own control, her vocal cords frozen along with the rest of her. Everything else happened too fast. Danvers turned from her, his power aimed at a new target. Random's footfalls sounded on the gravel as he ran toward her.

This couldn't be happening. She hadn't denied herself the brief time she might have had with him, hadn't compacted her emotions into an infinitesimal speck to ensure his survival just to watch him die in front of her. It wasn't that she thought he was helpless—she knew he wasn't—but his Aspect wasn't *normal*, either. He couldn't wield it in his defense like an ordinary Aspecter could. He could only let it *act* in his defense. And she wasn't going to take the risk that this time, it wouldn't make the right decision for him.

She slammed every ounce of her will against the chains Danvers held and shoved herself to her feet. Every tendon in her body felt as if it ripped from the bone as she flung herself in front of Random. Danvers's blast of Aspect hit her square in the chest. The impact knocked her off her feet, shoved her back into Random like a wrecking ball.

He didn't go down—he had better balance than she'd given him credit for. His arms came around her, steadied her as they skidded back together on the loose gravel. She blinked in rapid succession as her vision turned white. If she'd had an ordinary upbringing, she'd already be unconscious from taking a concentrated hit of Aspect with no shields in place. But she had practice with taking these kinds of hits. She'd done it every Friday of her sixteenth year.

She *would* pass out soon, but for now, she fought through it.

Random's body kept her upright when Danvers gripped her chains in a fist of Aspect and pulled. Random's arms around her waist held her to him when Danvers commanded her to moved forward. And then Random's Aspect did what it always did—it acted of its own volition in the manner it thought would serve its wielder best.

Random's power curved down her arms like a caress, slid carefully, gently, around her chains, and pried Danvers's grip from her. Then it sunk deeper, searching, testing. It felt along the inscribed lines of her bondage and then did the impossible.

Casually, as if it took no more effort than blinking, Random's Aspect sank into her chains and shattered them.

It was a profound, life altering moment and she didn't have the chance to appreciate it. A fresh wave of Danvers's Aspect surged toward her. She blinked through the white lights in her vision and snapped a shield into place.

It wasn't an ordinary shield. It also wasn't anything she had ever tried to use in actual combat, either. It was an idea, one she had played with over the years but never used in practice. Because if it had worked, she hadn't wanted her father to know.

Danvers's Aspect barreled into that shield. Rather than blunt his power, as a traditional shield did, hers embraced it, curving ever-so-slightly. It bent just enough beneath the blow to catch the attack, to hold it for a brief moment, and then rebound it upon its wielder.

Danvers didn't block—he didn't have time to, couldn't have prepared for something he'd never have expected—and his own attack hit him full-on.

He vanished.

Valkyrie lunged for the place where he'd been but her body refused to move, her sight whittled down to a narrow pinprick. She fought to tell Random that Danvers wasn't gone, that it was just illusion, but her throat was so tight she could barely suck air through it, much less speak. The sparkles in her vision went blindingly white and, much to her mortification, she passed out in Random's arms.

CHAPTER

FOUR

The only thing that kept Random from driving straight to a Council medical facility was the inescapable pull of his Aspect demanding that he take Valkyrie home instead. Considering the inconvenience his power became any time Valkyrie so much as needed a snack, he trusted it knew things he didn't, and she would be fine. Besides which, she'd probably kill him if she woke up in a hospital.

He'd pulled her Jeep into his driveway before he realized he'd brought her to *his* home instead of hers. She would likely be as pissed about waking up in his house as she would have been about waking up in a hospital, but he wasn't changing course now. Besides, she *had* told him to stay out of her house. He always respected a woman's wishes.

The lack of doors on the vehicle was a convenient aid to his getting her out of it and carrying her inside. He wished he could say he swept her into his arms, but it was slightly less graceful than that. He considered himself to be in excellent shape but Valkyrie had an inch on him in height and she was a freight train of solid muscle.

As he climbed the five steps up to his front porch, he was forced to admit there was absolutely nothing graceful about his hauling her up them, and he was glad she was unconscious for the ungainly event. Especially the part where he had to half set her down to open the front door.

She woke up when he was five feet from the couch, because of course she did. She couldn't even stay passed out for a length of time that befitted the amount of damage she'd taken. No, she was Valkyrie Winters, and she had to do everything slightly faster and better than everyone else.

He didn't even try to hold her. He dropped her at the first sign of movement. She landed on all fours like a cat, immediately sliding into a sweep that would have taken his legs out from under him if he hadn't backed well away from her the second he'd let her go.

"Not the enemy here, love." The endearment rolled off his tongue before he could stop it.

She zeroed in on him and stilled. He watched her take him in, then take in the room, then settle back on him before the tense lines of her shoulders eased.

"Where are we?" she asked.

"My place."

She frowned. "You live in a condo."

"I did. Now I live here."

She stalked for the door. He stepped in front of it.

"Get out of my way," she ordered. It was a good tone for ordering people about, appropriately terse and with all the right undercurrents promising terrible things would happen to him if he didn't comply.

Too bad for her, not complying was what he did best. "You just got knocked unconscious. Where do you think you're going?"

"After him."

"He's gone."

"He didn't vanish," she said in a patient tone—so patient it was condescending, "he's an Illusion Aspecter."

"Since I didn't think ceasing to exist had suddenly become a new branch of Aspect, I did gather it was something like that. He did, however, get into a vehicle and drive away."

"You let him go?" she growled.

"Couldn't see him to stop him, love."

"Why are you calling me that?"

Because I'm an idiot who can't help himself. "Because it irritates you," he lied. "I am irritated by tonight's turn of events, so I thought I would share the joy."

"So sorry if I interrupted your *date*, but I never asked you to come after me."

"I wasn't on a date, and you're physically incapable of asking for help when you need it."

"Lauren Hale seemed to think it was a date, and I didn't need help. If you hadn't come rampaging after me I wouldn't have had to throw myself in the literal line of fire, and I might actually have what I need right now." Her eyes flashed with the anger that limned her entire body, as if she were a vessel storing righteous indignation, and once she hit critical mass she'd go off. If he wasn't still recovering from the fear that he'd almost lost her earlier, he would poke her just to see if she exploded.

And why did she keep bringing up the date he hadn't even been on?

"Lauren did think it was a date. I corrected the misunderstanding. And forgive me, but you did need help. I watched you sit still and get punched in the face by a man who had literal Aspect chains around you. So what the fuck is going on?"

"It's work."

"Your work for the Council took you to a bar to meet a dangerous man *without* backup?"

"Yes."

"I already heard DuPont canned you. Lie better, Kyrie."

"It's none of your business." She lifted her chin defiantly. Did she have to be so goddess-damned beautiful when her eyes were telling him to fuck off? He was a masochist if ever there was one.

"Fine. You want to play it that way? Illegal use of Aspect occurred in Council territory, to which I was a witness." He pulled out his phone. "I feel the need to do my civic duty and report it."

"Don't."

His thumb hovered over his contacts list. "Give me a reason not to. Talk to me."

Her mouth stayed resolutely shut.

"Since words are so difficult for you, why don't I start with what I know? There are no Illusion Aspecters in Seclusion powerful enough to do what this one did tonight. I can think of precisely one in the entire country who is, and he nearly killed us all six months ago. He's also conveniently the only person I know who does weird experimental shit with Aspect like carve chains into people.

"There. I talked. Now it's your turn."

Valkyrie looked down at her wrists. She still couldn't believe the chains were gone.

"How did you destroy them?"

He shrugged, as if wiping away sixteen years of bondage in the space of a breath was nothing. "I didn't like them." He sank a world of meaning into the statement. "How did he get them on you in the first place?"

Her breath left her in a rush. Random didn't know. Whatever his Aspect had shown him when it severed her bonds, it hadn't shown him how old they were. She'd been so sure he would know, had prepared herself for the questions he would have about *that*.

Part of her had been relieved, had been selfishly glad the truth would finally come out. But it hadn't, it wouldn't, and that was good. That was better. Safer. For him.

"I don't know. I don't understand how the chains worked."

That much, at least, was true. If she had understood them, she would have removed them herself. "Thank you."

He jerked back. "What?"

"Thank you," she repeated. "For removing them." He didn't understand the depth of what he'd done, but *she* did.

He walked up and pressed his palm flat against her forehead. She went completely still. His body was barely a foot from hers, close enough to reach out and touch, to bury her head in the curve of his shoulder and breathe in his scent.

She batted his hand away. "What are you doing?"

"Checking for a fever," he murmured.

"Why?"

"You just thanked me."

"Isn't that what normal people do when someone helps them?"

"Yes. It just isn't typically what *you* do." He gave her a half smile, more a slight curving of lips than anything else. "Especially not when it comes to me."

There was something a little wistful in his voice. Combined with the intensity in his eyes as he looked at her, she could almost believe that the things he'd spent the last year telling her were true. That she wasn't just another phase for him. That he actually wanted her.

She realized she'd stopped breathing, stopped doing anything other than staring into his eyes.

"Kyrie?" His voice was thick and heavy.

Those two syllables cut through her walls like nothing else could. He was the only person who had ever called her that. She'd clung to it over the years, as if it were a separate identity she could lose herself in. When being Valkyrie or Ms. Winters was too difficult, when she hated both of those people, she could pretend she was Kyrie. Imagine the kind of person Kyrie *could* be.

But she couldn't be Kyrie right now, because Kyrie wanted to close the space between them and take his mouth with hers, wanted to lose her body in his, and the way he'd spoken her name told her Random's thoughts weren't far from her own.

"He has my father," she blurted out. The words had the intended effect of chilling the warmth in Random's eyes, of making him take a careful step back from her.

~

"DOES everything in your life come back to Elijah fucking Winters?"

Valkyrie's face shut down. Random took a deep breath and ran his hand through his hair. "I'm sorry. That was uncalled for."

Blood dripped off her hand to plink on the hardwood floor. He shook his head, retrieved a first aid kit from the bathroom and used the time to consider the situation logically, unemotionally. When he returned, he set the kit on the table and gestured her over.

"Give me your hand." Amazingly, she did. He set to work with the kit's tweezers, picking out bits of glass. She never so much as flinched, even when he had to dig in for a particularly stubborn sliver. "What was all the glass-breaking about anyway?"

She shrugged. "Something pissed me off. Nothing to do with you."

The very fact she felt the need to qualify that made him pretty certain it *had* had something to do with him. Wasn't that interesting?

He finished picking out all the glass, moved on to antiseptic, and segued back into the real conversation. "We don't know that Danvers has Elijah. Siren didn't actually see your dad when Danvers had her in captivity. She just saw an illusion of him.

"He has him."

"Valkyrie—"

"He knew things about me only my father knows. He has him."

He let out a frustrated breath and tore open a package of gaze, pressing it to her palm. "Okay. Say he does. Who is he? And how did you find him?"

"He told me to stick with calling him Danvers."

"Figures."

"And I didn't find him. He found me."

He grimaced. "The envelope you brought to my office?"

He'd known something was off when she'd stormed in, but he'd ignored it. Ignored it because she'd pissed him off, because he'd needed distance from her after what she'd said to him at Jace's wedding. That wasn't the first time she'd cut him to the core, but he *had* intended for it to be the last. Now here she was in his kitchen and he'd lost all of his senses a minute ago and almost asked if he could kiss her. *Would* have asked, if she hadn't spoken.

"Yes." He wished she was saying that to the question he hadn't asked, rather than the one he had. "Whoever delivered it got through the estate's wards without damaging them. The only person I know who can do that is you. Or the person who made the wards."

He finished taping the gauze down and reluctantly let go of her hand. "*You* built new wards when Siren was living at the estate." Valkyrie's now sister-in-law had tumbled into their lives with a mountain of problems on her heels, and she'd been attacked twice on the Winters' estate before Valkyrie had laid her own set of wards inside the ones her father had built.

"I took them down after she left."

"Why would you do that when you *knew* there was an issue with the wards your dad left on the estate?" He cursed in two languages as the answer dawned on him. "Bait? Please tell me you were not playing bait."

She said nothing. Loudly.

"Did you think your father was somehow involved in the ward breaches all along? Because Siren's life was on the line and you didn't say anything."

"I didn't think it then. Not with the first attack on her. That one broke the wards. It was the second instance that made me think it was a possibility Elijah was involved and I *did* do what was necessary to protect her after that. But she isn't living on the estate anymore. And she's strong enough now she doesn't need anyone's protection."

Random squeezed his eyes shut and didn't bother to point out that *Kyrie* still lived on the estate. Telling her to protect herself was a losing argument.

"Why would your father tell Danvers anything? He's been hunting the man for years. Danvers kidnapped your mother. He experimented on her Aspect, he—"

Raped her. Shit.

"Yes," Valkyrie said softly. "Odds are good that you met my *real* father tonight."

"Does he know?"

Valkyrie shrugged. "My mother wasn't very far along when Elijah rescued her. Danvers may not have realized she was pregnant."

"Are you okay?"

"I'm fine."

"Kyrie—"

"I'm *fine*, Random."

He held at bay every instinct that told him she *wasn't* fine. Denied the urge to take her in his arms. She didn't want his support. She didn't want his concern. She never had.

"Why would your father give him anything?" Random repeated. "Elijah Winters doesn't strike me as the kind of man who breaks under duress."

"I don't know."

She was lying to him. He'd have bet everything he owned on the fact because he knew *her*. Had known her since they were kids, before she'd closed herself off completely. Back when he could still talk her into playing cards with him and Jace. She'd trounced her little brother every game, but Random, Random had only lost when he wanted to. He knew her tell, and it was nothing as simple as a physical movement, a tick.

It was in her voice, in the slight shift in timbre when she had something to hide. If he'd wanted to win a game, he'd simply told her *he* was going to win it. She would inevitably tell him he wouldn't and he would know, by the way she said it, whether she had a decent hand or not.

She didn't have a decent hand right now. But if he called her out on it, if he tried to push her, he wouldn't win the game. She would simply walk away from it.

Before Jace had left for his honeymoon, he'd told Random that he thought Kyrie was keeping something about their father from him. And Random had long thought there was something *off* about Elijah Winters. To put it simply, the man had always given him the creeps. His great aunt, Ella, had never liked Elijah either, which told Random pretty much everything he needed to know.

After Elijah had gone missing, it had been the first time in years that Random had seen any glimmer of the Kyrie he remembered. That day she'd come home with him, when they'd —he shut the thought down and gave himself a good, hard mental shake.

This wasn't about him and her. She didn't want him. She didn't love him. He could accept that. But he couldn't change how he felt about her. He'd been fine with the idea of running away from those feelings until this mess landed in his lap.

He hadn't liked Kyrie and Jace's father when he'd thought the man was just an asshole. But if there was something more going on, he couldn't walk away. Not when her psychopath of a biological father was in the mix, too. Because Kyrie wouldn't ask anyone for help, and he was the only one suicidal enough to try to make her accept his.

That decision made, it was easier to take an emotional step back from the situation and think logically. "What does he want?"

"What?"

"Danvers. What does he want? You wouldn't have gone to meet him if he hadn't dangled an offer in front of you. Tell me what he wants and we'll figure out how to proceed."

~

VALKYRIE'S BLOOD CHILLED. "*We* are not proceeding. You wanted to know what was going on, I told you. That was the deal."

Random shoved his hands into his pockets and leaned against the kitchen's breakfast bar, his entire body going liquid and relaxed. That was bad. The more calm and seemingly indifferent Random got, the more dangerous he became. It meant his brain was working overtime.

"We didn't have a deal, love."

She used to watch him in court. Whenever she'd had a really shitty month, she would quietly hunt up his schedule and slip into the back of the courtroom, careful not to be noticed. The cases he took weren't always easy to listen to, but *he* was—smart and calculating and graceful. He cared about people, and it made him relentless in his pursuit of justice.

Whenever he had a really difficult case, he would look just like he did right now. And when he looked like he did now, he never lost.

"You said you'd leave it alone if I told you what was going on."

"No, I told you to give me a reason not to call the Council. So far, all I've heard are a litany of reasons *to* call them."

"It isn't their concern."

Random arched an eyebrow at her. "The man who is number one on the Council's most-wanted list is in the stronghold of their territory and it isn't the Council's concern?"

"They'll only get in my way. This is personal."

"Not a good enough reason."

"Fine. Call them. I'll deny everything. There's no evidence.

He'll have Scoured the scene, there won't *be* anything to Track. It'll be my word against yours. And Meredith won't Truthfinder this mess because she still wants to be BFFs with me."

"Then I'll call Jace."

"Don't you dare." She hadn't been through everything she'd been through, hadn't sacrificed everything she'd sacrificed to protect Jace only to have him thrown into a scenario likely to get him killed.

The intensity of her refusal was a tactical error, however. She knew it by the way Random's gaze sharpened, and though recovery was likely impossible, she tried anyway. "He's on his honeymoon. Don't bother him over something trivial."

"I don't think he would consider his sister being on an apparent suicide mission *trivial*. If that's the lever I have to pull, Kyrie, I'll pull it."

He would, too. She saw it in his eyes, in the set of his jaw, and didn't understand it. Didn't understand why he cared what happened to her.

He'd said he loved her. A year ago, a lifetime ago, he'd said those words. But he hadn't meant them. He *couldn't* have meant them.

She straightened her shoulders. "What will it take to keep you from calling him? What's the *deal*, Random?"

"The deal, love, is you tell me what he wants from you. We agree on a plan, and I am glued to your bloody side until this is over."

"I don't need your help."

"Don't care. Take it anyway, or I call Jace."

The muscles in her shoulders bunched. Either she refused, keeping Random safe and risking Jace, or she kept Jace safe and risked Random. Jace wasn't a fighter. Oh, he had many of the necessary skills—Elijah had seen to that—but his heart was never in it. Random's Aspect made him difficult to counter in a fight, and his mercurial nature made it impossible to predict what he would do in any given situation.

Random was the obvious choice, on paper. She didn't want to choose at all. But if she refused, if he did call Jace, Random wouldn't simply wait quietly for her brother to come home. He'd sunk his teeth into this problem and he wouldn't let it go. If Random was going to be involved in this, she'd have a better chance of protecting him if she kept him with her. And if she wanted to protect him forever, she'd just have to make certain she accomplished her objective.

"All right. Fine. We work together, and Jace doesn't hear about any of this. Ever. That's the deal."

"Agreed. We can discuss the particulars tomorrow. It's late and you're barely standing—"

"I'm fine," she said automatically, even though he was right. Because she'd never been allowed to admit she *wasn't* fine. Because any sign of weakness she'd ever shown had always been met with punishment.

"Forgive me," he said, his voice laden with sarcasm. "Of course you are fine. Should I pretend *I'm* barely standing and you should go to sleep because I need to? Will that do it for you?"

She didn't dignify that with a response. The keys to her Jeep were in the middle of the living room floor, no doubt dropped when Random had dropped *her*. She retrieved them. Random put himself in front of the door and leaned back against it, arms folded across his chest.

"I can't go home and sleep if you don't move away from the damn door."

Not that she'd get any sleep at home. The house was too large and empty and filled with memories she didn't need to relive. It had been bearable when Jace and Siren had been living there, but they'd moved out months ago because they were normal human beings who wanted their own space.

After their departure, it had been bearable because Random had started showing up every morning. Knowing he would be there had kept her from feeling like she was walking through her own tomb, just waiting for the silence to kill her.

"What part of 'glued to your side for the duration of this mess' was unclear?"

She narrowed her gaze. "I assumed you meant when I was investigating. You didn't specify otherwise."

"Mine was an all-encompassing statement. Failure to specify was on your end."

"You want me to *live* here?" Incredulity twined with stupid pleasure hit her like a strange, wondrous cocktail. At that moment, it didn't matter that he only wanted her to stay because of some sense of obligation toward her. It only mattered that she wouldn't have to go home to the vacant emptiness that awaited her there.

"I recognize it isn't the luxury you're accustomed to," Random bit off, and she realized too late how her words must have sounded, "but I hardly think it's slumming it. My bedroom is through there."

He pointed to a short hallway across the living room. Every nerve in her body went on high alert. Surely the whole glued-to-her-side thing didn't literally mean at all hours of the day and night? The idea of being in the same bedroom with him, in the same *bed*, sent an ache of longing through her, which in turn produced a feeling of sheer panic. She struck back out of self-preservation, her voice cold and harsh.

"To be clear, I agreed to work with you. I didn't agree to anything else."

She regretted the words the instant they left her mouth. Random stiffened, and she thought he would have looked less hurt if she'd hurled him off a two-story building.

"I'll be on the couch. You have the room to yourself." His words were perfectly even, the smooth monotone that came out when he was angry but holding that anger inside him.

"Random." His name was the only word she could form. She wanted to say she was sorry, that she knew he would never use leverage over her for *that* purpose. He'd never tried to force her to do anything. She had always known that if she told him to leave her alone, he would. It was why it had taken her so very long to do it.

He watched her, waiting for her to continue. But she didn't have anything else to say. Better, if she had hurt him. Best, if she had finally hurt him enough he wanted nothing to do with her.

"Go to bed, Kyrie," he said softly. "I can't talk to you anymore tonight."

For the first time in her life, she did what she was told without even wanting to argue. She fled for the relative safety of the bedroom and the closed door it put between her and him. Unfortunately, it took less than a breath inside it for her to realize nothing about this room was safe for her. It *felt* like Random, and when she kicked off her boots and climbed into the large four-poster bed, the sheets smelled like Random.

She stared at her carefully bandaged hand, remembering the feel of Random's fingers against her skin, the gentleness with which he'd cleaned the shallow cuts. She wanted everything she'd been terrified of minutes before. She wanted him in here with her, next to her, touching her. The weak part of her whispered that he was already in danger. That he was involved in this mess now and sleeping with him couldn't possibly make him any less safe than he already was.

But even if that was true, it wasn't safe for *her*. Having him again would only make her want him again. Random didn't do long-term. She'd never seen him with the same woman for more than a month. His tenacity in hounding after *her* stemmed from a misplaced sense of guilt, and she didn't want to be anyone's pity-fuck. Least of all his.

She buried her head in his pillow, breathed in his scent, and knew she wouldn't sleep.

RANDOM STARED down the hallway where Valkyrie had disappeared behind the closed door of his bedroom. Every time he thought she couldn't possibly manage to hurt him more, she outdid herself. That was his Kyrie, always reaching previously unimagined heights.

He should have just climbed into the damn Jeep with her and let her drive back to the Winters' estate. It would have been better than seeing the contempt on her face at the thought of spending a night in his home.

From the moment he'd started designing the house, he hadn't bothered to lie to himself. He'd built it for her. Goddess knew *he* had no need of a sparring room with several weapons racks, or the ten-stall barn out back that was currently empty.

He'd even chosen the damn interior design with her in mind. All dark wood floors and cabinetry and gray-toned blues because she didn't like anything bright. He couldn't build her a mansion—he didn't have the kind of money the Winters or Meredith had, the kind of money that ran in the old Aspect Society families—but he'd done well for himself. He could give her the things he'd thought were most important to her.

And she'd curled her nose up at the thought of staying here for a few hours.

He couldn't even be mad at her about it because she'd never once pretended to want anything he could offer. The only hope she'd ever given him was a few months of not outright refusing his attention.

He picked up his phone and called his real estate agent. A groggy voice answered and he belatedly realized it was past midnight. Still, he'd already made the call. And the man *had* picked up.

"Daniel, it's Random. I need to sell my house."

Several beats of silence followed this announcement. "The house you just moved into?"

"Yes, that one."

"So you want to take the condo in town off the market?"

"No." He'd had sex with Kyrie in that condo. He was never setting foot in it again if he could help it. "Sell that too."

"Okay, if that's what you want. What should I be on the lookout for?"

"Lookout for?"

"For your new residence? What did you have in mind?"

"Nothing. Don't look for anything."

The pause that followed had a weight of concern, transmissible even over the phone line. "Mr. Tremayne, are you feeling well?"

"Perfectly well."

"Why don't you sleep on this decision," Daniel said, his voice trying a little too hard to be calming.

"I don't need to. Just put the house on the market."

"I'm going to hold off on that. Why don't you think about it for a week and call me if you still want to sell. Maybe talk it over with someone."

"I don't—"

"Maybe someone professional. Goodnight, Mr. Tremayne."

The line clicked. Great. Now Random didn't have the peace of mind of knowing the house was going on the market and his real estate agent thought he was having a mental health crisis.

He tossed the phone on the kitchen counter in disgust. Then he rolled up his shirt sleeves and pulled the mixing bowls out of the cabinet. He clearly wasn't going to sleep tonight. He might as well fucking bake something.

CHAPTER

FIVE

Valkyrie woke—which was a surprise in and of itself because it meant she'd actually slept—to a mixture of delicious scents that had made it past the closed door into Random's bedroom. She opened the door and ghosted down the hallway on bare feet, the soft wood warm beneath her skin.

She took a moment to appreciate it. Did the man have to own her dream home? Why couldn't he still be living in the impersonal condo where they'd—no. She was not going to relive *that* memory. But at least the walls there had been an irritatingly bright white, the floors uninspiring brown tile. *This* house, with its cozy, muted colors, its warm wood floors and elegant but understated design, wrapped itself around her like it was made for her. Like it had been sitting here, waiting for her to come home.

She got a mental grip on herself as she hit the end of the hallway, and stopped dead in her tracks. The kitchen bar was littered with baked goods. A pie with a latticework top crust sat next to a platter of iced brownies, which in turn sat beside a plate of scones. A casserole dish of what looked like frittata perched on a cooling rack. Random was in front of the stove, his back to her, the smell of bacon sizzling from the pan in front of him.

Guilt twisted through her. Random cooked all the time. He only baked when he was upset or stressed, and by the looks of it he'd been going all night. She hadn't seen him bake this much since the week before his and Jace's Academy finals.

"I'm sorry," she said quietly.

The stiffening of his shoulders told her he hadn't realized she was there until she'd spoken, which wasn't really a surprise. She'd moved soundlessly out of habit, and Random had a tendency to get lost in his own head.

"For what?" He didn't turn, just methodically flipped the bacon in the skillet.

Everything, she wanted to say. "I don't know."

He shook his head and flicked off the burner. "Coffee's made, if you want some."

The coffeemaker rested on the counter next to the stove, between Random and the refrigerator. She would have to go stand next to him to get it. It felt too personal, too domestic. She'd slept in his bed, for goddess sake, and now she was going to go pour her own coffee like she had a right to be here, a right to stand close enough to him to lean in and kiss him good morning.

The thought sent a knife of pain through her chest. Domestic bliss had never been high on her list of life's priorities. Hell, it had never been on the list at all. Even in those rare moments when she'd allowed herself to admit she was human, that she *did* have wants, those wants hadn't extended to ever imagining something like this.

Simplicity. Comfort. Shared spaces.

To imagining that she would even want something like this. She thought that if she took Random out of the equation, replaced him with anyone else, the whole domestic thing wouldn't appeal anymore.

But standing there, watching him, it had a draw she couldn't deny. She wanted him to want her here. In his house, in his bed, in his kitchen. She wanted to know that if she walked over and stood beside him, he would *want* her to kiss him good morning.

She acknowledged the desire and then let it go, arranging her face into the mask that had seen her through so much of her life. It had taken her years to perfect it, to make it so expressionless that her father could no longer tell what she thought, what she felt. It was her battle mask, and if this wasn't a battleground, she didn't know what was.

She set her shoulders and walked to the coffeemaker.

Kyrie stood next to him like it physically pained her to be in close proximity to him. She pulled a mug from the wooden rack beside the coffeepot and filled it. The movement was graceful. Not in a delicate, polished way, but in the way that strength and surety, the way that something deadly, was graceful.

She was close enough he could wrap an arm around her waist, tug her to him and kiss her. Here she stood in his kitchen, in the house he'd built for her, and none of it was the way he'd imagined. He'd known he was an idiot for building it in the first place, and he'd been okay with that, with the knowledge that she would likely never set foot in it, no matter how badly he wanted her to.

He'd just never imagined that he would find himself in a situation where she was *here*, but she didn't belong to him. So it might hurt her to stand next to him, but it hurt him, too. Because this was so close to everything he'd wanted, only it wasn't.

The doorbell rang.

He barely had time to register the sound before she was across the room, a dagger in her left hand, her Aspect gathering around her like a storm cloud. She peered through the front door's peephole, her body a single, taut line of alertness.

His own Aspect hadn't flickered with any of the warning

signs it traditionally produced when danger was near, but then, while his Aspect tended to do what it thought was best for him, it could also be overly focused on what he wanted. Since the person he wanted most in the world was standing ten feet away, looking like the Valkyries she was named for, it was possible his Aspect could have been too misdirected to notice an approaching threat.

But he doubted it. Because the only thing he wanted more than Valkyrie here, was Valkyrie safe. So he wasn't surprised when she relaxed a fraction and opened the door. No one stood outside. Instead, a manila envelope lay on the doormat. She stepped over it, her gaze sweeping the area beyond.

He moved to the doorway, but when he tried to follow her outside she whipped around, the flat of her palm slamming into his chest with enough force to bump him back over the threshold.

"Stay inside."

"It's not a bomb, Kyrie, it's a letter."

"Yes. But it's addressed to me."

He looked down and saw she was right.

"It isn't ideal, but it isn't surprising Danvers knows who I am, and I *was* in your company last night. If he tried your place and found it empty, it's logical he would jump to mine. And since my wards don't suffer from the intentional loopholes yours do, he can't get in here without alerting us."

The envelope had been delivered via the Seclusion Courier, a private delivery service. A *Null* private delivery service. Aspect wards typically weren't set to keep out Nulls—both because they weren't much of a threat to anyone with Aspect, and because Aspecters, like most everyone else, preferred their packages actually arrive at their place of living—and Random's were no exception.

"There's no one here," he insisted. A blur descended from the sky and Nelsen hurtled down to land on the porch railing. Kyrie, who had readied and then relaxed her dagger in the space of a second after identifying Nelsen, gave the falcon a pointed glare, as if wondering how he could be so dumb as to appear out of nowhere at a tense time.

"Let's just ask Nelsen, shall we? Nelsen, is anyone on the property?" His Aspect caught the words and translated them for the bird, who replied with a series of noises that Random's Aspect translated into a mental image of a barren field.

"Nelsen says it's all clear."

"Forgive me if I don't take the bird's word for it. I need to clear the area. Which means I need *you* to stay inside."

"You do realize *I'm* the one who broke your mystical chains of bondage last night, right? I'm not helpless, Kyrie."

She gave him *that* look, the one that told him there was no point in arguing with her.

"Fine, I'll stay inside." But only because his Aspect hummed quietly inside him with the pleasant happiness it felt whenever Valkyrie was near, and none of the disquiet it felt when she was near and in danger. "But your coffee's going to get cold."

He bent down to retrieve the envelope.

"Leave it," she snapped.

"Yes, General." He gave her a sharp salute that she ignored. To Nelsen, he said, "I'm sure that somewhere, deep down, she apologizes for her rude behavior." Then he shut the door and went to put the bacon in the oven to keep it warm. For good measure, he dumped her coffee back into the carafe as well. She'd probably be half an hour before she was convinced the damn premises were safe.

VALKYRIE SWEPT the perimeter of the house, despite her relative certainty that nothing was wrong. She'd looked out the peephole in time to see the courier service driving away and her senses, Aspect-heightened by the possibility of danger, hadn't keyed in on anything more dangerous than a suicidal squirrel leaping through the tall pine trees that surrounded Random's house.

But Elijah Winters had trained her to be thorough no matter how benign a situation appeared, and she'd be damned if anything happened to Random because she'd been too lazy to take sensible precautions. He *wasn't* helpless, but he also wouldn't be in any danger at all right now if it weren't for her.

She should have asked him how large the property was, but while that would have made things easier it wasn't, strictly speaking, necessary. She cast her Aspect out and searched for the wards that protected the home of every Aspecter powerful enough to create them. They were easy to find. Like the stickers on Null house windows that proclaimed the home was protected by such-and-such alarm system, wards *wanted* to be noticed. Their primary purpose was to declare that the property they protected was more trouble than it was worth to breach.

Her power brushed against Random's wards, her Aspect whispering against his like the soft touch of velvet against skin. Long tendrils of her power left her, disappeared into the wards and weaved themselves into the structure, adding her strength to Random's cleverness.

It was an instinctual thing, more her Aspect's choice than hers, and it happened before she could think to stop it. Now that it had, she couldn't believe Random had allowed it. Wards weren't open to manipulation unless their maker wanted them to be. He would have felt her touch the moment she found the wards, could have kept her out with a lazy blink.

A joint work like this, mixing Aspect—it was personal. It suggested an almost intimate level of trust between two people, which was why the only people who typically worked together in this fashion, actually blending Aspect together, tended to be close family members or lovers.

Family. Random was her brother's best friend. They had all grown up together. Of course he trusted her. Beneath the sarcastic playboy lay a core of practicality most people would never expect from Random, and he would have recognized the value her enhancements could bring to the wards. That was all. It had nothing, absolutely nothing, to do with *her*.

She finished her sweep of the area around the house, her new connection to the wards obviating the need to physically search the entire property. Fortunate since, though she couldn't put an exact acreage to it, she had the sense the property was large. Nothing near the fifty acres her father's estate comprised, but maybe ten or so.

She'd never envisioned Random as the type to want any amount of land. When they were younger, he'd frequently complained that she and Jace lived too far away from anything fun. Her confusion only mounted when she found the barn. She swept the building to verify it was empty, which it was. Completely empty. No horses, no tack, nothing. Why the hell would Random buy a property with equestrian facilities? Much less one with a ten-stall barn, three turnouts, two round pens, and an arena?

Properties with these kinds of facilities did not come cheap, and while she suspected he did well for himself, she couldn't imagine why he would spend his money on this. It was more her style than his, and he obviously hadn't decided to buy an actual horse.

She stalked back to the front door and swept up the envelope. She didn't doubt Danvers knew her phone number and could have just as easily sent a text instead. He'd sent a letter for the same reason he'd put one in her house. He wanted her to know that he knew where she was. That he knew how to get to her.

She pulled out the slip of paper and her blood went cold.

Random Tremayne? Really, Ms. Winters, I'd have thought you'd have more sense than to get attached to anyone. Attachments can be so...fragile. So easily broken. I would hate for

something to happen to him. And your father would be so disappointed.

Valkyrie's fingers clenched, wrinkling the edges of the paper. She didn't like Danvers' continual references to Elijah. Because, like Random, she couldn't see her adoptive father bending to anyone's will, much less that of the man he'd been hunting ever since her mother's death.

Elijah Winters didn't have it in him *to* bend. Yes, torture could make a person say almost anything, but this was more than that. It was one thing for Danvers to know about her once-broken fingers, but this was different. It was in the tone of the words, the easy, casual knowledge that her father *would* be disappointed, and the implication of how Elijah's disappointment with her typically expressed itself.

It didn't flow like the information gained when one man tortured another. It flowed like the information gained from two people who spoke to each other often, conversationally. Two people who were close. But what kind of trickery, what kind of power, could make Elijah *close* with the person who had ultimately caused her mother's death? Her mother, the only person Elijah Winters had ever truly cared about.

She couldn't fathom it, had never heard of any branch of Aspect, even Dark use, that could twist a person's base nature in such a way. But experimentation was Danvers' dominion.

To her knowledge, her mother, Evelyn, had been his first attempt to twist a person's Aspect. Valkyrie still had no idea what he'd done to Evelyn. Her mother had never spoken about it when she was alive, and after she died, Valkyrie never asked her father because the one surefire way to break his hair-thin temper was to mention her mother. So Valkyrie had stopped thinking about it at all, until Siren had come into Jace's life.

Siren, who had been yet another of Danvers' experiments at changing Aspect, who had almost, almost managed to kill him.

He'd told Siren that she and Evelyn had been the first, and not the most interesting, attempts of his career. Who knew what uses he had twisted Aspect to in the intervening years? Who was she to say he *couldn't* turn Elijah to his will? And if that had happened…

If *that* had happened, then Random was in far more danger than she could have imagined.

She smoothed out the paper and forced herself to read the rest.

I propose a new deal. I will be at your home Thursday evening. Bring me the Council's adnexus by midnight, or we'll see how much you like Mr. Tremayne when he's missing all of his extremities. You'd be surprised what you can cut off a man and still keep him alive.

I'll be watching.

RANDOM WAS DEBATING how rude it would be to eat without Valkyrie when she stormed back into the house.

"Where's your luggage?" she barked.

"My luggage?"

"Luggage bags. Where do you keep them?"

"The closet. Why?"

She moved for his bedroom and he followed after her. What the hell did she need a bag for? Of course, it was Kyrie, so—

"If you have a dead body to dispose of I'd really prefer if you didn't use my suitcases for the job."

She didn't answer. She didn't even acknowledge that he was present, just flung open his closet door and pulled his suitcases down from the overhead rack.

"Seriously, Kyrie, I have trash bags. Heavy duty ones. Tarps, too. All of it much more appropriate for blood-soaked appendages than my luggage set."

That at least got her to glare at him but it was a short, side-long glare. She didn't look angry, didn't look murderous, she looked—scared.

In the seventeen years he'd known her, he'd never once seen her look scared.

"Kyrie, what's going on?"

She still didn't answer him. She opened his dresser and started throwing his clothes into the bags. She didn't even pay attention to what she grabbed, if her throwing all of his work ties into a case was any indication.

"Kyrie."

She grabbed an armful of T-shirts and tossed them on top of his ties, then went back for more. He was going to have redo all his laundry. She'd just wrinkled half his wardrobe in under a minute.

"*Kyrie.*" He took his life in his hands and grabbed her shoulders before she could abuse any more of his clothing. "What the hell is going on?"

She didn't shove his hands away. That was worrisome enough that he dropped them.

"You need to leave."

"Beg your pardon?"

"Leave." She turned back to the suitcase that contained all of his socks, all of his ties, and the majority of his T-shirts, and zipped it closed. "Get out of town. Out of the country would be better."

"Uh-uh." He placed his hand on the suitcase so she couldn't pick it up and haul it out of the room. "I'm not going anywhere, you and I had a deal."

"And I'm breaking it. You're not safe here, you need to go."

"I'm not any less safe than I was yesterday."

"Yes, you *are*. He thinks—" She cut off, her lips twisting into a grimace. "He thinks I care about you. He thinks he can use you against me."

The words cut. *He thinks I care.* Not, *I do care.* But even as he reminded himself, again, that she didn't, he *looked* at her. She could run miles without getting winded but she breathed heavily now, her chest rising and falling in marked movements. Valkyrie, who had taken her Academy finals at sixteen and trounced every record in Battle Aspect history without ever losing the mask of cool detachment on her face, looked wild now. Almost frantic.

Looked, he thought, like he'd felt when he'd seen Danvers punch her in the parking lot last night, seen the chains around her wrists.

"Would it work?" he asked softly. "Do you care, Kyrie?"

He'd never asked her. He'd spent the last year trying to prove to her that he was worth something, worth taking a chance on. Worth more than a one-night stand. He'd wanted her to give him a chance to make her care about him. He'd never considered that maybe she already did. Because it wasn't possible. Because if she *did*, then she was a better actor than he'd ever given her credit for. If she did, then she'd put them both through hell and he had no idea why.

"No. I don't care, Random. I never have."

Every instinct in his body shouted one perfect, glorious word: *liar*. The truth was there, in that shift in her voice, in the way she looked right through him when she said it, rather than at him. *Liar, liar, liar.*

It took everything he had not to grin like an idiot. He didn't call her out on it. Whatever her reasons for lying to him were, they weren't ones he was going to overcome by trying to make her admit the truth. And though he didn't have any proof, he would bet his own money that somehow it all tied back to Elijah Winters.

"Then there's nothing to worry about," he said smoothly. "You don't care, so I can't be used against you. Our deal still stands."

"I may not care, but that doesn't mean I want to see you hacked into small pieces."

"Is that what he threatened to do to me? It lacks originality, don't you think?"

"This isn't a joke, Random."

"I never suggested it was, love. I happen to take threats against my life very seriously. Which is why I'm not going anywhere. It's personal now."

Her hands clenched into fists. "What will it take?"

He raised an eyebrow in question.

"To get you to leave. What will it take?"

"Ah. That. If you want me to leave town, I will."

Her shoulders relaxed.

"If you come with me."

And she was tense again. "I can't."

"Why not?"

"You know why. Danvers has my father. I have to get him back."

"Why does it have to be you? You've worked enough body-guard details to know that when someone is fixated on a person, the best course of action is to remove that person and let another party handle the issue. Danvers is obviously fixated on you. Come away with me and let the Council handle him."

"No."

The stubborn set of her jaw told him she wasn't going to yield. He could ram his head against the iron wall of her will until his skull caved in, or he could retreat and skulk in the shadows until he found an alternative way around her barriers.

"Fine. Keep your secrets. But you're not getting rid of me."

"I can knock you out and put you on a plane to Switzerland."

"One, it is very difficult to put an unconscious individual on a commercial flight, and you don't own a private jet. Two, I'm the only Aspecter to ever successfully manage teleportation. It doesn't matter where you put me, I'll just come right back here."

"No one believes you actually teleported."

Fortunately, that was true, since the only witness to the fact would never admit to it. He'd been too young and traumatized at the time it had happened to realize convincing the Council of his ability to teleport would have been one of the worst things he could do. But he'd been all of eight when he'd done it, and his entire world had just been upended, so he had talked. The random nature of his Aspect meant he hadn't been able to replicate the feat, and he had quickly become a laughingstock. The Boy Who Cried Teleportation.

His first days at Academy in Seclusion had been terrible, and he didn't want to contemplate how miserable his childhood might have been if Jace hadn't befriended him. But even Jace, for all he had the Winters family name behind him, couldn't have entirely quashed the level of teasing aimed at Random if Valkyrie hadn't decided to step into the waters because her little brother was involved.

Anyone dumb enough to fuck with Valkyrie Winters didn't do it a second time. Even when she'd been twelve. That had been the beginning of his childhood idolization of her that had turned into a schoolboy crush when he was older, hopeless infatuation when he was even older, and now this. Head-over-heels, insert-your-preferred-cliché-here, love.

"Believe it or don't." He shrugged. "But we both know there isn't a cage you can put me in that I can't get out of. So you can waste time trying to get me out of the way, or you can accept that I'm going to be here."

"You are infuriating."

He flashed her a grin. "One of my untold number of charms."

"*Leave.*"

"No. I'm sure I can trust you not to let anything happen to me."

It was, perhaps, manipulative. A few of the bodyguard assignments she'd contracted with for the Council had been for witnesses in cases he'd been involved with. He'd seen her work. She had protective instincts a mile wide. Questioning her ability to protect him should make her dig her heels in.

Her face went carefully blank as it became the mask she

showed the world. Seeing her disappear beneath that ice would have hurt him before, because he hadn't believed she could look at him with that level of detachment if he'd meant anything to her. He thought differently, now.

"Fine," she ground out. "You can stay."

"Generous of you."

"But Random?"

"Yes, love?"

"You don't go *anywhere* without me."

His Aspect practically purred. "I'll manage, somehow."

"That includes work."

"I'm already on vacation." It was rapidly shifting from the worst to the best vacation of his life. Or it would be, as soon as they dealt with Danvers and he tricked Valkyrie into admitting she had feelings for him. "Come have breakfast, Kyrie, and tell me what was in that damn letter."

CHAPTER
SIX

Random whistled—*whistled*—as he walked out of the bedroom. Valkyrie had never seen a man so happy to be relieved of the burden of thinking she *liked* him. His entire demeanor had shifted when she'd told him she didn't care about him. As if he'd spent the last year carrying the weight of her supposed affection around like a boulder and now he'd gotten to cast it off.

She'd been right all along, couldn't believe some small part of her had thought he'd meant all the things he'd said to her. It had been hard *not* to believe him. He'd spent a bloody year trying to convince her he loved her, and she'd never let him touch her in all that time. Not until Jace's wedding.

He hadn't looked this happy when she'd told him to leave her alone *then*. Of course, then, she'd practically had her body wrapped around his right before she'd told him to leave. He'd probably thought she was about to sleep with him, because she *had* been about to sleep with him before she'd come to her senses, and he likely hadn't appreciated the sudden switch in her temperature.

She followed him into the kitchen and sat down at the bar, gritting her teeth at the cheerful look on his face. If he was so damn happy to think she didn't want him, why had he insisted on sticking to their deal?

Guilt, she decided, as he poured a cup of coffee and put it on the counter before her. She always came back to guilt as his primary motivating factor. She just needed to make him understand he had nothing to feel guilty about.

That night—he hadn't done anything that night except what she'd asked him to. And despite the pain of seeing him so happy right now, if his safety weren't a factor, she wouldn't go back and change what had happened.

But his safety *was* a factor. She had quit trying to convince him to leave because she knew him. The more she told him to do something, the more he'd try to find a way around it. They had that in common. If someone pointed them both at a brick wall and told them not to get to the other side of it, they would both end up on the other side. The difference between them was that she would bash a hole through the wall and everyone would see her coming a mile away. Random would sneak around somehow, and no one would even know he'd reached the other side until he got bored and revealed himself in some spectacular fashion.

Better if he thought she'd agreed to let him stay. And, truthfully, because she needed him. Getting what Danvers wanted wasn't going to be easy. Random's Aspect, his uncanny ability to luck into the things he wanted, might be the only thing that would allow her to acquire it within the timeframe Danvers had specified.

Once she *had* acquired it, though, then all bets were off. Then, she *would* knock Random out and send him across the ocean if that was what it took. Because she didn't believe for five seconds that he could teleport. She'd lost track of the number of kids she'd intimidated, threatened, and beaten up when necessary after Random had first moved to Seclusion. The Aspect Society Academy prized strength, and instructors tended to look the other way where childhood bullying was concerned. If she hadn't stepped in, Jace and Random would have been bruised and bloodied more days than not.

She hadn't minded. It had given her something to focus on other than her mother's recent death. Something good to do with the skills her father had drilled into her. To say that everything had changed after her mother died wasn't quite accurate. It was more that everything had...intensified. Elijah had never broken her bones while her mother still lived.

"So what does Danvers want?"

The question took her from memory into the present. Random set a plate of frittata, bacon, and hashbrowns in front of her as her stomach rumbled. Goddess, she missed his cooking. She shoveled an obscenely large forkful of hashbrowns into her mouth and stifled a moan. She closed her eyes. Nothing had a right to taste this good.

"Do you and the hashbrowns need a moment alone?"

She flicked her eyes open to find him opposite the bar from her. His forearms rested on the counter. He leaned forward with that trademark wicked look in his eyes that had gotten so many women into his bed. The look that promised he was skilled and fun and absolutely worth it. She happened to know it was a promise he could deliver on.

"Of course, if you don't want to be alone, we could always make it a threesome."

Her throat went dry as she swallowed. Goddess curse it, now that he thought she didn't *care* about him, he'd decided she was safe enough to flirt with again.

She pointed her fork at him. "Do you want me to carve your heart out with this?"

He put a hand to his chest. "No point in taking what's already yours, love."

Valkyrie snorted. His heart belonged to her about as much as the Eiffel Tower did. She should have told him she was madly in love with him when he'd asked if she cared about him—maybe then he'd still be all serious and morose instead of flirty and heart-stopping sexy—but the truth had never been her area of strength.

"Danvers?" Random prompted.

She put away the plate's contents before she answered. His food was too good to ruin with unpleasant conversation.

"The Council is in possession of an item. He wants it."

"And?"

"And I need to acquire it for him or else."

"I could fill a book with the things you're not telling me."

She didn't answer. The answer held so many tangled threads she was afraid they would all unravel at his feet the moment she opened her mouth.

"What's the item? And before you lie to me, I'll remind you that what he had planned for Siren isn't exactly a secret. He wanted to use her power to destroy the Council. That didn't pan out for him and now he's manipulating you into taking something they have? I don't think I need three guesses to figure out why.

"Aunt Ella is on that Council. I know she frightens the living daylights out of most people but she took me in when no one else would. I'm not going to let her get hurt."

Valkyrie stiffened. When she was around Random, she forgot what other people said about her. What they thought about her.

Heartless. Selfish. Soulless. Bitch.

She'd heard it all whispered behind her back over the years, and she'd worn it like a mantle because it was either that or *feel* the sting. Random had never treated her like that. She'd believed he hadn't *thought* of her like that. Clearly, she'd been wrong, if he thought she would put her own life above everyone else's, above his aunt's.

She reached for the unfeeling fog of indifference she'd lived most of her life wrapped in. It was harder to find than usual, but eventually her fingers closed around it and she drew it on.

"Do you forget that I have a vested interest in keeping the Council alive as well?" Not the reason he would think, not her father's connection to the Council, but still, a reason. "I have no intention of giving Danvers anything. But I need him to think I will. Which means I need to steal what he wants."

"And what would that be?"

Getting Valkyrie to actually talk was like trying to brush a cat's teeth. It didn't *have* to be a big deal. The whole thing could all be over in a few minutes if she would just stop fighting, but instead it was going to drag out for the next half hour and he'd likely be bleeding by the end of it.

He wasn't sure what he'd said to make her shut down in truth instead of just presenting the façade, but the ice she brought to the room now could have frozen the Sahara.

"The Council's adnexus."

Random blinked. "Their what?"

She frowned. "Aunt Ella never told you what *makes* the Council the Council?"

"That would be the Aspect Charter? The laws upon which our society is founded?"

She shook her head. "I'm not talking about their legal authority. I'm talking about the reason they're so difficult to kill. The reason an appointment to the Council is for life. The reason a councilor can't abdicate their seat unless they die."

"There's no law that says a councilor can't abdicate."

She looked at him like he was being intentionally dense. "In the history of Aspect Society, name one councilor who has ever abdicated their seat."

Random forced his memory to dredge up his fifth year Academy history class, when he'd had to memorize the name of every bloody person to ever hold the title of councilor. His brain hurt after going through the first century's worth, and he couldn't remember half the names, so he gave up.

"I'm sure there was someone."

"No," she said softly, "there wasn't. And there never will be. When you join the Council, Random, you are *bound* to it. The magic that ensures that binding is older than the Council itself. You cannot be unbound except in death. And while a councilor *can* be killed, it's exceptionally difficult. That is why Danvers needed Siren's Aspect if he hoped to take them all out before a new Council could be formed. That's why he didn't simply pick them all off in their sleep.

"The adnexus is the tie that binds them together, the vessel that holds them. Destroy that adnexus, Random, and you destroy the Council."

"You seem to know a lot about this," he said carefully.

She shrugged. "Father talked a lot."

There it was again, that shift in her voice. She wasn't lying, precisely, but she wasn't telling him the truth, either. Not all of it. However she'd learned about this adnexus—he was still having difficulty with the idea that Aunt Ella would ever willingly bind herself in such a way—she hadn't learned it in idle chats with Elijah Winters.

"Let's say you're correct and this is all true. You want to steal what would then be the most important thing the Council possesses? The *Council*. We aren't just talking about a jail sentence, Kyrie. They'll kill us and not even Aunt Ella will be able to veto them on it."

"I don't intend to get caught."

"Said every thief ever."

"I *won't* get caught."

Clearly, that line of logic wasn't working, so he switched to a different one. "Do you even know where this adnexus is? How to get it?"

"Yes."

"Where, how, and why do you know?"

"The less you know, the safer you are."

Random gripped the edges of the counter. There was not enough time in the world to do the amount of baking he would need to do to lower the heights she raised his blood pressure to.

"I may not be able to convince the Council about what happened with Danvers last night if you deny it, but all it will take is one anonymous tip mentioning an adnexus no one is supposed to know about to ensure it's locked down so tight you won't get to it."

Valkyrie had an unparalleled ability to talk through clenched teeth and she exercised it now, answering his original questions in reverse order. "Like I said, Father talked a lot. I need blood from DuPont and your aunt, and it's beneath Council head-quarters."

"Just DuPont and Aunt Ella? Not the other councilors?"

She opened her mouth, shut it.

Shit. "You already have the others, don't you?"

She didn't say anything, which was answer enough.

"Kyrie, how long have you been planning to steal this thing?"

She sighed. "Since Siren confronted the Council in her home. When she fought them, her Aspect showed her the nature of their connection. She thinks that if she has the adnexus itself she can dismantle it and break the Council's bonds without killing anyone."

"And why would you—and her, for that matter—be so inter-ested in doing that? Do you have a secret plan to dominate Aspect Society that I don't know about?"

"Don't be ridiculous."

"Then what?" he snapped.

"My father has been missing long enough that the Council wants to replace him. I've already lobbied for two extensions on his behalf and I don't know if I can win another. As I told you earlier, there is no abdicating from the Council. If they want to replace him they will have to remove him from the adnexus. It will kill him."

There was something else, something *more* going on she

wasn't telling him. He was certain of it. He was equally certain he wouldn't be able to pry it out of her. He'd have better luck calling Siren and trying to pull it out of *her*. So he let it go, for now.

"How much blood do we need?" If they needed a blood bag he was going to have to tell her this was suicide.

"A few drops is fine. Soaked into a napkin, cloth, whatever, is fine too."

"How much time do we have?"

"The sooner the better."

Would it kill her to tell him anything without him having to drag it out of her? "Let me think about how to handle Aunt Ella. As for DuPont—he has dinner at StellaMia's with his wife every Saturday evening at seven."

She frowned. "Why do you know that?"

"I find it useful in my career to know things about people." It was technically true, and it sounded better than, *My assistant reads the society pages.* "I'm sure if we go, something will work itself out." That was how his Aspect tended to function.

"*Today* is Saturday. StellaMia's books out weeks in advance."

"I can get us in." At the incredulity on her face, he added, "I can *probably* get us in." He'd started eating at StellaMia's once a month, at Mrs. Harrington's insistence that he be seen in respectable establishments with some regularity. He'd continued going because the food was phenomenal, and because Stella and her partner, Mia, were lovely people.

"But I'd have to plead a special occasion to the owners. You're not going to like it."

"What kind of special occasion?" she asked, suspicious.

"A date."

The only problem with people as blissfully in love as Stella and Mia was that they always wanted everyone else to settle down and be as happy as they were. They kept telling him that eating alone was a surefire way to be alone for the rest of his life.

They would be thrilled, likely to an unbearable level, if he told them he wanted to bring a woman to their restaurant.

"A *date* is a special enough occasion for the most exclusive restaurant in Seclusion to find you a table?"

"Stella and Mia happen to believe in the power of true love, and they desperately want me to be happy. I am going to need you to at least *try* and sell the date image, though. They can smell bullshit a mile away."

She struggled with it before she ground out, "Fine."

"That means no visible weaponry."

"I said fine."

"Please don't accost anyone or break anything. I like eating there and don't want to get kicked out."

"Any *other* rules I should know about?"

"Yes. I consider Stella and Mia friends. Please be nice to them."

"Why wouldn't I be?"

"Just promise."

"Fine. I will be nice. Are we done here?"

"Just one more thing. The adnexus. It's a physical item?"

She nodded. "A scepter."

"How big is it?"

She frowned. "I don't know, exactly. Maybe sixteen, eighteen inches long? Why?"

"Because you want to steal a magical item that is bound to five of the most powerful people in Seclusion. If they can feel its magic, they will be able to find it." He tapped into his Aspect, felt his power searching, hunting, and then a black stone box popped into his hands. "Would this be big enough to hold it?"

"I think so. But it's just a box, Random."

"Can I have one of your daggers?" She held a blade out to him. He glanced at the naked steel. "I meant one of the imbued ones."

She grimaced, but she traded the plain dagger for one with runes etched along the blade's length. Every Aspecter felt the need to use their Aspect. If it built up too much inside them, they became like a vessel trying to hold more than it was meant to contain. Valkyrie built up Aspect like she was a battery with constant access to a supercharger.

She could only burn off so much from training, so much from the contracting work she used to do for the Council. So she channeled a lot of into her weapons, into the runes she inscribed for strength and stealth and true aim.

Her weapons were as much a magical artifact as the Council's adnexus. He took the dagger, placed it in the box and closed the lid. The power imbued in it naturally filled the box, then leaked out, reaching for the ties it held to the person who had made it.

"I can still feel it," Valkyrie said.

"That's because I haven't *done* anything yet. Tell me when you can't feel it."

Though Random's Aspect didn't fall into a defined category, he had personally always thought of his affinity as Desire. What he wanted at any given moment, his Aspect tried to make happen, and it often created things for which no recognized spell or affinity existed.

But it had to be a genuine desire, and one that wasn't entirely selfish. He had frequently desired a million dollars, but somehow that had never come into his possession. Right now, he wanted to ensure that when Valkyrie stole the adnexus—because Valkyrie never failed at anything, so she *would* end up with the bloody thing—she wouldn't end up in a Council holding cell five minutes later.

So he needed this box to be able to contain the Aspect signature of a magical object. His Aspect caught the flow of his thoughts, and once it realized that this was connected to *Kyrie*, it leapt into his hands, flowed out of them into the box, eager to begin.

Sometimes he wasn't sure who was more in love with Kyrie —*him*, or his goddamn Aspect.

His power flowed around the box, feeling the magic signature of Valkyrie's dagger within, considering. Then it sank into the box itself, weaving into the stone, creating a latticework of lines that formed a pattern Random had never seen before, and would probably never be able to intentionally recreate.

"Holy shit," Valkyrie said.

He couldn't entirely stop the satisfaction that thrummed through him. "Nothing?" he asked her.

"No." She stepped next to him and placed her hand on the stone lid. "I can't feel it at all. It's...creepy."

He held the box out to her. "One creepy, magic-hiding box. As promised."

She didn't take it. "Maybe you could just put it somewhere until we need it?"

He sighed. "You try to give a woman nice things. Fine." He walked to the living room bookcases and placed it on an empty shelf. "There. It could be decorative now."

She didn't look convinced. If he'd known a magic-hiding box would freak her out and impress her that much, he'd have made one years ago.

"So... *now*, are we done here? With the talking and everything? You feel as if you have been appropriately included in all the details per our agreement?"

She really knew how to ruin his moment. "Yes, we're done here. I'll call Mia and work things out for tonight."

"Good. Then I'll just, ah..." She looked around idly, her left hand tapping against her thigh, clearly unsure of what to do with herself.

He took pity on her. "The gym is down that hallway on the left."

Her expression went carefully neutral. "I'll probably just go for a run—"

"This way." He gave her a playful shove down the hall. He hadn't built the damn gym with her in mind for her to turn her nose up at it without ever having seen it.

⁓

Valkyrie decided that letting Random herd her to his "gym" was easier than arguing. She would try to find a way to let him down delicately, but she had no interest in being stuck in a windowless room the size of a closet with a Bowflex and a treadmill, or whatever most people thought constituted a home gym. Not that there was anything wrong with a Bowflex or a treadmill per se, they just bored her out of her mind.

"Look, Random," she began. She immediately cut off when he opened the gym door. She did not see a Bowflex or a treadmill. The room was large and airy, the size of a small dance studio with high, arched ceilings. Sunlight spilled through the window that ran almost the entire length of the long side of the rectangular room, giving a burnished glow to the dark wood flooring.

An Olympic weight bench rested in the corner diagonally across from her. A heavy bag hung in the opposite corner, a row of free weights in the stand that lined the wall across from the window. The wall to her left was a rock climbing wall that stretched to the top of the high ceiling. Climbing ropes hung nearby, just far enough to make it an interesting challenge to leap from the top of the wall onto one of the ropes, or vice-versa.

"This is perfect," she said, the words out of her mouth before she could stop them. Random looked pleased. No, she decided, he looked smug. Oh, for goddess sake, it wasn't as if he'd designed the room himself. "Whoever had it built clearly had good taste."

This additional sentence did not wipe the satisfied cat-with-the-cream expression off his face.

"No doubt," he said cheerily. "I'll leave you to it, then. Wouldn't want you to get carried away in here and ruin my pretty face before our date."

"It's not an actual date," she growled at his retreating back.

"Methinks the lady doth protest too much," he called back over his shoulder.

She closed the door. Forcefully.

Insufferable. He was absolutely insufferable.

She dragged out and pieced together the rubber workout mats leaning against the wall next to the free weights. Even after fifteen minutes of stretching and tumbling to warm up her muscles, her clenched jaw hadn't relaxed. Relaxation didn't come until she settled into a rhythm on the heavy bag. Punch, punch, punch. Duck. Upward jab. Reset. Punch, punch, kick.

She'd like to say she imagined punching the satisfied look off Random's face while she hit the bag, but she just...couldn't. Aside from the sparring matches she'd been able to talk him into when they were kids, she'd hit him for real precisely once in her life. On his eighteenth birthday, no less.

She hadn't *wanted* to. He'd just strolled into her backyard, seen her and zeroed in, looking like a man going to the gallows. He had walked right up to her with that look of impending doom on his face and said, "If you don't stop me, I'm going to kiss you."

She figured it must have been a dare. *Bet you don't have the balls to kiss Valkyrie Winters,* someone might have taunted and Random, well, he hadn't been good at turning down challenges at that age.

She hadn't ever expected those words to come out of his mouth, not pointed at *her*, so she'd stupidly stood there and let him follow through. She'd even had the idiocy to kiss him back. For a moment. Before reality took hold. Before she'd seen the flicker of movement in her peripheral vision that told her her father watched from his study window.

So she had done the only possible thing she could to keep Random safe. She'd hauled back and punched him. She hadn't pulled the blow, and she'd walked away and left him without a word. Because violence followed by obvious indifference was the only possible thing that might convince Elijah it meant nothing to her. That Random meant nothing to her.

She hadn't realized he *had* meant something until he'd kissed her. At least, something other than her brother's best friend. She'd always felt so much older than him and Jace, but she wasn't, not really, and when he'd kissed her she'd realized he wasn't a kid anymore.

She'd spent the next day, the next week, the next year, afraid the hit hadn't been enough. That her father would use it against her. She hadn't relaxed until Jace had gotten himself disowned and left town. Once her brother was gone, Random had left for a while, too, and with the only two people she cared about out of Seclusion, she had dedicated herself to doing whatever Elijah wanted. To not giving him a reason to go after Jace or Random.

But it had cost her. Jace and Random were the only two people who had ever treated *her* like a person. The only two people who hadn't seemed to understand that she was irreparably broken. Once they were gone, it had made her life easier. But it had made it worse, too. And when Random had moved back to Seclusion, when she'd seen him again, it had sparked something inside her. Something that had made her realize she wasn't as hollow and dead inside as she'd thought. Something that had kept her going when she hadn't understood what the point in continuing was.

No matter what else had happened between them, she would always be grateful to him for that. Even if he would never know.

CHAPTER

SEVEN

Random held his phone two feet from his ear in a futile attempt to save his hearing from the damage Mia's excited shriek was certain to cause.

"She finally said yes?"

He frantically lowered the volume while he kept his gaze trained on the hallway that led to the gym. Kyrie only had above-normal senses when she actively used her Aspect, but one could never be too cautious.

"She, who? I never said who I was bringing."

"Valkyrie Winters, obviously."

His usually on-point brain could not come up with a single smart thing to say to that. "How did you…?"

Mia snorted. "Oh, please. You could find a way to bring that woman into a conversation about ice fishing."

Kyrie would no doubt be excellent at ice fishing. The cold wouldn't bother her at all, and her weapons aim was exceptional. Not to mention—oh, hells. Mia was right. That didn't mean he had to admit it.

"I'm relatively certain that's untrue."

"Remember Axe to Grind?"

"I don't have amnesia, Mia." He'd gone with her and Stella to the hatchet-throwing venue a few months ago.

"Good. Then you'll remember how the first thing you said when it came time to select your hatchet was, ''Valkyrie wouldn't dignify this craftsmanship with the name of weapon?' In front of the owner?"

Random winced. "I'm sure I didn't say that out loud."

"You did. Then you explained the place shouldn't even be called Axe to Grind because they didn't have any axes, only hatchets."

"Did I?"

"Then, when it came time to throw the hatchets at the targets, which was supposed to be the fun part of the outing, you went on and on about how the hatchet wasn't properly weighted, and Valkyrie once showed you—"

"All right, all right. I see your point. Sorry I wasn't good company."

Mia harrumphed. "We weren't precisely expecting you to be, you've been in a funk all year."

"Have not."

"Have to, and we'd like to see you out of it. So I'll find you a table tonight. You said seven?"

"Yes. Thank you."

"She'd better be worth it."

"She is," he said softly. "But Mia? Try not to get *too* excited. She's not—I have no idea how this is going to go."

He could feel Mia's hesitation before she said, "I hope it goes well. I'm sure it *will* go well. But if it doesn't? Please let it go. You deserve to be happy and this—it isn't healthy."

He sighed. "I know. I was *going* to let it go and things...happened."

"Things will keep happening forever if you let them. Trust me, Random, I know a thing or two about wanting the unattainable. But when I finally let that go? That's when I found Stella. I'll see you at seven."

She hung up and Random tossed his phone on the kitchen counter. The rational part of him understood that Mia was right. Yes, he'd determined Kyrie cared about him, but he didn't honestly know in what capacity. Yes, she thought the gym was perfect, but she also thought someone else had designed it, and at the end of the day all her liking it really proved was that he knew her. Perhaps a little too well.

And the date wasn't a real date.

Unfortunately, getting his head to convince his heart that he shouldn't be hopeful was a losing battle. More unfortunately, where his heart went, his Aspect followed. Though he'd lived with the strange way his Aspect manifested his entire life, he couldn't control what it did all the time. It was desire-based, and while he could get it to do what he wanted by intentionally desiring very specific things, *stopping* it from acting on desires he wasn't even fully aware he had was a much more difficult task.

The latter required not wanting anything at all, and he couldn't shut his emotions down enough to achieve it. He'd tried a handful of times because of the sometimes inconvenient results of his subconscious power use—he'd lost track of the number of neighborhood pets he'd had to return to their owners over the years when he'd felt lonely only to turn around and find a friendly dog or cat pawing at his back door—but every time he'd closed himself off to the level necessary to stop his Aspect from acting on its own, he'd spiraled into such a dark place he'd been afraid he wouldn't be able to crawl out of it. It hadn't been worth it.

Still, when he looked out the window and saw what was in his backyard, he wished his Aspect could be a little less of a pain in his ass. Because he had no reasonable way to explain to Kyrie the situation unfolding outside, and he would prefer to simply hide it so she never had to know.

Damn it, Krissi usually *called* him when this happened. He tugged on his boots and headed down to barn.

THE SIXTH TIME Random's phone rang, Valkyrie decided to hell with politeness, and left the gym to yell at him to answer the damn thing or turn it to silent. His phone lay on the kitchen counter, buzzing incessantly. Random was not in the kitchen. He wasn't in the living room, or the bedroom either.

She didn't feel comfortable exploring the rest of his house without him, so she yelled for him at the top of her lungs. It wasn't so large a house that he wouldn't hear *that*. But he didn't answer. The phone cut off, then immediately rang again. She couldn't help but see the name on the display: Krissi. She only knew one person who spelled her name like that, and Seclusion was a small town.

Why the hell was her stablehand calling Random? The obvious answer didn't fit, because Krissi wasn't interested in men. She wasn't interested in anyone of any gender. According to her, she just "didn't see the point in all of it." Valkyrie was pretty sure Krissi and Random weren't friends, either, which led back to the question of why Random had thirteen missed calls from the woman and counting.

As a rule, Valkyrie did not believe in answering other people's phones. But with everything going on, she wasn't willing to risk a possible emergency for the sake of Random's privacy. She picked up and Krissi started talking before Valkyrie could announce that she wasn't Random.

"Why weren't you answering your phone? Are the horses at your place? You said this would stop happening but they're gone and the back gate's open and what am I going to tell Ms. Winters if she comes home?"

"I imagine," Valkyrie said, sounding much calmer than she felt, "you would tell me that the horses are missing." She stepped outside and around the side of the house, the phone still pressed to her ear, and looked down toward the barn. Random stood in the paddock to the right, by all appearances trying to convince Abaddon, her six-year-old mare, to walk into the barn.

"Ms. Winters?" Krissi squeaked. "Oh shit, am I fired?"

"That remains to be seen. Explain. Everything."

"Well, it started maybe six months ago? That week you were out of town? I came back from the feed store and the horses were gone and the back gate was open and I swear I didn't leave it open. I was going to call you when Random called and said they were at his place, and well, everyone *knows* his Aspect's really weird so I just took the truck and trailer and brought them back.

"It only ever happened when you were gone for extended periods, and the last time Random swore it wouldn't happen again, and it hasn't, not for three months, and I really thought he had the problem ironed out."

"Did he say *why* this happens?"

"No. But the horses were never hurt and Random said it would just upset you to know about it and I just thought...*am* I fired?"

Oh, Random had thought it would *upset her*, had he? Krissi should have known better. She *should* have told her. Still, Random could literally charm anyone. He just had that charisma that made a person certain that whatever came out of his mouth, he must be right about it. And Krissi's personal situation had been a bit of a disaster when she'd come into Valkyrie's employ, so she couldn't blame the woman for not wanting to lose her job.

"Since I am currently amused by how much trouble Abaddon is giving Random, and since I suspect this is all his fault? No, you're not fired." An audible sigh of relief carried across the line. "But Krissi? If anything of this nature ever happens again and you *don't* tell me, immediately, I *will* fire you. You will never be in trouble for things that are beyond your ability to control. You will be in trouble for lying to me. Am I clear?"

"Yes ma'am. Should I bring the truck and trailer over?"

Valkyrie considered it, but as irritated as she was, having the horses here was probably a prudent solution. Especially since she *knew* Danvers would be on her property soon, if he wasn't skulking around it already.

"No. Load up their gear and feed and drive it over. The horses will be staying at Random's until further notice."

A long pause followed this announcement. "Okay. What about me?"

"You're on paid vacation until further notice. At least a week, possibly longer. Don't return to the property until I tell you to."

Valkyrie ended the call and walked down to where Random was still trying—and failing—to entice Abaddon into the barn. The man had a lot of explaining to do.

"Seriously, Abaddon? Do we have to do this every single time?" Only Valkyrie would give a horse a name that meant destruction. The damnable creature was a Friesian—they were *all* Friesians, because Kyrie had a type when it came to horses and the type was tall, large, and black—and the mare absolutely hated Random.

Well, hate was a strong word. It was more, he thought, that she didn't take him seriously. She understood full well that she could walk all over him, and she did so to her heart's content. Any time he got within two feet of her, she ran away.

Honestly, all four of the creatures were nightmares. The only manageable horses she'd owned had been the three out-to-pasture retirees that Jace and Siren had taken with them when they moved into Siren's place.

"Just put on the nice halter and go in the nice barn, and the nice lady will come to take you back to your own place."

"Perhaps you should tell her it will be a *nice* trailer ride and there will be *nice* treats and she will suddenly realize she wants to do what you say," a derisive voice said.

Kyrie's voice. Shit.

He turned. She didn't look *too* pissed off. He tried a charming grin. She scowled at him.

"Give me that, you're teaching her bad habits." She held out her hand for the halter and lead, which he happily relinquished.

"I'm not teaching her anything."

"Everything you do around a horse teaches it something. Right now, you're teaching her she can run away whenever she doesn't want to do what you ask." Valkyrie walked right up to the mare, who stood placid as a lamb and even obligingly bumped her nose into the halter when Kyrie positioned it.

"Yes, well, I can see it's had a detrimental effect on your ability to handle her."

She shot him a sidelong glance. "I've trained her since she was two. One person handling her badly won't affect *me*. It's you she's going to keep taking advantage of."

"Well, she isn't my bloody equine."

"No, she isn't." Kyrie's voice was soft as she reached up to gently rub the mare's forehead. It was more affection than she'd ever shown *him*. Abaddon put her head in Kyrie's chest and looked like she was about to go to sleep, as if she hadn't had him chasing her all over the damn paddock moments before. "And since she isn't, why don't you explain what she's doing here? What they're *all* doing here?"

"Ah, well," Random started, following Kyrie and Abaddon into the barn.

"Is this like your thing with the damn bird?"

It was nothing like his connection with Nelsen. The bridge of understanding his Aspect had forged between him and the falcon was not one it had ever repeated with another animal. But it would be much easier to let Kyrie think that than it would be to explain that one of his deepest desires was for her to call this place home, and that any home she had would have her horses, so his Aspect kept pulling them here.

He gave a casual shrug. "You know how my Aspect is. Probably just trying to be neighborly."

She walked Abaddon into one of the barn's large box stalls. It wasn't until she'd slipped the halter off that his words seemed to hit her.

"Neighborly? Random, how far from my house are we?"

He swallowed. "Are we talking on foot at a leisurely stroll, or—"

"*Random.*"

"Like a two minute drive."

Her eyebrows furrowed. "You bought the Addams' place."

He had really, really hoped she wouldn't think about it that much.

"You don't even *like* the country."

"It has its charms. Besides, the city wasn't good for Nelsen, and this way I'm closer to Jace and Siren."

She nodded, but she had that little twist to her lips that meant something still bothered her, something she couldn't quite put her finger on.

Dear goddess, don't let her realize the Addams never put a house up on this land. Much less a state-of-the-art equine facility. Hells, he'd never intended for her to *be* here in a situation where he would find it uncomfortable to explain all of this. Fortunately for him, Krissi's truck chose that moment to trundle down his drive.

"Where's the trailer?" he asked.

"We don't need it. Much as I dislike the unorthodox way they arrived here, I'd rather everything living was off my property until this is over. That is, if you don't mind?"

"May as well get some use out of the place." His stupid Aspect didn't seem to understand that this wasn't winning. It just understood that the horses were staying, that Kyrie was staying, and it did happy little somersaults inside him the entire time he helped Kyrie and Krissi unload grain bins and hay bales.

Krissi, apparently, didn't understand it either, because as they hauled the last bale into the hay shed she grinned at him and said, "Congratulations, by the way."

Dear goddess, was there *anyone* in Seclusion who hadn't realized he had it bad for Valkyrie?

"Congratulations on what?"

Krissi blanched at the ice in Valkyrie's voice as her employer rounded the corner. She looked from Random to Valkyrie and back to Random.

"On, you know..."

"Our date," Random stepped in. "Couldn't keep it to myself. Terribly excited."

"And where would this date be happening?" Krissi asked.

"Nowhere," Valkyrie said, at the same time Random answered, "StellaMia's."

Krissi looked at Valkyrie. "*You're* going to a fancy restaurant for a date?"

"Isn't that what people do on dates?"

"I guess, I just figured you'd be more the type to, ah—" She cut off at the look on Valkyrie's face. "You know what? Never mind. Have a good time. I'll just go start that vacation." She sped back to her truck and made her escape in record time.

"Was it necessary to tell her that?" Valkyrie's perfectly calm demeanor told Random precisely how pissed off she was.

"The more it seems like a real date, the less cause DuPont will have to connect us to anything. She's free press. She'll have spread it over half of Seclusion by the end of the day."

"Maybe I don't want half of Seclusion to know."

His temper snapped, even though he knew it wasn't rational. But if she couldn't stand even the *possibility* of her name being romantically attached to his, then he'd clearly been an idiot to think she could actually give a damn about him. "Of course not. You wouldn't want your precious reputation sullied by being connected to me, of all people."

"That's not—"

"How about I make it easy for you? No one ever said it had to be a happy date. By all means, throw a glass of wine on me by the end of the night. Everyone will blame me. After all, I'm not the serious type. They'll assume I said something insensitive and you realized what a huge mistake going out with me was."

"Random—"

"You can even say it loudly. *This was a mistake, Random.* That is how you feel about me, isn't it? About fucking me? Just one big mistake. You may as well air all your grievances in public. Hell, maybe it'll be cathartic for both of us."

VALKYRIE WATCHED Random disappear inside the house, dumbfounded. He'd been whistling an hour ago because he was happy to be rid of her and now he was upset because he thought she didn't want to be seen in public with him? His damn mood swings were giving her whiplash. She could've brushed it off if he hadn't sounded so bitter, hadn't looked so hurt.

She let out a frustrated breath and walked back into the barn. The horses were all calm as daisies, and no reason they shouldn't be if they'd been to Random's place several times of their own accord. She turned Lilith, Azazel, and Dagon out into the large paddock, and led Abaddon to the cross ties.

The mare huffed out a deep breath, as if to say *Why me?*, but she stood patiently while Valkyrie brushed her down and tacked her up. The wonderful thing about horses was that they were difficult to bullshit. If her attention wasn't completely focused on them, they knew it and took advantage. Which was only fair, to Valkyrie's mind, since if she wasn't willing to give them her best, she didn't feel she deserved theirs.

So Valkyrie put Random out of her mind, and for the next hour the only things that existed were her and Abaddon. She'd only had the mare under saddle a few months, so she warmed her up slowly, taking her through all her gaits until the mare relaxed into the work. She hadn't ridden her in a few weeks, unable to find the time, the right head-space, so she started today taking her back through all the basic maneuvers she'd begun teaching her: forehand and hindquarter turns, side-passing at the walk and the trot. She moved on from there into trotting and cantering circles with her balanced and curved inward, on from there into flying lead changes.

A lot of people in the horse world liked to claim that mares were contrary and stubborn. Unpredictable or more trouble than they were worth. But the truth was, a mare would give you one-hundred percent every time. You just had to earn it from them.

As usually happened, by the time she'd cooled Abaddon down and turned her out with the herd, whatever tension Valkyrie had been carrying had eased. With her thoughts in less of a tangle, she could try and look at Random's reaction from his point of view.

No one wanted to be thought of as a mistake. No one wanted someone else to be ashamed of being seen in public with them and that...that must have been how her words had come across.

She couldn't tell him the truth. *Sorry I got pissed, but I'm worried my father will suddenly turn up again. If he at all thinks you're important to me, he'll probably kill you if I don't kill him first.* No, she could never tell Random *that*.

She walked into the house to find him baking. Again. "How do you possibly have any sugar left?"

He didn't verbalize an answer, didn't even look at her. He just pointed at the counter where a very large, clear storage container was half full of sugar.

"I guess if you buy that much it's hard to run out," she muttered as he extracted a baking sheet from the oven. A dozen cookies were spaced in even rows. They were the degree of perfectly round she'd thought only existed in mass-manufac-tured products. They were also her favorite: chocolate cookie with chocolate-chips.

"Did you need something?" he asked.

Shit. She'd come in here to try and smooth things over and instead she'd judged the amount of sugar in his possession. Why was she incapable of ever saying the right thing around him?

Why was it that whenever she meant to be nice, or neutral, she turned into a complete bitch? Maybe she should try to say horrible things to him. Maybe then she'd end up saying things like, *The cookies smell amazing*, or, *You look nice today*, or some other kind of inane conversation starter.

He set the baking sheet on a cooling rack and leaned back against the stove, his arms folded across his chest, one eyebrow lifted in silent demand.

"It's not about you," she tried.

"Few things ever are."

"I mean the...date." She nearly choked getting the word out. "Not wanting a lot of people to know. It isn't about you. About being seen with *you*, specifically."

The long line of his body tensed. "Are you seeing someone?"

What? "No."

"Then what are you concerned about?"

"I can't explain it. Look, I just thought you should know, okay? It isn't you. I'm sure there are lots of women who would be happy to publicly go on a date with you."

He stared at her, like he was trying to figure out if she was putting him on. Then he burst out laughing. Full-on, doubled-over, hands-on-his-knees laughing.

She felt her cheeks flush hot. She was never fucking apologizing to him again. "What is so damn funny?"

He straightened, still laughing, and wiped tears—actual fucking tears—from his eyes.

"You just gave me the, it's-not-you-it's-me-and-you'll-make-someone-else-a-wonderful-boyfriend-someday speech and we're not even in a relationship to break up from. You're fucking priceless, Kyrie."

He transferred a cookie to a small saucer and handed it to her. She stared at it, confused. "So are you mad at me or not?"

He shook his head. "What's the point?"

That didn't seem like a question that had an actual answer, so she steered the conversation in an opposite direction. She lifted the saucer. "I don't suppose you have..."

He rolled his eyes and pulled a whipped cream canister from the fridge. It wasn't the pre-made kind found in grocery stores. No, it was one of the sleek, silver canisters like baristas used, the kind that required a CO2 cartridge and made whipped cream from actual heavy cream when the trigger was depressed. Because of *course* it was.

She settled onto a barstool, ate the cookie, and tried not to feel guilty about hurting Random's feelings. Then she watched him eat his own cookie and lick whipped cream off his fingers and tried not to feel anything at all.

She failed, miserably, and suddenly she was remembering him licking *her* in some rather interesting places, and wondering what it would be like if he was licking whipped cream off of her, and—

She stood up so fast she sent the bar stool skidding backwards. "I need to go home and pack clothes."

Random stared at her. "Right now?"

"Yes. Right now."

"Okay." He stretched the word out.

"So, I'll just go." She grabbed her keys and headed for the door.

He sighed. "Glued to your side, remember?" he said, and followed her out to her Jeep.

CHAPTER

EIGHT

Valkyrie tossed yet another black tank top out of her closet. Her wardrobe was not something that had ever concerned her before, so she'd never paid much attention to it. An in-depth inspection proved it consisted of jeans, yoga pants, tank tops, and the evening gown she'd worn to last year's Gathering Ball. Approximately eighty-percent of the clothing was black, and none of it was appropriate to wear on a date.

At least, she didn't think it was. She didn't really know anything about dates. Even if she'd been willing to risk wearing something in her closet, none of it qualified as casual elegant, which was the dress code listed when she'd Googled StellaMia's. What the fuck did casual elegant even mean?

Valkyrie had never understood this stuff. She'd never had any interest in it, and her mother had never tried to force it on her. After her mother had died, her father had taken over her life so completely she'd never have even figured out how to put on makeup if it wasn't for YouTube. Even then, she'd only had the patience to watch the videos long enough to figure out how to pick a foundation shade and not stab herself in the eye with mascara.

"It didn't take you nearly this long to pack *my* clothes." Random stepped into her bedroom.

"I thought I told you to stay downstairs."

"I got bored. It's not like I've never seen your room before." He frowned. "Though I don't think I've ever seen it in this state. Did a tornado blow through here?"

Valkyrie grabbed the pile of tank tops off the floor and shoved them into her suitcase. She turned back around in time to see Random picking her bra off the floor. One of her actual bras, not a sports bra. It dangled lazily from his index finger as he held it out to her, a grin teasing at the corners of his lips.

Well, if he hadn't realized she had no boobs to speak of before, he certainly had now. She snatched the lingerie from him and threw it in the suitcase.

"I hadn't pegged you as the lace trim type. I do love it when a woman surprises me."

She refused to blush. She was too damn old to blush. "It was on sale," she said shortly.

He stepped closer, and his eyes took on that interested smolder capable of destroying women the world over. "Was anything else lacy on sale?"

The matching underwear had been, as a matter of fact. "Why do you care?" she asked.

"Just gathering information. Would Random Tremayne really take a woman to dinner if he couldn't tell you what her underwear looked like?"

"You'd be more likely to know than I would."

"That's just the thing though. I don't. Never taken a woman dinner before."

As if. "I don't believe you've never eaten dinner with a woman."

"Eating dinner with a woman is much different than taking a woman to dinner. I've done the former plenty. Never bothered with the latter."

"Then we'd better hope we both manage to convincingly fake it."

"Indeed." He stepped closer. Too close. Whatever aftershave he wore smelled like it was probably named something like *Waterfalls and Sin*. It made her want to bury her face in the curve of his neck and breathe him in. "Which is why we should probably practice."

"Practice what?" He shouldn't be allowed to stand this close to her. It screwed with her head.

"Kissing."

Her gaze had been burning a hole in his collarbone, but it snapped up to meet his, now, and that was a mistake. His dark brown eyes held a touch of heat, and she couldn't help but note that the two of them were conveniently right next to a bed.

"I don't need to practice. I know how to kiss you." *I'd really like to do it right now.*

"I'm not sure you do. The first time we kissed, you broke my nose. The second time, you jumped me. The third time, you destroyed my soul. I'd like to know that if I need to kiss you tonight, none of those things will happen, as none are appropriate for public consumption."

Yes, her body agreed, *let's practice.* "In what scenario do you envision us actually needing to kiss?"

"Let's see, you and me on a date? It's a hard pill for most to swallow. You'd be surprised what a well-placed parking lot kiss can do for the credibility of a fake date. So may I?" He lifted his hand, brushed the backs of his fingertips along her cheekbone.

Yes, she wanted to say, *yes, you definitely may.* "It isn't necessary. I can guarantee none of the previous reactions will occur." Which was a complete lie. Oh, she could guarantee she wouldn't punch him. She could also guarantee she wouldn't destroy his soul, because that was an exaggeration. He was prone to those where she was concerned. It was his pride she'd destroyed, and she could avoid doing so again.

No, it was the not-jumping-him outcome she couldn't guarantee wouldn't happen again. Because when he touched her, she never wanted him to stop.

"Perhaps I need to be convinced," he murmured.

Perhaps she needed to convince herself. "Fine."

She kissed him. She'd intended for it to be a brief, dispassionate action, but the second her lips touched his, he came alive. His mouth met hers hungrily. His hands settled on her waist and she stupidly wrapped hers behind his neck, let her fingers bury themselves in the soft silk of his hair. His tongue parted her lips, thrust inside her.

She wanted to press her body against his, to arch into his touch like a satisfied cat. She wanted to rip his clothes off and throw him on the bed, to have him beneath her. The thought almost made her moan, but she couldn't do that. If she did, he would know exactly what affect he had on her. He would know she wanted him, and she'd never be able to resist him if he was hellbent on giving himself to her.

Sex was what Random *did*.

She broke the kiss and leaned back against the hold he had on her waist. She held her breathing steady, held his gaze, which had gone from heated to a full-on bonfire.

"As promised," she said, her voice even and cool. "I haven't harmed you, fucked you, or said anything cruel."

The warmth in his eyes dimmed. His hands dropped from her sides and he stepped back, brushing his hands off on his shirt. Brushing *her* off, she thought.

"Wonderful. I'm glad that's settled."

She felt anything but settled, but she said, "Me too."

"I'll let you finish packing. Meet you in the car."

He turned and walked out. Slowly, casually, and without even a hint of the aching need that rampaged through her.

~

WALKING out of Valkyrie's room was the hardest thing Random had ever done. What the hell had he been thinking? *Kiss me, Kyrie, prove it doesn't mean anything.*

She hadn't been able to hide the desire in her eyes, no matter how calmly she had spoken to him. Not that it mattered. So what if she wanted him? She clearly didn't *want* to want him. Just because her body wanted to fuck his didn't mean *she* did, and he didn't want her body. Well, he did, he just didn't want *only* her body. He wanted her. Kyrie.

Why did he torture himself like this?

He climbed into the passenger side of her Jeep. Apparently he was only allowed to drive it if she was unconscious. She'd been very clear on that fact when he'd tried to wheedle the keys from her after she insisted she needed to go pack her things *right now* if she was going to stay at his house.

The sooner they got off this property, the better. He didn't like being here, didn't like Kyrie being here now that she'd told him about the vulnerabilities she'd purposefully left in the estate's wards.

Bait. She'd been playing bait for months, had admitted as much. He could have lost her at any moment and he'd never have even known it was coming.

He drummed his fingers on the dashboard and stared at the closed front door. As much as he was bothered that she'd intentionally left herself open to danger, what really bothered him, what he kept circling back to, was who she'd been playing bait for. Because no matter how he tried to twist the facts in his head to fit together, they did not lead back to Danvers.

Valkyrie hadn't been looking for Danvers for the last year. She'd been looking for her father—obsessively looking for him—since before she'd even met Siren, before she'd had any idea who Danvers was, much less had reason to suspect he'd have her father.

No, everything, every stray detail, circled back to Elijah Winters. To the fact there'd been no sign that he'd gone missing under suspicious circumstances. He'd simply dropped off the map. As if he'd chosen to leave. Whenever Random had pointed out that fact, whenever he'd pushed her, trying to understand why she couldn't accept that the man had probably just blown a fuse and abandoned her, she'd always answered that she needed to find him.

Not that she *wanted* to find him. Not that she wanted him home, or needed to know he was safe. No, it was always, unerringly, that she needed to *find* him. And there was that little fact that before Jace had left for his honeymoon, he'd said he was certain there was something about their father Valkyrie wasn't telling him.

Random glanced at the front door again. Valkyrie didn't appear likely to walk out it any time soon. He dug his phone out of his pocket and had to call four times before Siren picked up.

"Is anyone dead, dying, or likely to be either in the next hour?" she asked.

"Not technically, no."

"Then I am hanging up."

"You wouldn't really hang up on me, would you, darling? What if I'm in an emotionally dark place and I need a friend?"

"Are you?" she asked suspiciously.

You have no idea, he thought. "No more than usual, I suppose."

"Random," she growled, "I am on my honeymoon."

"You're at the end of week two of a month-long honeymoon. You can take one phone call."

She huffed out a breath. "Okay. Fine. What do you need?"

"I can't just be calling to see how you're doing? Wondering if you're bored of Jace yet and realizing his much handsomer, much more entertaining best friend is still single and available?"

He *felt* her roll her eyes from an ocean away. "Please. You may be single, but you have never been available. Jace and I are very, very happy. And if you don't tell me why you called in the next thirty seconds I will begin to explain, in graphic detail, the numerous inventive ways Jace and I have had sex since tying the knot."

"You wouldn't be that cruel." He assuredly did not want descriptive details of his best friend's sex life. Some things a man was just better off not knowing about another man.

"You know how we're renting a place on the beach, and Jace has an elemental affinity for water? You would not believe the incredible, mind-blowing things he can—"

"*La-la-la,* okay, you win. I called because I need to talk to Jace."

"Why didn't you call him?"

"One, he would never have picked up. You're an easier target. Two, I sort of promised someone that I wouldn't *call* Jace, but I never promised not to *talk* to him, so I called you."

"You promised, huh? Can I assume that means you and Valkyrie are hanging out? Have you two done it yet?"

"Geez, Siren," Jace's voice cut in, "*please* do not talk about my sister like that in front of me."

Ha. Random had had a feeling Siren wouldn't be able to resist putting him on speakerphone.

"He lives," Random said. "So tell me about this water thing."

"Random, if I live to be a hundred, I am never telling you how I fuck my wife."

"And thank the merciful goddess for it. Just had to make sure that was actually you, and Siren hadn't run off with a handsome Irishman."

"As if," Siren said. "So have you? Done it?"

Random could already feel the beginnings of the migraine this conversation was certain to produce. "No, and we aren't going to."

"Jace was supposed to tell you not to be subtle with her. Babe, did you tell him not to be subtle?"

"I was about as unsubtle as a brick. She isn't interested." *Leave it alone, Siren. Just leave it.* He wasn't in the mood to be pushed, not when he'd just had his mouth on Kyrie's before she'd coolly stepped away from him like it was nothing.

"No, she is. You must not have done things right. If you just—"

Random's temper got the better of him. "I realize it's highly inconvenient for *you*, personally, that the love of my life has no feelings for me. I am very sorry that *you* are having to go through that disappointment right now.

"Let me take this moment out of my own personal misery to assure you that I have tried every possible fucking thing. I have beat my head against the brick wall that is Valkyrie Winters and lost. She. Doesn't. Want. Me.

"Now that you have clear insight into my current emotional torment, can we move on from this topic?"

A long ten seconds of silence greeted that rant before Siren responded, her voice barely a whisper, "I'm sorry. I'll let you talk to Jace now."

He heard the shuffle of her standing, of the phone being handed off before it clicked off speaker.

"I'm going to give you a pass because I understand how it feels to be in love and miserable about it. But Random? Don't ever talk to my wife like that again."

He didn't need Jace's reprimand to feel like an asshole. He hadn't meant to hurt Siren's feelings. She hadn't meant to set him off. She just wanted everyone to be happy. She'd spent the last six years of her life completely alone before she met Jace, and now that she'd claimed Random, Valkyrie, and Meredith as her family, she desperately wanted them all to be as happy as she was.

And now that he'd been a jerk, he couldn't ask her about the adnexus. Especially since it occurred to him that Jace must not have a clue about it—because Jace would have said something to *him*—and no way in hell was Random going to be responsible for the lover's spat the airing of that secret was sure to create.

"I'm sorry."

"Tell it to her. I recommend accompanying it with apologetic cupcakes."

"Noted."

"So why are you bothering me on my honeymoon?"

He almost told Jace to forget it, but he'd already called. "I had some questions about your father." He swallowed. "You said you thought Valkyrie wasn't telling you something? Any idea what that might be?"

"Has something happened?"

"I'm not at liberty to say."

"Is she in danger?"

"No more than usual."

"Random."

"She will literally kill me, man."

"We're coming home."

"No. Whatever you do, don't do that. Unless you want to find my corpse buried in the backyard." Random would bet good money Jace was pinching the bridge of his nose right now.

"Do not let anything happen to my sister."

"I won't."

"Promise me."

"I promise. Just because things didn't work out the way I wanted, it doesn't change how I feel about her. Anything you would do for Siren, I'd do for Kyrie. I'll keep her safe."

Jace exhaled heavily. "I'll hold you to it."

"So about your dad?"

"I can't really explain it. Just a feeling that she knows something she isn't telling me."

"I never really saw your dad much." Random had spent a lot of time at Jace's house while they were growing up, but Elijah Winters had been a busy man. He'd always been off somewhere, and more often than not, he'd taken Kyrie with him. The man had shown so little interest in his son that Random was still a little surprised he'd cared enough to go to the trouble of disowning him. "How would you describe his relationship with Kyrie?"

"What do you mean?"

"Did it seem like they had a happy father-daughter dynamic?"

Jace couldn't keep the incredulity from his voice. "You do remember my dad, right? He doesn't have an affectionate bone in his body."

"And Kyrie?"

"She was devoted to him. She did everything he ever asked."

"And you don't think that's a little odd? Your father is a complete ass. Kyrie's almost thirty. And right up until the time he disappeared she was still doing every single damn thing he told her to. She had no life of her own."

"I didn't think you'd be the type to judge her."

"I'm not judging her. I'm trying to understand."

Jace sighed. "You know it bothers her—where she came from. That he's not her real father. She wanted his approval."

Movement caught Random's peripheral vision. Kyrie stepped out of the house. For all she'd been up there an extra fifteen minutes, she only had one small bag packed.

"Look, where are you going with this?" Jace asked.

He was going down a dark road he hoped he was wrong about. "Nowhere. Look, I've gotta go. Enjoy the rest of the honeymoon."

"Ran—"

Random hung up as Valkyrie tossed her bag into the back seat. His eyes followed her wrists, remembering the chains of Aspect he'd burned off her in the parking lot. So much had happened last night that he hadn't thought about them enough, but now that he did, he found things didn't quite add up.

Valkyrie hadn't been surprised by the chains. She hadn't been curious about them. She hadn't been infuriated by them. That lack of reaction didn't mesh with what he knew of her. Her reaction to being slapped in magical handcuffs should have been to get pissed off, and then replay the entire event to determine exactly how it had happened so it could never happen to her again.

Instead, when he'd asked, she'd just said she didn't know how Danvers did it. Then she'd thanked him, *thanked* him, for breaking them. Valkyrie didn't express gratitude. Certainly not for his help removing a few minutes of bondage.

But a lifetime of it? He could see her being grateful for that.

"Is there something wrong with my hand?" Valkyrie asked.

"No."

"Then stop staring at it. I need to swing by Meredith's."

Random raised an eyebrow. "I thought you two were only talking whenever you wanted to use her guilt over Jace to get her to do something for you."

"We are."

"What do you need from her?"

"It's personal."

"If it's related to what's going on, I need to know."

"It's not. Like I said, it's personal. I can drop you at your place on the way."

"No, you cannot. Are you going to make me reiterate the terms of our deal yet again?"

She muttered something under her breath that sounded suspiciously like, "Bloody lawyers," but when she pulled off the property, she took the turn that would lead them straight to Meredith's rather than the one that would meander by his place first.

CHAPTER
NINE

Valkyrie pulled into Meredith's driveway, the Jeep's rumbling idle a balm to the raw edges of her nerves. Meredith hadn't answered the call button for the estate's property gate, so Valkyrie had tried the code she'd used when they were kids.

The code had worked and now here she sat, outside Meredith's brilliantly white mansion, wondering why all of Aspect Society's old families felt the need to spend their excessive wealth on abysmally large houses. Goddess knew she'd hated hers ever since she was a little girl. Hated it more when her mother died and her father let all of the staff go and it was just her and Jace, alone in that big empty house with their father, trying not to set him off.

He'd been so angry after their mother died, and the rages he'd gone into...well. He might not be her biological father, but Valkyrie understood well enough where her temper came from. She'd kept Jace from most of it. She'd learned to pick up on all the little signals that told her when a rage was coming, and how bad it would be, so she could get Jace away. When they were kids, Jace would do almost anything she asked, and she'd become a master of coming up with on-the-fly tasks that needed to be done *right then* to get him out of the way.

Except for when Elijah was using Jace as a lever to keep her in compliance, he could forget his son's existence for long stretches at a time. Valkyrie hadn't been able to stop the emotional damage Elijah had done to her brother, but she *had* stopped the physical. Oh, she hadn't stopped him from lashing out—*that* was impossible. No amount of perfect behavior or excellence in training could truly please her father—but she could redirect that anger towards herself. So she had. She had made sure Jace never saw it, that he'd never known. That he never *would* know.

"Did you want to talk to Meredith, or stare at her house?"

She was too well-trained to actually startle, but her heart slammed into her chest at Random's voice. She'd been so deep in her memories she'd forgotten he was even there. She looked into those fathomless brown eyes she could drown in and lost herself in a different memory, one that had started in this stupid Jeep a year ago.

She'd foolishly picked him up after finding him broken down on the roadside. On the drive home, he'd been talking his usual line of seduction and she hadn't been able to resist it anymore. She'd dared him to act on it. He had obliged. Part of her was still amazed she'd had the presence of mind to tell him to take her inside instead of climbing on top of him and taking him in the passenger seat.

"I know I'm pretty, love, but is there a particular reason you're staring at me?"

"No." Goddess, she was a mess. She twisted the key out of the ignition. "I don't suppose you'll stay in the car?"

"Not a chance."

She slid out of the Jeep, booted feet landing on a sidewalk as blindingly white as the Townsend mansion. Did Meredith have the concrete power-washed every week?

She walked up to the front door and hit the bell. It was a

large house. It was reasonable that, depending on where Meredith was inside it, if she was even home, it could take her some time to reach the front door.

Valkyrie didn't care. She proceeded to jab the button over and over, continually restarting the annoying, chime-like tone she could hear on the other side of the wall.

The door jerked open.

"Touch that damn button one more time and you'll find yourself eating every ugly truth you've ever run away from." Meredith looked like she'd either just woken up or never gone to bed the previous evening. Her usual covering of flawless makeup was gone, and in its absence the dark shadows beneath her eyes showed prominently.

"I need to talk to you." Valkyrie swept inside. It had been a decade or so since she'd been inside the Townsend home, but she remembered the layout well enough to head for the kitchen.

"By all means, come in," Meredith said. She strode into the kitchen on four-inch heels that were practically an extension of herself. As long as Valkyrie could remember, she'd never seen the woman wear flats.

"Thanks."

Meredith narrowed her eyes. "That was sarcasm. You get that, right?"

"I'm not an idiot, I just don't give a damn."

Random had stopped in the doorway, as if he couldn't quite decided if it was safe enough to enter a room that contained both of them, and he winced now. "I'm sure what Kyrie meant was—"

"Oh, I'm sure she said exactly what she meant," Meredith interrupted. "She usually does. And since when are the two of you talking again?"

Valkyrie shrugged.

"It's complicated," Random said.

"It always is with her. I thought you'd broken the cycle. Freed yourself. You're too nice for her. Go find someone who doesn't eat people for breakfast, lunch, and dinner."

"And who do you suggest he go and find?" Valkyrie asked before she could stop herself, a warning rumble in her voice. She might know she wasn't good enough for him but that didn't mean she wanted her face rubbed in the fact.

Meredith rolled her eyes. "Oh, for goddess sake, Val, *that* was also sarcasm. Even if I had the inclination, I'm not dumb enough to go sniffing around territory you've already claimed. I happen to like breathing."

Random coughed. "Ladies, please. You're embarrassing me."

"I grew up with you, Random. You're incapable of embarrassment." Meredith turned back to Valkyrie and stared at her. Valkyrie stared back. Meredith swiped a glass of what looked like ice water—but was more likely gin if the mostly-empty bottle next to it was any indication—off the kitchen island. She drank half of it like it *was* water before asking, "So what do you want?"

"I need to talk to you."

"Then talk."

"Privately."

"If you wanted to talk privately, why did you bring him?"

"He brought himself. You know how he is."

"True. This way, then." Meredith topped her glass off with gin and moved for the sliding glass doors that let out onto a large veranda.

"Hey," Random said. "Is this going to take long? What am I supposed to do?"

"Bake something," they said in unison.

"All right. Fine. I get it. A man's place is in the kitchen, is that it?"

Valkyrie glared at him over her shoulder as she followed Meredith out. He blew her a kiss. She closed the sliding door more firmly than was, strictly speaking, necessary.

"You think he'll actually cook?" Meredith asked.

"Probably. You hungry or something?" Upon closer inspection, Valkyrie thought Meredith could use a meal or ten. Her curves had all but disappeared, and her designer clothes hung too loose on her frame.

Not that she cared, Valkyrie reminded herself.

"Not really. I have everything I need right here." Meredith tilted her glass of gin back and forth, the ice cubes clinking against the cut crystal sides. She turned and looked through the glass doors into the kitchen, where Random had indeed pulled an assortment of pans out of a cabinet. "What's it like?" she whispered.

Valkyrie frowned. "What?"

"Having someone love you like he does."

The strangest pain tore through Valkyrie's chest. "He doesn't love me."

Meredith laughed. "Goddess, you actually believe that, don't you?"

"It's the truth."

"Want to bet?" Meredith waggled her fingers and Aspect sparked at the tips. "I bet if we call him out here right now and ask him if he's madly in love with you, he'll say *yes*, and it'll be the truth."

"No."

"Come on. It'll be fun. A lot more fun than skulking around bushes, which seems to be the only thing you contact me for these days. Unless you have a different request today?"

Valkyrie gritted her teeth. Ask. All she had to do was ask. It couldn't be that bad.

"Please tell me I don't have to go skulk in the bushes again."

"No. I need—" Oh, hell. She couldn't do it. "Never mind."

"You need to know what to wear to a date at StellaMia's."

Valkyrie gaped at her.

"Don't look so shocked. Gossip is currency in this town. That," she pointed through the glass doors at Random, "is the favorite rebound candy of every single, straight woman in Seclusion, and he's been mysteriously unavailable for months.

"So you'd best believe when your stablehand told BettyLou at The Knitting Needle that Random was taking you, of all people, on an actual date, it made the town rounds in under two hours. Twelve people have texted me about it. Word on the street is Lauren Hale had an apoplexy. Bet you a hundred bucks she's at StellaMia's tonight."

Valkyrie closed her eyes. She wouldn't touch that bet with a ten foot pole, and this was precisely what she hadn't wanted.

"It doesn't take a detective to figure out you wouldn't have a clue what to wear. And with Siren gone, I'm the only female you could possibly ask." Meredith smiled. "I told you one day you'd wake up and realize not having friends sucks. Just didn't think it'd be the next morning."

"Are you going to help me or not?"

"For a price, certainly."

"What do you want?"

"What I've wanted for a damn year. To explain about what happened with Jace."

Valkyrie's jaw clenched. Her father had disowned Jace at eighteen, and Meredith had casually broken his heart the same day. Had told him he wasn't worth her time without his father's legacy, his father's money.

What explanation could Meredith give that would possibly make *that* okay?

"*He's* forgiven you," she pointed out. "Random has, too. Hell, even Siren likes you. Why do you care what I think?"

Meredith threw the hand not holding gin up in exasperation. "Because we were friends." At Valkyrie's lack of reaction she deflated a little and added, "Weren't we?"

Yes, they had been friends. If Valkyrie was honest with herself, which wasn't a task she ever found easy, that was the real issue here, the real reason she'd avoided this conversation.

Jace could forgive Meredith for what had happened between

them if he wanted to. It was his business, his hurt. And everyone else could accept Meredith back into the fold now that the issue that had caused the rift in their friendship had been repaired.

But Jace wasn't the only person Meredith had hurt. She'd turned her back on Valkyrie, too.

Valkyrie pulled a chair out from the patio table and dropped into it. She rested her right ankle on the opposite knee, leaned back and crossed her arms. "Explain away, then. Give it your best shot."

Now that she'd been given permission, Meredith didn't seem to know where to begin. She paced back and forth on the other side of the table, perfectly manicured French nails tapping against the glass in her hand.

"I did love Jace, you know," she said finally.

Valkyrie snorted. "You threw him away like garbage at the lowest point in his life because he wasn't useful to you anymore."

"And you were right there beside him picking up the pieces, were you? You're pretty fucking hypocritical for someone who didn't lift a finger to help him because her daddy told her not to."

Valkyrie's blood boiled. "I had my reasons."

"So did I, and I'd wager they weren't much different from yours."

"Oh, I doubt that."

"I don't." The tips of Meredith's fingernails pressed into the glass, the skin beneath them turning so white Valkyrie thought the nails might actually pop off. *That* would a bloody mess.

"Do you know why I started dating Jace in Academy? Why I became friends with you?"

"No."

"Because my mother told me to. Everything I ever did was because she told me to. She had ambitions in Society, and I was going to achieve them for her. She married my father because he had money, and she wanted money, but he didn't have status. It's why she made him take the Townsend name. *Her* family's name meant something, even if they'd landed themselves in financial ruin.

"Do you know what her Aspect was?"

Valkyrie shook her head. She'd been too busy surviving to give Meredith's mother much thought in her youth. Her Aspect would have been registered with the Council, of course, but those records weren't public. If an Aspect user didn't wish to disclose their abilities to the rest of the Society, they weren't required to.

"Agonia." Meredith gave a short bark of laughter. "Funny, how they like to dress up pain with a Latin word, as if it makes it all more civilized."

Valkyrie felt the first hint of uncertainty. She'd been so sure that nothing Meredith could say would account for anything, but Agonia? If Jace were here, he would likely explain how the various branches of Aspect were a product of evolution, like anything else about people. How Agonia had probably developed as a defensive branch—it was very difficult for an enemy to attack you if they were in so much pain they couldn't see straight.

"Your health problems?" Valkyrie asked tersely.

When they were kids, Meredith would disappear from Academy for days at a time. When she came back, she always looked as if all the vitality had been drained out of her, but she never had a physical mark on her, nothing to indicate anything was wrong with her other than the vague immune issues she referenced anytime someone asked.

"Mmm," Meredith agreed. "I never could do anything right, you see. I thought when I finally got Jace it would mean something to her. Your family's bloodline goes right back to the Council's founding, to Seclusion's founding. She wanted to be attached to it. She wanted the status and the influence. Never was my mother as happy as the day yours died. She thought she'd sweep in and comfort Elijah and he would fall into her perfectly augmented breasts."

Valkyrie blinked. "But your father..." She trailed off. She'd been about to say that Meredith's father had still been alive, then. Except he'd died a week after Valkyrie's mother.

"Yes. My father." Meredith's face softened, and old pain flashed across it. "My father, who was still useful because he was making money, but not as useful as a newly-single Elijah Winters would be. Dad died of a heart attack." She swallowed and looked Valkyrie in the eyes. "Do you know how much pain it takes, carefully applied to all the right systems of the body, to induce a fatal heart attack?"

Water welled in Meredith's eyes, but the tears that spilled down her cheeks didn't affect her voice. Valkyrie didn't think she even noticed them.

"I don't know how long I listened to him scream. I didn't do anything. I didn't try to stop her. I was too scared. I just sat in my room, hugging my knees and wishing for it to stop. It stopped when he quit breathing."

"You were just a kid," Valkyrie said.

"It's no excuse. My father loved me. He figured out soon enough after their marriage that my mother was petty and vindictive. He would have left her if it wasn't for me—because he didn't want to lose *me*, and he knew if he divorced her she'd never let him see me again.

"He honestly thought I had immune issues, you know? She was so, so careful, and I was too scared to say anything. And then, when his inconvenience outweighed his usefulness, she killed him. And for nothing. I would have laughed at how thoroughly your father rejected her, except she'd killed mine for it and took the failure out on me."

Meredith smiled. "And then she decided if she couldn't have Elijah Winters, that when I was old enough, I would have his son."

"That's why my father disliked you so much."

"Undoubtedly. When I finally *got* Jace my mother was so pleased she almost turned into a normal person. I could go entire weeks without her hurting me. And she never did it badly enough I couldn't hide it anymore. I would have loved him just for that reprieve, but then it turned out he was a good person, too." Meredith sighed. "And then Jace had to go and get himself disowned.

"It was all over then. My mother was furious. She expected me to fix it, as if *I* could make Elijah change his mind. And I think if I'd asked Jace to try and make it work with your father, he probably would have. But I saw how he looked when he told me what happened. He looked free. And I wanted that for him. When he asked me to leave with him..." Meredith smiled. "I'd never been happier."

"So why didn't you?"

Meredith turned an all-too-knowing look on her. "The same reason, I suspect, you never left home. She wouldn't have let me go. I was the only commodity she had left and I wasn't going to put Jace in the middle of that."

Valkyrie tried and failed to sort through the tangle of her emotions. She wasn't used to having so goddess-damned many of them. The overpowering one was guilt. That Meredith had been living through the same hell she had and she'd never noticed.

She'd been so caught up in her own misery, and she'd been quietly, desperately jealous of Meredith. Of how pretty and perfect she'd seemed. How she was allowed to be soft and vulnerable when Valkyrie wasn't. She'd never held it against her, but she'd coveted it, because she'd seen how Jace had cared about Meredith, and she'd known that no one could ever—would ever—love her like that.

She wasn't soft or pretty. Maybe once she'd known how to be vulnerable, but that time was long past.

"You could have told Jace the truth," she said. "Let him make up his own mind." But she wasn't really talking to Meredith. She was talking to herself. She could tell Random the truth. Let *him* make up his own mind.

Meredith made a derisive noise. "Like you told Jace the truth about your father?"

"I don't know what you're talking about." And with those words, she knew she would never tell Random anything. Because Meredith understood about her father, and Valkyrie couldn't even bring herself to admit the truth in front of *her*.

"Please. My mother never left an outward trace but you had bruises for days. Too many even for a Battle Aspecter. Our parents were both abusive fucks, whether you want to admit it or not.

"You know, I couldn't figure out why you were so obsessed with finding Elijah after he disappeared, but then I realized, it's the same reason I didn't go with Jace. The same reason that, now my blessed mother is dead, gin is my new best friend. You're afraid that without him, you'll realize there's absolutely nothing left of you but what he made you."

"You're wrong, there."

"Am I?"

"There's nothing to be afraid of. I already know there's nothing left of me but what he made me." She couldn't go back and change that. She could only hope to move forward.

"Then why the bloody hell would you want him back?"

"Earlier, when you said I didn't lift a finger to help Jace because my daddy told me not to, you were right. Because everything he ever told me to do or not do came with subtext. Do this, don't do this, or I take it out on Jace."

Meredith's lips were a thin line. "Did Jace know?"

"Of course he didn't know. The idiot's damn sense of honor would have gotten him killed. He's *my* brother, he's *mine* to protect. I made sure he never found out what Elijah really was."

Meredith's breath left her in a rush. "Good."

There was something in her old friend's face, in the tone of her voice, that convinced Valkyrie of what her words alone never could have: she *had* loved Jace. Maybe she still did. Valkyrie wondered, then, what it had cost her to stand in Siren's bridal party and watch her new friend marry him.

Valkyrie imagined having to stand a few feet away from Random while he smiled adoringly at some theoretical bride. She could never do it. If Random ever did decide to get married, she'd be halfway across the world and drunk off her ass on the happy occasion, because if she wasn't she'd be tearing the damn wedding venue apart.

"Jace has Siren now," she made herself say. "She can protect him. But Random doesn't have that. And despite my best efforts, it appears half of Seclusion now thinks the two of us are involved. And if my father comes back of his own volition, that won't end well for Random.

"I don't want to find my father because I want him back, Meredith. I want to find him because I want him dead."

Meredith drained the rest of her gin. She stared at Valkyrie, her fingernails drumming against the now-empty glass. "You want help with that?" she said finally. "Because I wish to gods I'd had the guts to put my mother into her grave myself instead of letting cancer do it. Maybe I'd have some fucking closure if I had."

Of all the reactions Valkyrie had prepared for, full-fledged support had not been on the list. Something tight in her chest, something she hadn't even realized was there, broke. She started laughing, and she couldn't stop. Not until the sliding door opened and Random leaned out.

"Oh good," he said to Meredith, "you're still alive."

"Why wouldn't she be?" Valkyrie demanded.

"I thought I heard you laughing."

"So you thought I killed her? I don't laugh when I kill people."

"You don't laugh at all."

"I do."

"No," Meredith said, "you really don't."

"So what were you two ladies talking about?"

"Nothing," they said at the same time. There was a reason, Valkyrie thought, that they'd been friends.

"Well, a deal's a deal," Meredith told her. "Come with me."

VALKYRIE STARED through the door into Meredith's closet, unwilling to step inside. She was accustomed to large closets—it was part and parcel of living in an excessively large house—but this one exceeded even unreasonable expectations. It was the size of a bedroom in its own right, plushly carpeted in the same china-white scheme as the rest of the house, and so brilliantly lit it hurt Valkyrie's eyes.

There was a bloody couch in the middle. Who spent so much time in their closet they needed a place to rest within its confines?

"I promise the dresses don't bite."

"Your clothes aren't going to work on me."

Meredith pulled a black dress off the rack, frowned at it and put it back.

"We're actually a much more similar build than you'd expect. You just turned all of yours to muscle so the presentation is different. If we stick with the stretchy, non-zippered options, it should work."

"It still won't work. You're pretty."

Meredith raised an eyebrow. "While I always appreciate a compliment, I'm not sure what that has to do with anything."

"I'm not. Pretty," she added, when Meredith didn't look like she understood.

"Even if you honestly believe that to be true, which it isn't, the fact would preclude you from wearing pretty clothes because...?"

Valkyrie opened her mouth, snapped it shut.

"That's what I thought. Here." She held out an indigo blue

dress. "This is the one. Try it on while I go to the other closet for shoes."

The woman had *another* closet? What was wrong with just one?

Valkyrie shrugged out of her clothes and into the dress. As promised, it was stretchy—slinky was the word she would have chosen—the fabric smooth and cool against her skin. It was a one-shoulder affair that fit her like a glove and ended mid-thigh. If she closed her eyes, she could imagine she looked pretty in it because it felt comfortable enough. But when she looked in the mirror all she could see was an over-muscled train wreck.

Meredith returned holding a pair of black heels and whistled. "Damn. I knew that was the one."

"I look like a She-Hulk."

"You look hot. Random's going to drool when he sees you in it."

"If he drools it will be because the horrors have broken his brain. I look ridiculous."

"Are you serious right now? Many, many women would kill to have your thigh muscles. And that annoying bra-fat thing? You don't have it. You know what? I'm not even arguing with you over this. The Internet can prove me right." She lifted her phone.

"What are you doing?"

"Taking a picture for Instagram."

"No, you're not."

"Oh, yes, I am."

"I *will* kill you if proof of me wearing this exists on the Internet."

"Coward."

"Nice try, but you're still not getting that picture."

"Fine. But when Random loses his goddamn mind upon seeing you in that, just make sure it's my voice in the back of your head saying, *I told you so*. Try these on." She held out the shoes.

Valkyrie tried. She really did. But she was never going to be able to walk in high heels. After a few minutes of attempted instruction, Meredith admitted defeat. She left the room and returned with a pair of strappy, mercifully flat sandals.

"I didn't think you owned anything without a heel."

"I have plenty of flats. Just don't wear them."

"Then why do you own them?"

"Therapy."

"Your therapist told you to buy shoes you won't wear?"

Meredith laughed. "Not unless my therapist's name is American Express." At Valkyrie's blank look she said, "Shopping, Val. Retail therapy. Buying things you don't need to fill the void in your soul."

"Oh. Does it work?"

"No. But it does mean I have cute sandals to give you."

Valkyrie got out of the dress and back into her own clothes, then realized she had another problem. How was she supposed to get this stuff past Random without him noticing? She'd never live it down if he found out the urgent reason she'd needed to come here was fashion advice.

"Put them in here," Meredith held out a canvas bag. "Oh, and I almost forgot." She dashed back into the closet, came out holding a tiny black bag.

"What is that?"

"It's a clutch. For your things."

"That thing will barely hold my phone."

"Phone, ID, one credit card, lipstick." Meredith agreed. "That's pretty much your limit."

Valkyrie took the clutch and popped the clasp open speculatively. There was no hiding a weapon under the damn dress. It was too tight and too short. But though the clutch looked ridiculous, if she left her phone in the car and—

"Do *not* put a knife in the clutch, Val."

"You don't know that I—"

"No knives, no throwing stars, no weapons of any kind."

"And people say *I'm* no fun," Valkyrie muttered. "When do you want this stuff back?"

Meredith waved her hand dismissively. "I don't."

"I'm not a charity case."

"Let me put it this way. After what is likely to occur in, around, and near that dress, I have no interest in taking it back."

Valkyrie rolled her eyes and gathered everything into the canvas bag. There wasn't any real point in disillusioning Meredith about the fake nature of the damn date. And it was...nice, that she'd gone to this much trouble. She could have just told her what type of thing to wear and sent her off to a department store, but she hadn't.

She started to shrug it off, to walk out of the room without a word, like she would have done a day ago. Maybe even an hour ago. She didn't want to need anyone. When Elijah was still here, she hadn't, because there hadn't been room for anyone else. He had been the demonic god around which her existence pivoted.

Once he was gone, she'd been able to pretend she still didn't need anyone, because Random had stepped into that void. But he would be gone, soon, too. Once this business with Danvers was resolved, he would be free to live his life without her. She'd had the last two weeks to understand how alone she would be without his constant check-ins and funny quips.

There wouldn't be another Random for her, but that didn't mean she had to be alone. "Meredith? About what you said. About Jace. I get it."

Meredith lifted an eyebrow. "Is that forgiveness?"

"I don't know. I'm not sure I fully understand the concept. But I think—I think maybe I could use a friend, after all."

A smile spread across Meredith's face, the first real one Valkyrie had seen all day. "That makes two of us."

Despite renewed friendship, Valkyrie still wasn't good with the emotional nonsense that followed these types of situations, so she hefted the canvas bag like a duffel and started downstairs.

In the kitchen, Random was closing the dishwasher door and hitting the "start" button.

He turned around as they entered and zeroed in on Meredith. "Are you aware that the only well-stocked part of your kitchen is the liquor bar?"

"It *is* the most important part." She sniffed at the tantalizing aroma coming out of the oven. "It smells like you managed just fine."

"That's because I'm a culinary genius and my Aspect managed to direct me to the one jar of pasta sauce in your cupboard that was hiding under a metric ton of plastic bags. You know those things are really bad for the environment right?"

"I'll be sure to jump on the reusable bandwagon right away. What did you make?"

"Calling it lasagna is a stretch given what I had to work with, but it's the closest approximation I have. Take it out of the oven in twenty minutes when the timer goes off. And for goddess sake, actually eat some of it."

Meredith looked at Valkyrie. "I'd forgotten how bossy he is."

"It's a problem," Valkyrie agreed.

"Good luck with that."

Random's eyes narrowed. "I think I liked it better when you two were sniping at each other. It's less fun when you gang up on me."

"There, there. I'm sure Val is more than capable of tending to your wounded ego."

"Oh?" Random turned a speculative eye on Valkyrie, and he had *that* look in his eyes, the one that said something wildly inappropriate was about to come out of his mouth. "I find my ego is best tended by frequently engaging in—"

"Time to go," Valkyrie said.

"But I haven't—"

Valkyrie shoved him out of the kitchen.

TEN

Valkyrie had been ready for the not-date for the last fifteen minutes. She just couldn't find the courage to leave Random's bathroom.

She tried and failed to convince herself that this was like the Gathering Ball, or Jace's wedding. On both of those occasions, the dresses had blissfully covered her to the ankle. And they might have been form-fitting, but at least they'd had substance. This thing was so thin it made her feel naked.

Why hadn't she told Meredith to find her something else? Maybe a nice pantsuit?

At least her hair wasn't a disaster. She was confident on that point, since Siren had insisted on teaching her how to use a curling iron, which had annoyed her at the time, and for which she was now grateful.

As for her face...she was never going to be beautiful, and she was never going to be comfortable in a lot of makeup. But she'd played up her eyes, and they matched the dress, and she thought maybe she at least didn't look bad.

She gripped the annoyingly-small clutch and wished it was a weapon. Any weapon. How did normal women do this? Always trying to present their best selves and getting their souls sucked out for it? The great thing about never putting any effort into her appearance was that she didn't have to worry about being judged for it. People *did* judge her, yes, but it didn't matter, because she wasn't trying to impress them.

Putting on a dress and makeup blatantly said, *Hey, look at me. I'm trying.* It invited scorn and derision. She couldn't even retaliate properly against inflammatory comments people might make because if she got into a fight in this dress she'd end up showing the world a lot more of herself than she was interested in revealing.

Random knocked on the door. "Not to push you, but I can't guarantee they won't give the reservation away if we're late."

"I'll be right out."

She could do this. She could. She would just pretend it was her Academy trials all over again. She straightened her shoulders, put on her expressionless war mask, and stepped outside. The bedroom was empty. She relaxed a fraction, until she walked into the kitchen.

Random leaned against the island and he looked—goddess, he looked good. In dark pants, with a dress shirt and tie beneath a black blazer, he looked like he was about to go on a date with a woman he actually wanted to impress.

He straightened and stared at her. Just...stared. She hoped maybe it was a good stare, but then the seconds continued to tick by and he still didn't say anything. The longer the silence went on, the more certain she was that this was not a good reaction.

RANDOM WAS RELATIVELY positive he possessed functioning lungs, he just seemed to have forgotten how to operate them.

Snap out of it. You've seen her in a damn dress before. The very male part of his anatomy was keen to point out he hadn't seen her in a dress like *this* before.

"You look…" *Perfect. Beautiful. Stunning.* "Nice," he finished lamely. "Excuse me. I forgot something."

He retreated into the bedroom and shut the door. It was that, or make an idiot of himself. Since that was all he seemed to do around her anymore, he wasn't interested in staying to do it again.

It's not a real date, he reminded himself. But damn if she hadn't turned out like it was. How was he supposed to sit next to her all night and pretend to be infatuated with her without the reality of his actual infatuation seeping through?

Easy answer there: he wasn't. There was no show like the real thing. And if he was going down that road, he might as well go all in. He walked over to his nightstand and rummaged through it until he found the small black box he was looking for. He'd bought it from some up-and-coming jewelry artist in the local art scene a few months back.

He'd wanted to give it to her for her birthday, but it hadn't been the right time. He knew now there wasn't ever going to be a right time, and if he couldn't give it to her properly, she might as well still have it.

VALKYRIE WINTERS DID NOT CRY. This was a truth universally acknowledged. But she was the closest she'd come to it in a long, long time. She'd known, *known,* how ridiculous she looked, but some small part of her had hoped maybe Meredith had seen something she couldn't. Meredith had been wrong.

You look…nice. It had taken him long enough to come up with a neutral, one syllable word to describe her. He had fled the room at the mere sight of her.

Her gaze went to the black box on the living room bookshelf. She'd retrieved the blood samples she had for the other councilors when she'd packed her clothes earlier, and she'd stowed them in the box. She reminded herself that *that* — blood acquisition—was why she was going on this fake date. She had a goal to accomplish tonight. It didn't matter what Random thought of her.

But that didn't stop embarrassed heat from flushing her cheeks when Random came back out of the bedroom, carefully looking anywhere but at her. She couldn't believe she'd gone to the trouble to try and look nice. And she was wrong—she couldn't do this.

"We're calling this off," she said.

"What? Why?" His head jerked up, and he carefully directed his gaze at some distant point over her left shoulder.

She shrugged.

"This is our best chance for an ''accidental' meeting with DuPont on short notice. Even if you can come up with a legitimate reason to set up a meeting with him, he'll remember that."

"I don't care. I'll find another way to get to him. One that doesn't involve me looking like a bull in spandex."

"You look nothing like a bull in spandex."

She channeled every ounce of insecurity she felt into fury and leveled it at him in a glare. "You can't even look at me."

"It isn't because you look *bad*."

"I'm not so pathetic I need you to lie to me." She didn't have to stand here and listen to him soothe her out of pity. She could go take off this stupid dress, find a knife, and stab something. Even if it was just the punching bag in his gym instead of her usual sandbag course. Stabbing things always made her feel better. It was a soothing activity.

Maybe she would go stab DuPont. He *had* fired her, after all. It would be cathartic and achieve her goal of blood acquisition. All she had to do was make it look like a mugging. Except, of course, that someone of DuPont's caliber of Aspect had the means to deflect ordinary muggings, which meant if she succeeded, he'd know it had been done by someone in the Aspect community. He'd be on alert.

Well, there was still stabbing punching bags to cheer her. She brushed past Random toward the gym. He muttered something in Spanish and stalked after her.

"You want to know why I can't look at you, Kyrie? *This* is why I can't look at you." His arms encircled her and pulled her tight against him. He was almost the same height as her, which meant her ass pressed back against his cock. His exceptionally hard cock.

"You're so fucking hot I can't see straight," he whispered in her ear. "But you've made it painfully clear you have no interest in sleeping with me again. So you'll forgive me if I need a few minutes of not looking at you to desensitize."

He let her go, stepped back and held out a small black box. "This is for you."

She took it on reflex, too stunned by what had just happened to do anything else. Somewhere in the back of her mind, Meredith's voice whispered, *Told you so.*

She stared down at the box. "What is it?"

It was his turn to shrug. "Not even you're good enough to hide a knife under that dress. I thought this might make you feel a little less...naked. I'll go warm up the car."

She waited until he was gone to lift the lid. Inside, a necklace nestled against blue velvet. The black chain was thin but strong, the pendant hanging from it a black titanium sword with a sapphire set into the pommel.

She liked it. It was pretty, but also strong. Against her better judgment, she put it on and walked into the bathroom to check it in the mirror. The chain was short, and the tiny sword settled against the hollow of her throat.

Random was right. It did make her feel less naked.

Damn him for knowing it would.

AWKWARD WAS FAR TOO TAME a word to describe the atmosphere in the car on the drive to StellaMia's. Random's house was only twenty minutes from the establishment, but every minute felt like an hour.

Random kept both hands on the wheel and his attention laser-focused on the road, as if they were driving in six lanes of high-speed traffic instead of an empty, single-lane road. Short of his asking her if the temperature was acceptable and her replying that it was fine, they hadn't talked.

She fiddled with her new necklace. No matter how hard she tried to think about something—anything—else, her brain kept replaying Random pulling her to him, the proof of his interest pressed against her. He'd known that would convince her where nothing else could.

She groaned internally. He'd done it so she would know she didn't look terrible, and it had worked, but it had had other unfortunate results as well. Every time she remembered it her inner walls clenched and desire flared through her. She was on the verge of being embarrassingly wet.

Thank the goddess he couldn't tell.

Wait, he couldn't tell, right? Did men have a fifth sense about that sort of thing?

She sneaked a glance at him. His jaw was locked tightly enough that a muscle twitched along it, and his eyes remained on the road. She returned to looking out the passenger window, but he'd clearly noticed the momentary inspection, because she felt his gaze shift briefly to her.

She couldn't sit in this much tension for the rest of the drive. They'd both arrive at the restaurant looking like they were in pain and then no one, absolutely no one, would believe they were on a date. She had not put herself through this much discomfort for their cover story to fail.

"This is a nice car," she blurted out. Wonderful. A truly inspired conversation starter. She hadn't even known he owned a car, since his motorcycle seemed perpetually affixed to his person, but it still didn't qualify as decent conversation material.

He unclenched his jaw long enough to say, "I got a really good deal on it."

Don't ask him about the financing. You can come up with something smarter to say than asking about the financing.

"Good APR?" She officially wanted to die.

"Yeah, and I talked the salesperson down five grand and—goddess, are we really talking about the deal I got on my car?"

"Yes? What do people normally talk about on dates?"

"I'm not sure. I think you're supposed to ask me about my job and listen with rapt attention while I bore you out of your mind with what I consider to be interesting details about my life."

Valkyrie shivered. "What do I talk about?"

"I don't think you do. You just bat your eyelashes and laugh at my bad jokes."

"Dating sounds terrible."

"Why do you think I've never done it?"

She swallowed as he pulled into the parking lot at Stella-Mia's. "You really haven't? Not even when you were in Academy?"

He didn't answer until he'd pulled the car into the space and killed the engine. "No. Not even then."

She wanted to ask him why. She didn't.

"Since this is supposed to be a date, I should probably get the door for you." He opened his and got out without waiting for her to respond. He walked around the front, opened her door and held out his hand. She took it and stepped out of the car.

She hadn't relaxed any. Every muscle in her body was tense. She had the insane urge to bolt off into the darkness, only seven o'clock appeared to be a popular time for StellaMia's—maybe they were always popular—and people would notice if she impersonated a fleeing animal. They would notice if she walked in this on-edge too, though.

She knew of only one thing—one person—that could turn her muscles liquid when she was this uptight, and he was still holding her hand. Kissing him would be stupid. But if she didn't kiss him she'd walk into that restaurant so stressed that absolutely no one would believe they were on a date and then this entire charade would have been for nothing.

Before she could overthink it and ruin everything, she leaned in and pressed her mouth to his. Random stiffened and drew back, and heat flushed her cheeks.

"Shit. I'm sorry, I should have asked first." Just because *she* found kissing *him* relaxing didn't mean he felt the same way.

"I'm not complaining, love," he said slowly. "I'm just confused."

"You said a well-placed parking lot kiss could sell a fake date." Hadn't that been the entire point of "practicing" earlier? Or, as she remembered it, him torturing her. "We're in a parking lot."

"I don't think—" He cut off, shook his head. "Never mind. You're absolutely right. But there's a proper way to do this."

His hands settled on her waist and he pushed her gently back against the car, his body covering hers as he leaned in and claimed her mouth. She yielded to him, closed her eyes and slid her arms around him as their tongues brushed.

He might not be any more experienced at the official dating part than she was, but he had plenty of experience in other areas, and goddess, he could kiss. His hands traveled up her back, raising gooseflesh in their wake. As thin as the fabric of the dress was, he might as well have been touching her bare skin. She melted against him, all of her tension releasing as she lost herself in the taste of him.

To her left, a woman coughed disapprovingly. Valkyrie broke the kiss to glare at the woman—she'd *just* been starting to feel mellow—who turned out to be Jenna DuPont. Jenna made a startled noise, her eyes going wide in astonished recognition. Her husband, who hadn't bothered looking in Valkyrie's direction until his wife reacted, did so now. If his wife's eyes were large, Martin DuPont's practically took over his face.

"Evening, Mr. And Mrs. DuPont," Random said with casual politeness. He was still pressed against her, trapping her neatly between him and the car.

Jenna DuPont managed a brittle, "Evening, Mr. Tremayne," and rushed her husband toward the restaurant.

"Well," Random said once they were gone, "I'd say we sold the fake date to precisely the right people." He pulled her away from the car. His hands idly stroked up and down her spine, and she didn't think he realized he was doing it. Then again, that sort of casual touching was probably second nature to him.

"I guess we should go in, then." She didn't want to. She wanted to stand in the circle of his arms forever, to hold on to this one moment in time, where she wasn't afraid or angry or haunted.

He nodded and stepped away from her, but when his hands left her back, his right trailed down to clasp her left.

"For appearances," he said, when she looked at their joined hands.

What other reason would there be?

RANDOM WASN'T sure what impulse had stopped him from telling Valkyrie that the parking lot kiss that could sell a fake date usually came at the end of the evening, not the beginning. Maybe it was because it had seemed, for once, like she actually wanted to kiss him, *needed* to kiss him. Masochist that he was, he hadn't been able to stop himself from taking what she offered.

He also couldn't stop his thumb from tracing circles on the back of her hand as they walked into the restaurant. If she decided to point it out, somehow he didn't think she'd buy that *that* was for appearance's sake too. But she didn't comment on it, and as the hostess led them to their table, she kept his hand. Even when the paths between tables narrowed, not quite wide enough for two people to walk side-by-side, and she had to trail her arm behind her to keep hold of him, she didn't let go.

He knew precisely when people noticed them because Valkyrie stiffened, her already perfect posture going just a little bit straighter, fingers clenching around his. Especially when they passed a table that contained none other than Lauren Hale. Given how the previous night had gone, he decided it was absolutely fine to enjoy the look of shocked outrage on Lauren's face.

Once they passed her, he didn't give her another thought. When they reached their own table—a small round affair designed specifically for two—he slid Valkyrie's chair out for her. As she sat, he leaned over her shoulder and whispered, "It will be fine."

She gave a small, sharp nod, and he took his seat across from her. He'd barely settled into it when the server appeared.

"Can I get you started with something to drink?"

"Wine?" Random asked Valkyrie. He had a suspicion they were both going to need it.

"Goddess yes," she answered, enthusiastically enough that the server's eyebrows shot up. He handed them each a long, slender wine menu.

Random could tell, by the growing combination of panic and irritation in Valkyrie's eyes, that she had no idea what to make of it. As long as he could remember, she'd never drank. Not until her father disappeared.

He could have cheerfully murdered Elijah Winters had the man been around. Not because he thought everyone should be drinking alcohol left and right, but because the more he thought about it, the more certain he was there wasn't a facet of Valkyrie's life the man hadn't kept iron control over.

For goddess sake, Random was a domestic abuse lawyer. He should have fucking seen it before now. He reminded himself he hadn't been a domestic abuse lawyer in his teenage years, which was the last time he'd spent any real time around her before her father disappeared. After the man was gone...well, Kyrie hadn't really been talkative enough for him to put it together until now.

"Should I choose?" he asked. At her nod, he picked a merlot. "It's basically dessert," he told her once the waiter left.

"Great." She sounded hollow. She kept bumping the table and he suspected that beneath it she was twisting the cloth napkin on her lap into knots. The table was intimate enough he could reach beneath it and take her hand. He did, and she stilled. Then she squeezed his hand back tight enough to cut off his circulation.

"Everyone is staring," she whispered.

"Yes, but it's surreptitious staring."

"How does that make it better?"

"It's supposed to make it easier to ignore."

"It doesn't. I can't do this."

"You can. You gave a speech to the most stuck-up members of Aspect Society at the Gathering Ball. There were a lot more people staring at you then."

"That was different."

"How?"

"It was a role. One I was taught how to play. I know what Aspect Society expects of me. I don't know what role I'm playing here. I don't know who I am."

He lifted their joined hands around the side of the table, brought hers to his lips and brushed a kiss across her knuckles.

"You're a beautiful woman, having dinner with a man who's absolutely wild about you." He swallowed, wishing he could leave it there, at the truth, but knowing he couldn't. "And you're wild about him. That's the role you're playing tonight."

The server chose that moment to return with the wine.

VALKYRIE SLIPPED her hand from Random's, grabbed the wine glass and took a large swallow, one that made the server's eyebrows raise almost to his hairline. She didn't care. Before Random had added that last, *That's the role you're playing,* she could have believed he'd meant the words he'd spoken.

Get your head on straight. He'd given her the role, and if she thought about it like that, it helped. Playing that role wouldn't be hard, either. Because she *was* wild about him, and she had complete permission to let it show, this one time. After...after, he'd never need to know it had been real.

She realized the server had been saying something and tuned back in.

"—need more time with the menu?"

Valkyrie scanned the menu—it was select, what she supposed was probably referred to as *curated* in these types of establishments—so she made quick enough work of it.

"I don't think that will be necessary." Goddess, it felt good to have some confidence in her voice again. "He'll have the vegan mushroom Wellington, I'll have the lemon garlic scallops, and we'll start with the artichoke dip."

The shock on Random's face was priceless. The server shot him a questioning glance and Random nodded his confirmation of the order.

"How did you do that?" Random asked.

"What? You think I didn't know you're a vegetarian? Except for bacon." She frowned. "I never could figure that out."

"I'm a hypocrite," he said sheepishly. "Bacon is bacon. I shouldn't, but sometimes I have it. You know, Jace is my best friend and he never figured it out. I had to tell him."

"Jace's head is so perpetually stuck in the land of theoretical Aspect equations, fictional characters, and now Siren, that he wouldn't notice a bulldozer if it was about to flatten him."

"There were three other vegetarian options on the menu," he pointed out.

"One had eggplant and one had rosemary, neither of which you like. It was a toss-up between the Wellington and the butternut squash linguine. But you seemed more in a Wellington mood."

The look he gave her was...she had no idea what it was.

"I, too, find it useful to know things about people," she said. It sounded better than, *I've noticed everything you do for a long time.* Much better. Much less creepy. She should change the subject.

"You've never really explained how your Aspect works." She'd picked up on the obvious—that it tended to do what he wanted or needed—but often it appeared both more and less specific than that. More specific, more controlled, when he wanted to do something like get through a property ward. Less specific when unintentional things happened, like her horses wandering onto his property. Goddess only knew what had made *that* happen.

"Are you asking me to explain it now?"

"No." He had a right to his privacy, and if he'd wanted to explain it, he would have by now. "But sitting here while my mark is fifteen feet away and waiting for things to just work out is not in my nature."

The DuPonts were seated two tables over. Jenna radiated a stiff disapproval in their general direction—apparently she vehemently disapproved of people making out in parking lots—and Martin kept sneaking glances at Valkyrie like she'd sprouted dragon fangs and was merely waiting for the chance to sink them into his neck. Which, truthfully, wasn't far off the mark. If nothing else, Valkyrie was pleased she'd clearly ruined their evening.

Random smiled. "You're getting antsy, is what you're saying?"

"I'd like to know the plan. Is he going to magically develop a nosebleed or something?"

"Truthfully? I have no idea. But probably not a nosebleed. I can do a lot of things but I can't bridge over into Life or Death Aspect."

"Then how am I—"

He reached across the table and took her hand again. She was already entirely too accustomed to him doing so, and her fingers reflexively twined with his.

"What do you want to happen, love?"

"I thought your Aspect was all about what *you* wanted."

"Humor me."

"I just want this to be over. I want to be free."

His fingers tensed briefly. "Free from what?"

She really had to stop opening her big mouth. "Nothing." She was grateful, this time, when the server reappeared. He handed Random a card and then retreated.

"Looks like I have to go pay the piper for this reservation," Random said, waving the card. "Mia wants a word. May I suggest you look longingly in the direction of my disappearance while I'm gone?"

"Don't push it."

"Perhaps you could rest your chin in your hand and sigh dreamily?"

"Now you're just being ridiculous."

He grinned at her. "I thought you knew. Ridiculous is exactly what I am." He stood, stopping on his way past to lean down and whisper in her ear, "Try not to look *too* happy that I'm gone."

She watched him walk away, because he was a pleasantry to the eyes at all angles, and because it allowed her to observe the DuPonts without giving the appearance of doing so.

When she was nineteen, two years into her work contracting for the Council, she'd come to the conclusion that Martin DuPont was the single most boring man she'd ever encountered. A decade had done nothing to improve him, and it appeared even his wife had given up pretending to be interested in him. The couple didn't look at each other and they weren't talking. DuPont's entire focus was on the steak in front of him, and his wife's was on noting who else was in the restaurant.

Valkyrie tracked the servers' paths through the dining area and calculated her odds of tripping one at the right trajectory to send them sprawling into DuPont. It was doable, and she could make it look like an accident on her part, but the odds of the server falling into DuPont with a sharp object were slim.

She took another sip of the wine—it really *did* taste like dessert—and the velvet smooth liquid was halfway down her throat when Danvers walked in. He wore yet another new face—a younger, more handsome face—but it didn't matter, now. She'd cataloged the way he carried himself, the mark of his stride, the things an illusion couldn't quite hide, if one knew where to look.

Her power was a deep rumble in her chest, both a comfort and a warning, as Danvers walked to her table. He took care to make the walk look like the lazy amble of a powerful man taking his time, but Valkyrie saw the stiffness beneath it that hinted at pain. She felt a bone-deep satisfaction to know she had cost him something in their encounter the previous evening.

He sat in the chair across from her. Random's chair. She wanted to growl at him to get out of it, but she wouldn't let him goad her into speaking first. She held his gaze, ignored the badly-disguised curiosity of those seated nearby, and took a small sip of wine to steady her nerves.

Danvers *tsked* in disapproval. "Alcohol muddles the senses."

Valkyrie swirled the burgundy liquid and took another deliberate sip before she set the glass back down. She chose her reply with care. "Disapproval is hardly your place. After all, you're not my father."

The seconds ticked by, one then two, then five, then ten, and she thought either that she'd been wrong, or that he wouldn't take the bait. Then the corners of his lips curled and he said, "Oh, come now. We both know that isn't true."

Fury shot a jolt of adrenaline into her. Its harsh tendrils shuddered through her chest, down her arms to twitch and dance in her fingertips. Her Aspect hummed, begged and demanded to be unleashed.

"You knew," she gritted out. "You *knew* Evelyn was pregnant."

He looked mildly surprised. "Of course I knew. That was the entire point."

Valkyrie jerked back.

"You never put it together? I thought you would, after Siren brought so much of my work into the light. Evelyn was never special. But she wasn't a failure, either. She was simply a vessel. Everything I changed in her, I changed to create you."

Horror churned through her. "No."

"Oh, yes. The earliest manifestation of Aspect on record? Obliterating all the records for Battle Aspect in your Academy trials? How swiftly your Aspect regenerates? That's not coincidence, daughter mine."

"I am *not* your daughter."

"But you are. Blood speaks, Valkyrie. It is a shame. You could have been so much more. Given Elijah's interference, you didn't have quite the upbringing I'd intended. Still, he did push you, once he saw your potential. A little. Not enough."

Not enough? The sadistic son of a bitch had broken a quarter of the bones in her body. And that had only been the beginning.

"What is your connection to Elijah? Did you know him? Before Evelyn?" She had been on the verge of putting it together at Savado's, but the pieces hadn't quite clicked together for her until just now—the way Danvers talked about Elijah, as if they were familiar, as if they were close. Closer even than a year of holding the man prisoner could make them.

"You might say we were contemporaries, of a sort." His words held just a trace of amusement. "Before the idiot went and fell in love with Evelyn. Our paths diverged after that."

Contemporaries. Valkyrie swallowed against the bile that rose in her throat. She clasped opposite hands to opposite wrists, over the internal scars where her chains had been.

"Yes," he said, noting where her hands had gone, "those were my design, originally. Such beautiful work and that *anomaly* had to go and destroy it all in a temper tantrum." He reached for her right wrist.

She snapped her hands back, out of his reach. Her Aspect uncoiled, shadowed the air behind her like the wings of the battlefield Valkyries for which was she was named, power poised to strike.

"Touch me, and you will regret it." Her voice was loud and clear. Too loud, in the quiet, elegant restaurant, the classical music piped through the room too soft to mask either her words or her fury. Even as well-bred as the establishment's patrons were, some were no longer bothering to disguise their interest in the goings-on.

"Why are you here?" she asked, softly this time, so it wouldn't carry to nearby ears.

"To make sure you understand something. Random Tremayne is nothing more than a spoiled playboy who thinks a defect in his Aspect makes him invulnerable. He isn't. He can't save you."

Anger rode her, demanded she explain to Danvers just what would happen to him if he touched a single hair on Random's head. But if Danvers and Elijah were working together, she couldn't risk that information getting back to Elijah. Couldn't risk showing that she cared.

She leaned back against her seat and affected boredom. "Random is a means to an end. Getting what I need" —her gaze flicked pointedly to DuPont before returning to Danvers— "isn't easy. And with the timeline you've put me under, I decided to take advantage of his apparent interest in me.

"All *you* are doing here is interfering. So get out. Before I decide I'd rather put you on your ass here and now and get Elijah back from you that way."

"You could try," he snarled. "You'd never manage it. You'd never *find* Elijah without me."

She shrugged, to all appearances unconcerned. "Want to find out?"

~

"HOW IS IT GOING?" Mia asked. She was five feet three inches of curvy, bubbly excitement, and Random was not entirely sure they were far enough away from his table that Kyrie wouldn't feel the waves of enthusiasm radiating off the woman.

"You mean how *was* it going before I left my date at the whim of another woman?"

Mia rolled her eyes. "You're avoiding the question."

"It's going just fine."

"That was convincing. You don't sound happy. You don't *look* happy. Why aren't you happy? I have it on good authority you were making out in the parking lot—speaking of, what are you, sixteen all of a sudden?—and you were holding hands, so what's the problem?"

"The only problem is the length of time I have been gone from my date."

Mia crossed her arms. "This isn't one of those hetero male things where you finally secure the affections of your beloved and then decide you don't want her anymore, is it?"

"Of course I still want her." A little too much. "But I am fairly positive she doesn't want me."

"She ordered for you, didn't she? Accurately, I'm told."

"It's hardly a sign of true love that she can pick a menu item for me and goddess, woman, do you have that poor server reporting our every interaction back to you?"

"Poor nothing. Liam is well-paid and—"

"Walking toward us like his ass is on fire?" Random suggested.

Liam came to a breathless halt in front of them. His eyes darted between Mia and Random, as if unsure which of them to address. He eventually settled on the space between them. "There's someone here."

A vague feeling of unease crept up Random's spine, even as

Mia said, "You're going to have to be more specific than that, Liam."

"At the table. With Ms. Winters."

Random was already moving when he felt Valkyrie's Aspect punch the air. It roiled through the restaurant like a dark cloud, a swift-moving storm of her fury. He rounded the corner to the aisle that led to their table, and the cold violence in her eyes told him precisely who sat across from her.

Her gaze flicked to him for less than a second, but he read the message in it loud and clear: *Back off, I've got it handled.*

He couldn't back off. Not even for her. *Because* it was her. His Aspect sensed a threat to her and surfaced with a vengeance, a tidal wave spurred by the winds of her anger. His need to protect her was instinctual, undeniable.

The restaurant's windows rattled in their frames, as if set in motion by the beginning tremors of an earthquake. He heard hairline cracks etch through the glass, had no doubt the windows would have shattered if Kyrie's Aspect hadn't streaked forward and wrapped around him.

Her power slid over his skin, strong as steel and soft as spider silk, more heady than any wine. That touch alone might have been enough to bring him down, to dim the red haze in his vision long enough for him to accept that she didn't want his help. But she didn't stop there.

Her Aspect found his own and brushed against it, a tentative question and an offer. He couldn't have rejected her even if he'd wanted to. His Aspect opened to her completely, invited her in, and she came. Their power twined together, merged, until he couldn't tell where his ended and hers began.

Disbelief coursed through him. Blending like this was personal, intimate. Like opening up the darkest parts of your soul to another and asking them to accept you. This was something lovers did. True lovers, partners who trusted each other implicitly.

She wound against him like a caress and he felt what she

wanted from him in that connection: *Calm*, her power whispered. *Don't give him anything.*

He couldn't be calm. But he could give her the veneer of it, if that was what she wanted. He straightened his tie, slipped his hands into his pockets, and walked to stand next to her.

The face Danvers wore was much younger and handsomer than the one he'd chosen the previous evening, and Random could guess how this altercation would be taken as it made Seclusion's gossip rounds.

"You're in my seat," Random said. His tone was mild, but his power thrummed along beneath it, twined with Valkyrie's.

Danvers leaned back in the chair. "Am I? One could argue it was mine, first."

"It was never yours, and it never will be. You should leave. If I lose my temper, I can't guarantee you'll make it out in one piece. If she loses hers, I assure you that you won't."

Random had lost track of Mia when he'd made for the table, but she appeared now, two burly individuals behind her. Stella-Mia's wasn't a club, so they didn't have bouncers, but Mia had found the nearest available approximation.

"You don't have a reservation," she told Danvers, her voice brittle. "I'm going to have to ask you to leave."

Danvers smiled. "I see my welcome has worn out. I look forward to calling your bluff, Valkyrie." He stood and looked at Random, his mouth curling up in a sneer. "Tremayne. I dislike it when people borrow my property without asking. You'd be wise to rid yourself of it."

The words were so detached that Random didn't understand what—*who*—Danvers had meant by "property" until the man was halfway to the door. And though it was undoubtedly the reaction he'd counted on, Random couldn't stop the anger that fueled his response.

His Aspect detonated.

CHAPTER
ELEVEN

Valkyrie felt for all the places where her and Random's Aspects connected and clamped down. What had promised to be a truly spectacular—and spectacularly stupid—retaliation simply...dissipated.

It startled her so much she almost dropped the connection. She'd been prepared to throw her strongest shields around him, but it was as if his Aspect had recognized it would have to go *through* hers, and wasn't willing to do it. He was still furious, his power simmering just below a boil, but he was contained.

Only the thinnest sliver of his power escaped, and DuPont's muffled curse a moment later told her well enough where it had gone. The top of DuPont's wine glass was cracked, and the jagged edge at the rim had cut his lip. The small wound bled more profusely than one might expect, and he had the restaurant's fancy cloth napkin pressed to the wound.

The woman who had told Danvers to leave rushed over to DuPont's table, and he spoke irately at her while she removed the offending wine glass and made apologies.

"Stella or Mia?" Valkyrie asked Random.

"Mia." He bit the two syllables off. He hadn't moved from his place next to her chair. His face was bloodless, his lips pressed into a thin line.

Valkyrie had been told before, and often, that her rage was a suffocating force. She had an inkling of what that felt like now, sitting next to Random. It was as if she lay in the shadow of a mountain, waiting to see if it would topple over onto her. She understood, suddenly, why people fled when they saw her coming. Why Jace, and Random, and Meredith had been the only people who could stand to be near her when her temper rose.

Because if she didn't know that Random would never take his anger out on her, every hackle in her body would be standing on end. As it was, it was still uncomfortable, and she didn't know if her need to reduce his tension was because of that feeling, or because of her Aspect still tangled up with his.

But because of the latter, she understood what would ease it. Random responded best to physical touch. He was not, she thought bitterly, a creature made to be alone. Not like her.

She took his hand. His fingers threaded reflexively through her own, and his tension eased a fraction. He shook himself, like she'd woken him from a trance, and shifted to look at her.

"Perhaps now would be the time to leave?" Her gaze flicked pointedly to where Mia was leaving DuPont's table, broken wine glass and bloodied napkin in hand.

"I'll make our excuses to Mia," he said smoothly, but his fingers tightened on hers. "I think it would be best if you didn't let me go, just yet."

She understood he wasn't talking about his hand.

"I won't."

As he dropped her hand and walked after Mia, she let her Aspect curl a little more snugly around his. Because she wanted to. Because she could. Because, for the moment, he had accepted her, and she wanted to memorize the feeling.

Even if she took care of Danvers and Elijah, even if she found freedom, she knew she would never do *this* with another person again. Would never be this close, this connected, to anyone else.

She still couldn't believe Random had let her do it, but he'd taken her in as easily as he'd allowed her power to join with his property wards that morning. As if she belonged with him.

She'd done it because she'd needed the reassurance that she could stop precisely what she had: Danvers taunting Random into a reaction that would get him killed.

She hadn't expected to like it so much. She hadn't expected him to ask her to keep doing it, for any reason.

She didn't know how she was going to let him go.

THERE WAS no good way to explain to Mia what had happened, so Random didn't try. He made his apologies for bringing an unpleasant situation into her establishment, filched Dupont's bloodied napkin from the trash, and tried to remember that DuPont's blood was the actual reason they'd come here in the first place.

Mission accomplished. He should be happy.

He was furious. Kyrie's power stroking alongside his own was all that was keeping him in check. It was the only thing that had stopped him from going off the proverbial deep end earlier, and he was grateful for it, since even he would have a difficult time explaining to the head of the Council why he'd thrown all his Aspect around in public in what would, to the casual observer, look like nothing more than a pissing match between two men over a woman.

Fortunately, Valkyrie had locked him down tightly enough that no one but her would have felt how close he'd come to losing it. They'd have felt *her* power, but people expected public threats from Valkyrie—no one would think she'd have actually *done* something with that power in public.

She stood when she caught sight of him, a question in her

eyes. He answered with a nod. As they walked out, the too-interested gazes of Seclusion's elite upon them, he slid his arm around her waist. He needed to feel her—safe and warm and alive beneath his touch, and no one's property but her own—and once they were out of the public view he wouldn't have an excuse, wouldn't have her permission, to touch her anymore.

They reached the car too soon. Neither spoke as he saw her safely into the passenger side before taking his own place behind the wheel. He didn't ordinarily break the speed limit but he did so now, taking the curves of Seclusion's back roads at highly inadvisable speeds.

They were halfway back to his house before she asked. "Did you get it?"

He reached into his blazer pocket and pulled out the damn napkin, placed in the plastic Ziploc bag he'd conveniently found in the trash next to it. He didn't quite throw it at her, but it was close. A touch more force and he couldn't have passed it off as a toss.

She caught it, stared at it, didn't say anything. Not that he could blame her.

He pulled into the garage, turned the car off and stared at the steering wheel, hoping it would impart some calm or wisdom to him he couldn't otherwise seem to find.

"Are you okay?" she finally asked.

"He called you his fucking property."

"I'm aware."

"You're not a *thing*, Kyrie."

"Also aware," she said softly.

"Does he know?" He turned to look at her. "Tell me he doesn't. Tell me he doesn't know you're his daughter. That he didn't sit there and treat his own child like that."

"I can't tell you that, Random."

"The son of a bitch deserves to die."

"Yes, he does."

He didn't understand how she could look so calm, so

controlled. "How do you do it?" he asked. "How do you sit there and keep it contained like it doesn't fucking matter?"

She snapped, then, and he was selfishly glad, so relieved to see any emotion from her, anything other than that implacable calm she wore like a second skin. "Because what I feel has *never* mattered, Random. What I *feel* only gets me in trouble."

His gaze dropped to her lips and lingered. *Fuck it.* "And what do you feel when I do this?" He leaned across the console and took her mouth with his. He wasn't gentle, wasn't restrained, and she returned the kiss with the same ferocity. When he drew back, they were both breathing heavily.

"Everything," she whispered.

He'd expected any answer, save that one. "You're killing me, Kyrie." He brushed his nose against hers, his Aspect mimicking the gesture against her power. "Tell me I don't mean anything to you. Tell me you don't want me. Tell me if I walked away right now, you wouldn't care."

VALKYRIE CLOSED her eyes and pressed her forehead to Random's. It should get easier, telling him the things he'd asked her to. She'd done it before and she'd thought, if she did it enough, that one day she would wake up and believe it was true. But all being around him seemed to do was prove that it wasn't.

"I should tell you that. But I can't seem to make myself do it, tonight."

He pulled back from her and got out of the car. She didn't have time to feel angry or hurt at the abrupt withdrawal because his Aspect moved around her, a reassuring caress, and then he was at her door. She let him open it and draw her out, let him take her hand as they walked inside his house, even though there was no one here to put on a show for, no appearances that needed to be maintained.

There was only him. Only Random.

He shut the door behind them and drew her to him, his hands on her waist. His thumbs traced the muscles on her stomach. The way he touched her, reverently, made her feel beautiful. Desired.

She wanted to kiss him again. She wanted to forget everything and lose herself in his body. But she knew it wouldn't be fair to either of them right now. Because the way Random had reacted to Danvers tonight, the way his power still twined with hers, the emotion in his voice when he'd spoken to her in the car —well, she was starting to think maybe she'd been an idiot. That maybe, just maybe, if a man spent a year trying to prove he loved you, it was because he did.

And in this moment, with her emotions on edge, she might be willing to admit she felt the same way. But tomorrow? She didn't know about tomorrow. Because he would always be safer without her.

If he *did* love her—if he did, then she'd hurt him. Badly. She didn't want to hurt him again. But every nerve ending in her body pulled her to him. She pressed her face into the curve of his neck and shoulders, so she couldn't be tempted to kiss him again. So she wouldn't have to see whatever passed through his eyes when she spoke.

"I want you." Even that admission was hard enough to put into words. "But I'm not thinking clearly."

It was something she would never have felt comfortable enough to say to another man. But he was Random and she knew, somehow, that if she was honest with him in this moment, he wouldn't let her down.

"I don't think either of us is thinking clearly right now, love," he murmured.

"So what do we do?"

"You act like I know what I'm doing." She felt his smile, even if she couldn't see it. "The truth is, I'm just as lost as you are. But if you'd let me, I'd like to hold you for a while."

That sounded more intimate, more dangerous, than sex. But

she didn't want him to let her go. Didn't know for certain that if he let her go, she wouldn't leave this house and do something very, very stupid.

"Okay." The word was barely more than a whisper, and if her face hadn't been right next to his, she doubted he would have heard. He led her to his bedroom, and she was eternally grateful he didn't turn the light on, didn't talk while they took off their shoes. His hand found hers in the dark as they climbed into the bed.

She'd always had this image of herself as some hulking barbarian, too large to be held. As if being spooned was something reserved for petite, magazine-cover-pretty people. Turned out she was wrong. Random's arm came around her stomach and he tucked her against him. His legs fit with hers and his head rested on the pillow behind her, his breath a soft warmth against her hair.

She felt his heartbeat against her back, felt the rise and fall of his chest.

"Don't run away," he whispered. "Not again."

She almost didn't answer, because it was easier to simply lie here with him and not talk. Because if she never talked about that night, she never had to learn the truth. "You ran away first," she said softly.

"I've never run away from you, Kyrie."

"Not physically." She swallowed. She'd started this, so she had to get the damn words out. "But it was on your face. After we—when we—you know."

His arm tightened around her. "I don't think I do."

Goddess, he was going to make her say it. "When we had sex. You realized I'd been a virgin beforehand and it freaked you out. And I thought—I always thought that's why you were so *attentive* after."

He didn't say anything for a long minute, and she had the distinct impression he was struggling for emotional control.

"Kyrie, please, for the love of our probably-made-up

goddess, *please* tell me you didn't think I professed to love you because I took your virginity."

She shrugged. It had seemed logical at the time.

"You weren't the first virgin I'd slept with. I didn't tell any of *them* I loved them. And you can't honestly believe that I, of all people, hold virginity sacred. I'd have to be ten kinds of hypocritical."

"I remember the look on your face." It was burned into her memory, the way his expression had shifted when he'd seen the blood between her thighs. "I've never seen you look like that. You were horrified."

"It wasn't because you were a virgin. It was because I didn't *know* you were a virgin."

She wasn't sure that made it any better. "I don't really see how it was any of your business."

"It was my business because I would have done things differently. In case you didn't notice, I'm told it hurts the first time. I took you up against a goddamn *wall* and I wasn't gentle about it. I was afraid you'd hate me and you'd have every right to. If I'd taken five goddamn seconds to pay attention I should have figured out you hadn't done any of it before."

"That's what bothered you? That you weren't gentle?"

She wasn't making fun of him, but it must have come across that way because he snapped, "I'm sorry if you think it's funny that I thought I should have been considerate."

"I don't think it's funny, Random, it's just... as far as pain goes? That was *nothing*. It hurt way more the first time Dad broke my nose." *Or my collarbone. Or every one of the fingers on my left hand.* Really, the entirety of her childhood had hurt a lot more than the temporary pinch she'd felt when Random had thrust inside her. Since she'd still been in the grips of the orgasm he'd licked her to she really hadn't given a single damn about the pain.

Random tensed around her, and his voice was a low, warning

rumble. "The *first* time? How many times has your father broken your nose, Kyrie?"

Shit. She hadn't meant to say that. Keeping her mouth shut had been a lot easier when she hadn't had anyone to talk to. "It doesn't matter. The point is, it really didn't hurt. And I liked the wall." She'd liked everything about their encounter, right up until the end. "Is that—thinking you hurt me—is *that* why you kept hanging around, then? Guilt, or—"

He swore and flipped her around to face him.

"Kyrie, I want to be very, very clear about something. You don't have to do anything with what I say. I don't expect anything from you, but I need you to understand it.

"I. Love. You. I have *always* loved you. It has nothing to do with your damned virginity. If you'd fucked everyone in Seclusion before we'd had sex, the words still would have come out of my mouth because I was idiotically incapable of stopping them. You were the first woman I ever kissed."

"You were eighteen by then," she whispered.

"Not everyone starts young. Besides, I was a romantic idiot. I wanted you to be my first kiss. Maybe if I'd practiced before-hand you wouldn't have punched me." He shrugged. "The point is, when you didn't feel the same way, I tried to forget you. But I never did. And then you finally noticed me last year, and I knew I wasn't ever getting over you.

"When you let me keep hanging around, I thought maybe I could convince you I was worth it. That I was at least worth trying. There hasn't—you should know there hasn't been anyone since you."

That comment Meredith had made about Random being "unavailable" for the last year cast itself in a new light.

"Random." She couldn't get anything out other than his name. The full impact was settling onto her, the memory of every time she'd snapped at him in the last year. Every time she'd made snide comments about his sex life and implied that someone with his tendencies wasn't really capable of love. She hadn't meant any of it. She'd just meant he wasn't capable of loving *her*. Because who could?

"It's okay." He smiled at her, a small, sad smile that broke her heart. "I know you don't love me."

He was so very, very wrong about that.

"But if there isn't anyone else, if you want me at all—I'll take anything you're willing to give me."

Valkyrie's heart thudded in her chest. The voice of caution, the one that had been with her since the first time her father had threatened Jace, urged her to be careful. But careful had gone out the window the moment she'd walked into StellaMia's at Random's side. Had probably gone out the window in the parking lot at Savado's.

What did holding back from him now accomplish, except to make them both miserable? If she couldn't be honest with him now, when he'd just bared his soul to her, when could she?

Maybe she couldn't tell him she loved him. She didn't think the words would go past her lips, for the visceral terror they incited in her. But she could tell him *something*.

"Random, I—"

Her phone's message tone cut her off. She would have ignored it, but it sounded again. And again. Random's chimed soon after, and then the phone calls started. She retrieved her phone, a sick feeling in her gut, and opened the message from an unknown number first.

You said you didn't care what I did with Elijah. Let's see if that's true.

The other two messages were from Meredith.

Has the Council contacted you yet?

Call me as soon as they do.

The missed call was from DuPont. She had a feeling she knew what it contained before she started the voicemail, but she listened anyway.

"Ms. Winters." DuPont sounded as if he struggled for composure. "It's your father. It's Elijah. He's—he's returned.

Call me back and report to Council headquarters immediately."

Valkyrie ended the voicemail and called Meredith.

"You heard?" Meredith asked.

"Yes."

"DuPont wants me to come in. He left a message, I haven't spoken to him yet. I'm the only Truthfinder of any real power in the state. Whatever they want me for, if I don't go, it'll take them a day at least to contact someone else and fly them in. What do you want me to do?"

Given the length of time Elijah had been gone, the Council wouldn't reinstate his full legal authority without an in-depth investigation of his missing time. With a Truthfinder of Meredith's caliber, that could be as simple as a Q-and-A session.

"You're out of town. And I mean that literally. Out of the state would be better. Out of the country would be best."

"What the hell is going on, Val?"

"I don't know. But I'm going to find out."

She ended the call but couldn't bring herself to look at Random, and busied herself with putting on her boots. "Elijah's back," she said, her voice dull. She didn't think she would ever manage to call him her father again. "The Council's summoned me to headquarters. I have to go, I have to leave, I have to—"

"*Kyrie.* Look at me."

She stopped and looked, realized her entire body was trembling. Her hands, frozen on the laces of her boots, shook. That wouldn't do. She couldn't see Elijah like this—this unwound. But the tactics that had seen her through life failed her now. She couldn't breathe her way to calm this time, couldn't will her heart rate into slow submission, couldn't force her hands to steadiness.

Because the last two days—the events of this evening—they all added up to the one thing she'd fought so hard against. She loved Random Tremayne—and if she didn't fix this, she was going to get him killed.

~

RANDOM CAUGHT Valkyrie's shaking hands in his. They were even paler than usual against his own. She'd gone the white of death and she was cold.

He'd never seen her like this. The closest to it was when she'd tried to pack his things and make him leave. Even with that, before this moment, he would have told anyone who bothered to ask that truly rattling Valkyrie Winters was impossible.

She was rattled, now. She hadn't changed out of the dress but it was her combat boots she was frozen in the midst of lacing. The incongruity between the two alarmed him only because she hadn't seemed to have noticed it herself.

"He's back," she repeated, and there was a world of disbelief and fear in her voice.

"I know." He'd gotten the call, too, if only because DuPont had seen them together at StellaMia's and tried Random when Valkyrie hadn't answered her phone.

He rubbed her hands in his, trying to bring even a little warmth into them. She hadn't looked at him since she'd listened to DuPont's message. She stared unblinking at a spot on his chest, and he knew what this was. He'd seen it enough times before, on enough clients' faces.

Trauma.

He cursed himself again for not understanding sooner, even as he knew that sometimes these things were so well-hidden it was difficult to. Victims of domestic abuse often bore up better—outwardly, at least—while it was still ongoing. Because their bodies were on constant alert, constant survival mode. It was later, when it was over, that their bodies, their minds, gave them leave to fall apart.

Kyrie had been in survival mode her entire life and he thought, even once Elijah was gone, that she'd only halfway come out of it. Because she had expected him to come back at any moment, she had never been able to relax. Now that he *was* back, it would all be crashing in on her again.

"Don't go," he told her.

"I have to," she whispered. "DuPont—"

"Doesn't matter. There is no legal statute that says you have to be present for that asshole's return."

"You don't understand."

"Don't I?" He ran his thumbs gently along her wrists. "Those chains I broke. It wasn't Danvers who put them on you, was it?"

Her gaze flicked to him briefly before returning the spot she'd picked out on his chest. "No."

He'd suspected—known, really—but hearing her confirm it made it real in a way it hadn't been before. "When?" he asked tersely.

"After Mom died. Everything got worse after Mom died."

"The chains are gone now," he growled. "You don't need to see him again. You don't ever need to go back to that house again. You can stay here."

She shook her head. "I can't."

He didn't take it personally. He understood well enough how that might feel like trading one unwanted dependence for another.

"Then somewhere else. If you don't want to take things from me you know damn well Siren will do anything for you without wanting something in return."

"You don't understand," she said again, and then the words started tumbling out of her. "It wasn't the chains. It never really was. I fought them the moment he put them on, and I kept fighting him. Every day, every minute. I made holding the leash difficult.

"It took a toll on him, and I would have broken them eventually. I knew it. He knew it. Breaking my bones didn't stop me, though it did slow me down."

She said it so casually he could barely keep a grip on the rage that flooded through him. But this wasn't *about* him, so he held it down, even as she turned her left hand over, the one he'd noticed shook ever-so-slightly whenever she talked about Elijah.

"The day I almost broke free, I destroyed his concentration so badly he lost a business deal he'd wanted. So he broke every finger on this hand. I was left-hand dominant, before that. But I think he knew that wouldn't keep me down for long." Her lips twisted bitterly. "So he found something worse to threaten me with. He told me how very easy it would be for him to kill Jace and make it look like an accident."

Random's blood turned to ice.

"He never liked Jace," she said softly. "I ran him off whenever Elijah got bad, so he wouldn't know. Kept Elijah busy with me so Jace wouldn't get hurt. And he didn't. Elijah never hurt him." A sheen of water filled her eyes, tears he knew would never fall, and a desperate need to be believed limned her voice. "I never *let him* hurt Jace. I protected him. You have to believe that."

"I do, love." He took her face in his hands, his heart breaking for her. He'd only felt this helpless once before in his life. He couldn't take away her pain, couldn't undo what she had lived through. All he could do was offer her words, and truth, and he didn't know if they would help. "But Kyrie, if he *had* hurt Jace, that wouldn't be your fault. Elijah's sins aren't yours to pay for."

"Aren't they? I can live with everything else. But I can't live with it if he hurts Jace." She finally met his gaze. "I can't live with it if he hurts *you*."

The words, the intensity in her voice, gave him hope he hadn't had since Jace's wedding. And wasn't he a selfish bastard if the thing he was thinking right now was, *Maybe she could love me, after all.*

"I'm sorry," she said. "I'm so sorry."

"You have nothing to be sorry for."

"I do. Your birthday. When you kissed me the first time. He was watching." She touched her fingers to his cheek, to the exact place her knuckles had landed her punch. "Hitting you—I didn't know how else to keep you safe. To make you both think I didn't care.

"And then I saw you again, after he disappeared, and I wanted you. I knew better, but I wanted you anyway, and I was selfish enough that I took you. And I told myself it would be fine because you don't get serious with anyone, but then you..."

"Then I told you I loved you," he finished for her, "and I wouldn't let you go."

She nodded.

Her attempts to drive him away without ever really telling him to go made sense now. Because she hadn't wanted to let him go. He didn't know if she loved him, didn't know if that was something she would ever be capable of admitting to, even if she did. But he knew, now, that she hadn't wanted to let him go anymore than he had her.

"I'm still not giving you up." He tilted her chin up. "I'm not afraid of Elijah Winters. And I'll damn myself to hell a thousand times before I let him touch you again. Bringing charges against a councilor won't be easy, but—"

"*No.*" Her hands gripped his shoulders. "You can't take him to court."

His frustration hit its peak, and it took everything he had to calmly ask, "Why not?"

"Even if you could get the Council to convict him, and no matter how good you are, I don't know that you could, it wouldn't be his fate you'd be sealing. It would be mine."

"I don't understand, Kyrie."

"I know."

"Then help me to. Jace and I—we can protect ourselves if we know what's coming. You don't have to worry about us."

"It isn't that. Isn't *only* that. There are things I can't tell you."

"Can't or won't?" he asked, and he couldn't keep the hard edge from his voice.

"I don't know. I'm *trying*." She slid her hands down to his and threaded their fingers together. "But I need you to trust me on this. I need you to trust me when I say that I have to walk into Council headquarters and see him. Trust me when I say I can handle this.

"Because if we do it your way, I'm going to die. And I don't want to die, Random."

Those words were the complete unembellished truth. He felt it when she spoke, and it terrified him.

"Tell me I'm not going to lose you, Kyrie."

"Trust me," was her only answer. "If you do love me, trust me."

He closed his eyes. Every instinct in him screamed to do the opposite of everything she'd asked. To hide her away somewhere safe and bury Elijah Winters so far in the legal system no one would ever find him again. But Valkyrie would never allow herself to be hidden. She would never allow herself to be kept safe.

"I do trust you." He squeezed her fingers, still entwined with his. "But I need you to trust me, too. We'll do it your way, but you don't do it alone. Let me help you."

For two long beats of his heart she held her breath. Then she let it out on a shudder. "Okay."

His pulse thudded in his temples. "We go to headquarters together. You don't try to cut me out. You don't go back to your house. He doesn't touch you again."

"Okay."

He could hardly believe she'd agreed. "What do you need from me?"

He expected her to say nothing. She never needed anything from him. Never needed *him*.

She shifted closer and her eyes fluttered closed for a moment before they opened into his. "I need this," she said softly, and kissed him.

~

Valkyrie poured everything she had into the kiss. All her need, all her desire, all her fear. She felt Random battle with himself in the way he yielded to her even as his hands went to her waist as if to hold her back.

He managed a few words between the joining of their mouths. "Probably" —kiss— "shouldn't be" —another kiss— "doing this."

Should or shouldn't had lost all meaning for her. There was only Random, here and now and vibrantly alive, and she needed him. Especially when he opened his mouth to her and her tongue swept inside, glided against his, stoking the growing fire inside her.

"You said you weren't thinking clearly," he tried again, when they came up for air.

She didn't need to think, didn't want to. She kissed his jaw, his throat, fumbled at the buttons of his shirt before losing all patience and ripping it open, buttons scattering in every direction on the hardwood floor.

"Shit," he breathed, then sucked the air back in on a sharp inhale when she trailed her lips down his chest, his stomach. His fingers dug into her hips. "Kyrie, love, I'm not made of superhuman restraint."

"Good." She bit at the firm planes of his abs and slid her fingers inside the waistband of his pants, grazing his head.

"Oh, *fuck*." His hands came under her thighs and dragged her onto his lap, her legs straddling him. His erection pressed at her core and she ground against him, enjoying the sound of pure male need the movement elicited.

He grabbed the hem of the dress and pulled it off her, revealing the bra he'd picked off her floor that morning...and the matching underwear.

"So something else lacy *was* on sale," he murmured, fingers skimming down her stomach, her thighs.

"Do you like it?" She'd worn it for him. She'd never thought he'd *see* it, but she'd worn it for him.

"Oh, I like it." His voice was all rough heat, sliding over her like molten honey. "I'm going to like it even better when it's on my floor." He unclasped her bra and let it fall, took her nipple in his mouth and sucked. An answering tug of need shot through her. She arched her back and ground against him, the rough friction of his pants against her nearly-bared flesh an exquisite torture.

She'd never been a particularly patient woman. She undid the button of his pants, then the zipper, and pulled the length of him free. He was hard and heavy in her hand, the velvet skin an exquisite contrast to the iron shaft it covered. She closed her fist around him and pumped once, an experimental slide that had him jerking in her hand.

Then she figured *what the hell*, this might be the last time she ever got to have sex, and leaned down to close her mouth over the hot, swollen tip. The low, male sound that came out of his throat sent a deep pull of need right between her legs, and she answered it by taking him deeper, running her tongue along the underside of his shaft.

Then his hands were beneath her chin, pulling her up.

"Did I do it wrong?" She'd thought she'd been doing it right —goddess knew it had *felt* right—but she supposed a person could only learn so much by skipping to the sex scenes in romance novels.

"If you did it any more right I'd be dead. But if you keep doing it, I'm not going to last."

"Shouldn't you have more stamina where this sort of thing is concerned?"

He laughed. "I told you, love, I'm a year out of practice."

Her heart stuttered, slammed back into rhythm. "You were serious about that?"

"Yes." His hands cupped her face, kept her from looking away from eyes filled with an intensity that scared the hell out of her. "You're all I want, Kyrie. You're all I've ever wanted."

She had to break that intensity or it would break *her*. "I take it that means you're clean?"

He looked slightly startled at the sudden change in conversational direction. "Yes, but—" He quit talking when she stood up and slid her underwear off before settling astride him again, positioning him at her entrance.

His eyes widened and he gripped her hips, holding her back when she would have sank down onto him. "We probably definitely should not be making a kid tonight, love."

"I got an IUD when you kept showing up at my house." She'd known if he ever kissed her again it was a fifty-fifty chance as to whether she'd say *no*, or *Goddess yes*. And she'd wondered what it would be like to have nothing between them. "So we don't need to—you know. If you're okay with it."

His answer was to ease her down, filling her inch by inch. When their bodies met, when he was fully inside her, he took her mouth with his, kissing her slow and deep as he gave her body time to adjust to him. He teased her with each stroke of his tongue, his hands skimming up to cup her breasts, until the multitude of sensations had her rocking her hips against him with pure need.

Her clit brushed the defined ridge of his abs and an electric jolt of pleasure had her gasping into his mouth. He swallowed it down, his thumbs stroking across her nipples, and though she felt his need he didn't move, leaving the reins in her hands. As if he knew she needed the control right now.

She rose up until he was almost out of her and then drove back down, rolling her hips to grind her center against him again. She didn't know if she could come like that but she damn well wanted to try. She settled into the rhythm, each rock of her hips building friction and tension, the deep seat of him inside her making her frantic with need.

She lost herself entirely to impulse, riding him faster, harder, her pleasure building and building until it hit a crescendo. Her orgasm shattered through her and Random finally lost control.

He let out a hoarse cry and thrust up into her, his hands falling to her hips to hold her down on him as his entire body jerked and he spilled himself inside her.

Her head fell to his chest as the aftershocks coursed through them, their breaths drawn in twin, ragged inhales. She felt like her world had just been obliterated and rebuilt.

Goddess, she wanted to stay here. But she couldn't. And the longer she did, the harder it would be to leave.

"We should go," she said softly.

His arms tightened around her, pulled her close before finally letting her go. "Yeah."

She didn't look back at him as she rose and went to the bathroom to clean herself off and put her clothes back on.

She wouldn't let anything happen to him.

She wouldn't.

CHAPTER

TWELVE

Valkyrie walked into Council headquarters, acutely aware of Random's presence at her side, her body humming with his nearness, with the memory of what they'd just done. He shouldn't be with her. Every instinct she had screamed at her to never let Elijah lay eyes on him again, much less in her company. But she'd promised Random she wouldn't leave him behind, and she would keep that promise for as long as she could.

They descended the stairs to the Warded Room and she paused outside the doors, unable to make herself open them, to walk through into the room beyond. She found her gaze inevitably drawn to the left, to the small alcove where a faceless statue of Aspect Society's goddess waited.

"That thing always creeps me out," Random murmured, following her gaze.

If you had any idea what hides beneath it, you'd really *be creeped out,* she thought. Her left hand started to tremble, and she cursed the stupid dress she'd mechanically put back on for its lack of pockets with which to hide the flaw.

Random's hand covered hers, his chest pressing against her back as he stepped close behind her.

"It's okay. I've got you."

She shouldn't depend on him like this, shouldn't let herself grow accustomed to the safety his touch made her feel. He wasn't safe with her. But she wanted him to be. She turned and kissed him, wrapped her arms around his neck and melded her body to his, trying to say everything with her touch that she couldn't say with words.

He held nothing back when he kissed her—every emotion he felt for her that she'd tried to deny expressed itself in the glide of his tongue against hers, in the wrap of his arms around her waist. When she finally broke away, he rubbed his nose against hers, the simple act jolting for its intimacy.

"Let's get this over with," he said.

She nodded, broke away from him entirely, and opened the doors.

The Council rarely used the Warded Room. The symbols inscribed onto every surface, be it floor, walls, or ceiling, all joined together for a single purpose: to contain any power unleashed in this room, and keep it from leaving. It took the perception of a very large threat for them to bother with its use.

The last time they had bothered was when Siren Savage had petitioned to join Aspect Society. Valkyrie wasn't sure what it said that they had opened it for one of their own councilors. That Elijah had the raw power to warrant the caution, there was no doubt. She was simply surprised they'd been ballsy enough to offend him by insisting on the protocol.

She kept her shoulders back, her head high, her face its careful mask, and walked into the room. The Council sat behind the table that rested on the dais on the far side of the room. Of the five of them, the only one who looked unruffled was Random's great aunt, Ella Tremayne. Then again, it took a lot to ruffle the Queen of Death.

Theodore Bronte had an air of quiet suspicion, Kara Barrow one of tight-lipped unease. Julian Astor, who was only an acting councilor, a stand-in for Elijah in the true councilor's absence, was the only one of the five foolish enough to look irritated.

He'd clearly thought, given the length of time Elijah had been missing, that the position would become his in truth. In all fairness to him, according to the Council by-laws, the seat *should* have gone open to vote months ago. But Random wasn't the only one who could use the law's loopholes to his advantage, and Valkyrie had pressed for an extension on the vote. It was the second such extension she'd managed to secure, one largely driven through by the approval of Martin DuPont. The head of the Council himself was currently sweating and fidgeting and trying to hide both. He looked precisely like what he was—a puppet leader whose master had unexpectedly returned.

That master sat at the petitioner's table facing the Council, his back to Valkyrie.

Walking forward was like dragging each foot out of nearly-dried cement. Yes, she'd intended to find Elijah. She'd made a public show of being desperate to find him—and she *had* been desperate. But she'd always meant to find him alone, so she could put an end to the horror, once and for all. If his body was ever found, no one would suspect that his devoted daughter had had a hand in it.

Now...now she didn't know how things would play out.

She stopped at the end of the table where he sat, Random's presence behind her a solid, comforting weight.

Elijah Winters turned to look at her and she took an involuntary step back, bumping into Random. His right hand settled on her hip, steady and supportive, and she needed it.

Her father looked as if an artisan had decided his exterior should finally match the monster within. His face, once handsome and striking, was a hell-scape of scars and pieces that looked as if they had been torn apart and put back together with more care for haste than appropriateness of placing. His lips were oddly slanted, his right eyebrow higher than the left and his hair, once jet black, was streaked through with coarse gray.

The only thing about him that hadn't changed was his eyes. A cold, acerbic blue, they took her in with the same icy detachment she'd endured her entire life.

"Not quite as you remember, am I?" he asked, and even his voice was different, rougher. "But then, neither are you."

His gaze drifted over her, cataloging the makeup she hadn't washed off. The necklace at her throat. The dress. Random's hand on her hip.

His eyes lingered on the last, and even through the odd new shape of his lips she recognized the sneer that twisted them. It took everything she had not to rip the dagger from her boot and slit his throat, witnesses be damned.

She forced herself to turn and look at Ella Tremayne. "It's really him?"

There was always the chance, however small, that Danvers had chosen to come wearing Elijah's visage.

"I have confirmed his identity, Miss Winters." The Queen of Death had not missed her nephew's hand on Valkyrie's body any more than Elijah had. But where Valkyrie understood what her father's expression meant, Ella's was unfathomable to her.

"Good," was the only response she could manage.

DuPont found his voice. "It seems your father was in Danvers' captivity, as Siren suggested was the case. We had reasons for believing this improbable, but it seems we were incorrect."

It was fortunate, Valkyrie decided, that in addition to not having a loving relationship with her father, he'd never insisted on the outward pretense of one. On her devotion? Yes. But that devotion had always been detached. No one expected her to burst into tears and hug Elijah.

Truthfully, she didn't know *what* anyone expected. They all waited in the silence that followed DuPont's explanation, as if they'd expected Valkyrie's arrival to make the situation made sense. Because they all seemed to recognize that something wasn't quite right, but no one could put their finger on what the not-quite-right thing was.

Valkyrie could. It was in the fact that all of Elijah's wounds were months healed over, that his clothes were clean, that his demeanor was not that of a man who had recently escaped imprisonment.

"Is he free to leave?" she asked.

"Yes," Ella said. "Though he will not be formally reinstated to his duties on the Council until he has undergone a psychological evaluation, and a Truthfinder of sufficient talent can verify his statements." She turned a dragon-like smile on Elijah. "Not that your testimony is in any doubt, of course. Formalities, you understand."

"Of course." The coolness in Elijah's voice told Valkyrie all too well that he had fully expected to be swept back into his place without incident. He probably would have been, if it wasn't for Ella. She was the only councilor Valkyrie thought Elijah had ever truly feared. He stood. "I think I would like to go home now. Valkyrie?"

Frustration bit at her—she was missing something. Why would Danvers give up Elijah *now*? Yes, he obviously understood the effect Elijah's return would have on her, and she'd pissed him off at StellaMia's, but that couldn't be the whole of it. She couldn't see him doing this unless there was another reason, another advantage.

He wanted the Council destroyed, and to that end, he needed the Council's adnexus.

It hit her, then. He wanted the *Council* gone. And no matter the preachings of anarchy to the contrary, people who sought to destroy the structure of power typically wanted to slide something new into its place. And Elijah could be that something, because he *wouldn't* die with the adnexus's destruction: Valkyrie would.

Valkyrie, who could take the fall for everything. Valkyrie,

whom no one liked. Valkyrie, who had always been so devoted to her father. Devoted enough to want to place him as the only power in Aspect Society?

She could see precisely how it would play out. If Danvers destroyed the adnexus, then with the councilors and Valkyrie dead it wouldn't be hard for Elijah to spin the tragic tale. No one outside of the Council knew about the adnexus, so it would be a simple case of how Valkyrie had killed them all, and died in the doing.

Elijah would be appropriately heartbroken, while at the same time admitting how her fanatic loyalty had frightened him at times. How is iron control over her life had been necessary to curb her dangerous tendencies. How he had thought she would grow out of it, into her own person, but she never had, and his return from captivity had driven her into a manic state.

"Valkyrie," Elijah repeated, her name a warning, as if he understood she was on the precipice of diverging from the path he wanted her to follow. "Take me home."

The path he *wanted*, the expected path. She had come here to keep up public appearances, because she had thought that publicly being at odds with him was the thing likely to cast suspicion on her. And he had known that, expected that, when the opposite was true. When letting the Council have a hint of how she truly felt about her father was the only thing that might save her after all.

"No," she whispered. A whisper was all she could manage. She hadn't told him *no* since he'd first threatened Jace. But Jace wasn't here. He was in Ireland, he was safe for the time being, and Random—Random wasn't leaving her sight. Not until he was somewhere safe, and she could finish this.

"Valkyrie." Elijah's voice had lost any pretense of affection. "Take me home. Now."

"No," she repeated. Her voice was still soft, but it was strong, and she might as well have shouted for how loud she sounded in the stillness of the room. "Take yourself home, Elijah. I don't live there anymore. And I'm never going back."

He advanced on her. She was all too familiar with the threat that hovered in his eyes, and she didn't have to feign the fear that thundered through her veins, an instinctual response born from years of helplessness. She stepped back again, flush into Random, whose arms came protectively around her. For a moment, she thought it would be enough to shred Elijah's razor-thin temper in public.

Then he stopped, a ripple-like shiver running through him as he took control, smoothed his voice into something patronizing, something that told her she'd been precisely right about the light he'd have cast her in once the Council was gone.

"Valkyrie, you're hysterical. You don't understand what you're saying."

Everyone save Ella looked unsettled, but they didn't look unsettled at Elijah—no, they looked unsettled at *her*—and she understood that he must have laid the groundwork concerning her for years. In case getting rid of her ever became a necessity. An offhand comment here and there, a father concerned about his daughter's mental state.

"She understands exactly what she's saying." Random's voice rumbled in her ear.

Elijah's gaze turned as cold as she'd ever seen it, then, his voice the special level of calm it had been when he'd broken her left hand.

"You don't understand what you're tangling with, boy." Elijah closed the distance between them. Only Ella stood when he advanced, only Ella's Aspect readied to act, but Valkyrie held no illusions that the Queen of Death would interfere on her behalf. No, she would interfere on behalf of her nephew.

"I understand everything," Random said. "And you're never touching her again."

Elijah reached for her. Random's Aspect blanketed her in a

thick mist. The pattern it wove itself into was like nothing she'd ever seen before, felt like nothing she'd ever experienced. It closed tight around them both like a cocoon and everything just...dissolved.

CHAPTER

THIRTEEN

The world swam into focus slowly, like the blurred image on a television screen coming together pixel by pixel. It resolved, not into her father's face, or those of the Council, or the room they had been standing in, but into Random's living room. She stepped out of his arms and turned in a slow circle, taking it all in. Sectional sofa, coffee table, entertainment center, open floor plan that led into the kitchen, and Random.

He stood with his hands in his pockets, his jaw clenched, fury an amber blaze in his dark eyes. He didn't look at all surprised by their new surroundings.

"You teleported us," she said, and she didn't think she'd ever sounded that incredulous in her entire life.

He gave a short, sharp nod.

"From inside the *Warded Room*."

Another nod.

"You *actually* teleported us. How?"

"I don't know. I've only done it once before. And you know wards have never been a problem for me."

Knowing that didn't make it any easier to accept what had just happened. The Warded Room was one of the oldest parts of Council headquarters, a room that had been built centuries ago. It contained thousands of runes, all drawn and formed together for a single, specific purpose: to contain any Aspect used within its bounds. To ensure that Aspect did not escape the room.

Random had just used Aspect to blink right out of it. In front of the Council.

"You shouldn't have done that."

He shrugged. "It was instinctual. And I didn't do anything illegal. If they want to punish me for doing what I once told everyone I could, I'd like to see them try."

Her mind was still reeling from the whole teleportation thing. No one in the recorded history of Aspect use had ever done it. It wasn't a recognized branch of Aspect, it wasn't a recorded ability.

"Your Aspect is desire based," she said softly.

"Yes." His vocal cords sounded as if they were so tight they might break.

Random had wanted to keep her father from touching her so badly—had wanted to protect her so badly—that he'd performed an impossible feat. One he hadn't managed to replicate even when he'd been a kid being mercilessly bullied, when one little teleport would have turned him from a pariah into a golden child.

He'd *teleported* them. For her. And now he looked like he was afraid she'd run from him for it. She hated herself for doing that to him, for putting that wariness in him. She couldn't change the last year. But she could try to change now.

She closed the distance between them and kissed him, long and slow, until he looked slightly dazed when she pulled back. "Have I ever told you you're amazing?"

He blinked. "That would be a definite no. Usually you tell me I'm insufferable, or cocky, or ridiculous, or—"

"You're amazing," she said, and kissed him again, parting his lips this time, her tongue delving inside. She pressed the length of her body against his, needing to feel closer to him, to erase the terror that had flooded her system at seeing Elijah again.

She could tell herself a million times, a million ways, that Elijah would never control her again. But no reassurance could change years of conditioning that told her she was powerless in his presence. That no matter how hard she fought, she would lose. Her body remembered every bruise, every broken bone, every iota of pain he'd ever exacted. Remembered, and feared.

She hated being afraid, hated feeling powerless. So she lost herself in Random. Because when she touched him, she didn't think about anything other than him. And when he held her, the only thing she felt was safe. Wanted.

She slid her hands beneath his shirt, ran them up the firm muscles of his back and felt him stir against her in response.

He groaned. "I can't believe I'm saying this, but shouldn't we be talking about what just happened?"

"It happened." She bit his lower lip, released it. "It's done." She kissed her way across his jaw, down his throat. "What's there to talk about?"

"How about what actually happened back there? Pretty sure your original plan was not to publicly tell Elijah to go fuck himself."

"I don't want to talk about that right now." She attacked the buttons on his shirt, wanting to just rip it off, but figuring she shouldn't ruin two of his shirts in one day. She was halfway down when his hands caught her wrists.

"Kyrie."

She sighed. For a man who'd spent a year chasing her, she kept having a remarkably difficult time getting him to sleep with her. "You have two options," she told him.

"Do I?"

"Option one, you keep pushing me on this."

"How does that go for me?"

"I push back, we both get pissed."

"Option two?"

"You could fuck me in the shower." His body was entirely on board for option two, if the statement his cock was making against her was any indication. The man, however, was in the mood to push. Valkyrie saw it in the set of his jaw. So she leaned back and pulled the dress over her head, noting with satisfaction his sharp intake of breath.

"That is cheating."

"Winning's winning," she answered.

"We're going to have to talk about what happened sometime."

"Sometime," she agreed, noting that for once the lawyer in him had failed to specify a time frame. Apparently the secret to winning an argument with him was taking off her clothes. "But not now. So what's it going to be?" She stepped back, shucked her bra and underwear. His eyes turned molten and she knew she had him.

"Fucking you in the shower?" he offered.

"Good choice."

VALKYRIE TURNED the water off and stepped out of the shower to find her clothes were gone. She'd been suspicious when Random had insisted she stay in the shower to *luxuriate*—whatever the hell that meant—and she had now walked into a bedroom that was missing her duffel bag of clothes.

A single midnight blue dress shirt was folded on the bed. She recognized it as Random's. Every time he wore it he looked like sex personified and she found it impossible to take her eyes off him. Now that she thought about it, he'd worn it a lot around her.

A note rested on top of the shirt and she plucked it off, scowling at Random's elegant scrawl. *I put your clothes in the wash. Try this on for size. I bet you look sexy as hell in it.*

She was going to kill him. She pulled the shirt on and,

because she wasn't precisely slender, it was almost a perfect fit. Her scowl deepened as she realized he hadn't left her anything *else*, and the shirt barely covered her ass. She stared at her reflection in the dresser mirror. She didn't look sexy. She looked like a woman wearing a man's dress shirt that just happened to fit her.

She stopped her brain from going down the dark rabbit hole of wondering if any *other* women—perhaps prettier, smaller, softer women—had ever worn Random's clothes. She was never going to be any of those things. Truthfully, she didn't want to be any of them, would go insane if she tried.

And those other women, they weren't here now. She was. And if she wanted to have something with Random, something real, she had to let those faceless women go, had to stop being bitter about all the years he hadn't been hers.

It had been her choice to stay away from him. It had been the right choice, the one she'd had to make, and she would make it again. She couldn't blame him for not having spent his entire life lonely. She was glad he hadn't. Goddess knew if she could have drowned her sorrows in someone else's body without putting their life in jeopardy, she'd probably have done the same thing.

And she mattered to Random. She fingered the sword pendant at her throat and something that felt perilously close to a smile tugged at her lips. That would never do. She was supposed to be pissed off he'd taken her clothes, not grinning like an idiot.

Well, there was one way to solve that.

"Random," she yelled, opening the bedroom door and heading for the living room. "Where the hell are my clothes?"

He didn't answer her. She understood why when she found him in the living room, staring at the room's other occupant.

Ella Tremayne stood just inside the doorway, and the Queen of Death did not look pleased.

FOURTEEN

Valkyrie had spoken with Random's aunt many times. She'd known Ella Tremayne almost her entire life.

So why did it feel like she was meeting her boyfriend's mother for the first time?

Possibly because, given Valkyrie's state of dress, it was pretty damn impossible not to guess what she and Random had just been doing. Fine time to wish she'd put on a pair of Random's sweatpants, but she refused to shrink from Ella's gaze. Valkyrie Winters did not shrink. She straightened her shoulders, crossed her arms, and lifted her chin, as if she wore battle armor and not a dress shirt that barely covered the important bits.

"Aunt Ella," she said, unsure which subconscious part of her clearly longed for death by calling the woman that. Jace called her Aunt Ella, had never called her anything else, but while Kyrie called her that when referencing her to Jace or Random, she couldn't recall that she'd ever addressed the woman as Aunt Ella to her face.

Neither of the two women were under any illusion that she did so now out of anything other than mulish stubbornness.

"Random," the Queen of Death said, "please give Ms. Winters and I a moment."

Random had, until this moment, been mimicking a statue. A very surprised, adorably confused, statue.

"Aunt Ella," he began soothingly, "I don't think—"

"Don't you 'Aunt Ella' me, boy." She cut him off in a tone that brooked absolutely no disobedience. "It wasn't a request."

Valkyrie had a feeling that, for all the devil-may-care ways of his youth, Random had never once disobeyed his aunt when she used that tone on him. Because when he didn't immediately leave the room, Ella turned and lifted her eyebrows at him in inquiry.

"Promise me nothing will happen to her."

Aunt Ella's eyes softened the barest fraction. "I'm not going to hurt her, boy. You have my word."

He nodded, but instead of walking out, he walked to Valkyrie and took her in his arms. She hadn't unfolded hers from across her chest, so she ended up oddly smooshed against him. It wasn't entirely unpleasant and, despite Aunt Ella's presence, she couldn't help but lean into him a little.

"I promise she's not as scary as she seems," he whispered. "I'll be right outside."

"You should be more concerned for yourself," she whispered back. "Because of you, I have to talk to her in your damn shirt. You're going to pay for that."

"Do you want a kiss for luck?"

She glared at him and he laughed. He did kiss her—on the cheek—before he dropped his arms from her. Aunt Ella tracked his path from Valkyrie out the front door. Ella considered the closed door for five seconds, ten, before she flicked her hand at it and a spark of Aspect leapt from her to flare through the door and frame.

Random yelped. "Was that really necessary, Auntie?"

"Waylon Jennings Tremayne, do not even think about eavesdropping on this conversation."

Valkyrie's eyes widened. On some level, she'd known Random couldn't be his real name, but Waylon Jennings?

Really? Someone's mother had clearly had a thing for country singers.

"Low blow, Aunt Ella," Random called. Then he tromped loudly off the front porch and appeared framed in the kitchen window a few seconds later, a respectable fifteen feet from the house walls. He waved at them as if to say, *See? I can behave.*

Valkyrie snorted.

"Yes, he does have that affect on a person." Ella Tremayne crossed her arms and tapped her fingers against her biceps, considering her nephew through the window.

"Do you know why I'm here?"

Valkyrie debated a multitude of responses and discarded them all. She figured, when people asked that question, they didn't actually want you to answer it.

"No."

"Random's Aspect isn't as mercurial as he and I have made it out to be. But it was safer for him if Aspect Society viewed him as a trivial oddity." She turned her gaze from Random to Valkyrie. "Yes, his Aspect is tied to his desires, but want alone couldn't bring him to teleport two people from inside the Council's most heavily warded room. In the entirety of his life, he has teleported precisely once before."

Valkyrie couldn't entirely suppress the flicker of surprise that showed on her face. When Random had been the new child laughingstock in town talking about teleportation, he'd said he could prove it, that his aunt had seen it. Ella Tremayne had staunchly denied that any such occurrence had happened. Since Random had been all of eight at the time, no one had felt it necessary to get a Truthfinder involved in determining the legitimacy of a claim of magic use no one believed was possible in the first place.

"Yes, Ms. Winters, I lied to the Council. You cannot have failed to notice, after Siren's entrance into our world, that they do not like anything that is different. They treat it either with forceful suspicion or dismissive contempt. It was better for the boy to be ridiculed than to spend his childhood under a Council-assigned tutor who would poke and prod him to find out what his limits were. When he was older, he understood why I'd done it."

"If you dislike the Council so much, why did you join it?"

"To protect him, of course. Because that first time he teleported, Ms. Winters, was to *me*. I am sure you're aware that the idea of teleportation has long fascinated the Aspect community. It's theorized that if it could be done, one would need a very distinct knowledge of both the origin point and the destination point that would involve complex preparation and spellwork.

"Before Random appeared in front of me, there was no preparation. No spellwork. The boy had met me precisely once in his life. When he was two. I don't believe he even consciously remembers it. His mother was still living here then and her life was, as it always was, a disaster.

"I went to the apartment she was living in and tried to convince her to give Random to me. For all her faults, she did love the boy, and she wouldn't do it. I told her that if she ever changed her mind, I would be there for him. She left Seclusion two days later and I never saw him again.

"Understand that he had never been to my home. When Random teleported, he didn't do it to a specific place, but to a person. He came to *me*, because some part of him remembered that I had promised I would take care of him. Has he told you anything about that day?"

Valkyrie shook her head.

"You know he came to me because his mother died?"

"Yes." Valkyrie had a desperately bad feeling that she knew where this was going.

"He was holding her in his arms when he teleported into my kitchen. He was eight years old and his mother choked to death on her own blood with her head in his lap."

"Why are you telling me this?" Valkyrie managed. It was

horrific, it was personal, and if Random had wanted her to know, he would have told her himself.

"So you will understand something. Random's mother jumped from abusive relationship to abusive relationship. It's why Random took the path with his legal career that he did. From what I understand, though admittedly the boy's records are spotty given how frequently his mother shifted towns, he hadn't managed a single use of his Aspect before then. Everyone thought he was a Dud.

"Because while his Aspect does try to give him what he wants, that isn't his true trigger. It's love. Love—and fear—for his mother made his first ever use of Aspect to teleport her away from the man who beat her to death.

"So tell me, Valkyrie, why was my son so afraid of you being near your father that he revealed to the Council something we have successfully hidden his entire life?"

Valkyrie didn't answer. She couldn't.

Aunt Ella held out her hand, and Valkyrie knew what the woman was asking.

"No."

"It wasn't a request, child."

"You don't have the right."

"I have *every* right. That boy out there," she pointed out the window, "is *mine*. In every way that matters he is *my* son. I raised him, I loved him, and I watched him turn into a shadow of himself over the last year and I know damn well that was because of you. I need to know if you're worth it."

Ella's Aspect surfaced, the full strength of it a dark cloak swirling around her. Her chocolate brown eyes, so like and unlike Random's, deepened to pure black, the promise of death filling the kitchen like a thunderous fog. Her hair seemed to shift and twist, writhing as if the tendrils were living things that promised to sprout fangs and deliver a stony un-death.

"So you may not like it, but I am not leaving this house until I have the answers I need to keep him safe."

"We both know I can't stop you," Valkyrie spat. She could shield herself, yes, and her Aspect was strong enough that she could hold even the Queen of Death off for some time. But she wasn't willing to kill Random's aunt, and that was precisely the force that would be necessary to stop the woman from doing what she intended. It didn't mean Valkyrie had to like it. "But I'll be damned if I give you permission. You want to do a blood delineation, you do it knowing it is fully against my wishes. I won't grant you absolution because you think you have the right."

"I'll bear that in mind," Ella Tremayne said. She strode across the room and gripped Valkyrie's wrist.

A blood delineation didn't *have* to hurt, and if Valkyrie hadn't fought the invasion of Ella's Aspect, it wouldn't have. But she was incapable of *not* fighting. Ella's Death Aspect might be the opposite of Siren's Life, but they were of the same coin. Both women could see a person's history written in their physical body, and Valkyrie had no desire to give away her history.

The breaks in her bones, the memories of cuts and bruises and blows, they were *hers*. No one had the right to see them unless she offered them. No one had the right to read them like a book. But Ella did, and because Valkyrie fought it, the woman's Aspect burned like acid through her veins.

She didn't know how long it went on for. It felt like she'd stuck her hand on a live power line and couldn't let go, but couldn't die, either. When Ella finally dropped her hand Valkyrie crumpled, barely able to get her hands beneath her to break the fall.

She sucked in air through a constricted throat, her chest tight, and it took several breaths before she could turn her head to glare at Ella. Random's aunt was as pale as the physical state her Aspect was named for, and she'd taken two steps back after she'd let Valkyrie go.

"Did you like what you found?" Valkyrie asked.

"No," was Ella's soft answer.

Valkyrie understood, then. Understood, and laughed. "You bought it, didn't you? You don't even *like* Elijah and you bought it. Battle-happy, slightly-unhinged Valkyrie. Good thing she has Dear Old Daddy to keep her in check. I guess a bastard man's always more believable than a cold-hearted bitch."

Ella grimaced. "You have my sincerest apologies."

"Fuck your apologies." Valkyrie pushed off the floor. "Did you think I lied to Random? Did you think I knew his history so I told him some sob story about my father to push all the right buttons and get him invested in my survival?"

Ella's flinch was answer enough.

"I wouldn't have told him *anything* if he hadn't figured out too much on his own."

"I had my reasons for believing otherwise."

"Did you? I'd love to hear them."

"I know what Siren discovered when she touched the Council's adnexus. I know it is you, not Elijah, that's bound to us."

Valkyrie's blood chilled. "And you thought I *wanted* that? I was *six* when my father joined the Council. Was I a cold-blooded demon child plotting world domination in my fucking cradle?"

"You have to consent to being bonded to the adnexus," was Ella's only defense.

"What is the consent of a child who doesn't understand what they're doing? A child who spent her entire life having her father tell her he *wanted* to love her, but she wasn't really his. She was the daughter of a monster, and daughters like that had to try harder. They had to *work* for it if they wanted to be loved.

"I consented because I wanted my father to love me. I didn't even understand what I'd done until I was in my teens. By then, nothing mattered." Valkyrie shook her head, wishing she could shake away the memories. "Are we finished here?"

"No."

"No? What other accusations would you like to level at me? I can't wait to learn what *else* I've done."

"I know you have DuPont's blood. And Kara's and Theo's. Does Random know *why* you've taken them?"

"Yes."

Ella's lips thinned. "And once you've stolen the adnexus, what do you intend to do with it?"

"Siren said if she had it, she thought she could break it without killing us."

"Siren's across the ocean. Why move for it *now*? Why involve my son?"

"Because I didn't have a choice. Because Random got himself involved and there was nothing I could do about it. Because to keep him safe, it has to be now."

Ella's lips thinned. "Your father threatened him?"

"No, not Elijah." Then, because she figured it didn't matter at this point, she said, "Danvers."

"Danvers?" Ella's eyebrows lifted. "You really don't know, do you?"

"Know *what*?"

But Ella just shook her head. "I don't think you'd believe me if I told you. And if you did? Well, that might be worse. If you're fortunate, you'll never have to know."

"Is cryptically refusing to relay information a side effect of joining the Council?"

"No." If it weren't that circumstances forced it to be otherwise, Valkyrie suspected she and Ella could make an entire conversation out of that two-letter word. "I have sympathy for what you've been through—"

Valkyrie snorted. Ella's sympathy was worth absolutely nothing to her.

"—but you cannot expect me to sit idly by while you hand the adnexus off to Danvers."

"I'm not an idiot. I'm not going to give it to him. But he will be watching me. I can't tell him I have it if I don't, and I need him to meet with me. If I kill him, Random is no longer in any danger.

"You understand why I can't simply take this to the rest of the Council? It won't matter to them whether I had a choice in how I was bound. It will only matter to them that, in truth, *I* am the Council's fifth member.

"I wasn't voted in. I wasn't approved. With the exception of Siren destroying the adnexus, which they would never sanction, I cannot be removed except by death. They would kill me."

"A death vote would have to be unanimous."

"And you think it wouldn't be? Would *you* have voted against it if you hadn't walked in here and read me?"

Ella chose not to answer that. "You understand that the second that adnexus leaves council headquarters any one of us will be able to track it. You can't hide it long enough to get what you want."

If she was pointing that out then there was a chance, however slight a one, that Ella wouldn't simply haul her in to the Council right now.

"I can't," Valkyrie agreed. "But Random can."

"You would involve him that far?"

"He's a grown man, Ella, not a child. However you may still see him. He makes up his own mind. I had the choice of cutting him off or keeping him close where I could protect him. I chose the latter. The only question is, are you going to help me or are you going to get in my way?"

Ella considered her. "Let us assume you were to reach the adnexus. It was never meant to be held by a single individual, even for a short span of time. The magic that binds us all is very old and very dark. I am not at all certain that, should you grasp it, its magic won't consume you."

"A risk I'll take."

"Very well." Ella reached for the sugar bowl on Random's counter, dumped the contents out into a small mound, and held her fingertip poised over the ceramic dish. Her Aspect opened a slice in her skin and blood flowed, plinking down into the bowl.

"Why are you helping me?" Valkyrie asked. She understood

Ella not turning her in—it would ruin Ella's relationship with Random—but she didn't have to do this. "Are you hoping I'll get myself killed?"

"As things stand now? No. But let me be very clear about something. If your actions get my son killed, you would do well to follow at the same time. Because the death I will give you will be far less kind than any you could find on your own."

She took a handkerchief from her pocket and pressed it to the wound.

Valkyrie stared at the blood welling into the white cloth. "You haven't asked what I intend to do about Elijah."

"No, I haven't. It may be that I think one problem will be solved by another." Ella walked to the door and paused, her fingers on the handle. "And Valkyrie? I well understand that this may mean nothing to you given our...interaction here today. But you should know that I hope this all turns out for the best. Not simply for my son's sake, but for yours, as well. Because I would much rather call you my daughter than kill you."

Valkyrie stared at Ella as the woman opened the door. Had she just gotten the Death Queen's approval to date her son?

Ella opened the door. Random came through it a moment later, took in the shallow bowl of blood on the counter, and Valkyrie. Whatever he saw on Valkyrie's face, he clearly didn't like.

"Aunt Ella—"

"You can relax, dear. It's only her pride I hurt. For now." She reached out and cupped Random's face in her palm, a more tender gesture than Valkyrie would have thought her capable of. Then again, maybe that was the pot calling the kettle black.

"Be careful, boy. It's a very dangerous game you're playing and I can only help you so much."

FIFTEEN

As soon as his aunt was gone, Random walked across the room and took Valkyrie in his arms. It was as if he was afraid that, if given the chance to think about it, she wouldn't let him do it.

"Should I be apologizing right now?" he asked.

She tried for levity. "For your aunt or for this shirt?"

He winced. "Both? In all fairness, love, you just threw your clothes into a bag and left them. They were wrinkled."

Yes, she thought, *that* would *bother Random.* "I would have preferred meeting your aunt in wrinkled clothing to meeting her in something that barely covers my ass."

He ran his hands up her back and worked at the knotted muscles between her shoulder blades. It felt so good that she wanted to lean into him and forget the entire conversation. Devious of him.

"I didn't know she was going to storm in. And besides." He flashed her his trademark wicked grin. "I was right. You *do* look sexy as hell."

She summoned her best glacial tone. "I am sure that was at the forefront of your aunt's mind. 'Yes, Valkyrie has beguiled

Random into helping her with her personal vendetta, but hey, at least she looks sexy'."

"Beguiled?"

"That would be the politest way of putting what she accused me of. Did you know you're very easy to manipulate? She thought I used your interest in me to sell you a fake story about an abusive father, shed some tears, and throw myself at you for political advantage."

"She *what*?"

Valkyrie gave a small shrug. "She had her reasons. They were shit reasons, but she had them."

"I would be delighted to hear them," he said coolly.

"You seem not to have noticed what everyone else sees, so let me enlighten you. I am a selfish bitch, Random. I don't care about anyone but myself. I am not nice. I am not pleasant to be around. There is no possible way I could secure *your* interest without resorting to emotional manipulation."

"That's bullshit. Everyone is an idiot. Aunt Ella, of all people, shouldn't judge you on a façade she perfected decades ago."

"Maybe not. But Elijah laid his groundwork well."

He didn't answer that statement immediately. She could see him puzzling through the words, no doubt adding them to her unexpected reaction to Elijah earlier. She hadn't told him precisely what she'd intended to do when she saw her father, but he'd already guessed the original plan hadn't been to publicly cut ties with her father.

"What do you mean?"

"I believe he's been painting me as unstable for years."

"Why would he do that, Kyrie?" His voice was that careful, low timbre that usually only reared its head when he was about to obliterate someone in court. She loved that timbre and the state of mind that went along with it. Loved it, and needed it now. Because she wanted someone to come up with an alternate explanation for the things she'd learned, and the things she suspected.

"Danvers plays a long game. He altered Siren's Aspect and left her for sixteen years before he tried to do anything with her. He left the two Empaths with their adoptive fathers."

"Okay," Random said, "but we're not talking about Danvers and his penchant for experimentation. We're talking about Elijah and you." When she didn't answer he added, "Aren't we?"

"At StellaMia's Danvers told me—" She cut off. She didn't want to tell him what Danvers had said, didn't want Random to look at her differently. "He told me my mother was never the experiment. He said I was."

Random's hands, which had paused their gentle circles on her back, resumed working at her knotted muscles. "He was probably just trying to fuck with your head, Kyrie."

"Maybe." Danvers didn't seem like the type to bluff. He was too cocky, too sure of himself.

"You don't think he was."

"No. I don't."

"Come here." He led her over to the bar, nudged her down onto one of the bar stools. He stared for a moment at his aunt's blood before delicately picking up the bowl and removing it to the opposite counter. Then, as if they were done talking about everything, he switched gears and said, "You need to eat something, you never got food at StellaMia's."

"Random."

He was verging into caretaker mode, which meant he was concerned and upset. He opened the refrigerator. "I made fried rice yesterday, or there's some roasted garlic soup from the day before."

"Random."

"Or I have leeks, I could make—"

"*Random*. I'm fine."

He wasn't. She could see that from the way his hand clutched the refrigerator so hard his knuckles were white.

"Whatever it is, just say it," she told him.

"What kind of monster thinks of his own daughter as an experiment?"

"The kind who doesn't think of family in the same way as other people. He has no emotional attachment to me. Using himself as a stud in his own experiment would have been the natural choice in his mind. I don't know precisely what he aimed for with my creation, but he mentioned the early age at which I manifested."

"And all of the Aspect records you broke?"

"Yes, those too."

He closed his eyes briefly. "Say that you're right. What kind of long game is letting Elijah Winters raise you? I understand why he left Siren for years. He left her with people who worked for him. But Elijah destroyed Danvers' initial operation and stole you and your mother from him."

"Danvers said that he and Elijah were contemporaries, once. It sounds crazy, but I think they might have been working together. Danvers said Elijah fell in love with my mother. That that's when everything went wrong.

"You never met my mother." She had died just before Random arrived in Seclusion. "You never saw my parents together. He *did* love her. I don't think it was a very healthy love —it bordered on obsession—but I don't think she ever let herself recognize that. To my mother, Elijah was forever going to be the white knight who rescued her.

"And he was so careful around her. The monster never showed when he didn't want it to. And all those times he disappeared for weeks and months on end, 'hunting' Danvers? How is it, do you think, that someone with Elijah Winters' connections, drive, and resources never managed to find him in over twenty years of dedicated searching?"

"Unless he didn't have to," Random said.

"Exactly. The things Danvers knows about me—he's too familiar with my life for it all to have come from an interrogation of Elijah. It's more like he received the information as it happened."

"You think every time he was off 'hunting' Danvers he was just reporting to him?"

"Why not? I was firmly under control. And Elijah's position with the Council was too useful for Danvers to give up."

Random finally closed the refrigerator door and leaned back against it. "Why did Elijah leave a year ago? Why come back now?"

"I don't know for sure."

"I'll take a guess."

"Danvers had been looking for Siren for six years by that point. And he had recently obtained Lucille, an Oracle. Their visions may be difficult for the uninitiated to decipher, but I'd wager he gleaned from her that if Elijah 'disappeared' it would lead Siren to him.

"Because that's what happened, isn't it? When my father left, I called Jace home. I didn't know where Elijah was, so I wanted Jace close." She hadn't been willing to take the chance that Elijah would decide to get rid of the son he blamed for his wife's death. She'd needed Jace here, where she could protect him. "And Jace was the thing that made Siren sit still long enough for Danvers to try and reacquire her.

"As for sending Elijah back now—he did that to fuck with me. And—I think—so Elijah could quietly remind everyone that I'm unstable. Everyone thinks I'm completely devoted to him. Maybe I'm unhinged and devoted enough to take out the entire Council and put my father in their place."

Random looked at the bowl of his aunt's blood. "How much of this does Aunt Ella know?"

"Most of it, I suspect."

"Then why the hell is she giving you her blood to steal the adnexus instead of taking this to the Council and having them throw Elijah's ass in jail?"

"Because she cares about you."

"What do *I* have to do with this?"

"You love me," Valkyrie said softly. Random's gaze snapped to her at those words, as if he couldn't believe she'd actually said them out loud. *She* couldn't believe she'd said them.

"I do," he agreed cautiously.

"If Ella takes her suspicions about Elijah to the Council, if she convinces them that those suspicions are true, they won't throw Elijah in jail. They will remove him from the Council. They will do that by severing his connection to the adnexus. When a councilor's connection to the adnexus is severed, they die."

"Where is the problem here?"

"The problem is that Elijah isn't bound to the adnexus, Random. *I* am."

Every time Random thought Valkyrie couldn't shatter his world any further, she managed it with ease. "No."

"Yes."

"How?" he managed to spit out. "How did it happen? How did the Council not know? How did *Aunt Ella* not know?"

"Your aunt quit looking at people with her Aspect years ago unless it was required in the course of her official duties."

He stared at her. Last time he'd checked, Valkyrie and Aunt Ella didn't meet for tea and exchange small talk about how they did or did not use their Aspects.

"Ella talks to Siren, Siren talks to me," Valkyrie said. "Your aunt joined the Council *after* my father did. If she'd already been a member when he substituted my bond to the adnexus for his, maybe she would have noticed. But she wasn't, so no one did."

Random shook his head. This couldn't be fucking happening. "There must be a way to undo it. How did it happen?"

"I don't know."

"What do you remember?"

"Nothing."

"Nothing, as in it's been a long time since it happened and everything is fuzzy, or—"

"Nothing, as in almost the entire event is a fog."

"There isn't an Aspect branch that affects memory."

"There doesn't have to be," she snapped at him. "Not every situation has a magical explanation. Goddess knows the Null world has drugs that fuck the memory over just fine, no Aspect needed."

Random shoved off the refrigerator.

"Where are you going?" she demanded.

"To kill Elijah Winters the normal way. If he's dead he can't hurt you anymore."

"You can't do that, either."

He paused in front of the door, his hands curling into fists, and strove for a calm voice. A reasonable voice. A lawyer's voice. "Why not?"

"I told you the councilors are difficult to kill? Because of the benefits being bound to the adnexus confers? Elijah bound *me* to the adnexus for a reason. However he managed it, I suffer the disadvantages and he reaps the benefits."

"Are you saying that if I kill him, I kill you?"

"I don't know," she said in that voice that told him she absolutely did know and wasn't inclined to reveal the particulars.

He fought to process the problem logically, to not simply react. "Which part is unclear? Explain the mechanics to me."

"If a councilor is injured, the adnexus pulls from the other four to help repair the damage done. It doesn't leave a corresponding mark on the others—if someone stabbed DuPont, the other four wouldn't gain matching knife wounds—but it does draw from their energy to repair it.

"It isn't an exact correspondence, either. The adnexus amplifies what is given to it."

Random tried to accept what she told him without interrupting her, but it defied reason. "There is no Aspect use that can do what you're describing."

"No, there is no *legal* Aspect use that can do it." Her gaze flicked briefly to the blood-filled sugar bowl.

"Blood magic," he spat. "You're telling me the Council, the head of our society, the foundation that made our laws, is built on breaking the first law they ever enacted?"

"What better way to maintain power than by making sure no one else is allowed access to the same Aspect that ensured the Council's supremacy in the first place?"

It wasn't as if Random had previously held some rosy image of the Council's beneficence that was now being shattered—he'd never been that naive—but he'd more or less thought that any less-than-savory actions by one of those members would be just that: an action by *one* member.

An individual might gain a prominent position and decide they liked the influence they wielded, might decide that that influence gave them a license to do what they wanted. That individual could then be tried in a court of law and removed.

But this—this wasn't power turning a single person's head, wasn't a corruption that could be excised from the whole. This was a failing at the heart of Aspect Society, a breach of trust and integrity so profound that to fix it would necessitate the removal of the whole in its entirety.

He would deal with that revelation later. After he'd ensured that the woman he loved wasn't going to die.

"Continue," he said, with a great deal more calm than he felt.

She frowned at him. "What's going through your head?"

"Things. Explain the rest of it."

"There isn't much else. If one councilor is sustaining damage, the adnexus won't draw from the others enough to kill them for the sake of the one. There is a threshold for how much can be taken, so it *is* possible to kill a single councilor."

"If there is a threshold, where is the danger?"

"Because the adnexus might not pull from me past a certain point, but Elijah can. And I don't have any doubt that if it's him or me, he's going to choose himself."

"You're telling me he could kill you at any moment?"

"If he was sadistic enough to stab himself in the heart and transfer the death to me? Sure."

Random opened his mouth, shut it. He hadn't felt this helpless since his mother had died. At least then he'd been a kid, too young to really understand what was happening, and his Aspect hadn't manifested yet. They were good excuses for his failure to prevent what had happened, even if he couldn't make himself fully believe them.

But he wasn't a kid anymore, and his Aspect was more or less his to command. He fully understood what was happening. He wanted to walk to Valkyrie, to take her in his arms and prove to himself that she was here, and alive, and well. He wanted to bury himself in her body and give in to the illusion that simply loving her could solve this problem.

It wouldn't. All it would do was distract them both when they needed to focus.

His brain scrambled to come up with a solution. "You said Siren could destroy the adnexus. She knows about this? That it's you bound to it?"

Valkyrie nodded. "She discovered it when she had her little showdown with the Council. What she saw wasn't the adnexus itself, but the connection it draws between all of the councilors. She couldn't figure out how to disperse it then, but she thinks if she has the adnexus itself, the physical anchor for it, that she might be able to destroy it without killing any of us."

"So that's why you already had Kara's and Theo's blood?"

"Yeah."

"Kyrie..." He trailed off, not sure how to say what he wanted to, and certain this wasn't the right time. But there never seemed to *be* a right time with her. "Kyrie, I think we should talk. About us."

∾

VALKYRIE COULDN'T BREATHE. It was like she'd been hammered in the chest with a Battle-Aspect-strengthened punch and had no chance to shield against the impact.

She didn't know much about relationships. She knew she and Random weren't really in one. But she also knew it was not a good thing when the man she was fucking said they should "talk."

She breathed in short, shallow sips, willing the tightness in her chest to ease. It didn't.

"Kyrie?" Random sounded concerned. Of course he did. He was a good man. He didn't like to hurt people.

He loved her. She knew that. She also knew love didn't fix everything. Her life wasn't a book, or a movie, or a love song. Real love was complicated, and messy, and sometimes people decided it wasn't worth it.

Who *wouldn't* run away from her after learning everything he'd just learned?

"It's fine." Getting the two words out let her breath come a little easier. "You don't need to explain. I understand."

He swore. "I'm not pulling the plug on us, Kyrie."

"I may be inexperienced, but I'm not an idiot. I know what *we should talk* means. And I get it. This isn't what you signed up for." Loving her despite her many flaws was one thing. Loving her after finding out she was a magical experiment with her life tied to a blood magic spell was...something else.

"I signed up for *you*, love." He came to her, reached for her, but she held up a staying hand.

"Please don't." He shouldn't touch her now, if he never meant to do it again. Some part of her wished he would anyway, but Random wasn't the kind of man to disrespect the boundaries a person set.

"Kyrie, love." His voice was pleading, now. "Wherever you went in your head just now, don't go there. I don't want you to leave. I want you *here*. But things can't keep going on the way they have been. I need more from you."

More. He didn't need more, he needed different. Someone who wasn't her. Someone normal. "I can't be what you need me to be."

He was silent for a moment before he said, voice dangerously soft, "And what is it you think I need?"

"A normal woman. A *nice* woman. Someone who fits here." She waved a hand indicating the house, the kitchen. "I'm never going to be domestic."

"When have I ever asked you to be? When have I ever said, 'Kyrie, you'd be perfect if only you'd put on a dress and some pearls and bake a fucking casserole'? I don't want any of that shit, I want *you*.

"And as for you *fitting* here, you are the only woman who ever will. I built this house for you. Why do you think I have a bloody stable? Why do you think the gym is perfect for you? I even picked the goddess-damned color scheme with you in mind."

The revelation was so obvious it should have slapped her in the face long before now. Random, who'd always been more disposed toward the city than the country, had bought property out here. She'd known the build was new, she just hadn't put together that it had been *his* new build.

No wonder he'd been so smug when she liked the gym. No wonder her horses liked the damn barn so much. No wonder she'd felt like she was home the morning she'd woken up in his bed and felt soothed by the "goddess-damned color scheme."

"You built this for me?"

"Yes." His voice was hoarse.

"When?"

"I had the plans drawn up the day after." He didn't specify which day after. He didn't have to. There was really only one, for them.

"What would you do if I didn't want it?"

Pain flashed across his face, as if he thought her asking the question guaranteed that she didn't want any part of what he'd built. But he answered her. "Sell it. I'd never live here with anyone but you."

The idea of him selling the house—her house—of anyone else living here, was one she didn't like it. Maybe it was naive and foolish to want this. Maybe it was crazy to think a relationship with him could work, that they could just fit together with no experience. Maybe they would crash and burn. But she did want it.

"What's the more you need?" she asked.

He offered her his hand, palm up, and she took it. "I need to be your partner, Kyrie. I need you to trust me. I know that isn't easy for you, and I understand why. But at every stage of this mess, I've told you I need the truth, and you only ever tell me part of it."

His free hand cupped her face and his thumb stroked against her cheekbone. "I love you. And I just found out I could have gotten you killed at any moment because you weren't honest with me. Because you still don't factor me into your decisions.

"You don't owe me anything. If I'm not what you want, then tell me that."

She couldn't tell him that. Not now. She had managed to before, but she never wanted to do it again.

His hand slid down to the nape of her neck. "But if Elijah is the only thing that's kept us apart, if you want to be with me, I need it to be equal. I'll follow your lead. I'll trust you to know what you're doing. But don't ask me to stumble in the dark with half the information while you risk your life.

"Don't ask me to wake up one morning without you, wondering if I could have changed everything if I'd known what you know. I can't lose you like that." He swallowed. "I can't lose you."

Valkyrie had no intention of being lost. But she understood in that moment that *she* was going to lose *him*.

Why couldn't he have waited one more day to have this conversation? Just a day, when she could be on the other side of this mess and give him the promise he wanted? But the adnexus, Elijah, Danvers—they were all too dangerous for her to risk involving Random any more than she already had.

She could—would—end this. Tonight. But she couldn't take him with her when she did.

"Then don't lose me," she whispered, the words more request than command. She leaned in and brushed her lips across his. "Make love to me, Random."

She threaded her fingers in his hair and pulled his mouth back to hers. She sank every ounce of her pent-up longing and need into that kiss, hoping he would take her passion in place of a promise.

"Kyrie." The syllables were prayer and plea, desire and hesitance, as were the hands he settled on her waist, his fingers curling against her. He was too smart not to realize she hadn't promised him anything. But he was also a man who wanted her badly, and she had no qualms about using it to her advantage.

"I want you." She kissed the corner of his lips. "I need you." She kissed the opposite corner. "Make love to me," she repeated.

Because they hadn't really done that yet. Everything about their physical encounters had been hot and explosive and it had been wonderful. But she was asking for the opposite side of the coin, now. For sex that neither of them could pretend was *just* sex.

"Kiss me like you did after Jace's wedding."

His eyes softened. She had him, then, and they both knew it. He took her mouth, softly but intensely, like a drowning man who'd just found oxygen. Just like he had when he'd found her after Jace's wedding. She felt everything in that kiss: his love, his need, his fear.

She parted his lips with her tongue and tried to say everything she didn't know how to put into words: *I love you, I trust you, I'm sorry.*

She turned him toward his bedroom and walked him back to it with kisses and touches. At the side of his bed they paused, and he undid the buttons on her shirt with deliberate slowness, his mouth claiming every inch of skin as he exposed it.

"You are so beautiful," he said when the shirt was finally gone, and she believed it, because he did. He guided her back to the bed and she laid down, content for once to let him do what he wanted, to let him take control.

He kissed her breasts, his tongue teasing her nipples to hard peaks before his lips trailed lower, before he settled between her legs with a groan. He licked and sucked at her outer folds, his slow, thorough devotion making the ache growing within her nearly unbearable.

"Random." She curled her fingers into his hair. "You're killing me."

He made a low, pleased rumble that vibrated through her, but he didn't stop. His tongue thrust into her. She'd *thought* she remembered how good it was the first time he'd done this to her. But they'd been frantic with need, then, and he'd made quick work of her.

There was nothing quick about the attention he gave her now. It was soft, slow, exquisite torture. When he finally worked his way up to her clit she was so desperate she couldn't stop herself from grinding against him.

He made another one of those noises that indicated he thoroughly approved of this behavior and his hands slid underneath her to cup her ass. He rocked her forward with each flick of his tongue, the steady movement and the sensation of him against her building her pleasure with each stroke, until her breath came in sharp, ragged gasps. He sucked her clit into his mouth, rolled it gently between his teeth, and she screamed as release tore through her.

She didn't let herself relax. He'd made her shatter and he hadn't even taken off his clothes. She pushed him back, rose to her knees and pulled his shirt over his head. She fumbled with his pants, waited while he slid off the bed to step out of them, until he was perfectly, gloriously free.

He slipped back onto the mattress and she fell back beneath him, the length of him hot and hard against her stomach as he kissed her. When his mouth broke from hers she guided him to her entrance, needing to feel him there, to feel him everywhere.

He pushed inside her a scant inch and leaned down to suck her nipple into his mouth. She bent her legs and arched her hips, trying to take him deeper. He leaned back, his hands coming to rest on her knees, and only gave her another inch.

"So impatient," he murmured. He sounded like sin and heaven all rolled into one, and given the excruciating slowness with which he filled her, she thought he might be the devil. He *still* wasn't fully inside her when he drew back, so far he almost left her entirely, and paused, waiting.

Waiting for what, she didn't know. "Random?"

"Yes, love?" His voice was a low purr.

"Do you have a death wish?"

He grinned. "Maybe. But only for a little death." He held her gaze and buried himself to the hilt in one hard, defined thrust that made her toes curl. He built a rhythm that was almost lazy in its slowness, glorious in the time it gave her to savor the sensation of him moving within her.

When she slid her hand between them to stroke herself he halted, his fingers digging into her knees, his eyes half-lidded with barely-controlled lust. She clenched her inner walls around him, demanding movement again.

He complied and he lost the slow control, moving with fast, steady thrusts. She met his tempo. Her fingers worked her pleasure as their breaths grew shorter, their movements more desperate, until the ache inside her peaked and she came in a hard wave, bucking against him.

He rode her orgasm until his entire body went taught and he emptied himself into her with one final thrust.

She wasn't sure if he collapsed onto her or if she pulled him down, but she wrapped her arms around his back to hold him there, his weight on top of her a comfort. He nuzzled the side of her neck, pressed a line of kisses up to her mouth before he rolled onto his side and pulled her with him so they lay face-to-face.

Now that need and lust were fading, exhaustion was evident in the lines of his face. She had no idea what time it was, only that the sun had gone down hours ago.

"We should get some sleep," he said, his eyes already closed. "Problems will wait for the morning."

She wished that were true. But one way or another, their current problems wouldn't see the dawn. They would be replaced with new ones, and if she survived, she didn't know if he would forgive what she was about to do. She didn't know if she would forgive him, if their places were reversed. But she couldn't make herself change her mind.

"Random?" she said softly, not sure if he was still awake.

"Hmm?"

"Could you say it again?"

The corner of his mouth quirked up, and his arm around her waist pulled her closer. "I love you, Kyrie."

She drank the words in. She laid awake and memorized his face, the way his hand felt on her hip, the way he twitched in his sleep like a cat in the grip of some strange dream.

Then she made herself get up, silently so as not to wake him, because the longer she stayed, the harder it was to leave. She found her clothes in the dryer, got dressed, and retrieved the magic-masking box Random had made from the bookcase.

She paused in the doorway and looked back inside the house, at the kitchen where she could see him if she closed her eyes. It would have been a good life, here with him. But that life was a fantasy, and she had her feet both firmly planted in reality.

Reality dictated that she had an adnexus to steal and a father to kill. And Random—Random couldn't be a part of that. If saving Random Tremayne destroyed her, she would die with a smile on her face so long as she knew it was done.

CHAPTER

SIXTEEN

Valkyrie glanced in the rearview mirror. Someone was following her. The car had been on her as soon as she pulled out of Random's drive, and the driver wasn't trying to hide the fact that they were tailing her. They hadn't tried to run her off the road or otherwise get her attention, but when she sped up they didn't let her lose them either. They kept the same distance behind their vehicle and hers no matter how erratic she made her speed, and they did so with a precision that spoke to exceptional driving skills.

Without warning, Valkyrie stood on the brakes. The car behind her halted immediately, maintaining the six feet of space between them perfectly. Valkyrie threw the Jeep in reverse and floored it. The car behind her sped backwards without missing a beat.

Valkyrie hit the brakes again, pulled the Jeep off to the side of the road and got out. The car pulled up next to her, and she was utterly unsurprised when it revealed itself to be a silver Porsche Spyder. The door opened and Meredith emerged, outfitted in surprisingly practical clothing—for Meredith, at least.

"That was fun," Meredith said. "We should do it more often.

Though maybe you could get something that drives faster than a turtle waddles."

"This *turtle* has ground clearance and four-wheel drive."

"That's about all it has." Meredith sniffed. "At least it's a stick shift."

"I thought I told you to leave town."

"What, and miss all the fun? You said we were friends again. I want to help."

"I get that I'm unfamiliar with the friendship concept, but I think friends just call."

"I did. I texted, too. Your phone is dead."

"No, it's n—" She pulled her phone out and tapped at the screen.

"Dead," Meredith said sweetly.

"So you decided to lurk at the end of Random's driveway waiting for me to leave?"

"I wasn't lurking, I was listening to an audiobook and doing my nails." She waggled her fingers, the tips of which were now a pastel green. "What do you think?"

"They look like mint ice cream." Valkyrie hated mint ice cream. She finally caught up to the fact that Meredith *had* been lingering by Random's driveway and her brain did a one-eighty. "Wait, how did you know I was at Random's?"

"As though I couldn't have guessed you'd be there. But if you must know, I heard all about the earlier drama from Julian. Did Random seriously teleport you out of the Warded Room?"

"*Julian?* You talk to that asshole?"

"As a matter of course, no. But he's still hoping I'll sleep with him someday so he tells me things. Now talk to me about teleporting. Was it sexy? Did you fuck Random's brains out after?"

"There is nothing sexy about teleporting."

"You definitely fucked him, though. You're blushing. I reiterate that I do not want that dress back."

Valkyrie pinched the bridge of her nose. "I don't have time

for this. I'm not out on a lark, Mer. I'm about to steal from the Council so I can try and kill my father and you're following me so you can talk about boys and—"

"*Ha,*" Meredith said, a note of triumph in her voice. "So we're stealing something before murder, then?"

Valkyrie narrowed her gaze. "How did you do that?"

"You'd be surprised the things people will start saying when they want you to shut up about something else. Let me help, Val."

"No. Leave town."

Meredith crossed her arms. "No."

"I am trying to keep all of you safe. Why does no one see that? Why is everyone so damn determined to get dragged into hell with me?"

"Because we care about you. Because you're not the only one capable of doing things. The rest of us may not be *you* but we're not helpless. I don't really have the right to be pissed because we're just now friends again, but if I were Siren or Jace or Random, you'd best believe I would be. Does Random even know you're gone?"

"No. And if you dare tell him and something happens to him I will never forgive you. I don't have *time* for this." The only head start she had on Random was however long he would naturally stay asleep. Drugging him was pointless—his Aspect would just clear it from his system, and the use would alert him to the danger. She hoped he was still mostly tapped out from teleporting them earlier, but the rate at which he regenerated Aspect was as seemingly random as his use of it, so she couldn't be sure.

She needed to move, and the only expedient way of doing so appeared to be giving Meredith what she wanted. "Fine. If you insist on landing in the Council's dungeon next to me, get in the damn Jeep. Your car couldn't drive over a rock without scraping the undercarriage."

Meredith gave Valkyrie's vehicle a disapproving wrinkle of

her nose, but she tapped the Porsche, which then took on the appearance of a dilapidated Toyota Corolla, and jumped into the Jeep's passenger seat.

"What's that phrase?" Meredith asked, her voice entirely too chipper. "Something about good friends bailing you out and best friends helping you bury the body?"

"I have no idea what you're talking about."

"No, I suppose you wouldn't. If I may ask, where *are* you planning on burying Elijah's body if you do kill him? I should warn you I'm not very good with shovels."

Who would have thought pretty, perky Meredith would have such a macabre underside? "You're really stuck on the whole killing thing, aren't you?"

"What? I'm living my parental-murder fantasies vicariously through you. So fill me in. What are we going to steal? And for love of the goddess, why?"

This was the problem with having *people* in her life. They constantly wanted to know things. How was it she'd successfully kept her connection to the adnexus under wraps for nearly two decades and in the last twenty-four hours she'd told her lover, the woman who had raised him, and now it seemed she was going to tell her best friend? Because if Meredith insisted on coming, she should know what she was getting herself into.

If Valkyrie had hoped telling Meredith that they were breaking into Council headquarters to steal illegal magic would convince the woman to bail on the excursion, she was sorely mistaken.

"That is fucked up," Meredith said, her voice still cheerful.

"Thank you for describing my life so succinctly." Valkyrie pulled the Jeep onto the forest road that led to the Council's headquarters.

"I can't decide whose childhood was worse, yours or mine."

"Is it a competition you're keen on winning?"

"I'm just trying to cope with the horrors I've experienced through the liberal application of humor."

Valkyrie shifted her gaze from the winding dirt road long enough to give her a dubious look.

"I'm just repeating the explanation my therapist gave me," Meredith said innocently.

"Does it work?"

"Gallows humor?"

"Therapy. Well, either one, I guess."

"No to therapy, and sort of on the humor. I mean, I only went to therapy once, but it was boring, and the therapist just lied to me a lot. Sometimes being a Truthfinder sucks."

"Were you holding hands with the therapist?" Truthfinders required a physical connection to a person to actually tap into their truth-telling abilities.

"As if I needed to. Growing up as a Truthfinder means you can spot most people's bullshit a million miles away, no Aspect needed. Trust me, she lied a lot."

Valkyrie pulled up right beside the cabin that served as the Council's headquarters. She didn't bother to turn off the lights or kill the engine.

"They don't have *any* security?" Meredith asked.

Valkyrie shrugged. "As far as anybody knows, there's nothing in there to steal. If they put a guard on it, they'd only alert people to the fact that there's something worth having inside. Besides, if the Council hasn't unlocked it, the front door doesn't open for anyone but a councilor."

"It's still beyond bizarre that you're a councilor."

"I'm not *actually* a councilor."

"You know what I mean. So what do you want me to do?"

"Mask my trail so a Tracker can't find it and drive the getaway car?"

"No way, I'm coming in with you."

"Meredith, I'd like to think I know what I'm doing, but I am about to steal a magical artifact hidden in a secret room. It will be dangerous. There's no point in us both going in. If I don't come back in half an hour, leave."

The cheery façade slipped and Meredith's eyes filled unexpectedly with water. "Please don't die, Val. I don't—I'm not doing so hot on my own. You dragging me out on your damn recon missions has been the only thing holding me together. I don't have anyone besides you and I'm a selfish bitch. I don't want to be alone."

There was naked truth in Meredith's voice, in her words. Every emotion Valkyrie had buried too deep to feel—anger and terror and bleak hopelessness—was mirrored on the other woman's face. They were sisters, her and Meredith. Maybe not by blood, but by experience.

Valkyrie did something she never in a million years would have thought she'd do before that moment. She leaned over the gear shift and hugged Meredith. Meredith clutched her back, so fiercely Valkyrie felt every bony edge of her. Clearly, the woman needed calories from something other than gin. If Valkyrie survived this mess, she was going to sic Random on the woman. His cooking was impossible to resist.

"We both know I'm too mean to die," Valkyrie said.

Meredith huffed out a laugh, and they broke apart, awkwardly retreating to their own sides of the Jeep.

"And you know you have more than me. You have Jace and Siren."

"The man I should have married and his wife?"

"They like you," Valkyrie insisted. "And you have Random, too."

"Maybe. But they don't understand me. And as for Random, you're delusional if you think he'll ever speak to me again if I let you get killed."

All this talk of death was making Valkyrie paranoid, making

her think of all the things she hadn't said to Random. "Look, if something *does* happen to me, tell Random I—"

Meredith's eyes rounded.

"Oh, never mind." It would have sounded like a bad movie line anyway. *If I don't make it, tell Random I love him.* She jumped out of the Jeep.

"You love him?" Meredith finished.

"Yeah," Valkyrie said, her throat tight. "That." She opened the Jeep's back door, pulled out the backpack holding the box and slung it over her shoulders. She felt the little tendrils of Random's magic in the lining of the box and it bolstered her, like she had a tiny piece of him here with her.

She stopped in front of the cabin's door, pulled out a dagger and made a small nick on her chest. She'd never understood why characters in movies slashed open their palms every time they needed blood for something. Instant healing wasn't a thing for anyone but Siren, so why anyone would go around intentionally injuring one of their most useful appendages was a mystery to Valkyrie.

She rubbed her hand against the nick, smearing blood over her palm, and then pressed it to the cabin door. The magic of the door's ward-lock reacted to her, tested her, tasted her, the blood on her palm flashing in a hot sizzle before it turned black and crumbled off. The ward-lock clicked open. Valkyrie swept inside and went straight for the door opposite the reception desk. It opened onto the stone stairwell she'd followed earlier that day to reach the Warded Room.

As far as most people knew, the Warded Room was the last stop on the stairwell, the lowest level of the Council's headquarters. Valkyrie knew better. On the landing she turned left, past the Warded Room to the alcove that housed the faceless statue of Aspect Society's nameless goddess.

If anyone needed proof that that goddess had been made up from a man's imagination, she thought those two features should have done it. Nameless and faceless, a blank female slate upon which to write in whatever a man wanted. Typical.

She shrugged the backpack off and set the box on the floor, opened it to reveal the vials of of blood inside. She barely remembered the day that had wedded her fate to the Council's. She'd only been six, and she'd already been in somewhat of a haze as she came down here.

All she really remembered was that the other councilors had only spoken to her father, as if they hadn't realized she was even there. They *couldn't* have realized she was there, or they never would have let her go into the room below this statue.

How to open the room—that part she remembered. It was as easy as the ward-lock had been, only it required five offerings rather than the one.

She opened each vial and poured the blood over the statue's head. The cold marble drank the liquid in, red vanishing into the white. She swiped her thumb through the nick on her chest and added her own blood to the goddess' figure. Her crimson fingerprint faded into the stone.

The ground shuddered. The statue sank below the floor, then slid aside to reveal another, narrower staircase. No lighting illuminated the passageway. She summoned a globe of Aspect light and placed it to hover above her right shoulder. Then she threw the empty blood vials into the backpack, picked up it and the box, and descended.

The staircase was carved so that it brought an individual directly beneath the Warded Room before it turned into a spiral and wound down another twenty feet. The press of the earth was a heavy weight around her. She wasn't quite claustrophobic but she'd never like small, deep spaces, and she had a feeling that dislike could be traced back to the room that resided at the staircase's base.

It was small and circular, approximately six feet in diameter, its only feature the stone pedestal at its center. The adnexus rested atop the pedestal, a golden scepter with a dark, blood-red jewel at its apex.

As in the Warded Room, symbols were carved on the room's walls and floor, a continuation of those above. Here, like there, this space was built to contain and shroud, to hide both the existence and nature of the magic that dwelled within it.

That magic reached for her, thin, smoke-gray ropes unfurling from the scepter. Valkyrie snapped a shielding ward into place on instinct but it did no good. The magic that came for her was *of* her, in part, and it slid through her barriers as if her shield was no more than mist.

The tendrils curled over and around her, dark and viscous. Her fingers twitched, wanting the reassuring hilt of a weapon in her hand, but a blade would do her no good here. This was not the kind of magic that could be fought with the physical. And she didn't *need* to fight it. All she needed to do was get the scepter in the damn box.

She set the box on the floor and flipped the lid open. Then, because she was Valkyrie and she needed a blade in her hand whether it was useful or not, she wrapped her left fist around the sword pendant that rested in the hollow of her throat and stepped up to the pedestal.

The tendrils of magic undulated more wildly about her, the adnexus excited by her nearness. Five items clung to the scepter's shaft, held there like metal to a magnet. She recognized the one she must have given it all those years ago. A rose-gold band with a star sapphire at its center. It had been her mother's, and though she'd been too young for such jewelry, she'd liked it so much that her mother had given it to her.

She'd thought she'd lost it. All she'd known was that she'd woken up one morning to find it gone, and when her mother had asked her where it was, she hadn't had an answer.

She reached for the ring. She wanted to rip it free, but as soon as her fingers brushed the cool metal she felt a jolt of connection —to the scepter, to the ring, to the adnexus. If she removed the ring, she removed her connection to the Council. If she removed her connection, she died.

So even though her fingers ached to reclaim what was hers, she stretched them wide and grasped the scepter instead. She tensed, expecting the tendrils of the scepter's power to strike at her. Instead, they ceased their wild roving and brushed against her almost lovingly, leaving oily streaks against her skin. It was unpleasant, but it wasn't the annihilating force she'd expected after Ella had warned her that no one individual was meant to hold the adnexus.

She turned to place the scepter in the box. As she did, her Aspect slid over it, and through it she felt the adnexus's connection to the other councilors. The knowledge hit her, so simple she couldn't believe she hadn't seen it before, and she paused with her hand over the box: she held the Council's adnexus. She'd been so focused on discovering a way to dissolve her own attachment to them that she hadn't considered simply dissolving theirs.

She hadn't known it could be done before she'd held the scepter in her hands. Without the scepter, it would indeed take four councilors acting in concert to destroy a fifth. But she held the physical embodiment of their connection, held the magic that made their bond possible. Magic they had all agreed to be bound with. Their promises, the physical tokens of their willingness, were all here. She could simply...take them.

The tendrils of the adnexus stroked against her face, whispering how the feat might be accomplished, whispering that *she* was the one who deserved this power. She had been tricked into it when she was too young to understand its meaning. She had suffered as it took from her again and again to heal the wounds of others and she had never once been on the receiving end of its benefits. Even now, the Council would try to kill her if they came to know of her connection to them.

Why not kill *them*, instead? Pull their power into the scepter? She felt the points where the others were bound, felt the edges of their Aspects, and sipped at them. Their Aspect flowed into the scepter and then into her, a heady mixture that hit her like a jolt of adrenaline-soaked euphoria.

This was the power she needed, the piece of the plan she'd been missing. Draining the councilors wouldn't kill Elijah, because he wasn't bound to them correctly, but with the power of the Council contained in one vessel, in *her*, she could not fail to end Elijah *and* Danvers. Random would be safe.

Random.

Reality slammed into her, cold and hard. She was sucking the Council's power into the scepter. They would all die. Random's aunt would die. He would never look at her the same. He would never want to touch her again.

She halted the influx of the Council's Aspect and dropped the scepter—or tried to. The power of the adnexus flowed over her, coercing, promising. Lassitude stole over her.

She shouldn't drop the scepter. It was the way to gain her freedom, to save Random. He wouldn't need to know how the Council had died, wouldn't need to know—

Valkyrie clenched her left hand so hard around the sword pendant that its tiny, sharp metal tip pierced her skin. The pain brought her a flash of clarity and she forced her right hand open. The scepter fell, straight into the box, and she slammed the lid closed. The whispers, the promises, died as Random's magic contained the scepter's.

Valkyrie unclenched her hand from the pendant and stared at the tiny pinprick of red on her palm. Who would have thought a piece of *jewelry* would prove useful in a magical battle of wills? If she survived, she would really have to thank Random properly for the gift.

Blood magic—a small shiver went through her at the remembrance of oily caresses against her skin—no wonder it had been outlawed.

She didn't have long to contemplate it. The room shuddered and the runes on the walls and floor flickered as a pulse of light went through them, as if they were searching for something. She'd made the foolish assumption that these runes were just like those in the Warded Room, that they had been etched simply to contain any magic within the room's boundaries. But what if they had instead been made to guard a specific magic? One they couldn't now locate because it was hidden behind the box's magic?

Valkyrie grabbed the box and sprinted up the stairs. She was halfway to the top when the scrape of stone told her that the room had found its occupant missing, and decided to lock down. She poured Aspect recklessly into her body, her legs gaining strength and speed. She took the steps six at a time, reached the top as the statue was already three-quarters returned to its place.

She hurtled herself at the opening, pouring so much Aspect into the sheer vertical jump that the stone step she pushed off of cracked from the force. She felt the kiss of stone against her toes as she cleared the opening, the statue's pedestal snicking into place behind her. Valkyrie barely gave the faceless goddess a glance. She just kept running.

The Council might not be able to track the scepter when it was in the box Random had made for it, but they would have felt the pull when Valkyrie had drained traces of their power. They would converge on this location, and she needed to be gone before that happened.

Thank the goddess only Random could teleport.

Valkyrie flung herself out the front door and jumped in the Jeep's passenger seat. She didn't even have to bark out an order to drive because Meredith took one look at her face and hit the gas pedal before Valkyrie's ass was even fully in the seat. Valkyrie clutched the roll bar overhead as the vehicle bounced over bumpy terrain.

Meredith flew threw gears, apparently uncaring of the possibility of flipping—really, the woman should have been a race car driver—and Valkyrie didn't waste her breath on words of caution. This dirt road was the only path into or out of the Council's headquarters, and it was another mile back to paved asphalt. They needed to be out of the woods long before anyone else hit the entrance.

Meredith knew her vehicles. They were, near as Valkyrie could tell, the woman's only passion other than shoes. If the bumps and swerves made Valkyrie feel like she was on an ill-maintained rollercoaster, well—she was too much Elijah's creation to feel truly nervous, but she decided closing her eyes until the ordeal was over was a fine idea.

"You can open your eyes," Meredith said. The Jeep's front tires gripped onto gloriously smooth asphalt. "Where are we going now?"

Valkyrie snapped her eyes open. "Back to your car. I'll take it from here."

"I thought we discussed this. I'm coming with you."

"I'm going to fight my nearly-invincible father in physical combat and attempt to kill him. You're a Truthfinder and a Tracker, Mer," she said as gently as she could.

"So, what? I'm useless?"

"You barely passed Basic Defense in Academy, and only then because you flirted with the instructor."

"I was sixteen, I didn't know I'd need self-defense." Meredith threw her hands up in exasperation, and Valkyrie fought the urge to grab the steering wheel for the three seconds Meredith's hands were off it. "I thought I was going to marry your brother and live a life of quiet luxury. Besides, I'm not completely without natural defensive capabilities."

"From what I understand, for a Truthtelling to hurt a person, they have to have a conscience. Elijah doesn't."

"I'm not talking about a Telling."

"Then what *are* you talking about?"

"There has to be *something* you want to know from him."

Valkyrie stared at her. "You ranked high as a Truthfinder. You didn't rank high enough to *compel* truth from someone."

Meredith shrugged.

"You scored low on purpose?"

"Do you have any idea what my mother would have done with me if she knew I could *make* people answer me? No, just *no*."

"Theoretically, how many questions would I get?"

Meredith lost a little of her outward confidence. "I don't know. I only did it once and that was by accident."

"Who?"

"Does it matter?"

"Jace, then," Valkyrie said.

Meredith made an irritated noise. "How do you *do* that?"

Valkyrie shrugged. "For you to not want to tell me it would have to be someone I cared about. You wouldn't be stupid enough to do it to Siren, and your abilities don't work on Random." His Aspect had a way of slipping sideways out of other people's. That left precisely one person Valkyrie cared about. "So what did you want to know badly enough you forced it out of my brother?"

"I'm glad we're friends again and all, but some things are none of your business."

"He never mentioned it."

"He was drunk off his ass at the time. I doubt he remembers."

"Are we talking about the same Jace? I've never seen him go past tipsy."

"That's because you never saw him directly after Elijah disowned him and I broke his heart. So, are we agreed that I'm going with you, or do I need to go back to my car and follow you again?"

"This is Elijah we're talking about. He isn't going to just let you waltz up and interrogate him."

"Sure he will," Meredith said easily, as if it were the most obvious thing in the world. She did not elaborate, clearly wanting Valkyrie to ask.

"Okay, I give. Why would he do that?"

Meredith smiled at her. "Watch and learn." She pulled the Jeep off to the side of the road and made a phone call. "Martin? It's Meredith."

Valkyrie couldn't make out the words of DuPont's response, save that it was clipped and irritated.

"You sound stressed, is everything alright?" She paused, then, "You did say to call at *any* time once I returned to town. Should I verify Mr. Winters' statement immediately?"

She tapped her fingernails on the steering wheel while DuPont's angry voice issued out of the speaker. Meredith had the nerve to cut him off. "Yes, yes, I'll record everything for the legality of it all. You'll call ahead to let him know I'm coming? Wonderful." She hung up and turned to Valkyrie. "See? One doesn't *have* to go in sword drawn."

"You just irrevocably tied yourself to this entire mess. There's no hiding it now."

"Oh, wake up, Val. There was never any hiding it. From the moment you took that," she pointed at the box that held the scepter, "it was all over. All I did by masking your trail at headquarters and calling this in was buy us some time.

"You said the second that *thing* comes out of the box they'll know where it is. So we're going to get caught. The only question is, are you going to be able to do what you need to first?"

"You came with me expecting to get caught? Why would you do that?"

"Because the situation is seriously fucked up. It's wrong. The whole thing is wrong. Elijah, the Council, blood magic, everything. It needs to change."

"You can't change centuries of ingrained corruption."

"Then we overthrow it. Wasn't that your plan?"

"I didn't have a plan." Not past making sure her father was dead and Random was safe. Nothing else mattered.

"Well, I do. It's called you're banging a lawyer. Hell, you're banging *the* Aspect defense lawyer. If he can't blow up a scandal like this six ways from Sunday, no one can."

"I don't want him involved."

"We don't always get what we want." Meredith put the Jeep in gear and pulled back onto the road, heading towards the Winters' estate. "And at some point, Val, you're going to have to stop trying to make everyone's decisions for them."

CHAPTER

SEVENTEEN

I n the end, Meredith reclaimed her Porsche for appearance's sake, and Valkyrie now followed the silver sports car through the gates onto Elijah's estate. She could no longer think of the place as her own. In truth, it hadn't felt like her home since her mother died. Even in Elijah's absence it had only felt mildly like a home for the brief time Jace and Siren had lived there with her. With their departure it had simply become a cold, empty, too-large space, filled with ghosts that refused to move on.

Now, as the towering gates closed behind her and she approached the house, she couldn't shake the feeling that the mansion was nothing more than a mausoleum that had patiently awaited her death for years. She parked in the circular drive out front rather than the garage, directly behind the Porsche, and met Meredith as she exited the vehicle.

"You're sure about this?" Valkyrie asked.

"A little late now if I'm not. But yeah."

"As soon as you lose your hold on him, run. I'll ensure he's too busy to follow."

Meredith wiped her palms on the thighs of her jeans. "You're certain you'll be all right?"

"Positive," Valkyrie lied. The scepter, in its spelled box, was tucked under her left arm. Elijah would no doubt guess what the box held the moment she walked inside, but he wouldn't *do* anything about it until Meredith left. He would want to play everything above board until the witnesses were gone.

Even if he suspected she was up to something by arriving with Meredith, he wouldn't truly believe the Truthfinder could be a danger any more than Valkyrie had seriously considered she could be an asset. An arrogant oversight, on both their parts.

She let Meredith ring the doorbell. They could have simply walked in—the doors were never locked—but Valkyrie no longer belonged here, and guests waited for an invitation. Besides, waiting at the door forced him to physically answer it, which was better than walking into a house with no idea of where Elijah lurked within it.

Her weapons were sheathed in plain sight—the two short swords crossed at her back, one hilt rising over each shoulder, knives at her waist and thighs. There was no point in hiding them. He'd been the one who'd taught her *how* to hide them, after all.

The door opened, revealing Elijah framed in the doorway. He wore an expression of cordial geniality that chilled the blood in her veins. Valkyrie's heart slammed against the cage of her ribs. Her wrists burned, expecting the cruel jerk of chains that were no longer there.

Elijah's lips twisted, and she knew his thoughts had turned to the same subject as hers, that he had reached to deliver that hit of pain out of habit. He didn't look surprised when it didn't work, only mildly annoyed, confirming every one of her suspicions. What Danvers knew, Elijah knew.

"Mr. Winters," Meredith said, her voice bright. "It's such a relief to see you well." She was a hell of an actress—she actually sounded like she meant it.

Elijah turned a wide, convincing smile on her. "Thank you, Meredith. I find it such a comfort to be home. Though my daughter, apparently, feels differently. I admit, I didn't expect to find her on my doorstep. Have you talked some sense into her?"

His words were charming, teasing. They revealed no hint of the hollowness that lay beneath them.

Meredith waved a dismissive hand. "No need for that. I'm sure it was the stress of the moment. And I know you two must have a lot to catch up on, so I'll just get the formalities over with, shall I?"

"Please do."

He stepped back and ushered her inside. Meredith went. Valkyrie waited. She had no intention of presenting Elijah with a back in which to plunge a blade. His lip curled up in a sneer, but the expression smoothed when Meredith turned back to him for direction.

"The parlor," he told her. "You remember where it is?"

"Of course," she said airily, turning right.

Elijah stepped away from the door and followed Meredith. Valkyrie didn't miss how he held his left arm just a little farther from his body as he turned, the way he always did when a long knife rested in a shoulder sheath under his coat. It was hardly any tell at all, a mere centimeter more of distance that most people wouldn't notice. She noticed. She'd always *had* to notice. She'd also bet he had a dozen or more weapons hidden in the parlor room. It was what she would have done, after all.

Valkyrie stepped inside, shut the door behind her, and followed them both. The parlor was a room that had seldom been used after her mother's death. Elijah had rarely received guests in the house, conducting most of his business outside of it, and Valkyrie herself had certainly never had any use for it. She couldn't even remember the last time she'd bothered to go into it.

The room was practically a memorial to her mother, untouched since her death, a beautiful, serene expression of the woman Evelyn Winters had been. It was painted a soft robin's-egg blue. White lace curtains adorned the floor-to-ceiling windows on the two exterior walls, the furniture all pale pinks and golds. A sectional lounged in the middle of the large room, an ornate antique coffee table nestled in the curve.

A smaller table sat before the fireplace, low chairs seated around it, another similar setting grouped in front of the window that overlooked the front gardens.

She had a flash of her mother seated at the couch's center, smiling, the parlor filled with women and laughter during one of Evelyn's weekly socials. She had surrounded herself with people, as if she'd been determined to experience every moment of life she could.

Or as if she hadn't been able to stand being alone.

Elijah seated himself on the sectional, directly in the middle. Just where Valkyrie's mother had always sat and she knew, without doubt, that he'd chosen this room to unsettle her.

"Nothing to say, daughter mine?" He smiled at her.

"Oh, I have plenty to say. But it will wait until Meredith is gone."

He shrugged. To Meredith, he held out his hand. "Shall we commence with the formalities?"

Meredith took out her phone, set it on the table, and hit record. She took his hand without so much as a flinch and her Aspect rose to the surface.

"Are you Elijah Winters?" she asked.

"Yes."

"Have you been in the captivity of the man known as Danvers since your initial disappearance?"

"I was under his control, yes."

"How did you escape that control?"

"He let me go."

"Why would he do that?"

Elijah shrugged. "I imagine he thought it would be to his advantage, in some way."

The questions continued, Meredith tossing them out like a robot following a script. Sometimes it was the same question twice, phrased a little differently. Valkyrie could see her father growing weary of the inquiry. She didn't know if the lengthy repetition was necessary for Meredith to do what she needed to do, or if the other woman was simply working up her courage. Valkyrie did know Meredith needed to make her move, soon, or Elijah was going to put an end to the session.

As if the thought had sparked action, Meredith's power exploded from her without warning. Elijah stiffened as her Aspect wrapped around him like a vise. Sweat broke out along his forehead. He struggled to move and failed.

"Was it your decision or Danvers' to bind Valkyrie to the Council in your stead?"

"Mine." The single syllable seemed physically wrenched from him.

"Is there a way to remove her from the adnexus? If so, how?"

Elijah's face turned red with strain as he fought the compulsion, and an answering tremble went through Meredith. Finally, he answered, "Yes. If she can pull her ring from the scepter, her connection to the adnexus will be broken."

That much, Valkyrie had already guessed.

"What will happen to her then?" Meredith's voice shook.

"She'll die." He smiled. If he could smile, Meredith's grip on him was waning.

Valkyrie set the box with the scepter on the coffee table and pulled both her short swords. She would prefer to already have a blade at his throat, but any contact from her to Elijah, even if just from the metal of her sword, would interfere with Meredith's Aspect.

"Let him go, Mer." She hadn't gotten the answer to the most important question, but Meredith was almost tapped out. And if Elijah managed to break the connection instead of Meredith releasing it voluntarily, the woman wouldn't have the two to three second head start she would need to get away from Elijah so Valkyrie could get between them.

But instead of leaving, the blonde woman stubbornly shook

her head. Her grip on Elijah's hand tightened and another slug of Aspect surged from her. "Why will it kill her?"

With what looked like herculean effort, Elijah Winters turned his head to look straight at the Truthfinder, rage and the promise of death in his eyes.

"Meredith, run. *Now*," Valkyrie ordered.

Meredith didn't run. She clung to Elijah, the last of her Aspect hitting him in one final command. "Why will it kill her?" she repeated.

"Breaking a spell bound by blood magic causes a reversal of the intended effect. The spell is meant to heal when she is injured. The reverse is to harm her when she's not. And a spell that can call her back from the brink of death can lead her to it."

Sweat poured off Meredith's body. "But *you* receive those benefits," she managed.

"Yes, but she is the conduit. My taking what flows into her from the adnexus is optional. The backlash of the breaking will hit her alone."

Valkyrie wasn't sure why he offered the last bit of information—it hadn't been a question, so she didn't think Meredith had compelled the answer—until she felt Meredith's Aspect flicker and falter. She might not have used her power to force the answer, but testing its veracity had drained the last of her Aspect.

Valkyrie didn't have time to shout a warning, doubted Meredith could have run even if she had. Elijah surged to his feet. His power crested like a tidal wave and he backhanded her with enough Battle Aspect to send her flying six feet across the room. She slammed into an armchair and dropped, instantly unconscious.

At least, Valkyrie prayed she was only unconscious, but she couldn't risk going to check. Elijah moved toward the fallen woman, his eyes hot pools of rage, and if he got to her, Meredith would never wake up again. Valkyrie pivoted and stepped, the short sword in her right hand lunging for his exposed middle.

She hadn't expected the strike to land, and it didn't. He pulled the long knife from its shoulder sheath in a movement so practiced and graceful it was almost invisible. He parried and leapt back before the strike from her other sword landed.

It was the movement of a man who knew precisely where he was positioned in a room. He dove over the back of the couch, rolled, and came up with a short sword in the hand that had been empty.

Valkyrie did not immediately press after him. The parlor was an atrocious space for a fight. She couldn't go three feet in any direction without hitting a piece of furniture. She'd known she would likely fight him somewhere inside the house, had chosen short swords because the length of a long sword made swinging one in an object-cluttered room practically impossible. All she would do was hit furniture, herself, or otherwise aim strikes that had none of the necessary momentum to cause real damage.

The shorter length of her chosen weapons meant fewer things to avoid when she struck, but it also meant the necessity of getting closer to Elijah to land a strike. Additionally, a one-handed weapon couldn't hit with the same force she could deliver with a two-handed blade. Any advantage Battle Aspect gave her in an ordinary fight was more or less nullified by the fact Elijah's Battle Aspect was the equal of her own.

Or...was it?

He had always been larger than life, to her. An immovable force. A mountain the rocks of which were too steep and jagged to climb. A monster too vicious to slay. She had always known she couldn't kill him, because to kill him was to kill herself. And somehow, that knowledge had translated itself into the belief that he was better than her.

A better fighter. Better at his Aspect use. Smarter. More strategic.

That's bullshit, she could almost hear Random say, *and you fucking know it.*

Elijah wasn't *better* than her. That belief was predicated on her fears, on the fact that at one point she had been a child, and vulnerable, and he had chained her before she could grow into her power. So that by the time she *had* grown into it, she hadn't realized how much of it she possessed.

He had trained her, and she had never been good enough. Even when she'd bested him in sparring matches, she had always been *not good enough. Sloppy technique,* he would tell her with a sneer. *A lucky hit. I left that side wide open and how long did it take you to land a strike?*

Six months before her Academy trials, he had stopped sparring with her altogether. He had told her she was as good as he could make her, in a voice that implied she was an utter waste of his time. She'd been so relieved at the fact that his giving up on instructing her meant she had to spend less time with him that she hadn't given much consideration to the fact that, in the month prior, she had won every single one of their sparring matches.

She gave it thought now. Realized that, though he stood six feet from her, condescension and arrogance written in every line of his face, it was not the belief in his superiority that made him stand and wait for her to make the next move. It was uncertainty.

He didn't know who would win this fight. He didn't know if she would be willing to destroy herself if it meant taking him down with her.

Elijah Winters was afraid. Of *her*.

A wide, vicious grin spread across Valkyrie's face, and she launched herself at him.

CHAPTER

EIGHTEEN

Valkyrie scored another cut along Elijah's side, felt the answering drain in her body as he pulled from her to close it over. She couldn't continue this much longer. Already her body dragged with lassitude as the injuries she inflicted on Elijah took their toll on her own body.

It had taken what seemed like eons to wear him down even to this point. He might delight in the opportunity to use his wounds to weaken her, but his vanity had refused to allow him to take hits needlessly.

She had not sparred with him in over a decade and his style, though the same at its core, bore small differences. He'd rid himself of many of the weak points she'd once exploited, had gained a few new tricks that necessitated quick response.

But he had not fought as often as she had in that time period. And though his connection to the Council's adnexus, to her, allowed him to heal his injuries, it did not grant him eternal youth, or endless stamina. He was just past fifty years old and she had pressed him hard in the beginning, landing strikes that would have been fatal—to both of them—had he not blunted or turned them aside through Battle Aspect.

He could kill her at any moment by allowing one of those

fatal blows to land, but she knew him. His arrogance wouldn't allow him to let himself be bested. He didn't *want* her dead—he wanted her back under his control. Wanted her to submit, to beg him for mercy, to finally yield to him.

She would never yield. So she'd struck and spun until he'd spent his Aspect enough that her blade started tasting flesh instead of shield. He wouldn't have spent his power entirely—he wasn't reckless enough to leave himself with no defenses. No, he would have held a quiet reserve, waiting for her to spend her own power to the dregs, and then he would make his move.

It was the playbook he had taught her. He simply seemed to think she hadn't learned the lesson well enough. But she had. Her own Aspect shields dimmed as he landed hits—some genuine hits, others she intentionally allowed—until she quit shielding altogether, and his cuts drew blood.

She felt the quiet triumph in him, felt his certainty that he had won and only needed another opening to ensure his victory. She let him press her back, to maneuver her into a corner. Without her Aspect, and with as much as he'd pulled from her body to heal himself, it was almost a guaranteed victory for him.

She let herself falter and gave him an opening. He took it, his short sword aimed in a thrust at her wide-open left side. Valkyrie's Aspect snapped into place around her, coated her from head-to-toe in full Battle armor. She didn't have enough power left to maintain it for long, but she only needed it for a few seconds. She dropped the dagger in her left hand and used that arm to block, sweeping under the blade as Elijah thrust, diverting the strike upward.

At the same time, she pivoted, using her weight and momentum to slam him into the wall. She thrust the short sword in her right hand forward. It impaled him through the stomach, sliced through flesh and muscle to pin him to the wall.

His fingers went nerveless, dropping the blades in his hands, and he clutched for the sword in his stomach. Valkyrie drew his right arm away, held it to the wall, and pulled one of her daggers. She plunged it through his palm into the plaster, drew a second dagger and secured his left arm the same way.

He moved as if to shove himself off all three blades. She scrambled for the hilt of the short sword and held it into him, held him pinned. Her vision wavered as he spun her body's energy from her, took it into himself to staunch the flow of blood from his stomach, to stave off the death due him.

"Do you truly think you can hold me here?" Elijah spat through a mouthful of blood. "Every second I stay on this sword is a second you come closer to death. You cannot win this, daughter."

"I am *not* your daughter."

A grotesque smile spread across his face. "Oh, but you are." Aspect twisted around his body. His face flickered and morphed, became Danvers' for a moment before it resumed the likeness of Elijah's.

Her legs almost gave out, a combination of her life dripping slowly from her body and the truth she fought hard not to accept. The man before her *was* Elijah. The Battle Aspect he'd used, the way he'd fought, and the strength that even now flowed from her to him proved that beyond all doubt.

But the illusion Aspect that had changed his face seconds before—*that* had come from him as well. She remembered, back to what seemed like lifetimes ago, meeting Danvers at Savado's and thinking his movements looked familiar. She had explained Danvers' intimate knowledge of her life by accepting that Elijah had worked with him. But even then, some part of her had known that it didn't add up, that he knew *too* much even for that explanation.

She remembered Ella's words as she stood in Random's kitchen. *"Danvers? You really don't know, do you?"* And Ella—Ella would have. Ella, who could read a person's lineage with a touch, who had read Valkyrie's in Random's living room, would have known beyond all doubt that Elijah Winters was not Valkyrie's adoptive father, but her biological one.

She should have put it together before now—the pieces had all been there—but she hadn't, hadn't even considered it. Because it meant—it meant…

"You raped my mother," she whispered. But that wasn't the worst part. No, the worst part was that he'd done that, and then he'd taken on a different face and he'd pretended to "rescue" Evelyn, to love her. He'd tortured and used her and then he'd shared a home with her for the rest of her life in some mockery of a family, and for what? Because Valkyrie was the result of that experiment?

Elijah's face twisted into a snarl. "*Danvers* did that."

"You're the same person." Her voice was raw, savage.

He shook his head. He was agitated in a way she'd never seen him. "I created Danvers to do what needed to be done, to do the things that don't fit in society. *I* loved Evelyn."

He honestly believed it. She saw it in his face, in the fervent light in his eyes. Elijah Winters was legitimately, full-on psychotic. He'd put on a different face, built an identity around it, and thought it somehow absolved him of the sins he committed in that body. That Danvers wasn't truly *him*.

Another, worse thought occurred to her. "Tell me she didn't know. Tell me she never found out." If her mother had ever *known* what she lived with…

"No. I made certain she never found out about Jace, either."

The room seemed to stiffen and contract around her. She could barely stand. Moisture fled her body as Elijah drained her to stay alive, the skin around her knuckles cracking and splitting open. She needed to retrieve the adnexus, to end this, but she couldn't make herself move. She needed to know, *had* to know. "What *about* Jace?"

"Your mother didn't like to be left alone. But there were things I needed to take care of, things I couldn't entrust to others. Things I needed months to accomplish." He choked, coughed up a mouthful of blood and spat it out. "So I left my brother in my place. He shared my talent for illusion, so she never knew the difference. But he tired of it. He knew she wanted another child. Knew that it would kill her, eventually, to have one. So he gave it to her so he could be done with the charade.

"And by the time I found out, it was too late to make her abort it."

Valkyrie tried to process the information, what it meant, and found she couldn't. Her thoughts were slow and muddled, and she had the strangest sensation that her body was shutting down piece by piece, like a long hallway in which the lights were being turned off one by one.

Chills wracked her. She shivered, unable to control them, her body shaking so hard she clenched her teeth to keep them from rattling.

"I thought," Elijah smiled, "that would get your attention for long enough." He strained forward, using his body to work the swords and daggers from the wall.

Valkyrie stumbled back, the room spinning and spinning as she fought to stay upright—and failed. Her legs buckled and she went down.

RANDOM WOKE with the certainty that something was wrong. He reached for Valkyrie, only to find the other side of the bed empty. Cold.

His pulse pounded in his ears, his Aspect a soft echo alongside it. A worried echo. It was, he thought, what had woken him up. He was used to his Aspect waking him up for her—when she wasn't eating enough, wasn't sleeping enough. It would push and push at him until he gave up and drove to her house to fix whatever was wrong.

This was...different. His Aspect was still worn down to almost nothing from the teleport, but it was insistent within him, urging him up. He rolled out of bed and got dressed. He turned the lights on and swept through the house, hoping to find her in each room he checked and knowing he wouldn't.

He'd seen the look in her eyes when he'd asked her not to shut him out again and he'd known that whatever she had planned next, she intended to keep him from it. He'd *known* and he'd let her distract him anyway. Because he'd wanted that softer side of herself she'd offered him in that moment. Because he'd thought he had time. That he would wake up next to her and convince her to tell him whatever it was she still hid.

Only when he'd cleared the house, when he knew she wasn't there, did he think to check the bookshelf. Gone. The box was gone.

Shit. Idiot. He was a complete, flaming idiot.

He grabbed his phone and dialed her number even as he ran for his car. His Aspect burned with painful intensity behind his chest, regenerating at an uncomfortably fast rate it had only seen fit to do a handful of times in his life. There was a reason Aspect regenerated at a steady rate, over several days: like building muscles, or growing new blood cells, it required fuel and energy to accomplish the process. To replenish it faster meant it took from his body what it needed, burning any available energy and fat stores to convert one kind of energy into another. If it ran out of those, it tore into his muscles.

He didn't *have* much available fat at the moment. Fine time to wish he'd eaten more of his own cooking.

He slid into the car and twisted the keys. The engine barely had time to catch before he slammed it in drive and raced for the road that led to the Winters' estate, where his Aspect assured him he would find her.

He tried not to think about how the last time he'd driven this car, she'd been here next to him. Tried not to wonder if she ever would be again.

His phone clicked, sending him to Valkyrie's voicemail for the sixth time in a row. On a hunch, he called Meredith. When *she* didn't answer the cold dread that had been steadily building inside him evolved into something stronger, something darker. Meredith was *never* without her phone, and she was pathologically incapable of not answering it.

He pulled up to the massive gate that guarded the Winters' grounds, only to find that the code he'd used the entire time he'd known Jace and Valkyrie no longer worked. He reversed ten feet, put the car back in drive, and floored it. Metal screeched against metal and the car busted the wrought iron gates wide open. The estate's wards reached for him but his Aspect slipped him sideways through them, as if he passed through a viscous liquid that closed back around him once he was through.

His heart pounded in his chest, only grew worse when he reached the circular drive and saw Meredith's and Valkyrie's vehicles already there. He parked behind the Jeep and ran to the front door. He paused at it for the briefest moment to listen, but his Aspect gave no indication that a trap waited. It simply urged him on with that steady, burning certainty that he needed to hurry.

Inside, his Aspect tugged him right, toward the front parlor room he'd never seen any of the Winters actually use. Meredith lay prone on the far side of the room. He saw her chest rise and fall, knew she lived, and gave his attention wholly over to the wall where Valkyrie had Elijah impaled on a sword, his hands pinned to the wall with two daggers like some modern crucifixion scene.

Random didn't need his Aspect hammering behind his chest to tell him something was wrong. He saw it in Valkyrie's posture, in the pallidness of her skin. In the shock on her face. Elijah strained against the blades, as if he'd rip them all the way through his body to free himself.

Valkyrie fell back.

Random *moved*, jumping over broken furniture, and caught her. Elijah let out a snarl of rage and Random freed one hand to slam it against Elijah's chest, pushing him back against the wall to hold him immobile. The more Elijah moved, the more he damaged himself—and Valkyrie.

"Kyrie, love?" Random tried to keep the panic from his voice and failed. She was cold as fresh snow against him, her skin dry and brittle, and her heart beat like a hummingbird's, too fast and too shallow.

"Random?" She sounded dazed.

"Kyrie, what do I do?" He needed her to tell him, because there had to be an answer. One that didn't end with her dying in his arms.

At the sound of her name she stirred. Her legs took on a little more of her weight. She shook herself, like a dog that had smelled something bad and was trying to rid its nose of the scent. "Just—" She gasped in a breath, the sound rattling through her lungs like wind through dry leaves. "Hold him."

She pushed off him, fell twice as she stumbled to the coffee table and the box that lay atop it. She dropped beside them, her eyes half-lidding closed, and took the box in both hands. "Let him go and get out of the way."

He did as she asked, moved out of the line of sight between her and Elijah. He told himself it would be fine. She had an answer, she *had* to have an answer. She grasped the lid of the box, tore it open, and smiled at him. "I'm sorry," she said.

No.

It took less than a second for his Aspect to move him to her side. It wasn't fast enough. He appeared next to her just as her fingers ripped a ring from the scepter that lay inside the box. An invisible line of force drew taught between Valkyrie and the box, as if a rubber band connected them and was being stretched to its limit.

Valkyrie clenched her fingers around the ring. The band snapped. She slammed the box closed as a tidal wave of howling power crashed onto her—and hit the same odd shield she'd used against Danvers in the parking lot outside Savado's. Any ordinary shield would have fractured under the onslaught of power that raged against her. But he'd felt how this shield worked, knew it didn't try to absorb the impact but redirect it.

Hope flared in his chest. This shield didn't need to be strong enough to withstand the adnexus' rebound, only strong enough to send it at a new target—at Elijah.

But Valkyrie didn't have that much strength left. Her Aspect flickered and guttered like a dying candle. He slid behind her and wrapped his arms around her, wrapped his Aspect around her, and offered her everything he had.

He just needed her to take it.

VALKYRIE HAD KNOWN she didn't have enough left in her to hold the shield. She'd tried anyway. From the moment Elijah had told her that breaking the adnexus wasn't an instant death sentence, that death instead came by way of magical backlash, the idea of using the shield had formed in her mind. She'd known she would have a split-second, between the breaking and the repercussions, to deflect her death.

She hadn't expected to be this drained by the end of the fight —wouldn't have been, if she hadn't been so taken off guard by Elijah's words about Jace, if she hadn't needed to know. But even if she had broken the adnexus immediately after impaling Elijah, she didn't think it would have mattered.

The force that battered her was immense. Unfathomable. Her tattered reserves had barely managed to form the shield at all. Only the look on Random's face when she'd told him she was sorry, the utter desolation in his eyes, made her grit her teeth and hold the shield. Only his voice, echoing in her head, made her cling grimly to consciousness.

Don't ask me to wake up one morning without you, wondering if I could have changed everything if I'd had all the information.

For those words, for the pain her death would cause him, she tried. If she kept going, she'd spend her Aspect down to the last dregs and join the ranks of the Broken. Of course, she would be dead a second later, so her inclusion would be short-lived.

Random's arms wrapped around her. She hadn't seen him move across the room. He pulled her close, the warmth of his body a hot brand against the ice she had become.

He needed to let her go. To leave. She had only seconds before her Aspect failed, before she passed out and the backlash consumed her. If he was touching her when that happened…

She opened her mouth to order him to leave, but the words wouldn't come. She didn't think her mouth even actually opened. Her body was a numb, unresponsive husk she could no longer feel.

Then Random's Aspect enveloped her. It brushed against the fading spark of her own, seeking permission, as she had done with him at StellaMia's. She understood, then, that he wouldn't leave. Even if she could somehow get her mouth to work, to warn him, he wouldn't leave her.

If she wanted him to survive, *she* had to survive, had to hold the shield. To hold it, she needed power.

Valkyrie opened herself to him completely. His Aspect inundated her, twined against her own, melded with it, until she no longer knew where hers ended and his began. They were simply one force, one being.

Her shield blazed into brilliantly renewed life as Aspect patched the weak edges and gaps. The harshness of the scepter's assault faded, like stepping from brutal desert sun into cool, inviting shade.

Valkyrie leaned back against Random, let his body bolster hers, let his strength sustain her, and she held the shield. Held it, until the last of the adnexus's backlash dissipated, until the haze cleared from the air and she saw the charred remains of Elijah's body still pinned to the wall.

"Kyrie?" Those two syllables, spoken with raw need and desperation, were the last things she heard before the darkness dragged her under.

NINETEEN

"Kyrie." Random didn't know how long he held her, repeating her name over and over again, willing it to wake her. His Aspect, still entwined with hers, and the pulse beating faintly in her throat were the only things that kept him clinging to sanity.

But the pulse beneath his fingertips grew fainter each time it beat, and no matter how he much he willed his Aspect to *do* something, it didn't. It couldn't. For all the myriad uses it could adapt itself to, Life Aspect had always been outside his reach.

He wasn't Siren.

He thought he was hallucinating when a moment later, as if his thoughts had conjured her, footsteps sounded in the room. His gaze jerked to the doorway and there she stood, like a five-foot-five, red-haired desert mirage.

"Siren?" He didn't know how she was here, and he didn't care. All he cared about was that she took one look at them and ran to Valkyrie's side, Aspect limning the hands she put to Valkyrie's face and abdomen.

All color blanched from Siren's already pale skin. "Your Aspect," she said, "whatever you do, don't let go of her."

"I won't." He couldn't if he tried. Wasn't sure he would ever be able to let go of her again. He cradled her body in his arms, held the fragile, lingering spark of her Aspect within the well of his own power, and prayed to a goddess he didn't believe in.

A second set of footsteps—Jace's—came from the doorway. Random had been too concerned about Valkyrie, too relieved Siren was here, to wonder where Jace had been. He stood in the doorway and took in the scene—Valkyrie in Random's arms, Siren's power flooding into her—and fear lit his eyes.

"Is she—" Jace didn't finish the question, couldn't seem to make himself finish it. Random didn't answer.

It was Siren, a full two minutes later, who opened her eyes and said, "She'll live."

Random and Jace exhaled twin breaths of relief.

"But she isn't going to wake up any time soon. Possibly not for a few days. You can pull your Aspect back," Siren said to Random. "She'll be all right without it."

But he didn't. He couldn't. He needed the feel of hers, however shallow, twined with his own.

Jace looked from his unconscious sister to the charred body on the wall, and finally to Random. "What the hell happened?"

Random couldn't bring himself to meet his friend's gaze. He'd promised Jace he would keep Valkyrie safe and instead she'd almost died, would have died, if Siren hadn't walked in at precisely the right moment. How were they *here* when they were supposed to be in Ireland? And how could he hope to explain any of this?

More importantly, they needed to leave the Winters' estate. Now, before—

A dry, choking noise came from the doorway. "Oh, dear goddess." Martin DuPont stared at the body on the wall, turned around, and vomited. Kara, Julian, Aunt Ella, and Theo entered after him.

Instead of falling apart like their figurehead, Kara and Julian unleashed twin torrents of power. They were Immobilizers, their Aspect inducing paralysis in those it touched. But instead of touching anyone, their Aspect fetched up against a wall of brilliant white power, so bright it stung the eyes.

Siren stood, her eyes glowing with the same white flame as the barrier she held in front of them. Turning Aspect use visible was a conscious choice, and Siren was making a statement with hers. "I am getting very tired of doing this with you people," she said, her voice deceptively soft and melodic. "We had an agreement. Don't come after me and mine, and I will leave you alone."

The Council feared her, and with good reason. She'd spent the first twenty-two years of her life with her Aspect largely inaccessible to her, trapped behind an internal cage of Danvers' making. When the dam had finally burst, she'd held so much Aspect it had nearly killed her. But she had survived, and the Council's response to the trauma she'd suffered had been to be so afraid of what she might do with the unprecedented amount of Aspect at her disposal that they'd tried to lock her away.

She'd manipulated them into publicly admitting that she had done nothing wrong, and they had come to a tense cease-fire, in which they agreed to leave her and everyone she loved alone, and she agreed not to annihilate them.

"The scope of that agreement does not include immunity from the repercussions of theft and murder," Kara said icily. "No amount of power makes you or anyone else above the laws of this society."

It was the most hypocritical thing Random had heard in a long, long time. He didn't know if it was the statement alone, or it combined with the constant stress of the last few days and the fact he'd just held the woman he loved in his arms while she lay dying, but he laughed. Once he started, he couldn't seem to stop.

"You find that amusing, Tremayne?" Kara asked.

"I find it hilarious." He eased himself out from under Valkyrie and rested her gently against the side of the sectional. He picked up the box that held the Council's adnexus, and walked to stand next to Siren. "Hilarious," he repeated, "but delightful. I'm *so* pleased the Council understands that *no* amount of power is above the law. Do you know what the Aspect Charter says in relation to the use of blood magic?"

No one answered. "Allow me to enlighten you. 'Reasonable suspicion of blood magic use shall be punishable by the offender's immediate removal from any positions of influence within Aspect Society pending trial. Proof of blood magic use may be punishable by death'."

He looked to Siren and lifted the box. "You told Valkyrie you could destroy the adnexus ties without killing anyone. How confident are you about that?"

"Extremely."

"Good." He turned back to the Council. "Let me explain what is going to happen. As of this moment, you are all relieved of the burden of your office. You will undergo a very lengthy, very public, trial. You will spend the time leading up to that trial in your own holding cells. If you are very, very lucky, you may not die."

"You don't have the authority," Kara spat. "Do you honestly believe you can convince our own security to arrest us?"

"He won't have to." Aunt Ella, who had watched everything up to now with an air he recognized as detached resignation, now drew the gaze of every other member of the Council, including DuPont, who had finally decided to stop retching and pay attention. "I'll do it for him."

"And you will have my full support," Theo said, stepping forward to stand next to her.

Julian looked at the two of them, anger and incredulity written in every line of his face. "What the hell are you two playing at?"

Random couldn't help but wonder the same thing. Clearly, his aunt had expected some version of what was happening now. She was an intelligent woman—once she'd agreed to help Valkyrie, she would have made preparations. He'd just thought those preparations would have involved leaving town, not putting her own Council under lock and key. Whatever she'd decided, it appeared she'd involved Theo in those plans, as the man didn't look any more surprised by what was happening than she did.

"You understand," Random told them, "that your cooperation in this matter will not earn you preferential treatment. That you will be subject to the same restrictions, holdings, and trial as the rest of the Council?"

It hurt him. Aunt Ella had been more of a mother to him than his own ever had. She had raised him, she had loved him, and right now he wanted to grab her by the shoulders and shake her until she explained *why* she had involved herself in this madness. What could have possessed her to agree to being bound via the adnexus when she didn't even *like* being a part of the Council?

He couldn't understand why Theo had, either. Aside from Aunt Ella, Theodore was the only other member of the Council Random could stomach, the only other one who'd ever seemed like a decent human being.

"We understand," Theo said.

"If you think we're just going to stand here," Kara began, "and let you—" Kara dropped to the ground. DuPont and Julian followed suit a second later.

A pleased smile stretched across Siren's face. She turned to Aunt Ella and Theo. "I trust neither of *you* need an extended nap?"

"No, dear," Aunt Ella replied. Then she turned to him. "Random—"

He shook his head. "I don't want to hear it right now." He *couldn't* hear it right now. It was all he could do to keep it together while they waited for Council security to arrive. Siren woke Meredith, a liberal application of Life Aspect healing what had apparently been a spectacular concussion and some internal bleeding.

Random hovered by Valkyrie's side. Despite Siren's assurances that Kyrie was fine and just needed to sleep for a day or ten, he didn't think he would be capable of calming down until she opened her eyes. She would hate lying here, unconscious, vulnerable, in a room full of people.

Through it all, he avoided looking at his best friend. So far, Jace had been remarkably patient. The kind of patient he was when he understood that now wasn't the right time for an argument, but he had every intention of jumping at the right time the moment it appeared.

When the Council's security finally arrived, Random put on his bureaucratic face and went through the tedious necessity of explaining the letter of the law, calmly and efficiently, to people whose job had always consisted of serving the Council, never arresting them. For all his talking, it only took one smile from Aunt Ella to snap their mouths shut. They handcuffed everyone and left.

Random turned back to Valkyrie and found Jace in his path.

"What the hell is going on? Why is my sister almost dead, what's in that damn box, why and how did we just arrest the entire Council, and who the hell did Valkyrie crucify on the wall and burn to a crisp?"

Random looked past Jace to where Valkyrie slumped against the couch, unconscious. She wouldn't want him to tell Jace. Not about Elijah. But there was no explaining any of this without telling him. And whatever Kyrie might want, she hadn't left him much choice. She certainly hadn't respected what *he* had wanted.

It was Siren who gave him the out. "Does Elijah have something to do with the fact her left hand was broken in fifteen places when she was twelve? Or that her nose has been broken six times? Or the litany of other things I could list off?" She was practically incandescent with fury, with the knowledge of Valkyrie's history that healing the woman had given Siren.

Random forced himself to meet Jace's stunned eyes and said, "Yes." Then he summarized the massive absurdity that had been the last two days. The look on Jace's face when Random explained, as tactfully as he could, what Elijah had done to Valkyrie was...he'd only seen his friend look like that once before, when Siren had been abducted and they hadn't known if she was still alive.

But Jace didn't interrupt. When Random got to the point in the story of waking up and realizing Kyrie was gone, he handed the explanations off to Meredith.

She filled them in on what had happened between his house and them coming to the estate. "Once we arrived here, well..." Her gaze landed on the coffee table where her phone sat, miraculously unharmed amidst the wreckage of the rest of the room. She retrieved it and said, "I guess you can listen for yourselves." She hit play on a recording and turned up the volume.

They listened, and then they sat without speaking for a few minutes while the recorded sounds of steel hitting steel drifted from the phone. Meredith finally reached out to shut the recording off, but paused when Elijah's voice filtered out.

They listened and listened as the darker truths emerged from Elijah's lips. Siren wrapped her arms around Jace, who stared at the phone with a vacant expression. When Random's own voice came on, begging Kyrie to tell him what to do, how to help, Random reached over and turned the recording off. He didn't ever want to sound like that again. He didn't ever want to *feel* like that again. He stood, walked to Valkyrie, and lifted her into his arms.

Jace broke from his trance. "What are you doing?"

"Getting her the fuck out of this house. I don't ever want to see her in here again."

Random braced himself for an argument. Jace might have given Random his blessing to date Valkyrie at his and Siren's wedding, but that had been before. Before this mess. Before she'd almost died on his watch. He wouldn't blame Jace for never wanting to see Random around her again.

But when his friend opened his mouth he just said, "Take her to our place. There's plenty of room for you to stay, and I want her where Siren can make sure she's okay."

Random gave a short, sharp nod. He hugged Valkyrie to him, savored the soft, steady thump of her heartbeat against him, and carried her out.

CHAPTER

TWENTY

The first thing Valkyrie realized upon waking was that nothing hurt. The second was that she only wore her underwear and a tank top. She realized the latter because she'd flown out of the bed she was in the second her eyes opened, and the air conditioning from the floor vent beneath her bare feet was kissing cold air up her thighs.

Siren and Meredith stood on the opposite side of the room. Siren dramatically slow-clapped. Meredith said, "Top points on speed and form considering you've been unconscious for a week, but I'm going to have to ding you for your choice of weapon. It lacks originality."

Valkyrie looked down. Her right hand clutched a lamp. A familiar, ocean blue lamp. She was in Siren's house, in the guest bedroom she always used whenever Siren convinced her to stay over.

"How did you know she'd dive right instead of left?" Meredith asked Siren in a faux-conspiratorial whisper.

"It's the most strategically defensible side of the room."

"But she was unconscious. She didn't even know where she was."

Siren shrugged. Valkyrie deliberately replaced the lamp on

the bedside table. She stared at her fingers as they uncurled from the base, hardly able to believe they were functioning. That *she* was functioning. She was pretty certain she should be dead, and she couldn't for the life of her remember why.

"What's the last thing you remember?" Siren asked gently. Too gently. The kind of care a person used when something unspeakable had happened and they wanted to soften the blow.

Valkyrie's head snapped up, every muscle in her body stiffening. Her heart slammed against her chest, adrenaline roaring through her. "Random?"

"He's fine," Siren said quickly. "He's not hurt."

Valkyrie's legs gave out and she dropped onto the bed as relief tore through her. Random was fine.

Why had she thought he wouldn't be? The last thing she remembered was making love to him, watching him fall asleep before—before she'd left. It came back, then. All of it. Stealing the adnexus. Fighting Elijah. Understanding who Elijah *was*. Understanding she was going to die.

Then Random holding her, his power inundating her, strong and steady, letting her hold out long enough to finish what she needed to finish. He'd held her, he'd given her everything, and now he wasn't here. Her heart squeezed inside her chest. "Where is he?"

"He's barely left this room since we brought you here. Jace had to go to his house and pack his clothes for him, and I've had to force him to eat," Siren said, not answering the question. She hesitated, then pressed on. "You should have woken up two days ago. You were *ready* to wake up two days ago."

"And?" Valkyrie asked.

"And I finally had to lie to Random and tell him I was absolutely certain you wouldn't wake up in the next hour and force him to go to the store with Jace. Supposedly for the sake of his health. You woke up the second he got far enough away for his Aspect to disentangle from yours."

"You think I was avoiding him? In my *sleep*?"

"It is a very *you* thing to do," Meredith offered. "I'm all right too, by the way. Thanks for asking."

Valkyrie dragged her mind off the ridiculous assertion that she'd been subconsciously avoiding Random by *sleeping*, and scrounged up a modicum of human decency. "I'm really glad you're okay."

Meredith's hand went to her heart and her eyes fluttered wide open. "Is this genuine care? For me? I'm touched."

Valkyrie rolled her eyes. "Don't let it go to your head." She looked around the room again, looked at Siren and Meredith again, and frowned. None of this was right. "How are you here?" she asked Siren. "Shouldn't you still be in Ireland? And why am I not in a holding cell?"

"You're not in a holding cell," Meredith answered, "because I was totally right. You banging a lawyer was an excellent plan for not going to jail. Random pointed out that the Council had broken their own laws and used the Aspect Charter to suspend them from office pending a very public trial that starts tomorrow."

Valkyrie frowned. "And that worked?"

"Well, Aunt Ella did throw her lot in with him and convinced Council security to arrest them all. As for you not immediately going to jail, there was a sizable power gap after the Council's arrest. Apparently they're so arrogant there's nothing in the Aspect Charter about who power shifts to should the entire Council be out of commission.

"That gave Random enough time to brand your theft of the adnexus as a public service to Aspect Society, and to irrevocably prove that Elijah was Danvers. Trust me, honey, no one was putting you in jail after *that* shit came to light."

"And I'm here," Siren began, folding her arms across her chest, "because Jace and I are not idiots. When Random called us—"

"He did what? He specifically promised not to."

"According to him, he specifically promised not to call Jace.

He did not agree not to talk to him. So he called me instead." Siren gave her a pointed look and added, "That's what you get for banging a lawyer. Especially *that* lawyer. So, anyway, he wouldn't really tell us anything, but he was being just weird enough we decided we should cut the honeymoon short. Then Charles called and suggested we might want to cut it as short as possible, so we moved up the flight."

Charles. Bloody Oracles.

"Good thing, too, or you would have been dead and there wouldn't have been a damn thing I could do about it." There was enough pain and censure in Siren's voice that it drove guilt right through Valkyrie.

"I'm sorry." She'd gone her entire life without apologizing and now it seemed to be all she was doing.

Siren let out an angry breath. "When I agreed not to tell Jace about the adnexus, you said you would wait for me. That once you had all the councilors' blood we would work out a plan together—preferably a legal one—and that we would tell Jace before we did anything."

"Did it cause problems between you?" Valkyrie felt like an idiot even asking. Of course it would have caused problems. If she'd ruined her friend's and her brother's relationship…

"He wasn't exactly thrilled with me. Fortunately, he is a reasonable man. Between the logic of me pointing out that stumbling onto your dirty secrets doesn't automatically give me the right to divulge them, and the fact that I too was pissed off at you, he magnanimously forgave me. The enthusiastic make-up sex helped."

"TMI," Valkyrie and Meredith said in unison. Siren seemed to remember that, of the other two women in the room, one was her husband's sister and the other was his ex-girlfriend, and that she had indeed given too much information.

"Sorry," Siren muttered. "Anyway, why *didn't* you wait for me to help with the adnexus?"

Valkyrie suddenly found the sheet bunched in her hands fascinating. "I needed to take care of it. I couldn't risk waiting."

"Because of Jace and Random?" Siren asked softly.

Valkyrie's gaze jerked accusingly to Meredith.

"What? It was all going to come out anyway."

"And you're an idiot if you think anything Elijah did would make us look at you differently," Siren said.

"But he wasn't just Elijah," Valkyrie said softly.

"Listen to me," Siren snapped, "because I'm only going to say this once. I don't care about your father *or* Jace's. I don't give a fuck whose DNA made either of you. You're my *family*."

Siren was just cracked enough in the head to believe that, too. To believe that lineage didn't matter. That Valkyrie hadn't been irreparably stained by the plague that had been Elijah Winters. But Valkyrie knew better. She was broken. Broken in places so deep inside herself she didn't know if she would ever heal. Knew that even if she did heal, she would never be normal.

She could keep it together well enough on the outside. She always had. She could be Jace's sister, and she could be Siren's and Meredith's friend. Because they didn't have to see all of her. She could hide the darker parts. They would never need to know how often she woke in the middle of the night screaming, a knife in her hand. They would never need to know that some days she was nothing more than an empty shell, habit and necessity carting her body from place to place on autopilot, no one really home.

But a lover would know. A partner would know. Who could see all of that—live with all of that—and still love her? Love someone that broken? And if Random could, would it even be fair to ask it of him?

Siren's head lifted, tilting to the side. "Jace and Random just passed through the perimeter wards."

But Valkyrie hadn't needed Siren to tell her that. Random's Aspect had reached for her the moment he came onto the property. She wanted to pull him into her, to feel his power alongside her own and believe that she would never be alone again.

But she understood what she was, understood that though the nightmare might be over, the fairytale was too. The reckoning simply hadn't come yet. Right now, Random was too concerned to see straight. But soon he would understand that she wasn't going to die and it would all catch up to him.

He had told her that what he needed—the *one* thing he needed—was for her to be honest with him. To not cut him out. To let him help her. And she had immediately done the opposite.

Maybe, if she told him *why* she'd done it—that she'd loved him too much to risk him—maybe he would forgive her. Take her back. Tell her they could work through it.

The problem was, she didn't deserve to be forgiven. And Random—he deserved better than her. All she'd done was take from him—his love, his support, his body. What had she ever given him in return?

You're nothing, Valkyrie. Nothing without me, Elijah—Danvers —whispered in the back of her mind. In that moment, she knew she would never be rid of that voice.

Nothing. *That's* what she had given Random. That's all she *had* to give him.

So although Random's Aspect reached for her, she didn't let him in. Because the only thing she could give him that would make his life better was a life without her in it.

RANDOM COULDN'T THINK. He could barely breathe. Awake. She was awake. His Aspect had reached for her when Jace pulled into the drive, and instead of feeling the sleepy, quiet fog that had been his steady companion the last week, he'd felt *her*. Awake and vibrant and crackling with energy.

He barely managed words, barely waited for Jace's truck to

roll to a halt before he jumped out of the cab and tore into the house. He was just to the foot of the stairs when glacial walls descended around Valkyrie's Aspect and blocked him out.

He stumbled and caught himself on the balustrade. It felt like she'd severed one of his limbs. The rejection was so cold, so thorough, that for a moment he couldn't believe it had come from her. Not after everything they'd been through.

Dread replaced anticipation.

Siren had sent him off with every assurance that Kyrie wouldn't wake up while he was gone, had practically forced him out the door. He'd finally agreed to go because she wouldn't stop hounding him, and because she was never *this* wrong about something.

Bitterness coated his tongue. Siren had known that if he left, Kyrie would wake up. Apparently, the only thing the love of his life needed to get better was his absence.

He stopped trying to reach her with his Aspect and cleared the stairs to her room. Meredith took one look at his face, one look at Valkyrie's, and said, "Right. We'll just go." She grabbed Siren's hand and dragged her out, shutting the door behind them.

"You're awake," were the two brilliant words he managed to form.

"Yes," was Valkyrie's equally loquacious reply. The silence stretched out between them. She didn't fidget. She didn't give any indication that she was uncomfortable. She just stared at him, through him, as if he wasn't even there.

"That's it?"

"What do you want me to say?" she snapped, and there was a trace of *her* in the flash of anger in her eyes. He would take the anger over the emptiness.

"Something. *Anything.*" She didn't answer. "Tell me you're sorry. Tell me you want to work this out, tell me—"

"I'm not sorry." She cut him off. "And there's nothing to work out."

For a moment he just stared at her, dumbfounded. He'd thought a lot in the last week about what would happen when she woke up. He'd figured that after he finished reassuring himself that she was okay, they'd have a raging argument. She'd done precisely what he'd begged her not to—cut him out, left him behind—and she'd almost died because of it. He'd almost lost her.

So yeah, he'd figured they'd argue. She'd insist she'd done nothing wrong, that it was all to protect him, he'd tell her she didn't get to make those decisions for him, and they'd rail at each other until they met in the middle for some kind of under-standing. So they could move forward. Together.

But the woman he could have that argument with wasn't here. *Kyrie* wasn't here. Valkyrie Winters sat in her place, as silent and unfeeling as stone. It was as if everything that had happened between them in the two days she'd spent in his house had vanished. Every smile he'd coaxed from her, every truth she'd given him, every hint of *her* was gone now, hidden carefully beneath a shell of ice.

"I thought we were on the same page," he said finally. Why had she asked him about the house, asked him what he needed from her, if she hadn't had any interest in giving it to him? "I thought you wanted to try, I thought you wanted *us*."

She opened her mouth, shut it, shook her head. "I don't."

"Then what the hell were we doing together? What the hell were *you* doing?"

She shrugged. "I was off-balance. I needed a distraction and you were there. That's what you're good for, isn't it?"

Her words cut straight to that vulnerable part of him, the one built from every snide comment she'd ever made about his sex life, the part of him that had always feared she'd never think he was worth anything. Valkyrie had always known where to hit the hardest with him. Because it was easier for her to strike at him than it was for her to admit that he might matter.

"Bullshit. You asked me to make love to you. That's not what you say to someone when you want a fucking *distraction*. I get that this is new territory for you. I get that you're scared, but—"

"You don't *know* me, Random" she snapped. "You don't know how I feel, you don't know what I want."

"Then *tell me*. How do you feel, Kyrie? What do you want?"

"I feel like I made a mistake. And I want you to get out. Whatever you thought this was, it's done."

She was lying. He heard it in her voice. But for once, it wasn't him she was lying to. And he didn't think he could fix that. "You're wrong, you know," he said softly. "I *do* know you. I think you're the one who doesn't know yourself. I've waited a long time for you to figure it out. And I can wait longer. You've been through a lot. If you need time to deal with this without me, I'd understand. I can wait," he repeated, "if you ask me to. So ask me."

She didn't. Her hands went to her neck. She unclasped the necklace he'd given her and held it out to him. "You should take this back."

Invisible, skeletal fingers dug into his chest and twisted. He'd taken every hit she'd ever thrown at him, both literal and metaphorical. He'd fought to be worth something to her. He'd let her yo-yo his emotions back and forth because he'd thought he was getting through to her.

He stared at the black blade, at the sunlight reflecting off its dark surface. "Keep it," he said hoarsely. "Or throw it away. I don't care." He took a step toward the door and stopped, trying one last time. Because he'd been trying so long he didn't know how to stop. "I love you, Kyrie. But if you let me walk out this door right now, I'm done. *We* are done."

The last flicker of hope he held dwindled to an ember when she set her lips in a thin line. He turned and walked out, and when he crossed the threshold and she didn't try to stop him, that ember died too, leaving nothing but ash in its wake.

～

VALKYRIE HELD BACK until she heard the front door slam, until she heard Random's bike start, and then the sob tore out of her. She hadn't cried since her mother died. Tears were a weakness Elijah hadn't allowed. But what Elijah allowed or didn't allow no longer mattered. He was dead and he was never coming back.

But Random wasn't coming back either, and there was a raw, bloody hole in her chest where he'd been and it *hurt*. So she wrapped her arms around her legs, buried her face in her knees, and let herself cry for the first time in seventeen years.

She didn't know how long she was like that before Jace came into the room and sat next to her. She didn't look up, but she didn't need to in order to know it was him.

He was quiet for a few minutes before he said, "Want to tell me why you're crying and Random walked out of here looking like you gutted him?"

"No." She just wanted to go home. But she didn't *have* a home anymore. She wasn't sure she'd ever had one. She thought of Random's house, of the way sunlight played through the windows onto the dark interior colors and made it all feel warm and inviting. She thought of lying in his bed, his arms and legs tangled with hers. His soft, sleepy smile when he'd said, *I love you, Kyrie.*

Pain punched her right in the throat.

"Val…" Jace trailed off, taking a moment to collected his thoughts. He had always been like that. He could be quiet for days if that's how long it took him to figure out what he wanted to say about something. "Maybe this is none of my business. But you're my sister and he's my best friend. I'm pretty sure I know the two of you better than anyone else does. I know he's in love with you. And since I haven't seen you cry since Mom died, I'm guessing you feel the same way about him. So what happened?"

Valkyrie buried her face deeper in her knees and didn't answer. How could she? How could she tell him she'd intentionally broken Random's heart because it was the best thing for him? Jace had never hurt anyone like that. He'd never *had* to. Because he wasn't broken like her.

Jace sighed. "If you're not going to tell me, I'll just have to start guessing. Let's see, Random told you his secret dream is to be a rockstar and you told him you can't support that lifestyle?"

Oh no. Jace had decided to joke. He was almost as bad at it as she was.

"No? Okay, you want to sell off everything you own and donate it to charity, and Random was really hoping you'd be his sugar mama."

Had her little brother really just said the words 'sugar mama'? She groaned.

"He wants you to go vegetarian but you just can't live without steak."

She should not be on the verge of laughing right now, especially at Jace's pathetic attempts at humor. It was wrong on so many levels.

"You're pregnant and one of you doesn't want to keep it." She jerked her head up to glare at him. He grinned. "Thought that one might get your attention. Should I keep going or—"

"He's better off without me." There. She'd told him, and he could leave her alone to be miserable now.

"I'm sorry, what?"

"I can't make him happy, Jace." After that, the words wouldn't stop tumbling out. "I can't give him what he needs. I hear my monster of a dead father's voice in the back of my head all the time. I jump at fucking shadows. I barely sleep most nights, and on the ones I do I usually wake up swinging at something that isn't there." She dug her fingers into her knees. "I'm not worth it."

"That's complete bullshit, Val. And I have a hard time believing he wouldn't have told you the same thing." She didn't answer. Realization dawned on Jace's face. "Val, what did you actually say to him?"

She squeezed her eyes shut. But she figured he'd hear it from Random at some point, and she'd rather he heard it from her first. So she told him. She finished and he didn't answer. He didn't even look at her. "Say something."

"I don't think you want my opinion."

She probably didn't. "Tell me anyway."

"Fine. You're being an idiot. Are you a little fucked up? Definitely. But who wouldn't be in your situation? No one expects you to sweep this all under the rug like nothing happened and suddenly become a suburban housewife.

"Me, Siren, Meredith—we're all here for you. We all love you. We don't expect you to be perfect. But you can't keep pushing us away. Because if you do that, then it doesn't matter that you killed Elijah, because he's won. You survived a fucking nightmare, Val. Don't let him dictate your life from the goddamn grave."

Valkyrie opened her mouth, shut it. *No one expects you to be perfect*. She'd expected it of herself. Expected that Elijah's death would be some panacea that fixed everything, fixed *her*. That she would emerge from some metaphorical chrysalis and become something new, something he hadn't made.

But it didn't work like that. She was still the sum of her experiences. But she was also the sum of her responses to those experiences. *You survived a fucking nightmare, Val.*

She had. But it had taken Jace telling her that to make her truly see it. She'd done nothing but focus on her failures, her flaws, because that was all Elijah had drilled into her day in and day out.

But he was gone, and she was here. She'd protected the people who mattered to her. She was strong. She'd survived.

And she'd just made the biggest fucking mistake of her life.

If you let me walk out this door right now, I'm done. We are *done.*

Shit. "How do I fix this?" she whispered.

"I recommend honesty. And groveling."

"Can I borrow your truck?" She had to go after Random, had to find him before—just before.

Jace sighed, pulled the keys out of his pocket and handed them to her. "Try to bring it back in one piece."

She clutched the keys in her fist. "Thank you."

"Good luck. You deserve to be happy, Val. You both do."

CHAPTER

TWENTY-ONE

S omeone pulled the blinds up in Valkyrie's room, letting in a truly cruel amount of sunshine. She flung her arm over her eyes, shielding herself from the blinding brilliance.

"This has to stop," Siren said.

"It's pathetic," Meredith agreed. "It's been two weeks. As your friends, we are morally obligated to drag your ass out of bed."

"Try it," Valkyrie growled, "and I'll put you both on the floor."

"You're not as scary as you used to be," Meredith said sweetly. "It's hard to take threats seriously from a woman who's been lying in bed binge-eating Doritos, cupcakes, and beer for fourteen days."

Valkyrie removed her arm to glower at Meredith. It was a mistake, as the vicious sunlight made her squint. "I've never had a vacation in my life," she said defensively. "And I was never allowed to eat Doritos. Or cupcakes. Or have beer. I'm trying to live my best life."

"Then for goddess sake, try a different beer. Dos Equis is disgusting."

"I like it."

Meredith made a *hmph* noise and turned up her nose.

"And you?" Valkyrie said to Siren. "Anything you'd like to weigh in with?"

"Oh, I don't know, you two were doing such a good job, I felt superfluous. But since you mentioned it, yes, I'll second her command to get your ass out of bed."

"Why? What is the point?"

"This is so cute," Meredith snickered. "She never had her heart broken as a teenager so now she's getting to live all of its angsty joys out right now, complete with existential comments about the general pointlessness of life."

"Thank you for mocking me. Would it kill you to be nice to me? I am genuinely fucking miserable."

"We know, honey," Siren said. "We're here to fix it."

"You can't." Random was gone. She didn't know where he'd gone when he'd left her, but it wasn't anywhere in Seclusion. She'd driven the entire damn town twice. And he wouldn't answer her phone calls. She'd tried to prepare herself for the very real possibility that he wouldn't take her back. She hadn't considered that he might never give her the chance to explain anything at all.

He'd always been there when she needed him. He'd always taken her calls. And she hadn't realized how much she'd taken that for granted until he was suddenly gone.

She might have gone a little overboard with the number of times she'd called him, because he'd eventually blocked her number. She knew, because calls still went through from Siren's and Jace's phones. Not that he picked up when she called from their phones, either. And then Siren and Jace had suddenly become very conscious of where their phones were and she couldn't call at all.

She'd been certain Random would be spearheading the Council's trial, and had considered ambushing him after one of the hearings, but he hadn't been a part of them. Siren had gently pointed out that his aunt being on the Council, and Valkyrie being involved in Elijah's murder, were both conflicts of interest for him. Which was a gentle way of saying he didn't want to be involved with anything Valkyrie.

She hadn't even been able to dredge up enough emotional energy to care when the entire Council was definitively disbanded. Since they hadn't created the adnexus themselves—that creation belonging to the founding councilors a couple centuries dead—they weren't receiving the highest-possible punishment of death.

They weren't even going to jail. They *were* on a monitored probation that forbade them from leaving Seclusion, all were barred from ever holding office in Aspect Society again, and none of them would be released from holding until the adnexus had been destroyed. Something that would happen just as soon as Jace decided he'd run enough theoretical scenarios to reassure himself that his wife's plan to dismantle it wasn't going to kill her.

Since Aspect law had no contingency plan in place for a complete removal of the Council, a movement had gone through to vote in an interim figurehead to make decisions until a permanent choice was made on whether to vote in a new Council or change the power structure entirely.

Since it was a popular vote open to every member of Aspect Society, Siren had been elected as that figurehead, which surprised absolutely no one but her. Valkyrie had even managed to stop wallowing in her own misery long enough to cast a vote her sister-in-law's way. Goddess knew someone with common human decency needed to be in that position.

And what thanks did she get for that support? Siren had now taken time out of her busy schedule of meetings, dealing with bickering Aspect Society matrons, and reviewing every Aspect law on the books, to come hound Valkyrie and make her feel more miserable than she already did.

"Maybe we can't *fix it* fix it," Siren conceded, "but you are definitely not going to win Random back like this. When was the last time you even showered?"

"How should I know?"

"Up," Siren commanded. "Shower."

"You're not going to leave me alone until I do, are you?"

"Nope," Siren and Meredith chorused in unison.

"Fine. I'll shower. But don't expect any further miracles."

"Grace and benevolence, thy name is Valkyrie Winters," Meredith said.

"Oh, shove it, Mer."

"I'd shove *you*, but you might fall into the hazmat site that is this room and never be seen or heard from again."

Valkyrie flipped her off and disappeared into the bathroom.

VALKYRIE WAS IRRITATED to discover that showering made her feel better. She was equally irritated to find that the salad Siren presented her with upon emerging from that shower looked appetizing. Maybe she'd taken the Doritos a little too far. She accepted the salad and let Siren and Meredith lead her downstairs to the living room.

Who knew there was an entire world outside her room? She dropped onto the couch and dug into her food.

"I'm clean," she said around a mouthful of lettuce, "and I'm eating the damn salad. What more do you two want?"

"We're going to explain how this situation might be salvaged, but you require a great deal of background information you don't have." Siren picked up her laptop and turned on the television, which was mirroring her computer screen. The screen read, *How it Got Fucked Up and How it Got Fixed.*

"You made a PowerPoint? And you went with *that* title?"

Siren glared. "If you'd read any romance novels, you would know it's very common for one of the characters to fuck the relationship up seemingly beyond all repair."

"I read the damn romance novels you gave me."

"Skipping to the sex scenes doesn't count."

"How did you—"

"You asked for the smuttiest books I had and then returned all ten of them the next day, saying you'd finished. Some people might read that fast but you do not."

Valkyrie stabbed a piece of lettuce with her fork. "I am a technical reader. I needed to learn a new skill, so I read about it. Isn't that what self-starters are supposed to do?"

"Sure," Meredith said. "But you skipped half the lesson, and now you're going to get the summarized version."

What proceeded was a lengthy number of slides in which Siren had summarized the plot of romance novel after romance novel, followed by the promised how-it-got-fucked-up-and-how-it-got-fixed revelation. After the tenth one Valkyrie's brain hurt, and she'd secretly Googled *The Courtesan Duchess* on her phone to make sure Siren wasn't putting her on about woman-fakes-being-a-courtesan-to-achieve-pregnancy-by-her-husband being an actual book plot.

Finally, the slides were finished. Siren looked her in the eye, as if she were about to make a Very Important Point, and said, "This presentation is meant to help you figure out where you fall on the scale of fuck-uppery, so you can determine the required level of groveling and how you might manage it."

Valkyrie's remaining salad lost its appeal and she shoved it away from her. Amusing though the presentation had been, and secretly charmed though she was that her friends had taken the time out of their lives to make it, now that it was over she was just reminded of how depressed she was.

"Look, I understand that I am the asshole in this given scenario. I fucked it up. I get that. But you know what all of these resolutions have in common? Every time the asshole goes to make an apology, the person listens to them. Random won't talk to me. How am I supposed to fix anything if he won't talk to me? *You're* the one who said I had to stop calling him."

"If a man blocks your phone number, you are morally obligated to stop calling him. He clearly wanted some space."

"How am I supposed to give him space *and* fix things?"

Siren gave Meredith a look that said Valkyrie was a poor student, and clearly hadn't learned anything from their instruction. "Whatever you did, you're going to have to find a way to *show* him that if he gives you another chance it won't happen again. You need a final romantic gambit. Calling someone twenty times a day is not a final romantic gambit."

Valkyrie had no idea what such a gambit would be. But... "What if I come up with something and he still doesn't want me?"

Siren reached out and squeezed her hand. "Then you have to let him go. And Meredith and I will buy you ice cream for a week and watch all of your bad action movies."

Valkyrie dragged herself outside to the barn. The day after Random had left, Krissi had arrived at Siren's with the trailer and all four horses. She had guiltily refused to meet Valkyrie's gaze and only said that Random had asked her to bring the horses from his place to Siren's.

Siren had been taking care of them during Valkyrie's fit of self-indulgent convalescence, and she felt guilty when she stepped into the paddock and Azazel and Abbadon immediately descended on her, muzzles bumping her for attention. Lilith and Dagon, always more reserved than the younger two, wandered closer into her perimeter but didn't approach. Valkyrie scratched Abaddon's cheeks and the mare shoved her head into Valkyrie's chest.

Horses. Humanity didn't deserve them.

"What am I going to do girl?" she asked. "How do I fix this?"

Abbadon huffed out a breath and lipped at the hem of Valkyrie's shirt. "Don't nip," Valkyrie warned. Abbadon knew better but, like all horses, she liked to test her boundaries on occasion to see if they had shifted. Eventually, she got bored and her and Azazel went back to grazing.

Valkyrie settled onto the ground, leaned back against a fence post, and thought. Random had fought for her for over a year. She had said some unimaginably cruel things to him in that year and he'd never given up on her. But she hadn't let him *in* during that time. She hadn't let him bare his truths to her. She had hurt him with snide comments and feigned disinterest, but she hadn't been able to touch the core of him.

But during the time she'd stayed with him, he'd shared everything with her. Everything he wanted. Everything he dreamed of. The house he'd built for her. The house he'd said he wouldn't live in with anyone but her.

Then, after he'd waited by her bedside for a week, she'd woken up and told him she hadn't wanted it. Any of it. That she hadn't wanted him. And it had mattered more this time because she'd *known* with full certainty what she was doing to him.

All because she'd been scared. Scared, because she couldn't love herself so she didn't understand how anyone else could. Scared he'd leave her. Scared that if she admitted she might be able to have him, have something normal, it would vanish from her grasp. So she'd thrown it away and told herself it was for *his* benefit.

Goddess, she was an asshole. He probably couldn't stand to set foot in his own house because of her, and—

The pieces clicked together in her head, then. The house.

"What would you do if I didn't want it?"

"Sell it. I'd never live here with anyone but you."

She opened her phone, pulled up Zillow, and there it was. For sale. His house. Hers. *Theirs.*

She knew exactly what she needed to do.

CHAPTER

TWENTY-TWO

The house had sold. He should be relieved. No, he *was* relieved. Definitely relieved. He'd turned down multiple offers for no damn reason. Daniel had sent him the paperwork along with a mobile notary on the latest offer and told him point blank that if he didn't take this one, he could find a new realtor.

So he'd signed the damn papers. He hadn't even bothered to look at them. It was easy enough to tune out the notary as they droned on and just sign where they told him to. He hadn't cared who he sold the house to or how much they paid him. He'd just wanted it done, and now it was.

He paced the inside of his hotel room. He didn't know what city he was in, though he was vaguely certain he was somewhere in Ohio. Soon, he would have to pull himself together. He needed to go back to work—he'd tied up all of his current cases or shifted them to colleagues before allowing himself to sink into total self pity, but at the rate he was going he'd be lucky to have a practice to go back to.

Maybe he wouldn't go back. He'd moved away from Seclusion once before because of Valkyrie. There was no law that said he couldn't do it again. Except that the first time he'd left, he hadn't had her. He'd been able to bury himself in other women and pretend he didn't think of her.

He couldn't do that this time. Every woman he saw he just compared to her. Every time he considered bedding one he remembered Valkyrie asking him to make love to her.

His phone rang and his heart gave a little jolt of excitement before he remembered it wasn't Kyrie, that he'd blocked her number. At first, he'd been so angry he hadn't cared why she was calling. Why she'd *kept* calling. Then, he'd started living for seeing her goddamn name appear on the screen and he'd known he had to do something, because if he didn't, one day he'd answer just to hear her voice.

He wanted to pick up and have her tell him that she'd made a terrible mistake. That she knew she'd hurt him and she was wrong. That she wanted him. That she loved him. He wanted her to beg him to come home.

Except they didn't have a home anymore. He'd just sold it. And Valkyrie Winters didn't beg. Valkyrie Winters didn't admit she was wrong. Valkyrie Winters didn't love him.

Her refusal to ever leave a voicemail was proof enough of all those things. She'd probably only called to alleviate her own guilt, and she'd probably only kept calling out of sheer stubbornness when he didn't answer. So he'd blocked her number to remove the temptation to put himself through yet another round of misery.

His phone rang again and he glanced at the nightstand where it lay. Daniel.

What now? He resigned himself, picked up the phone, and resumed pacing. "Was something wrong with the paperwork?"

Part of him hoped there was. If he'd fucked it up somehow, he didn't have to go through with it. Didn't have to admit everything was all done and tidied, and he had no tie to Kyrie anymore.

"No," Daniel said, but he sounded questioning rather than certain. "Did you look at the paperwork?"

"I signed in all the right places, didn't I?"

"Did you see how much the house sold for?"

"Are you going to keep asking me pointless questions or are you going to tell me why you called?" he asked crossly.

"It sold for a million dollars."

Random stopped pacing. It was a nice house. It was a nice property. It was not worth a million dollars. Wonderful. "Daniel," he said patiently, "this is a scam." He wasn't sure how, but this was what he got for not reading the paperwork for the first time in his life. "Why didn't you mention this before you sent me the paperwork?"

He went to the hotel room's small desk, opened his laptop and turned it on. Now he had to fix this when all he wanted to do was be miserable.

"Because I knew you wouldn't sign it." Daniel was quiet for a moment, then, "She said the price tag was to get your attention."

Random's heart stopped. "She?"

"The buyer. It's all on the up-and-up, I can promise you that. And, well, frankly, I couldn't turn down a commission on that amount of money. She asked me to pass a message on to you."

Random's hand shook as he found the email with the scanned copies of the mortgage documents and opened the file. He knew what he'd find but it still punched him in the gut to see her name written there. Valkyrie Evelyn Winters.

"What was the message?" he asked hoarsely.

"This is a direct quote, mind you. It's not *me* saying it."

"Just spit it out."

Daniel cleared his throat. "'I loved it the moment I saw it. I should have stopped you. I'm an idiot. Please come home and yell at me.'"

"Thank you, Daniel." Random hung up and dropped his phone onto the desk. He almost picked it back up, unblocked her number and called her. But no. He wasn't going to go through this on a phone call.

He wasn't sure he was going to go through this at all.

CHAPTER

TWENTY-THREE

Valkyrie's eyes were dry and grainy, her back hurt from hunching over a computer, and if she never read another legal document, physical *or* virtual, ever again it would be too soon. Elijah had hidden his tracks well where his activities as Danvers were concerned, and in the last two weeks she'd barely even managed to tie New Beginnings, the adoption agency used to place Lacey and Taylor with the Anders, back to him.

"I don't know how you stand it in here." Jace stood in the doorway, his lips pressed into a hard line as he took in their father's old office.

"Necessity." Valkyrie stood, stretched, and what seemed like the entirety of her back popped in relief. At first, coming here *had* been necessity—the need to access Elijah's files, to try and find any remaining individuals he might have hurt. Lucille's oracular premonitions had stopped with Elijah's death—her grandfather, Charles, said it wasn't unusual for a young Oracle to need a focus for the things they saw, and Lucille's had apparently been Elijah himself—so finding any remaining victims of Elijah's experiments fell squarely on Valkyrie's shoulders.

Given that Elijah had a track record of dumping his experiments in the care of associates and not checking in on them for years, Valkyrie had no doubt there were people who still needed to be found and liberated. She intended to do both. She also had an absurdly large fortune to split among them.

Reparations had to be made, and they ought to be made with Elijah's money. She didn't feel guilty about the funds she'd used to buy Random's house, or the small sum she'd kept to keep her afloat until she figured out what to do with her life—she was a victim of Elijah's handiwork too. She deserved reparations the same as everyone else.

The only thing she wasn't sure what to do with was the estate. She'd put off any decision on it thus far because she didn't want to risk letting go of anything that might finally give her the full scope of Elijah's operation. Didn't want to risk anyone's life just because she didn't like being in this house.

So she'd come back to it—to this office, where so many terrible things had happened to her—day after day and tried find an answer. It shouldn't have been so hard. She'd lived here the entirety of her life. But something about Elijah's death had finally allowed fear and memory to swamp her as they hadn't when she'd known he was still alive.

The first time she'd come back she'd stood here, shaking so badly she'd bitten clean through her lip, repeating the same thing over and over again in her head.

Dead. He's dead. You killed him and he's never coming back. He won't hurt you or Jace or Random or anyone ever again.

Eventually, she'd accepted that. But while Elijah might be gone, his ghost wasn't.

On the bad days, she wasn't sure he would ever leave her entirely, wasn't sure his voice would ever stop whispering in the back of her mind, telling her that she was weak, that she wasn't good enough, that she was nothing.

In her heart, she had believed it. Random hadn't. For that alone, she owed him a debt she could never repay. Because he'd given her the strength to see it too—that she was worth something. That she deserved to be happy.

So she planned to be. Maybe she couldn't be as happy as she wanted, if Random never came back, but she could be *happy*. She could be—was—free. And she would never take it for granted.

She wanted to ask Jace if he'd heard from Random, but stopped herself before she did. If Random was talking to Jace again, it was none of her business. She wouldn't make it awkward for her brother by constantly reminding him she was in love with his best friend and she desperately wanted to hear anything about him.

She told herself it was fine. That *Random* was fine. That it was fine if he never wanted to see her again. She'd hurt him, and he didn't owe her his forgiveness. He didn't owe her a second chance.

"Did you need something or did you just stop in to see if I was alive?" The words came out more sharply than she'd intended, and she cursed herself for snapping at Jace when she was angry about things that weren't his fault.

Jace gave her an odd look. "I came by to get you. Big day and all?"

Big day? What could he—oh. She dug for her phone, saw the date, and wondered how the hell three weeks had passed since she'd bought Random's house.

"Well, then," she said with forced brightness. "Ready to go destroy an adnexus?"

Her brother's face paled. "No."

She rolled her eyes and shoved him out the door. "Siren will be fine. How many contingency scenarios did you run the math behind?"

"All of them." His voice was deadly serious. "I ran all of them. Five times."

His home office was probably knee-deep in papers covered in tidy rows of numbers from him running and re-running math that would make her head spin.

"And in how many of them did Siren die?"

"None, once I added in anchors from all the Aspect branches."

"See? She'll be fine."

Jace did not look convinced.

CHAPTER

TWENTY-FOUR

The Warded Room of Council headquarters currently contained more people than Valkyrie had ever seen in it at one time. Every single branch of Aspect was represented, and gathering those people alone had caused a one week delay in this gathering, since many of the Aspecters had had to be summoned from out of state. They'd had no shortage of volunteers, as it seemed everyone wanted to be part of making history.

The adnexus rested on a pedestal in the center of the room, tucked away inside the black box Random had made for it. Her chest twinged—he should *be* here, should at least be here to see this, if nothing else. For one crazy moment she thought she felt him, felt the soft brush of his Aspect, but then it was gone. A brutally thorough sweep of the room proved he wasn't here. She just missed him so her brain was conjuring the memory of him.

"If everyone could take their places, please." Siren stood in the center of the room, a foot from the adnexus, Ella Tremayne equidistant from her on the other side. At Siren's direction the mass of people in the room shifted, each moving to a different node on the complex pattern drawn on the floor.

It had taken Siren and Jace the better part of two days to

draw it and, truthfully, Valkyrie still didn't understand what the hell it was. Between Siren talking animatedly about the adnexus as if the structure it formed between the councilors was a living organism in and of itself, and Jace descending into explanations of theory so dense Valkyrie couldn't have pierced them with a longsword, she didn't really understand *how* they were going to break the adnexus without killing the entire former Council.

After poking at the adnexus for days, Siren had said that blood magic was so powerful because it contained within it *all* Aspects, no matter the affinity of the person who'd given their blood to the working. As she explained it, though genetics played a large part in determining what affinity a person wielded, each person had the *potential* to bear any branch of Aspect, and that potential was carried in the blood.

"I think that's why Random can do pretty much anything," Siren had confided to her, "I think he's so mercurial, so into everything, that he *couldn't* choose an affinity. Or, rather, he chose *all* of them. Sort of like how some people have secondary affinities, except he has all the affinities.

"But he couldn't have Life or Death because to have either of those requires absolute dedication, absolute resolve. It's why so few people are born to either of them—there isn't much wiggle room."

That potential in blood magic was why Jace had determined they needed a representative from each branch of Aspect present at the time of the adnexus' destruction, one at each node on the pattern that Siren claimed was a visual representation of how she saw the ties the adnexus formed between the councilors when she looked at it with her magic.

With the exception of Aunt Ella, whom Siren apparently needed close, the former councilors were all positioned at the corners of the room, outside of the pattern itself. According to Siren and Jace, blood magic exacted its vengeance for a broken work by exploiting all those affinity possibilities a person didn't actually possess. In essence, it struck back against a person with every branch of Aspect they couldn't defend against. So, in theory, with Aspecters of all the affinities gathered in the pattern, the rebound of the adnexus' breaking would first filter through the nodes, the person at each node handling the branch of the rebound that correlated to their Aspect. By the time the backlash hit the councilors, what was left would be too weak to actually kill them.

Aunt Ella and Siren took the greatest risks. Aunt Ella, as the only living person with Death Aspect, had to be inside the pattern, at a node, for the plan to work. But as she was tied to the adnexus, she wouldn't receive the buffering benefits of the pattern.

Valkyrie had tersely pointed this out since, if Random ever did come home, she didn't want to try and explain to him how she'd let his aunt die while he was gone. Ella had simply given her a dragon's smile and said, "I've cheated death before, dear."

It was the "dear" that had floored her. That was what Ella called Siren and Random and Jace, what she called people she...accepted. Why the hell would Ella call her that when Valkyrie was the reason Random was gone and probably never coming back?

In the center of the room, Siren opened the box. The silk-oil call of the adnexus radiated out but it was muted, jumbled, as if it had never before seen so many Aspects, so many people, at once and it didn't know what to do. Who to entice first.

Siren never gave it the chance to make a decision. Her Aspect streaked forward, precise as a scalpel, and neatly severed the ties that bound the former councilors to the centuries-old blood magic that had kept them in power.

The adnexus wailed, a howling shriek that split the air and tore through the room like a windstorm. The retributive power that lashed out, streaking for the four corners of the room, halted as it hit the bounds of the small circle where Siren and Ella stood on the first two nodes.

Trapped, the sundered power turned its fury on the only two

available targets...and crashed against the combined might of Siren's and Ella's Aspects like storm-tossed waves breaking against seaside cliffs. The thread of power that was Ella's own broken tie to the adnexus hammered against the woman. The Queen of Death *smiled*.

Siren's Aspect wound around Ella and vice versa, Life Aspect buffering the rebound of the broken tie, Death Aspect tempering the fury leveled at Siren for being the one who had done the breaking. As the rebound broke around them, the pattern on the floor dragged at it, pulling power past Siren and Ella, filtering it out to the other nodes, and the Aspecters waiting at them.

Valkyrie stood in the ring closest to Siren and Ella, as Battle was one of the primary branches of Aspect affinity. But it wasn't the assault of power against her shield that made her blink, made her heart stutter, made her world stop.

It was Random, suddenly in that same secondary ring, directly across from her on the other side of the circle, standing on a node that hadn't been there before. As if he'd decided he was needed, so here he was, and the pattern had simply shifted to accommodate him.

She should have known he'd be here, known he wouldn't leave Ella's and Siren's survival to chance. And Jace—Jace must have known he'd come. Because Jace wouldn't have left it to chance, either, and for every branch of Aspect to be represented, they would *have* to have Random.

Because Random could do things that didn't *have* a known branch of Aspect affinity—things like teleport—which indicated the potential affinity of Aspect extended to things that Aspect Society, for all its centuries of study, couldn't even guess at. But Random could *be* all of those possibilities, all of those unknowns. And because he needed to be them right now, he would.

Holding her shield against the onslaught of the adnexus' power until it spent the potential for Battle and moved around her, deeper into the pattern, was nothing next to looking across the ten feet that separated her from Random and feeling as if it might as well have been an ocean for the distance that radiated off him.

He looked good. He'd regained most of the weight he'd lost when he'd hastily regenerated his Aspect to come to her aid. His hair had grown out, long enough to fall across his forehead now, and the itch in her fingers to brush it back, to run her fingers through it, was painful.

She barely noticed when the power of the adnexus ran its course, lessening with each ring of the pattern, each node, until only a shadow was left to reach the former councilors in the four corners of the room. She didn't join in the triumphant cheers and frenzy of hugging and back-slapping that occurred with the destruction of Aspect Society's dirty little secret.

The entirety of her world had narrowed down to one point, one person, who finally lifted his gaze to hers. Random's eyes weren't quiet or triumphant. They were a chaotic jumble of want and hurt and confusion, and every instinct in her screamed at her to *fix it*.

She stepped toward him. He stepped back in tandem, as if an invisible rod stretched between them, forcing them to remain this precise distance apart.

"Random?" she asked tentatively, feeling like he was a wild animal, a mythical unicorn that would spook at the wrong tone, the wrong look.

He wavered, as if he might step toward her. Then he caught himself and shook his head. "I need some time." He turned and walked away, through the throng of celebrating Aspecters and out of the room. Out of her life. Again.

Then Siren was at her side, wrapping her in a hug. "He'll come back."

"Yeah." But she wasn't sure she believed it. Because she'd seen the devastation in his eyes and he hadn't looked like a man who was coming home. Ever.

"He *will*," Siren insisted. "He loves you too much to stay away."

But the depth of that love was precisely why Valkyrie was certain he was never coming back. Because if he'd cared about her less, what she'd done to him would have hurt less.

"In the meantime," Siren continued, releasing Valkyrie from the hug, "I've been thinking."

Valkyrie groaned. "It's never good when you think."

"Hey, I'm brilliant. Jace says so."

"Jace is biased."

"Whatever. So I've been thinking. You need a job."

"Not this again." So far, Siren had come up with a number of entirely unsuitable possible careers for Valkyrie's future.

"Since you're apparently incapable of doing anything non-battle-y, I think you should just keep doing what you're doing, but official and everything."

Valkyrie tried and failed to make sense of that. "Huh?"

"I want to hire you to find all the people like us, like the girls you found with the Anders. The people Elijah hurt. You're already looking for them, so you might as well do it in an official capacity and get paid for it."

"I—"

"And before you say no, I'll remind you that I'm obnoxiously persistent. I'll wear you down eventually. Besides, you *will* need backup for this. It's too much for one person and, as acting head of Aspect Society, I have the resources to hire you and a team.

"Besides which, it will be good for people to see *you* for a change. To see that you aren't what Elijah made you out to be. Do something good and let everyone see it."

"No one is going to want to work with me."

"Oh, please," a new voice said, "you aren't as scary as all that." Meredith walked up and slung an arm around Valkyrie's shoulders.

"Oh, look," Siren said innocently, "your new partner is here."

"You got roped into this mess?" Valkyrie asked.

"Turns out you're not the only one Siren thinks would benefit from 'gainful employment'." Meredith snorted. "Whatever the fuck that means. I also made the mistake of explaining to Jace that I was Tracking an oracular *hunch* when I found Lacey and Taylor, and I exploded the geek side of his brain."

"The geek side is the entirety of his brain," Valkyrie pointed out.

"Exactly. Anyway, he hasn't stopped making me try to Track weird shit since then, so I figured I might as well get paid for it."

"So can I put you on the payroll?" Siren asked. Her big green eyes were entirely too excited for Valkyrie to turn down.

"Fine," Valkyrie said, and Siren let out a squeal. "But don't be too disappointed when no one signs up to join the Valkyrie battle unit."

"Well," Meredith said, ticking things off on her fingers, "we've killed a creepy scumbag, defeated an ancient evil spell, and gotten me and Val to get jobs. We should probably go drinking."

CHAPTER

TWENTY-FIVE

Going drinking with Meredith was never a good idea. It was three days later and Valkyrie swore she still had a residual hangover. On the bright side, it gave her something to be miserable about other than the fact that Random still hadn't come by. Or called. Or probably even thought thoughts in her general direction.

She dropped the eight-by-eight glass dish containing the burnt husk of a casserole onto the kitchen counter and then opened all the doors and windows before the smoke detector could go off. She had decided that if she was going to be alone for the rest of her life, she might as well learn how to cook.

Casseroles were supposed to be easy. The fucking Internet said so. They weren't easy. This was her third attempt in as many days and she seemed to be getting worse with practice.

In the open kitchen window, a flutter of wings announced Nelsen's arrival. He'd started showing up a few days after she moved in, the bleakness in his falcon eyes telling her he missed Random just as must as she did.

Nelsen gave the casserole an odd look and emitted a series of *kaks* that sounded like an alarm. Even the bird thought her cooking was shit. Not that he was wrong.

"I'm doing the best I can, okay?" Her words did not reassure the bird. So much so that he flew off without listening to her ramble on. She rambled on a lot these days, and he was usually a very good listener, despite the fact she knew he didn't understand a word she said. She figured he was probably just used to listening to a human talk, and she was the closest replacement he had for Random.

A small zing went through her, a faint flicker dappling the property wards. Adrenaline spiked her veins. She had learned years ago that that slight ripple occurred when Random slipped past wards as if they weren't there. It was so minuscule, it wouldn't be felt unless a person was sitting around every second of the day hoping to feel it.

She waited, listening, but there was nothing else. The adrenaline faded, replaced by disappointment. It wasn't Random. She knew that. For one, he would have no need to sneak through the wards. Though he'd taken down the original property wards when he'd put the house up for sale, she'd keyed the new ones she'd put up to allow him through. If he wanted to come to the house, he could drive right up.

He wasn't here—it was just her imagination, wanting him to be.

She'd read about people experiencing phantom phone rings even when their phone wasn't in their pocket. This was like that. She wanted him to be here, so she kept inventing little signs that he was.

She'd been hopeful, after seeing him at the adnexus' breaking, hopeful that his seeing her again would at least make him want to come yell at her, or something. She'd been so sure that, if nothing else, paying a million dollars for this house would guarantee he'd come back to tell her he didn't need her charity.

But Random hadn't come home. Not to yell at her, not to forgive her, not to *anything*.

She'd resisted the urge to buy a burner phone and call him. She'd made her gambit, and it hadn't paid off. And she would respect the fact that he wanted nothing more to do with her if it killed her.

She turned her back to the open door and surveyed the ruined casserole. Maybe it was only burnt on the top and the middle was edible? She twirled a dagger out of her thigh sheath and poked at the crispy top.

"I think it's already dead," a voice said.

She dropped the dagger and spun to the doorway. Random leaned against it, his hands shoved into the pockets of his faded black jeans. He was only relaxed on the outside. Beneath, he was tense, his usually warm brown eyes wary.

She'd rehearsed what she would say to him so many times, but now that he was here, all the words fled her.

"Do you want to come in?" She felt strange, inviting him into his own home. He hadn't moved any of the house's furniture or kitchen contents out before he'd sold it, and she'd told the realtors to leave it all. It was still his house, exactly as he'd left it.

For a moment, she thought he'd say no, thought he'd turn right back around and leave. Then he stepped inside, looking around like he didn't recognize anything.

"I made coffee. Do you want some?" she asked, desperate to say anything to keep him from leaving.

A shadow of the normal Random surfaced. "Is it safer than the casserole?"

"I can make coffee," she defended herself. She wasn't entirely useless in the kitchen. She filled a mug for him, added a splash of cream to it like he liked, and set it on the counter. He walked to the counter but he didn't sit down. He just slid the coffee cup to him and stared at the placid surface of the liquid. Then he looked up at her, and all the hurt and misery she'd felt since he'd left was mirrored in his gaze. She reached for him but halted midway and let her hand fall back to her side.

She had to do this right. Her carefully planned speeches evaporated and a rawer honesty tumbled out. "I'm sorry. I never should have let you walk out that door."

"Then why did you?"

"Because I'm fucked up, Random. And that's not an excuse, it doesn't make it okay, and I know that. I just… I hated myself. I couldn't look at myself without seeing *him*, so I didn't understand how anyone else could, either." She took a deep breath, let it out. "And I thought you deserved more than that, more than me. Because you're the best person I know and you deserve to be happy."

Random's fingers tightened around the coffee mug. "Let me get this straight. You thought I was such a great person that you decided to hurt me as deeply as you could? When I was literally begging you to ask me to stay?"

She made herself meet his gaze. "I wanted you to give up on me so you could move on. And now I'm terrified that you have and there's nothing I can do to take it back."

"Do you know *why* I said I was done if you let me walk out?"

She shook her head.

"Because when it comes to me, nothing ever changes with you. I give you everything and I get one step forward and ten steps back." He ran his hand in a frustrated pass through his hair. "Everything you're telling me now—how do I know that doesn't change in a week? A month? How do I know you won't just lie to me the next time you *decide* what's best for me? The next time you—"

"I love you," she blurted out.

He went completely still. She couldn't read the emotion in his eyes, but his voice was harsh. "You love me?"

"I love you," she repeated, the words foreign and wonderful at the same time. "And I'm a selfish asshole and I want to keep you even if I don't deserve you. I'm miserable without you."

"You broke my heart, Kyrie."

She wanted to squeeze her eyes shut, but she wouldn't run from this. From what she'd done. Not this time. "I know."

"You lied to me. So many times."

"I know."

"You took everything I gave you and you used it against me."

"I know." Her voice broke. This was it. She had fucked it up beyond repair, and he was just here as a courtesy. He was here to say goodbye. Water blurred her vision, welled up and spilled down her cheekbones. Goddess, she could do without the crying. But ever since those floodgates had opened on the day he left, she'd never managed to shut them down again.

Random stepped around the counter to her. She froze. He cupped her face in his hands, his thumbs stroking across her cheekbones as he brushed away her tears. She stopped breathing.

"You destroyed me," he whispered. "So why can't I make myself hate you? Why is it that when you cry, all I want to do is make it better?"

"Maybe we're both idiots?"

A smile tugged at the corners of his lips before it faltered and disappeared. "I love you, Kyrie. But you knew that. And I can't go through this all again. I can't think I have you just for you to turn around and break it all. I won't survive, next time."

"I'm sorry." Her voice broke. "And I know that 'sorry' doesn't fix anything. I know you don't have any reason to trust me. But I love you so much. And I swear, there won't ever be a next time. If you give me another chance and we don't make it, it won't be because of this. I'll never lie to you again. I'll never cut you out again. I'll never send you away again."

"I want to believe you," he said, something desperate and pleading in his voice. "But I don't know how to trust you anymore."

She was torn between wanting to grab at hope with both hands and wanting to tuck her heart carefully into a box where she couldn't be hurt if he decided he'd been through too much to trust her again. But holding back, always shielding herself—that was what had gotten her here in the first place. That was how she'd lost him.

So she opened, instead. She took down every shield, mental and magical, and let her Aspect flow to him, let it surround him in a soft cloud, but she stopped just shy of touching him. She let the offer stand, and she waited.

He hesitated. Then his Aspect unfurled, moving with hers, *into* hers, filling the yawning chasm that had opened inside her when she'd lost him. She didn't try to hide her relief, or the misery she'd felt while he was gone. She laid it all bare, and though melding Aspect like this didn't give two people the ability to feel each other's feelings, she willed him to know hers anyway.

As if wanting it badly enough could make it happen. And maybe it did, maybe his Aspect *made* it so he did. Because he exhaled sharply and stepped in, pulling her to him, his forehead resting against hers.

"I missed you," she whispered, "*so* much."

"I missed you, too."

"Don't ever leave again."

"Don't ever make me."

Her instinct was to answer that she wouldn't, but she had to be honest with him now. Because she knew they weren't final, yet, weren't *finished*. "I have nightmares all the time," she made herself say. "I don't know if you'll ever get a decent night's sleep again around me. I'm controlling, I always think I'm right, and yet I paradoxically have abysmal self-esteem. If you stay, you'll probably spend all of your time sleep-deprived, arguing with me, and then fucking me until I feel better about myself."

She held her breath, waiting for his answer. His hands worked soothing, promising circles up her back.

"Kyrie, love, you may not know this about me, but I'm happy to fuck you whenever you want. I love arguing with you, and as for the sleep-deprived bit—I really don't give a damn as long as it's you I'm waking up next to."

She exhaled. "Does that mean you'll come home?"

"I already am, love." And then he kissed her. She hadn't

forgotten the taste of him, hadn't forgotten the exquisite mix of need and wonder that spread through her at the feel of his lips against hers, the glide of his tongue. But the memory—oh, the memory paled in comparison to having him here, having him *now*, having him touching her.

Feeling that, every emotion coming back to her at once, she couldn't stop from saying what she really wanted, even if it was foolish, even if it risked ruining everything.

"There's something else. Just one other thing," she said. "I don't want to be a Winters anymore. I don't want that name, anymore." Jace had decided the same, after everything that had come out about Elijah, and he'd taken the Savage name. Valkyrie hadn't done anything yet. She'd been waiting, holding out hope for this, for now.

Random frowned. "Change it to whatever you want, Kyrie. It doesn't matter to me what your last name is."

She swallowed, and dove off the cliff. "And if I want it to be Tremayne?"

RANDOM'S HEART SKIPPED A BEAT. She couldn't have just said what he *thought* she'd just said.

She ducked her head, which had to be the first time he'd ever seen her not look a battle in the eye. "I'd understand if you said no. Goddess knows I've given you more than enough reasons to. And if you do say no, it won't change anything between us." She smiled, and gave him back the words he'd once given her. "I'll take any scraps you're willing to give me."

He couldn't stop the grin that spread across his face. "Why, love, are you trying to make an honest man out of me?"

"Well," she considered, "you *are* the son of the Queen of Death. It's in my best interests to do the honorable thing." Her smile wavered. "So will you? Marry me?"

He was more than a little surprised when his heart kept on

beating instead of outright exploding in his chest. "I'd be honored to be your husband, Kyrie." He tilted his head, considering her. "But I want a big wedding."

Her face blanched, the horror on it absolutely adorable. "Big?"

"Mm-hmm." He rubbed his nose against hers. "Extravagant, even. Consider it recompense for all the hell I've been through. I want everyone in this damn town to know you love me so much that you'll get up in front of them in a nice pretty dress and say vows that only I can probably find endearing.

"I don't want to be your dirty secret anymore, Kyrie. I want everyone to know you think I'm worth something."

She cupped his face in her hands. "You're worth everything, Random."

She couldn't know how much those words meant to him, how much he'd needed to hear them.

"If you want a big wedding, then you'll have it. Just don't expect me to plan it."

He laughed, the final bit of tension he'd clung to fading. "Not even I'm *that* delusional."

"Random," she said slowly, her hands leaving his face to glide down his chest, his stomach, to settle at the waistband of his jeans. "My self-esteem is feeling low."

"Oh, no," he said, his voice laced with mock concern.

"Very, very low."

He backed her up against the counter, slipped his hands beneath her shirt to feel the warmth and strength of her. Then his hands roved lower and he dropped to his knees, settled between her legs, looked up at her and said, "I should probably do something about that."

WANT THE BONUS PREQUEL SCENE?

Curious about that first time between Random and Valkyrie? That bonus prequel scene is available exclusively to my newsletter subscribers, and you can sign up and get it here: https://michellemanus.com/newsletter/

Fair warning, the bonus scene is definitely a steamy one, so if those are not your favorite parts of books, you may want to skip this one.

If you enjoyed *Valkyrie's Call*, do consider leaving a review at your retailer of choice. Reviews really are the best way you can help support your favorite authors.

You can find me on my website michellemanus.com, or Twitter (@MichelleManus), Facebook (https://facebook.com/michellemanusbooks), or Instagram (@michelle.m.manus) if social media is your thing.

Thanks so much for reading!

Also by Michelle Manus

The Aspect Society Trilogy

Siren's Song

Valkyrie's Call

Truthfinder's Promise

The Nyx Fortuna Series

Guardian of Chaos

Guardian of Shadows

Guardian of Madness